Praise for *USA TODAY* Bestselling Author

Sarah Morgan

"Sweet, sexy and deliciously feel-good,
Christmas Eve: Doorstep Delivery is an outstanding romance
that will make you laugh and cry from the always fabulous pen
of multitalented international bestselling author Sarah Morgan!"
—*CataRomance.com*

"Morgan is a magician with words, and she thrillingly transports
readers to picturesque Sicily, where she spins a modern-day fairy tale
of grudges, feuds and forbidden passion. And her love scenes
should come with the warning: 'Reading may cause hot flashes.'"
—*RT Book Reviews* on *The Forbidden Ferrara*

Sarah Morgan

entertain, enrich, inspire™

Recycling programs
for this product may
not exist in your area.

ISBN-13: 978-0-373-83788-5

ANGELS IN THE SNOW

Originally published as *Snowbound: Miracle Marriage*
and *Christmas Eve: Doorstep Delivery*

www.Harlequin.com

Printed in U.S.A.

CONTENTS

SARAH MORGAN

USA TODAY bestselling author Sarah Morgan writes for both
Harlequin Presents® and Medical Romance.

As a child, Sarah dreamed of being a writer, and although she took
a few interesting detours on the way, she is now living that dream.
With her writing career, she has successfully combined business with
pleasure and she firmly believes that reading romance is one of the
most satisfying and fat-free escapist pleasures available. Her stories are
unashamedly optimistic and she is always pleased when she receives
letters from readers saying that her books have helped them through
hard times.

RT Book Reviews has described her writing as "action packed and sexy"
and has nominated her books for their Reviewer's Choice Awards and
their Top Pick slot.

Sarah lives near London with her husband and two children, who
innocently provide an endless supply of authentic dialogue. When she
isn't writing or reading Sarah enjoys music, movies and any activity that
takes her outdoors.

Readers can find out more about Sarah and her books from her website,
www.sarahmorgan.com. She can also be found on Facebook and
Twitter.

To Lucy,
whose happy smile and cheerful nature
never fail to brighten my day

SNOWBOUND: MIRACLE MARRIAGE

PROLOGUE

'I'M OVER him. Really. That's why I'm back.' Stella stamped the snow from her boots and levered them off on the doorstep of the converted stable. 'Two years is a long time. Long enough to gain some perspective on things.' She glanced at the man next to her and caught her breath because he was so like his brother. And yet so different. *This man hadn't smashed her dreams into a million tiny pieces.* 'Are you sure it's a good idea for me to live in your stable?'

'It's nearly Christmas,' he drawled, a gleam of humour in his eyes as he stood aside to let her pass. 'A stable is prime accommodation, haven't you heard?'

Stella smiled, but beneath the smile was a shiver of trepidation.

Christmas.

Once, it had been her favourite time of year. But that had been before every glittering silver bauble reminded her of the engagement ring she'd worn for such a short space of time.

Putting her life back together had taken time, effort and determination. And she was about to test just how far she'd come.

She'd kept her emotions safely boxed away, like Christmas decorations that were no longer needed. What if the box suddenly opened, spilling all those emotions back into her life?

For a terrifying moment it felt as though two years of healing was about to be undone and Stella stepped quickly inside her new home, hiding her feelings from the man watching her. He was a doctor as well as a friend. She knew how much he saw.

Her feet sank into the soft, cream rug that covered much of the pale wooden floor and she blinked rapidly to clear the tears, angry with herself. *No more tears,* wasn't that what she'd promised herself? 'I suspect this is a little more comfortable than the original stable. You've performed miracles, Patrick. When I last saw this two years ago, it still had a horse in it.' She was making polite conversation but it was impossible to ignore the gnawing anxiety in her stomach.

'Stella, will you drop the act?' He slammed the door shut on the snow and the freezing December air. 'You're a nervous wreck. Pale. Jumpy. Looking over your shoulder in case Daniel suddenly turns up. He isn't going to. He's up to his elbows in blood and drama at the hospital. It's just you and me. We drowned our sorrows together two years ago. If you can't be honest with me, who can you be honest with?'

Stella tugged off her gloves. 'He's your brother. That makes it awkward.'

'The fact that he's my brother doesn't blind me to his faults.' Patrick dropped the keys on the table. 'Neither does it affect our friendship. We kept each other going over that nightmare Christmas. Don't think I've forgotten that.'

Stella felt her insides wobble and wondered whether it was a mistake to pursue this conversation. In a way it had been easier living and working among people who didn't know— people who weren't watching to see how she was coping. 'I'm nervous about seeing him,' she said finally. 'Of course I am.'

'I'm not surprised. Stella, you were engaged.'

'For about five minutes.' She walked towards the wood-burning stove and stared at the glass. 'I just wish he hadn't broken it off at Christmas. It made it harder, somehow.'

'He shouldn't have broken it off at all.'

'That was inevitable.' She turned, resigned to having the conversation she'd hoped to avoid. 'Daniel doesn't believe he'd be a good husband and he definitely doesn't think he'd be a good father—you know how his mind works. The surprise wasn't that he broke off the engagement, but that he proposed to me in the first place. If I'd been stronger, I would have said no. I knew it wasn't what he wanted.' Lost in thought, dwelling in the land of 'what if', Stella lifted one of the logs piled in a basket, ready to be used on the fire, and rubbed her fingers along the rough bark. Then she looked at Patrick. 'Enough of me. How are *you* doing? If anything, that Christmas was worse for you than it was for me. Your wife left.'

'The difference is that Carly and I weren't in love. I was angry with her for ending it at Christmas, and I feel for the children not having a mother around, but for myself...' He gave a dismissive shrug. 'The one thing about being unhappily married is that divorce feels like a blessing. But I'm aware that I'm probably part of the reason that Daniel got cold feet.'

'I think it was more like frostbite than cold feet,' Stella said lightly, 'and it wasn't your fault.'

'Carly walked out on Christmas Eve. Daniel broke off your engagement on the same day. Believe me, there was a connection.'

Remembering just how awful that Christmas had been for both of them, Stella sighed. 'You and I spent it on our own, trying to smile around your kids, do you remember?'

'I remember that you were brave,' Patrick said gruffly, reaching out and squeezing her shoulder. 'After Daniel walked out, you disappeared for five minutes and then came back with your make-up on and a smile on your face, determined to give

my children a good time. Because of you, I don't think Alfie
even noticed that his mother wasn't there.'

'The children gave me something to focus on. And you and
I *did* share that bottle of champagne, which helped. And we
ate every scrap of chocolate from the Christmas tree.'

'Then I went and picked up a kitten from the farmer next
door, do you remember?'

It was one of the few happy memories among the miserable ones. 'Giving Alfie that kitten was an inspired idea. And
it was *gorgeous*.'

'That kitten is now a cat and has just produced kittens of
her own.'

'Really? Alfie must love that.'

'I've said he can keep two. I have to find homes for the other
two. Our life is chaotic enough without four kittens.' Patrick's
gaze settled on her face. 'You really were brave, Stella. I know
how much you love Dan. The fact that you held it together
was nothing short of amazing.'

'If you'd seen me two weeks later, you wouldn't have
thought I was amazing. I was in pieces.'

'I'm not surprised.'

Talking about the past had removed any awkwardness between them. 'I'm worried about how Daniel is going to react
when he finds out that I'm living in your stable.'

'I don't care what he thinks.' Tough, calm and sure of himself, Patrick removed the log from her hands. 'My property.
My decision.'

''Well, that's a non-confrontational approach.' Stella watched
as he opened the wood-burning stove. 'I don't want to cause a
problem between you. I don't want you falling out over me.'

'We have to fall out over something. It won't be the first
time it's a woman. I still owe him for stealing Nancy Potter

away from me when I was eight. I adored that girl. I've had a thing for pigtails ever since.' His smile was slow and sexy and Stella wondered for the millionth time why she couldn't have fallen for him instead of his brother.

You always have to do things the hard way, Stella.

Dismissing her mother's voice from her head, Stella slid her hands into the back pockets of her jeans and forced herself to keep it light. 'So—was this Nancy Potter pretty?'

'She had red hair and a fierce temper.'

'Sounds scary.'

'Relationships are always scary.'

She wasn't going to argue with that. 'You and I both want the same out of life. I met you and Dan at exactly the same time, that week I started at the hospital five years ago. Why couldn't you and I have fallen in love with each other?'

Patrick fed the log into the stove. 'Because you're a beautiful blonde and I hate stereotypes.'

Stella lifted a hand to her hair. 'I could dye it black?'

'Wouldn't make any difference. There was never any chemistry between us.'

Stella watched his muscles flex as he reached for another log. 'Do you remember that time you kissed me, just to check?'

'Daniel punched me immediately afterwards.' Patrick lit the fire. 'He didn't want you involved with me in case I hurt you.'

They exchanged a look, both thinking the same thing.

That, in the end, it had been Daniel who had hurt her.

'Am I going to be able to do this?' Stella was asking herself as much as him. 'Am I going to be able to work alongside him every day and not wish I was with him?'

'You tell me. Are you?'

Stella gave a murmur of frustration. 'I don't know. I hope so.' She paced the length of the living room, hating herself for being so unsure and indecisive. 'Yes, of course I can do it. And if it feels difficult—well, I just need to keep reminding myself that he and I don't want the same things out of life.'

Patrick coaxed the flame to life. 'You just need to keep reminding yourself that when it comes to women, Daniel is nothing but trouble. We Buchannans are *seriously* bad at relationships.'

'*You're* not.'

He rocked back on his heels. 'I'm divorced, Stella.'

'Your wife was clearly deranged.'

'Or maybe I'm not easy to live with.'

'No man is easy to live with,' Stella said dryly. 'You're a different species. I just wish I'd listened to you when you warned me about Dan.'

'It wouldn't have made a difference. Women never listen when it comes to Daniel. It's those blue eyes of his. For some reason I've never understood, he can seduce a woman with a single glance.' Patrick stood up and brushed the dust from his long black coat. 'I admire you. He wouldn't give you marriage so you walked away. You refused to accept less than you deserve.'

Stella watched as the fire whispered and licked at the logs and then flared to life. 'Why does that sound better than it feels?'

'Because the right thing isn't always the easy thing.' Patrick studied her for a long moment. 'Why now? Why did you come back now?'

As the room grew warmer, Stella unwound the scarf from her neck. 'Because I hated London. Because two years is a long time. Because I worked here for three years and I miss all my friends. Because I can see how wrong Daniel was for me. And because I really am over him.' *Dear God, please let her be over him…*

Patrick gave her a long, hard look. 'If you're over him, why haven't you told him you're back?'

Stella felt her heart lurch and she glanced from the stove to the exposed beams. 'How did you find time to do this up?'

'I didn't. I just wrote cheques. And stop changing the subject.'

'Why would I tell him I'm back? We haven't had any contact since that nightmare Christmas two years ago. Not once.' *They'd been so close, and yet he hadn't even contacted her to see how she was.* 'He doesn't know I'm planning to live with his brother. He doesn't know I've got a job in the emergency department. If I rang him and said I was coming back he might think I was dropping hints. Hoping to get back together or something. That would be awkward and embarrassing.'

'So, instead, you're going to walk into the emergency department tomorrow and surprise him.' Patrick gave a sardonic smile. 'I hate to disillusion you, angel, but I don't think that approach is going to steer you away from awkward and embarrassing.'

'Maybe not, but there won't be an opportunity for conversation. There's no time to talk about personal stuff in the emergency department, especially not at Christmas when it's so busy.' Stella flopped down on the comfortable sofa. 'And one of the advantages of having been engaged for less than twenty-four hours is that most people didn't know about it.'

Patrick spread his hands in a gesture of apology. 'What can I say? Dan's always shied away from commitment. Our parents' marriage was ugly, you know that. *Really* ugly. Not an example anyone in their right mind would be in a hurry to follow.'

'It didn't stop you marrying.'

'Maybe it should have done.' His tone weary, Patrick walked to the window. 'I suppose I wanted to create something I'd never had—I wanted the whole family thing. Dan just rejected it. And maybe he was the sensible one given that my ex-wife is now living in New York and my children no longer have a mother.'

'I'm sorry about your divorce,' Stella said softly, watching as Patrick's broad shoulders tensed.

'Don't be sorry for me. I'm fine. It's just the kids I worry about.'

'I'm dying to see them. They won't remember me.'

'Alfie remembers you.' Patrick turned with a smile. 'He was eight when you left and you've been sending him thoughtful birthday presents. He's dying to show you our kittens. And you won't recognise Posy, she's grown so much.'

'I can't believe she's three.'

'She's very mischievous. Generally creating havoc.'

'And what about you? Any women in your life?'

'Thousands,' Patrick drawled, a wicked gleam in his blue eyes. 'I find I can't get through the day without stripping at least one midwife naked.'

'You can joke, but I happen to know that ninety-five per cent of the midwives in your department would be only too happy to be stripped naked by you.'

'What am I doing wrong with the other five per cent?'

'He's a man.'

'Ah.' Laughing, he tilted his head. 'Your turn to tell all. Did you find yourself a decent rebound relationship to cure you of my brother?'

Stella straightened her shoulders. 'Not yet, but I'm working on it. It's my Christmas present to myself. A love life. I've made a list.'

'A list of men?'

'No!' Stella laughed. 'A list of qualities. You know—things I won't compromise on.'

'Like tall, dark, handsome, rich...' Realising what he'd said, Patrick threw her an apologetic look but Stella managed a smile.

'That sounds too much like Dan,' she said lightly. 'I was thinking more of must want marriage and children.' She glanced around her. 'Does this place have an internet connection?'

'High-speed broadband—why?'

'Because I've joined an internet dating agency. I've decided that this time I'm going to be more analytical about the whole thing. It was crazy, falling for Daniel. He had "unsuitable" stamped on his forehead. If I'd made him fill out a questionnaire he never would have passed "go". This time I'm weeding out all the men who aren't right for me. I posted a description of myself last month and I've had three hundred and fifty replies.'

'You're going to be busy.'

'Maybe you should do the same thing?'

'I don't have time to date. Between the children, the kittens and the hospital, I'm lucky if I sleep. And, anyway, I wouldn't expose the kids to another woman. Too complicated. Talking of which, I'd better get going. The labour ward rang half an hour ago to warn me they have a woman who isn't progressing as she should be. I need to check her out.' Patrick scooped the keys from the table and handed them to her. 'These are for you. You're my first tenant so if there's anything I need to know about the place, just tell me. They're forecasting constant snow between now and Christmas so if the heating isn't high enough, light the fire or adjust the thermostat.'

'I'll light the fire. It's so cosy. And if you need any babysitting, I'm right here. It's so good to be home. I've been away too long.'

'I hope you don't find it isolated after city life. If you're internet dating, surely you're more likely to find Mr Right in London?'

'I don't think so.' Stella stared at the craggy outline of the mountains in the distance. 'This place is in my blood. I need a man who understands that. A man who loves it as much as I do.'

'Well, I wish you luck.' Patrick strolled towards the door and Stella turned to look at him.

'Just one thing…' Her heart pounding, she tried to sound casual. 'Is Daniel seeing anyone?'

Patrick paused with his hand on the doorhandle. 'Are you sure you want me to answer that question?'

'Yes.' Stella licked her lips. 'I'd rather hear it from you. It will be easier if I'm prepared.'

'He *is* seeing someone.' Patrick's voice was gentle and his eyes held hers. 'She's a lawyer. Career-woman. Workaholic. About as maternal as a cactus.'

'Oh. OK.' Feeling suddenly cold, Stella rubbed her hands over her arms. Because Patrick was watching her intently, she smiled. 'She sounds perfect for him. Not the sort to want marriage and a family. That's good. Great. Really, I mean it. I—I'm glad he's happy.'

Patrick studied her face for a long time and then he opened the door, letting in a blast of ice-cold air. 'I said he was seeing someone. I said she reminded me of a cactus. I never said that he was happy.'

And, with that cryptic comment and an enigmatic smile, he closed the door behind him.

CHAPTER ONE

'THE mountain rescue team are bringing in a boy who slipped on a school adventure trip. It was a very tricky rescue, by all accounts. He was wedged in a steep gully, too badly injured to move. And the weather was too bad for the helicopter to winch him out.' Ellie, the emergency department sister, checked the notes she'd made. 'Nasty compound fracture of the tibial shaft. I'm guessing that the poor boy had more adventure than he was planning for.'

'Oh, the poor thing!' Stella felt a stab of sympathy. 'So how did they get him out?'

'One of the team abseiled down into the gully. Sat in the freezing cold with him and figured out a way to achieve the impossible,' Ellie said dryly. 'Heroic rescue by all accounts. I was hoping you'd take this one for me. It might be a bit complicated and you were always good with complicated. It's so good to have you back. I missed you. Did they teach you anything new in that fancy hospital in London?'

'Only how to deal with stabbings and gunshot wounds, which isn't a lot of use up here in Cumbria. I missed you, too, and I can't wait to catch up properly.' Her friendship with Ellie was another reason she'd come back. 'We ought to go out. Pizza? Movie?'

'Both!' Ellie hugged her. 'But it will have to be early. I have to be in bed by nine or I can't function. The kids are exhausting at the moment.'

Stella felt a sudden stab of envy. 'I can't wait to see them. Are they looking forward to Christmas?'

'Are you joking? They're so over-excited they can't sleep and there's still another three weeks to go. Ben and I will be frayed by Christmas Eve.'

But frayed in a good way, Stella thought wistfully, longing for the chance to be similarly frayed. She wouldn't *want* to sleep if she had a baby. She'd just want to lie awake all night, staring in wonder.

'I'll go and prepare Resus.' Knowing that it was stupid to dwell on what she didn't have, Stella walked with Ellie towards the resuscitation room. 'So which one of the team performed the daring rescue? Was it your Ben?'

'No.' Ellie pushed open the doors to Resus. 'It was your Dan.'

Stella stopped, feeling as though her heart had been left two metres behind her body. 'Daniel?'

'Yes. He's bringing the boy in now.' Ellie peered at her face. 'I think you've just answered my next question, which was going to be, "Are you still in love with him?"'

'I'm not in love with him.'

'This is me you're talking to.'

'I'm not in love with him.'

'All right, we'll argue about that some other time. For now what I need to know is whether you can work with him.'

Stella was grateful for the acting classes she'd taken as a child. They helped her pull her features into an expression that said 'unconcerned'.

In less than five minutes she was going to see him. This was the moment she'd been dreading. The whole thing felt like some sort of test. How far had she come? Had she recovered enough to be able to look at Daniel and not want him?

Aware that some sort of response was required, she nodded. 'I can work with him. He's a very talented doctor.' She consoled herself with the fact that at least the second half of that sentence wasn't a lie. 'Why would it be a problem?'

Ellie sighed and then gave her a quick hug. 'Stella, this is a big thing for you, I know. I watched you fall in love with Dan. I know what he meant to you.'

'And you watched when it fell apart.'

'You were engaged.'

'For about five minutes. Two years ago. *Big* mistake. I don't intend to repeat it. Dan and I are history.' Stella pulled away from her. 'And I have a date tomorrow. He calls himself "Caring of Cumbria". Blond, sensitive, loves romantic nights in by the fire and is looking for a long-term relationship with the right woman.'

Ellie laughed. 'Sounds the complete opposite of Dangerous Dan.'

'Who is dark, *in*sensitive, likes hot sex by the fire and short-term relationships with the wrong women. You see? If I'd analysed him properly I would have run a mile.' Gaining confidence from that thought, Stella walked across the room. 'All right, what am I likely to need?'

'Do you want me to hang around?'

'In case we kill each other?' Stella pulled on an apron and a pair of gloves. 'I hope we'll be more civilised than that. Is there anything else I should know about the patient?'

'Dan will tell you when he gets here. He's going to deal with it himself.' With that unsettling announcement, Ellie hurried out of the room and seconds later the door swung open again.

The man guiding the stretcher into the room was tall and powerfully built, his outdoor clothing adding bulk to his muscular shoulders. 'All right, Sam.' His voice was calm and confident as he talked to the boy. 'Now I've got some proper equipment, I can make you a bit more comfortable.' He turned to the two junior doctors who were flanking him. 'I put a line in at the scene, but I want you to get another one in straight away. He's had morphine and the leg is splinted. I need another bag of fluid and…' Daniel glanced up, saw Stella and lost his thread.

Their relationship had begun with a single look, *a single look that had altered the future for both of them.*

Non-verbal communication had been their speciality—a knowing glance, a touch, a smile that was more of a promise—and if she'd hoped that the damage that lay behind them would have changed anything, she was disappointed.

The sudden jolt of chemistry was powerful enough to have Stella reaching out to hold the side of the trolley. It was as if she'd touched a high-voltage cable and a thousand memories shot through her, all of them including a man with ice-blue eyes and a dangerously sexy smile.

But the smile wasn't in evidence today.

His lean, handsome face was serious, his expression doing nothing to soften the hardness of the man.

It was unfortunate that he'd come straight from a rescue, Stella thought weakly. Stubble suited him. The first thing she'd done every morning had been to drag her fingers over the darkness of his jaw, just before she'd kissed him…

Her stomach took a dive. 'Hello, Daniel.'

He unzipped the neck of his jacket roughly, as if it was choking him. 'Stella?' His voice was hoarse and shocked and suddenly she couldn't breathe because the memories were out of control.

His breath hot on her neck; his skilled, knowing hands on her trembling body; that same husky voice murmuring her name.

She gazed back at him, the only man who'd ever had this effect on her.

In London she'd hoped to meet someone who would make her forget Daniel. But how did you forget a face as absurdly handsome as his? How did you forget six feet two of arrogant masculinity? Who, out of the many doctors she'd met during her period of self-imposed exile, would have been capable of abseiling into a narrow ravine and masterminding the rescue of a severely injured boy?

Who would have had the ability to make her care so much that when it had ended, part of her had ceased to function?

Remembering the agony was what saved her. Stella turned back to the patient, reminding herself that 'Caring of Cumbria' liked long walks and was looking for commitment. 'Hello, Sam.' She walked over to the stretcher and smiled at the white-faced boy. 'I hear you've had a bit of an exciting day.'

He looked impossibly young and he turned his head to look at Daniel, fear and hero-worship mingling in his eyes. 'You promised you wouldn't leave me. You said—'

'I know what I said.' Daniel's voice was rough and he curved his hand over the boy's shoulder. 'And I'm not leaving you. But I do need to try and sort out that leg of yours. Trust me. Just do as I say and you're going to be all right.'

Always in control. Always in charge.

Trust me.

Stella gritted her teeth. *Trust me to break your heart.* But she noticed that his hand stayed on the boy's shoulder, providing the contact and reassurance that was so obviously needed as he gave the other doctors a series of instructions.

She guided the stretcher alongside the trolley. 'We're just going to move you across, Sam.'

'You're working here?' Daniel's harsh interruption made her flinch and Stella gently removed the blanket covering the boy.

Wasn't it obvious? 'I've called the radiologist.'

'Wait.' His hand covered hers, stopping her. 'We move him on my count, not before.'

She'd forgotten what it was like, working with him. When he was in Resus, he was the one in command. Which was why this particular hospital had such impressive success rates, she thought dryly. Her heart thumping, Stella glanced down at the strength of his fingers covering hers and gently eased her hand away. 'Fine. On your count.'

Registering her withdrawal, his jaw tensed and his eyes narrowed dangerously. 'Why did no one tell me you were back?'

'Because the medical staff aren't usually interested in nursing appointments,' Stella said calmly, wondering if he was even aware that the other medical staff in the room were watching them, wondering what was going on.

Nothing was going on, she told herself firmly. *Nothing, except an awkward first meeting.*

They transferred the boy from stretcher to trolley, and Daniel gave Stella a fulminating look that warned her that the conversation was far from over. Then he turned back to the frightened child and proceeded to demonstrate how he'd earned his reputation as a ferociously talented emergency doctor.

Maintaining a casual flow of conversation that distracted the boy, he examined him thoroughly, his skilled hands looking for injuries he hadn't already identified.

'How's that pain, Sam?'

'It's OK.' But the boy's face was grey and Daniel glanced towards one of his colleagues.

'Is that line in yet?'

'Just about to do that now.' The more junior doctor was obviously keen to ask questions. 'So what's the Gustilo classification? Was there extensive tissue loss? Much bone exposure? This is an orthopaedic emergency, right?' His tactless observation drew a terrified sound from the boy and he clutched Daniel's arm.

'I feel sick.'

Panic, Stella thought to herself and Daniel gave him a warm smile.

'You're doing fine, Sam. I'm not worried and if I'm not worried, you don't need to be worried.' He glanced towards the doctor who had spoken and Stella saw his eyes narrow dangerously. 'Get that line in,' he murmured softly, 'and I'll talk to you about the case later.'

And about other things, Stella thought to herself. Daniel Buchannan was too much of a perfectionist to allow the younger doctor's slip to pass without comment.

'Just breathe for me, Sam,' she said softly. 'I'm going to attach these wires to you so that we can monitor your pulse and blood pressure without having to disturb you.'

The boy looked at her gratefully. 'You probably think I'm a baby.'

'Babies don't climb in Devil's Gully.' Stella wrapped the blood-pressure cuff around his arm. 'I've seen it from the top. Never had the nerve to go down.'

Sam closed his eyes. 'My mum is going to kill me.'

'She'll just be glad you're all right.' Stella looked at the monitor, noticing the rapid pulse rate and the low blood pressure.

She looked at Daniel and he inclined his head briefly, but said nothing that would worry the boy.

'I'm going to give you something else for the pain and sickness in just a moment, Sam,' he said gently, checking the boy's abdomen. 'Stella, I want to do a FAST scan. There might be some bleeding here.'

Stella reached for the machine, still talking to the boy. 'I can't believe you climbed that bit of the mountain,' she said briskly, reaching for the drugs that Daniel was going to need. 'It's a tricky route, even in summer. Steep.' She talked as she worked, keeping the boy's attention.

'It was snowy and I went too close to the edge.'

Picturing the scene, Stella suppressed a shudder. The boy had been lucky to escape with his life. Knowing the harsh, unforgiving terrain, she also knew that Daniel must have risked his own life to save the child. 'That story is going to get you lots of sympathy over Christmas,' she said lightly. 'And bigger presents.'

The child's face brightened slightly. 'Do you think so?'

'I'm sure.' Stella grinned and put the syringes on a tray. 'Start planning your Christmas list now.'

The boy managed a smile and then groaned as a spasm of pain took hold. The groan turned to a sob and he looked at Daniel, his eyes terrified. 'Am I going to die? I feel sick. And dizzy. Like everything is far away.'

When he needed reassurance, he looked at Daniel, Stella noticed. He'd bonded with the man who had saved his life.

'You're not going to die.' Daniel spoke firmly, his hand still on the boy's shoulder. 'If patients die, I get fired. And I need the money.'

The sound the boy made was halfway between laughter and a sob. 'To run that fancy sports car you told me about?'

'Yeah—that and other things.'

'Women?'

Daniel's eyes gleamed. 'They're expensive things, women.' Without moving his eyes from the patient, he held out his hand and Stella slipped the syringe into it, knowing exactly what he wanted.

'Morphine and cyclizine.'

'I know my leg is a mess,' Sam murmured, still looking at Daniel. 'I saw it before you put the splint on. It looked disgusting. And that other doctor said it was a medical emergency.'

'It's nothing we can't deal with,' Daniel said smoothly, checking the drug before administering it. 'Take no notice of my colleague. We doctors love drama—makes us feel powerful and important. Don't you watch the TV? It's how we pull the girls. There's a pretty nurse in the room. He's trying to impress her.'

The boy gave a weak grin. 'Those medical dramas mostly make me feel sick.'

'Me, too,' Daniel said blithely, dropping the empty syringe back onto the tray. 'Probably why I'm still single. I haven't got what it takes to pull the girls. All right, Sam, this is what we're going to do. I've just given you another dose of medicine for pain and sickness because I can see that's starting to bother you again. And now my friend here is going to put another needle in your vein.'

The boy's eyes closed. 'I still feel sick.'

'That will pass in a minute,' Daniel murmured, his gaze flickering to the monitor that displayed the boy's pulse and blood pressure. 'I'm right here, Sam. Don't you worry. Everything is going to be fine. In three weeks' time, you're going to be eating your turkey and opening those presents.'

How could he possibly think he wouldn't make a good father? Stella wondered numbly. For a man who claimed to know nothing about children, he was astonishingly empathetic.

Sam obviously agreed because he never took his eyes from Daniel's face. 'I'll never forget you climbing down that slippery bit,' the boy mumbled. 'You deserve a medal or something.'

Daniel grinned, moving to one side while the radiologist prepared to take the X-rays. 'Unfortunately I never get what I deserve. What was your reward supposed to be for battling through the snow and wind?'

'My adventure badge. But I don't suppose I'll get it now because I didn't finish the trip.' The boy moaned as the radiologist moved his leg slightly. 'I wish I'd never signed up for it.'

'You were unlucky, that's all. When you're recovered give me a call and I'll take you up there. The views are fantastic from the top. You'll get your adventure badge—I'm sure about that.' Daniel was working, examining the boy properly and murmuring instructions in a voice so calm that the boy remained unaware of the seriousness of his injuries. 'Stella, how are the distal pulses?'

'Strong.' Stella checked that the blood supply to the lower limb was satisfactory while the casualty officer secured the second line and took the bloods that Daniel had ordered.

'Do you want me to uncover the wound and take a photograph?'

'I did that at the scene. I don't want the dressing removed. The next time that wound is being exposed to air is in the operating theatre. Camera in my left pocket.' Daniel turned slightly so that Stella could retrieve it and she tensed as she plunged her hand into his pocket.

His eyes met hers for a moment and she backed away, her fingers clutching the camera.

'Antibiotics and tetanus,' Daniel said roughly, and Stella

turned away to prepare the drugs, knowing that her face was pink.

This was turning out to be much, much harder than she'd anticipated.

Was this going to get easier with time?

She certainly hoped so.

It wasn't the working together that was the problem—that was as smooth as ever. It was the emotion behind it. It was impossible to switch off.

'Daniel?' Ellie put her head round the door, her face worried. 'I know you're not officially on duty but we're having a nightmare out here. I suppose it's the snow and ice—the roads are lethal. I've got a pregnant woman coming in. She and her husband were involved in a car accident. Might you be able to—?'

'Yes. As long as she doesn't mind being seen by a doctor in full outdoor gear.' Daniel injected the antibiotic into the cannula, his eyes on his patient's face. 'I've been in the mountains for eight hours. At some point I need to get back to base, drop the equipment and debrief. Where is everyone else? What's the ETA of your pregnant woman?'

'Ambulance Control just phoned. She's about eight minutes away.'

'That should give me time to get Sam down to Theatre. Give me a shout when she arrives.' Daniel glanced at Stella. 'Any sign of the orthopaedic guys?'

'We're here.' A slim man with sandy-coloured hair hurried into the room. 'Sorry. Black ice has kept us busy. I've only just got out of Theatre.' He looked at Daniel's bulky outdoor gear. 'Is this a new uniform for the emergency department?'

'Daniel?' The boy's hand shot out and clutched Daniel's arm

again. There was fear in his eyes. 'Are they going to put me to sleep? Will I feel anything? Did you get hold of my mum?'

'They are going to put you to sleep and, no, you won't feel anything.' Daniel's voice was soft. 'I spoke to your mum. She's on her way.'

'Will you stay with me until she gets here?'

A muscle worked in Daniel's dark jaw. 'Are you kidding? You're wearing half my equipment—and it's the expensive half. There's no way I'm letting you out of my sight. We're going to take you straight to Theatre and get that leg of yours stuck back together in time for Christmas.' His glaze flickered to his colleague. 'Are you ready?'

'You're coming, too?' The man looked startled but Daniel's gaze was cool.

'I'll stay with him until he's under.'

The orthopaedic surgeon picked up the charts and gave a brief nod. 'All right. Well, you're obviously needed back here, so let's move.'

'If my pregnant patient was eight minutes away three minutes ago then I have five minutes.' Daniel glanced at his watch. 'I'll be back in five minutes.'

He'd been out on an exposed mountainside for eight hours and he had five minutes in which he could have grabbed a hot drink. Instead he was going to accompany a frightened child to the anaesthetic room.

Stella gritted her teeth. All the reasons why she'd fallen in love with Daniel in the first place were still there. Nothing had changed.

'Go.' She started clearing Resus. 'I'll sort things out here.'

She barely had time to run through another bag of fluid and restock, before the paramedics arrived with the pregnant woman. After listening to the handover by the paramedics, Stella tried to make her patient more comfortable.

Her face was bleeding slightly from several small lacerations and a livid bruise was already forming over one cheekbone. 'I'm so worried about the baby. We've been trying for five years—' Her voice broke and she rubbed her hand over her swollen abdomen. 'If anything happens to him I'll—'

'We're going to check you *and* the baby, Fiona,' Stella soothed, glancing towards the door as Daniel strode in. 'This is Dr Buchannan, one of our consultants.'

Fiona looked in astonishment at Daniel's outdoor clothing and he shrugged.

'It's cold in this department,' he drawled, and she gave a choked laugh.

'I read an article about you last summer. You're one of three doctors in the emergency department that volunteer for the mountain rescue team.'

'That's right.' Daniel glanced at the monitor that Stella had connected to the patient, tracking the readings. 'There's Sean Nicholson, although we do keep telling him he's getting a bit too old for tramping up in the hills. And there's Ben—both of whom are treating other patients, which is why you have me. Technically I'm off duty but there's no rest for the wicked. I see Stella's already given you oxygen.' He turned to Stella. 'I'd forgotten what it's like to work with a nurse who is always one step ahead of me.'

Stella's hands trembled slightly as she attached Fiona to the CTG machine. 'This will help us get a feel for how your baby is doing.' She adjusted the elastic until she was satisfied with the reading. 'Daniel—do you want me to call Obstetrics and get someone down here?'

'I'll take a look at her first. Monitors only tell you so

much—I learned that lesson as a medical student when the monitor told me a woman wasn't having contractions. She delivered the baby five minutes later. I was more shocked than she was.' Daniel took off his jacket, washed his hands and pulled on a pair of gloves. 'Have you had any problems in the pregnancy, Fiona? Anything you think I should know about?'

If sexual attraction was enough to hold two people together then they would have stuck like glue, Stella thought helplessly, watching the flex of his biceps as he worked.

'It's all been really easy.' Fiona twisted her wedding ring round her finger. 'I've been doing everything by the book. It's our first baby. And I'm terrified.' Her voice wobbled. 'Do you have kids?'

Stella's gaze met Daniel's briefly.

'No.' There was a sudden coolness to his tone. 'I don't.'

'It changes you,' Fiona said simply. 'All I care about is this baby. I suppose that's part of being a mother.'

Daniel didn't respond and Stella stayed silent, too.

Marriage, motherhood, maternity—Daniel's three least favourite topics of conversation. And she should know. They'd had that conversation on numerous memorable occasions. *Memorable for all the wrong reasons.*

'It's natural to be concerned about the baby.' Daniel spoke the words the woman needed to hear, but Stella sensed that part of him was detached.

'Babies are surprisingly resilient,' she reassured the woman. 'And we're going to check him very carefully.'

Daniel conducted a thorough examination and Stella knew that he'd shut the conversation out of his mind with ruthless efficiency. He was looking for clinical signs that might suggest a problem. He wasn't thinking about babies or emotion.

He was palpating Fiona's abdomen when she gave a little gasp of fright and shifted on the trolley.

'Oh!' Her eyes widened with panic. 'I think I'm bleeding. Oh, God, am I losing it? Please don't say I'm losing the baby.'

More comfortable with a medical emergency than an emotional one, Daniel was cool and calm as he examined her. 'Stella—give my brother a call, will you? Tell him I need him down here.'

Meeting his gaze briefly, Stella moved to the phone and spoke to Switchboard.

Fiona put her hand over her eyes and started to cry. 'I can't believe I'm bleeding. I wish I'd never left the house. We were going Christmas shopping. I know there's another three weeks to go but I wanted to get it out of the way in case something happens. And now I've made it happen.' Great tearing sobs shook her body and Stella slipped her arm around the woman's shoulders, trying to imagine how she'd feel in the same position.

'You haven't made anything happen,' she soothed. 'You must try and calm down, for the baby's sake.'

'If I lose this baby—'

'Fiona.' Daniel reached for an IV tray, nothing in his voice betraying the fact that he was concerned. 'I want you to relax and trust me. My brother is one of the best obstetricians in the country and he will take a look at you.'

'*One* of the best?' Patrick strode into the room, a mocking gleam in his eyes as he looked at Daniel. 'I'm not one of the best. I'm *the* best.'

Fiona blinked in shock and Stella sighed.

'Yes, they're twins. Don't worry, you're not seeing double. Both of them as arrogant as the other.'

Fiona gave a feeble smile. 'Are they as good as they seem to think they are?'

'Fortunately, yes.' Stella adjusted one of the probes. 'Or maybe I should say *un*fortunately. I don't know. It makes them unbearable to be with, but I suppose it's good for the patients. Patrick? Do you want to take a look at this CTG trace?'

'I'm looking.' Patrick stood next to her, studying the trace in silence. 'All right—so there are a few dips there.'

Stella looked up and found Daniel glancing between her and Patrick. Then he focused on his brother's profile, so like his own. His jaw tightened, his blue eyes glittered dangerously and Stella felt a rush of trepidation. He'd obviously registered the fact that Patrick hadn't been surprised to see her.

Patrick looked up and met his brother's accusing gaze.

They were like a couple of stallions, Stella thought with exasperation, locked in a battle over territory. The interaction lasted less than a few seconds, but the impact was sufficiently powerful to leave her nervous of what was to come.

Why couldn't she have fallen in love with someone mild and gentle?

Pivoting back to the patient, Daniel fastened a tourniquet around Fiona's arm. 'I'm just going to put a cannula in your vein, in case we need to give you some fluid. Can you straighten your arm for me?'

'Stella—can I have a pen?' While Daniel set up an IV, Patrick was examining the woman's abdomen. 'I want to mark the height of her uterus.'

Stella swiftly provided him with a pen, wishing she'd never accepted Patrick's offer of accommodation. It was going to cause problems, just as she'd feared. She should have stayed somewhere else.

Then she frowned, cross with herself. The stable was lovely.

And she could live anywhere she chose to live. It was none of Daniel's business.

And if it was difficult for him—well, tough.

He didn't care, did he?

'Why are you drawing on me?' Fiona looked at Patrick anxiously and he slipped the pen into his pocket.

'You've had some blood loss. It's possible for some of the blood loss to be concealed, trapped behind the uterus. I want to make sure your uterus isn't bigger than it should be. Dan, is there anything else I should know about? Any neck injury? Spine?'

'No.'

'Then I want her nursed in the left lateral position.'

'Fine. I'm nearly done here.' Daniel filled the necessary bottles and dropped them on the tray.

Stella stepped forward and helped him connect the IV, the casual brush of his arm against hers sending a shower of sparks over her.

And he noticed her reaction.

His eyes shifted to her face. As a doctor, he was trained to detect changes in the human body and he was a man who knew women. A man who knew *her*.

'Everything all right?'

'Everything is fine,' she said sweetly, wishing he wasn't quite so astute. Nothing passed him by. Nothing. And as much as she'd hoped that working together would be smooth and easy, it was turning out to be anything but.

Focusing on the pain that went alongside loving Daniel Buchannan, Stella murmured words of comfort to Fiona and helped her turn on her side.

'Why do I have to lie like this?'

'Because lying flat on your back puts pressure on one of

your major blood vessels and that's not good for the baby.'
Patrick checked the baby's heart rate. 'That's better. Thanks,
Stella. That's great.'

Daniel shot him a look. 'It's good to have Stella back, isn't
it?' There was an edge to his tone that wasn't lost on his
brother.

'Definitely.' Playing with fire, Patrick smiled. 'I was so
pleased when she called me to talk through her plans.'

Stella threw him an incredulous glance. What was he doing?
He appeared to be asking for a black eye for Christmas.

'You didn't mention it.' Daniel adjusted the IV. 'It must
have slipped your mind.'

'Nothing slips my mind. I just didn't think you'd be interested.' Calmly, Patrick checked the monitor. 'What bloods
have you taken?'

'U&Es, FBC, cross-match, BMG, coagulation screen, rhesus
and antibody status and Kleihauer—why? Did I miss something?'

'No.' Ignoring the snap in his brother's tone, Patrick winked
at the patient. 'Now he'll be unbearable.'

Fiona shifted the oxygen mask slightly. 'Twins, both of you
doctors.' She sounded amazed. 'One of you is an emergency
specialist and one of you is an obstetrician?'

'That's right. My brother is the emergency specialist.' Patrick looked at Daniel. 'The work suits his personality. Quick
and dirty. All superficial, no depth or emotion.'

Daniel's firm mouth flickered into a smile. 'That's how I
prefer it.'

While they bantered, the two brothers worked together
seamlessly, exchanging information, conducting tests. Then
Patrick moved to the side of the trolley and put his hand on
Fiona's shoulder.

'Fiona, I think there could be some concealed bleeding behind your uterus.' He spoke gently, knowing that the news he was giving wasn't going to be well received. 'At the moment everything is fine and I'm not going to interfere, but I want to transfer you to the labour ward, just to be safe. We can monitor you there and if we need to intervene, we can.'

Fiona shifted on the trolley. 'What's causing the bleeding?'

'It's possible that a small part of the placenta has come away from the uterus—we call it an abruption. I want to keep you in hospital for now, see how things develop.'

Fiona swallowed. 'And if it gets worse?'

'Then I will deliver your baby.'

'But the baby isn't due until January.' Panic drove her voice up a pitch. 'I have another six weeks to go.'

'All the indications are that the baby is fine,' Patrick said calmly. 'And thirty-four weeks is early, that's true, but not so early that I'd be worried. We have an excellent special care baby unit here—we call it the SCBU—but at thirty-four weeks your baby might not need any extra help. Let's see how you go. My plan is to keep him inside you as long as possible.'

Fiona's face crumpled and she started to cry again. 'But this wasn't *my* plan. I've been reading all the books—I've gone to all the classes—I know exactly how I want my labour to be.'

Stella picked up a box of tissues, about to intervene, but Patrick took Fiona's hand in his. 'It's hard when things don't go according to plan,' he said gruffly. 'I really understand that. It happened with Posy, my youngest, and it shook me up. Nightmare. Nature has a way of keeping us all on our toes, but all that really matters is that the baby is safe, Fiona. Remember that.'

'Babies can die if they're premature.'

'There is no evidence that your baby is in trouble. And

from now on I'm going to be watching you.' Patrick pulled a
couple of tissues from the box Stella was holding and handed
them to Fiona. 'Once you have kids, life rarely goes according to plan. Chaos is part of the fun. Or that's what I tell myself when I'm tripping over children, kittens and unwrapped
Christmas presents.'

Stella felt a lump in her throat. Tripping over children, kittens and unwrapped Christmas presents sounded like paradise
to her. 'Is there anyone else I can call for you, Fiona?' Stella
yanked her mind back from its fruitless journey towards a dead
end. 'Your husband is just having a few stitches in his head
and then I'll bring him to wherever you are.'

'I keep thinking that this is all my fault. Perhaps I shouldn't
have worn the seat belt—'

'Wearing a seat belt is the right thing to do,' Daniel said
firmly. 'Contrary to popular opinion, wearing a seat belt does
lower the risk of serious injury. Fiona, just relax and trust us.
Patrick will make whatever decision needs to be made and it
will be the right one, believe me.'

Patrick lifted his eyebrow. 'You're saying I'm always right?'

Despite her tears, Fiona gave a choked laugh. 'Are they always like this?'

'No, sometimes they're really bad,' Stella said cheerfully,
squeezing Fiona's hand. 'I'll come with you up to the ward.
Then I'll go and check on your husband. He must be worried sick.'

'He feels horribly guilty, but it wasn't his fault. The roads
are lethal.'

'I'll go and see him as soon as we've settled you upstairs,'
Stella assured her. 'Is there anyone else I can call?'

Fiona closed her eyes. 'My mum? No, not my mum. You'll

just worry her. No one for the time being. But thanks. You've all been really kind.'

'Let's get you upstairs.' Patrick moved the trolley towards the door and Daniel's gaze settled on his face.

'I want to talk to you.'

Patrick smiled. 'I bet you do. But I'm busy, so it's going to have to wait.'

Daniel strode down the corridor, his tension levels in the danger zone after six hours of working shoulder to shoulder with Stella. Six hours of torture. At one point she'd leaned forward to pass him an instrument and he'd detected the faint smell of roses. Knowing that it was the shampoo she always used had set up a chain reaction in his brain. Thinking about the shampoo had made him think about her hair, long and loose. And thinking about her hair long and loose had made him think about her in his bed. And thinking about her in his bed had—

Daniel ruthlessly deleted that thought from his mind, but it immediately popped back again, taunting and teasing his senses until he gave a low growl of frustration, oblivious to the pretty nurse who gazed at him as she hurried past.

Without slackening his stride, he took the six flights of stairs up to the obstetric unit, too impatient to wait for the lift.

Nodding briefly to a consultant he knew, he made straight for his brother's office and pushed open the door.

'You knew Stella was coming back and you didn't tell me?'

Patrick leaned back in his chair and lifted an eyebrow. 'Next time, knock. I could have had a naked woman in here.'

Daniel planted his hands on the edge of his brother's desk, struggling with his temper. 'Damn it, Patrick—just how long have you been communicating with my ex-girlfriend?'

Patrick closed the file he'd been reading. 'Your ex-*fiancée*,' he said with gentle emphasis, 'and I've been "communicating" with her since you unceremoniously dumped her. On Christmas Eve. Not exactly the present she'd been hoping for, I'm sure.'

Daniel felt a sudden rush of cold. 'Why are you bringing that up now? That's history.'

'If it's history, why are you standing in my office threatening me?'

Daniel dragged his hand through his hair. 'I didn't dump her. She dumped me.'

Patrick stood up abruptly, impatience making his eye flash a deep blue. '*After* you told her you wouldn't marry her.'

'Not wouldn't—*couldn't*. It isn't that I don't want to get married,' Daniel said hoarsely, 'I do. But I *can't*. I just can't do it. I would make a lousy husband and a terrible father and I won't do that to a child.' Sweat tingled on his brow as he thought of how close he'd come to breaking his promise to himself. Only Stella could have driven him to that. 'I can't be what she wants me to be. I did it for her.'

'Funny. She didn't appear that grateful last time I looked.'

'She should be grateful. Better to let her down now than in five years' time.' Or at least, that's what he'd told himself when he'd driven the scalpel through her heart.

Trying to dispel that image, Daniel pressed his fingers into the bridge of his nose and Patrick sighed.

'Why would you have let her down?'

'Being a mother is really important to Stella. Sometimes I think it's the only thing that matters to her.' Trying to get a grip on his emotions, Daniel clamped his hands over the edge of Patrick's desk. 'And I knew I couldn't be what she wanted me to be. She has this picture in her head—the perfect family. Mum, Dad, lots of kids—probably a dog or two.' He gritted his teeth. 'And I'm not the guy in that picture. Fatherhood is the one job I'm not going to try. You mess that up, you take people with you.'

'I happen to think you wouldn't mess it up,' Patrick replied calmly, 'but I know you believe it. Which is why I didn't knock your head off two years ago.'

Daniel straightened. 'So you agree I did the right thing.'

'No. But I know you think you did. And I didn't want to watch you self-destruct and take Stella with you. She is a rare, special person. The sort of woman who would be by your side no matter what life throws at you. She wants marriage and a family—and she'll make someone a fantastic wife and mother.'

'And is that "someone" going to be you?' Anger roared through him like fire through a parched forest and Daniel strode around the desk and grabbed his brother by the shoulders. 'You're in need of a wife and a mother for your children—is Stella going to fill that slot? Is that why she's back?'

Patrick didn't flinch. 'You've just said you're not interested. Why would you care?'

'I never said I didn't care.' Daniel let his hands drop, stunned by his own reaction. *Since when had he picked fights with his twin?* 'I just don't think you're the right man for Stella.'

'I don't think you're qualified to judge. Relationships aren't your speciality, are they?'

Daniel stared at his brother for a long moment and then breathed out slowly. 'You're not having a relationship, are you? You're just winding me up.'

'Why would that wind you up? You decided you're not good for Stella. Right or wrong, that means she's free to be with another man. And with her long legs and her sweet nature, they're going to be beating her door down. You'd better get used to it.'

Sweat pricking his forehead, Daniel tried to imagine getting used seeing Stella with another man. 'That's fine. No problem. I just don't want her mixed up with someone unsuitable. She's pretty innocent.'

'She went out with you for two years,' Patrick reminded him dryly, 'so she can't be that innocent.'

Thinking about the steam and sizzle that had characterised their relationship, Daniel suddenly felt a rush of dangerous heat. The thought of Stella with another man made his stomach churn. 'I just don't want some man messing her around.'

'Like you did? Don't worry—if she survived you, she'll survive anyone.' Patrick strolled back to his desk and sat down. He took a set of notes from a pile and reached for a pencil. 'I need to do some work.'

'Why is she back?'

'Obviously she's got over you and felt able to come home. She has friends here.' Patrick scanned some results, scribbled something onto the notes and dropped them in a tray ready to be collected. 'A life.'

A life that didn't include him. 'And you're one of those friends?'

'Of course. I've known her as long as you have. She was my friend, as well as yours. She made Christmas for us that year you and Carly had your own mini-meltdowns.' He looked at Daniel, a warning in his gaze. 'I'll never forget how she picked herself up and got on with things. Her heart was breaking but she still managed to dance around the house wearing antlers to make my son laugh.'

'She was always good with children. That was our problem. All Stella ever wanted was children.' *And children were the last thing he wanted.* Daniel stared at the row of photographs of his niece and nephew that Patrick had hung on the wall. Alfie and Posy giggling on a sledge. The two of them covered in ice cream at the beach. Posy in a backpack, grabbing Patrick's hair. 'Those two human beings are totally reliant on you. If you screw up, they suffer.'

'Thanks for that vote of confidence.'

'Doesn't it terrify you?'

'No. I love them. And I don't intend to screw up.' Patrick toyed with the pencil. 'It doesn't have to be the way it was for us, Dan.'

It was something they rarely mentioned and Daniel felt the filthy sludge of the past slide into his brain. 'Christmas was the worst time, do you remember?'

The pencil in Patrick's lean fingers snapped in two. 'Yes.'

'I counted the days until it was over.'

'I counted them with you.' His brother's casual tone didn't fool him and suddenly Daniel wanted to know.

'So how have you managed to put it behind you? With that grim example of parenting shining in your head, how do you do it?'

'I love my children.' A faint smile touched his brother's mouth. 'And I suppose I treat our childhood as an education in how not to parent. As long as I'm doing everything opposite, then I'm pretty confident that it will turn out all right.'

'You're divorced.'

'Precisely. If Mum and Dad had divorced, they might have been happy.' Patrick threw the broken bits of pencil into the bin. 'I don't subscribe to the school of thought that says a miserably unhappy couple have to stay together for the sake of the children. Why are we talking about this? What does this have to do with Stella?'

'I'm reminding you why I don't want marriage.'

'I don't need reminding.'

'I did her a favour.'

'You truly believe that, don't you?' Patrick gave a humourless laugh. 'Dan, you proposed to her and then broke her heart. What I don't understand is why you asked her to marry you in the first place, given your serious allergy to that condition.'

Daniel ran his hand over the back of his neck, remembering that night. 'It was Christmas. I was crazy about her. It was what she wanted.'

'But not what *you* wanted.'

'For a brief moment I thought I did,' Daniel confessed in a raw tone. 'I thought maybe, just maybe, I could do it, but when your Carly—' Breaking off, Daniel threw his brother a glance of apology but Patrick shrugged.

'Don't mince your words. When Carly walked out on me, it reminded you that relationships are difficult, fragile things.'

'And Alfie cried himself to sleep at night for months!' Daniel's eyes slid to the photographs on the wall. 'I never want to do that to a child.'

Patrick eyed the stack of work on his desk. 'Could we talk about this in my kitchen over a beer later? Or was there something else you wanted to say?'

Daniel tried to clear his head. 'You should have told me that she was coming back.'

'I didn't think you'd be interested. You're dating that sleek, sexy solicitor, remember? You've moved on.' Patrick closed the file he'd been reading and placed it in a tray at the front of his desk ready to be collected.

Glaring at his brother, Daniel wondered how it was possible to love a person and hate them at the same time. 'Well, how long is she back for? Where is she living?'

'As far as I know, she's back for good.' Patrick leaned back in his chair and looked his brother in the eye. 'And she's living with me.'

CHAPTER TWO

STELLA walked into the treatment room and stopped the moment she saw Daniel. Her stomach flipped and her heart did a crazy dance. 'Sorry, I just needed to pick up a dressing pack.' Depressed by the effect he had on her, she backed towards the door and then noticed that he was putting an ice pack on his knuckles. 'Have you hurt yourself? What happened?'

'I hit my hand on something.'

Forgetting her own feelings for a moment, Stella stared at his profile, sensing his boiling anger. She knew him so well. Understood his moods, his volatility and his restless, brilliant mind. She remembered Patrick once telling her that if Daniel hadn't suddenly decided to be a doctor, he probably would have ended up in gaol. 'You hit your hand? Oh, God.' Her stomach lurched as the truth hit her. 'You've seen Patrick, haven't you? Please tell me you didn't—'

'No.' He growled the word angrily as he flexed his fingers. 'I didn't. Believe it or not, I have no intention of adding grievous bodily harm to my list of sins. I punched the wall.'

'Oh.' Relief poured over her. 'What had the wall done wrong?' But even while she was making a joke of it, her thoughts were spinning all over the place. This was because of her, she had no doubt about that. And part of her felt light-headed that her arrival had destabilised him because it meant that he still *cared*. And another part was angry with herself because that reaction was so infuriatingly illogical. She didn't want him to care for her and she didn't want to care for him.

She'd been there. Done that. Tested their relationship to the limits.

Watched it snap.

The glance he threw in her direction was dark and threatening. 'This isn't funny.'

'I agree.' *If they couldn't put the past behind them it certainly wasn't going to be funny.* Crisp and professional, Stella walked over to him and took his hand in hers, examining the bruising. But she found herself thinking about the strength in those fingers—the skill she knew he possessed. Skill in the resuscitation room. *Skill in the bedroom.* 'That's a nasty bruise.' Taking the ice pack from him, she repositioned it so that it rested on the worst of the bruising. 'I suppose I should be relieved that you've learned to hit the wall and not your brother, otherwise I would have had both of you in here and that would take some explaining. Are you going to have this X-rayed?'

'What for? Nothing's broken.' There was a rough note to his voice that told her he was as aware of her as she was of him. 'Who's the doctor here?'

'You are.' She was tempted to slide the ice pack down the front of her scrub suit to cool her overheated body. 'But you don't appear to be thinking clearly.' And she wasn't thinking clearly, either, with him so close to her. Suddenly holding his hand didn't seem like such a clever idea. The sight of those dark hairs shading his strong forearms was enough to make her think things she shouldn't be thinking and the sudden flare of sexual awareness was like a punch to her senses. Stella let go of his hand. 'I'll get you a bandage.'

'I don't need a bandage.'

'Then maybe you need an MRI to look at brain function,'

she said tartly, her tone reflecting her frustration with herself. 'Going around hitting walls isn't exactly the behaviour of a consultant.'

'I wasn't a consultant when I punched the wall. I was a man. Dammit, Stella.' He caught her chin in his undamaged hand, turning her face to his, his movements strong and confident, his tone raw and demanding. 'Why didn't you tell me you were coming back?'

The way he touched her rattled her self-control. 'I didn't think you needed to know.'

'But you told my brother.'

'Yes.'

'You're living with him.'

Stella moved her head but he had her trapped. 'Not *with* him. In the stable. Is that why you tried to knock a hole in the wall?' Watching his reaction, she shook her head in disbelief. 'For goodness' sake, Daniel! What is the matter with you? I've seen you handle drunks and drug addicts with calm and patience. I've seen you ice cold, resuscitating a newborn baby when the other doctors in the room were all shaking hands and sweating brows. You have more control than any other man I know. And more intelligence.'

'He said you were living with him.'

'*In the stable!* Can't you tell when he's winding you up?'

Daniel gave a grunt and let his hand drop. 'My brother knows which buttons to push.'

'You two don't change.' But she knew how close they were and felt a flash of guilt for causing friction. 'There's nothing between Patrick and me.'

'It's two years since Carly walked out. He's ready for another relationship.' His tone was rough. 'If that's what the two of you want, I'm relaxed about it.'

Relaxed?

Stella decided not to remind him that his knuckles had required an ice pack. It was natural, she told herself, that he'd feel uncomfortable about her being with Patrick. It was just too close for comfort. He was probably worried that he'd be tripping over her every time he called in on his brother. 'Is that what you're buying him for Christmas? A relationship?'

Daniel flexed his fingers, testing the injury. 'I think we both know relationships aren't my speciality. And you still haven't answered my question. Why are you back?'

'I'm back because this is where I want to live, Daniel! I love the Lake District—I love the hospital. My friends are here. The only reason I went away in the first place was because I just couldn't work alongside you after everything that happened. But I've moved on.' She hoped she sounded convincing. 'And so have you. If you're worried about awkward moments, then don't be. There won't be any.'

'Have you moved on?'

'Of course.' Stella thought of 'Caring of Cumbria'.

'That Christmas two years ago—'

'Let's not talk about it. There's no point.' Surprised and unsettled by his unexpected reference to their highly emotional break-up, Stella decided that the best thing was to show him everything was fine. 'I hear you're seeing someone. That's good. I'm pleased for you.'

Daniel discarded the ice pack. 'You are?'

'Of course. I only ever wanted you to be happy. I'm seeing someone, too.'

Daniel inhaled sharply and his eyes narrowed to two dangerous slits. 'Who?'

Stella suddenly realised that she didn't want to tell him she was using a dating agency. Why did that feel embarrassing? She didn't know, but it did. 'Just a guy.'

'So you don't know him very well.'

'That's why we're dating. To get to know each other.'

'How long have you known him?'

Stella was starting to wish she'd never begun the conversation. 'A couple of months.' Which was true, she reasoned. They'd been emailing each other since October.

'What does he do?'

'What does it matter?' She stared at him, exasperated and confused. 'Why do you care?'

'I'm just making conversation. Finding out what's been happening to you.' But the expression in his eyes said differently. 'Isn't that what friends do?'

'Yes, but we're not friends, Dan,' Stella said softly. 'We haven't been in touch for two years and I think we both know that was the right decision.' *Staying in touch would have been like squeezing lemon juice onto an open wound.*

'You don't seem to have any problems being friends with my brother.'

'Patrick and I have only ever been friends.'

'Whereas you and I were lovers.'

His husky, sexy voice sent a white hot arc of sexual heat shooting through her body and Stella felt everything inside her melt. 'It's in the past, Dan.' She stepped back, rejecting the fiery chemistry and her body's instinctive response. 'It's not going to give us a problem.' Picking up the equipment she'd come to fetch, she walked back towards the door. 'We're colleagues, that's all.'

'So you can work side by side with me and not feel anything.'

'That's right.' The lie came easily, but they were wasted

words because both of them knew the truth. 'We want different things.' It seemed like a good idea to remind them both of that fact.

'Are you going to marry him?'

Stella opened the door. 'I don't know.' That was true, she reasoned. She didn't know. 'And I don't understand why you would even care.'

'Are you having sex with him?'

'For goodness' sake, Dan!' With a gasp, she pushed the door closed again, hoping that none of her colleagues had been walking along the corridor at that point. 'What business is that of yours?' Her eyes clashed with the burning fire of his and, for a moment, he didn't reply.

Then he drew in an uneven breath. 'None,' he said hoarsely, running his undamaged hand through his hair like a man on the edge. 'None at all. And if you are—well, I'm fine with it. That's fine.'

Desperately unsettled, Stella held his gaze, not understanding what was going on in his head. They hadn't spoken to each other for two years. He was seeing someone else. There was no reason for him to react with anything other than indifference.

Except that their relationship had been so hot and intense that it had left scorch marks on both of them.

'I'm glad you're fine with it,' she said shakily, 'because who I date is none of your business. Just as who you date is none of mine.' Deciding that she'd never understand men, Stella left the room before she said something she knew she'd regret.

'So you've never met this person? How do you know he's nice?' Alfie was kneeling on a chair in the stable, watching Stella as she tapped away at the computer. One of the kittens was snuggled on his lap.

'We've been writing to each other.'

'By email?' Alfie looked knowledgeable. 'I have my own email address at school.'

'Really? That's impressive. I certainly didn't know how to email when I was ten years old.' Stella scrolled through her latest message, scanning the contents. 'He wants to meet me, Alfie. What do you think?'

'Let's ask Mary.' He lifted the tiny kitten. 'What do we think, Mary?'

'You called the kitten Mary?'

'It's Christmas. The two I'm keeping are Mary and Joseph. They're the marmalade ones.' He kissed the kitten on the head and rubbed his cheek over the animal's fur. 'It isn't safe to meet a stranger. My teacher says you should never give anyone your real name or address over the internet.'

'Your teacher is right. You shouldn't.' Stella typed her reply. 'And I haven't given any personal details apart from my name. He wants to meet me in a pub.'

Alfie stroked the kitten. 'What if you meet him and he's, like, *really* yucky?'

'Well.' Stella didn't reveal that she'd been wondering that exact thing herself. 'I hope he won't be. We've already talked about the things we like and don't like. So we have a feel for whether we're going to get on.'

'You mean you tell him you like computer games and he tells you he likes playing with Lego?'

'Something like that.'

'What if he's lying just so that you'll be friends with him?'

Stella lifted her hand and ruffled his hair. 'Smart, aren't you?'

'Not really. Harry Trent did that to me,' Alfie grumbled. 'He said he loved Lego, so I invited him to my house for a sleepover but when he got here he just wanted to nose around. And he kept asking questions about how much money Dad has. He wasn't interested in Lego.'

'I'm sorry to hear that,' Stella said softly. 'And if this guy is lying to me, I won't see him again.'

'Why can't you just meet someone normally? It's going to be *really* weird going out with someone you've never met.'

'Sometimes it's hard meeting someone "normally".' Stella stroked the kitten gently. 'We lead busy lives and the chances of just bumping into someone you want to spend the rest of your life with are pretty remote.'

'Why can't you just be with Uncle Dan? You were going to marry him. Two Christmases ago you sat on my bed and read me that story and you showed me the ring Uncle Dan had given you.'

Remembering how quickly her best Christmas had turned into her worst Christmas, Stella bit her lip. 'We managed to have fun that Christmas despite everything, didn't we?'

'Oh, yeah.' Alfie shrugged, more adult than child. 'It was hard at first, when Mum left. Christmas was the final straw for her. She was screaming and yelling like she'd gone mad. At first I thought it was my fault for opening one of my pres-ents early, but Dad told me it was his fault for going to de-liver those triplets on Christmas Eve when Mum had dinner on the table.'

'I remember the triplets. Your dad saved their lives.'

'I know. He's cool. But Mum didn't think so. She hated his job. And she hated Christmas.' Alfie looked puzzled. 'I don't get that, do you? How can anyone hate Christmas? Dad says it stressed her out.'

Finding it hard to feel sympathy for a woman who could leave her children on Christmas Eve, Stella leaned forward and hugged him tightly. 'Alfie…' she discovered that she had a huge lump in her throat '…this Christmas is going to be the best ever. I promise. And no one is going to be stressed out.'

'If Dad has to cook a turkey, *he'll* be stressed out,' Alfie predicted, with insight beyond his years. 'And I'll probably be stressed out if I have to eat it. Dad is better at delivering triplets than cooking. He needs lessons. He's going to advertise for someone who wants a kitten. Do you think I could advertise for someone to come and cook Christmas lunch?'

'You don't need to advertise. I'll give him a lesson,' Stella promised, kissing him on the forehead and then pulling a face. 'Sorry—are you too old to be kissed?'

'I don't mind it,' Alfie said generously, 'as long as you don't do it in front of my friends.'

'I'll remember that.' Stella shut down her computer. 'Have you made your Christmas list?'

'Yes. And I've posted it up the chimney.'

Stella looked at him, unsure whether he still believed in Father Christmas. 'And did he pick it up?'

'It wasn't there when I looked so, yes, I guess so.' He picked up the tiny kitten and kissed it. 'I hope no one wants the kittens. Then we'll have to keep all of them.'

'It would be a lot of work for your dad.'

'I take care of them.' Alfie tucked the kitten back on his lap. 'I wish you'd married Uncle Dan.'

Stella thought, *Me, too,* but managed a smile. 'Your Uncle Dan isn't the marrying kind.'

'I know. He thinks marriage sucks.'

Stella blinked. 'Are you supposed to use that word?'

'Probably not, but I know you won't tell.' Alfred slid off the chair. 'If you don't want to marry Uncle Dan, you could always marry my dad. Then you could cook the turkey. And be my mum. That would be cool.'

'Being your mum would be cool,' Stella agreed, closing her laptop. 'But unfortunately your dad and I don't love each other. Not in that way. And people who get married should love each other.'

'You'd have to have sex, and I guess that would be gross.'

Stella gulped. 'Alfie!' she floundered, not sure how to respond, but Alfie had already moved on.

'What's his name? This guy you're meeting?'

'Edward.'

Alfie wrinkled his nose. 'I don't like that name.'

'It's just a name, Alfie.'

'Does he drive a cool sports car like Uncle Dan?'

'I have no idea.'

'Is he in the mountain rescue team like Dad and Uncle Dan?'

'I don't think so.'

'I'm going to be in the mountain rescue team when I'm old enough. I think it's *so* great, going out into the mountains to save people. You get to slide down ropes and sometimes go in a helicopter. I'm going to get muscles like Dad and Uncle Dan.'

Dismissing a disturbing mental image of Daniel's muscular physique, Stella gave a weak smile. 'I'm sure you will.'

'Last winter he went all the way to South America and climbed a mountain no one else has ever climbed. How cool is that?'

'Pretty cool.'

'Does your guy climb?'

Stella took a deep breath. 'He isn't my guy and, no, he doesn't climb.'

'He sounds a *lot* different from Uncle Dan.'

'Yes,' Stella said breezily. 'He is.'

She was counting on it.

CHAPTER THREE

THE weather grew colder still and the emergency department was busier than ever.

Which was good, Stella reminded herself as she worked her third double shift with no break, *because work took her mind off Daniel.*

'I've never had a headache like it,' the woman moaned, holding her head as Stella checked her blood pressure. 'It feels as though someone is splitting my skull with an axe. We saw the GP yesterday and he said that we've all picked up this virus that's going around, but today when I woke up I felt so bad I was scared I was having a stroke or something.'

'The whole family has had the same bug?'

'My husband, John, has been really sick, but he had the headache, too. And the kids feel rough. They're supposed to be doing nativity plays and Christmas parties but they're too ill to be excited about anything. I left them sleeping this morning. Billy wouldn't even wake up when I went to tell him I was coming here and he's usually the first one up in the morning.'

'He wouldn't wake up?' Stella recorded the woman's blood pressure, but something in the patient's story made her uneasy. 'Are you sure? Did you try waking him?'

'Yes. This bug has totally wiped him out, poor thing.'

Stella looked at her for a moment, a suspicion forming in her mind. 'And your husband?'

'He was asleep, too. I wanted him to drive me here,' Diana

muttered, 'but I couldn't even rouse him so I had to catch the bus. Still, I suppose he needed the rest after being sick yesterday.'

'Perhaps.' Stella glanced at the clock. 'What time did you leave the house?'

'An hour ago. Eight o'clock.'

'Right. Just wait there—I'm going to ask a doctor to take a look at you.' She hurried out of the cubicle and bumped straight into Daniel.

His fingers closed over her arms, steadying her. 'What's the rush? Or have you suddenly realised that there's only another twelve shopping days until Christmas?'

Stella didn't laugh, partly because she was too conscious of his hands on her body and partly because she was still distracted by her patient. 'I have a woman in cubicle 2 complaining of a severe headache.' She pulled away from him, alarmed that even when she was talking to him as a doctor, she was still aware of him as a man. 'The whole family is down with a virus.'

'And?' His gaze lingered on her face, dropped to her mouth. 'What are you thinking?'

That she must have been crazy to think she would ever get over Daniel. 'I'm thinking that it might not be a virus.' Yanking her mind back to her work, Stella gave an embarrassed laugh. 'I'm probably overreacting.'

'I've never known you overreact.' His voice was soft. 'I *have* known you to see things other people miss.'

Stella was silenced by the praise. Thrown, it took her a moment to focus. 'She's had this headache for a while,' she croaked, looking past him down the corridor rather than at his face. 'Yesterday her husband and the kids were sick—'

'They saw their GP?'

'Yes, and he said virus. Gastroenteritis.'

'Sounds reasonable. There's plenty of it going around.'

'Yes.' Stella rubbed her fingers over her forehead and sighed. 'I'm definitely overreacting. If one member of the family has it then it's perfectly reasonable for the whole family to go down.'

Daniel's gaze was fixed on her face. 'Why are you worried?'

'Because when she left the house this morning she couldn't wake her kids or her husband. She thought they were just tired, but—'

'Are you telling me you think it might be carbon monoxide poisoning?'

'I hope not. I—I'm sure it isn't,' Stella stammered, suddenly feeling foolish. 'If it was just her husband who was tired, I wouldn't have been worried, but it's a bit odd not being able to wake a child who is normally bouncing around thinking of Christmas, don't you think?'

'How hard did she try?'

'I don't know.' Stella waved her hand. 'Will you take a look at her? See what you think? If there's a chance I might be right, we should call the police and the paramedics.' It occurred to her that she trusted his judgement implicitly. Whatever their differences, she'd never doubted his abilities as a doctor.

Daniel stared at her for a moment, his expression inscrutable. Then he turned and strode into the cubicle. 'Diane? I'm Daniel Buchannan, one of the consultants here. Tell me about your headache.' He questioned the woman as he examined her, his eyes sharp and attentive as he listened to the history and took some blood samples. 'And the other members of you family had nausea, vomiting and headache?'

'Yes,' she groaned, closing her eyes. 'I did wonder if it was something we'd eaten, but the GP said there is a gastric bug going around.'

'Her sats are fine,' Stella murmured, looking at the monitor.

'The saturation level equals the sum of oxyhaemaglobin and carboxyhaemoglobin, so it's unreliable. It isn't going to tell us what we want to know,' Daniel murmured. 'I want to give her the highest concentration of oxygen possible—use a rebreathing mask. I want to check her COHb levels. And let's do an ECG. Diane...' Daniel turned back to the patient '...I don't think this is a virus. I agree with Stella—I think you might have carbon monoxide poisoning.'

The woman looked at him blankly. 'What?'

'There's been quite a lot about it in the papers. It's a tasteless, odourless gas—it basically lowers the oxygen-carrying capacity of your blood. What sort of heating do you have at home?'

'We're in a rented flat,' Diane gasped. 'We have a gas fire in the living room. We tend to congregate there to save on heating bills. Do you think—?'

'I suspect that the fire might be a problem.'

'Oh, my God—the kids are in the house.' Panic flaring in her eyes, Diane struggled to sit up. 'My husband—'

'We're going to deal with it, Diane. Right now. Lie down and think about yourself for a moment.' Her tone soothing, Stella put the oxygen mask on the anxious woman, adjusted the flow to maximum and then looked at Daniel. 'Do you want me to call the house?'

'I'll do it. You do that ECG.'

Stella attached the leads to Diane's chest and had just switched the machine on when Daniel strode back into the room.

'Diane, there was no reply from your house,' he said gently, 'so I've called the fire brigade and the paramedics. It's just a precaution, but if we're right, we need to get the rest of your family in here as soon as possible.'

Diane's eyes were bright with tears. 'I had no idea! I just left them. I thought they were asleep!'

'We're getting someone round there now, Diane,' Stella said soothingly, but Diane just shook her head.

'What if it's too late?'

Daniel's mobile rang and he answered it swiftly, giving instructions to the paramedics.

'They're at the door now and there's no answer—is there a key anywhere?'

'Flower pot,' Diane murmured weakly, and Daniel relayed that message to the emergency services on the scene. Moments later he was nodding and smiling.

'You're sure? OK. Yes, I'll tell her that.' He dropped the phone into his pocket and smiled at Diane. 'Your husband is awake, Diane. They're getting the children out of the house now and they'll assess them in the ambulance.'

Diane closed her eyes briefly. 'Are they OK? Please tell me they're OK.'

'They're going to give them oxygen and transfer them straight to us.'

'Dan? Do you want to look at this ECG?' Stella stood to one side and Daniel scanned the strip of paper.

'That looks all right. Nothing there that worries me.'

'Why did that GP tell me it was a virus?' Diane fretted, and Daniel slipped the ECG reading into the notes.

'Unfortunately, it's all too easy to miss.'

'*You* didn't miss it.'

'We're a busy emergency department—we're more alert to the possibility of carbon monoxide poisoning than the average family doctor.'

'But if you hadn't thought of it—'

'You can thank this nurse.' Daniel's gaze slid to Stella. 'She was the one who was suspicious. And rightly so.' His eyes rested on her face for a moment and she smiled and then turned away, part of her wishing that they didn't work together so well. Maybe if she didn't admire him as much as a doctor...

A siren sounded outside the department and Daniel moved towards the door. 'That will be the rest of your family. I'll go and see to them and then I'll come back. Stella, if you need me, shout.' He strode out of the room, leaving Stella with a very worried Diane.

'Can I go and see them?'

'You're not well enough.' Stella encouraged her to stay on the trolley. 'Give Daniel time to assess them, and then I'll go and find out what is going on.'

But she didn't need to because Daniel walked into the room less than ten minutes later. 'I've done a preliminary examination and it does seem to be carbon monoxide poisoning, but they're going to be fine,' he assured Diane. 'Your husband is conscious and talking and the boys woke up once they were removed from the house. Your husband has contacted your landlord and the fire department will be dealing with him.' He checked the blood results. 'Her COHb levels are high,' he murmured to Stella. 'I'm going to talk to the infirmary— I'm wondering whether she would benefit from hyperbaric oxygen therapy.'

'I thought that was controversial?'

'I think it might be appropriate in Diane's case. I'll call them.' He strode out of the room again just as Ellie walked in.

'Diane? I've been looking after your lovely boys,' she said, 'and I wanted to let you know that they're doing fine. We've given them oxygen and they're sitting up and chatting. They've told me everything that's on their Christmas lists and all I can say is I hope you won the lottery recently.'

'They're all right?' Diane clutched Stella's hand. 'It's because of you,' she said hoarsely. 'It's because of you they're alive. I can't believe I just thought they were tired. You saved our lives.'

'She's a miracle,' Ellie agreed, winking at Stella, 'but don't tell her too often or she'll expect a pay rise and we don't do things like that around here.'

Stella smiled at her friend and squeezed Diane's hand. 'I'm just relieved that your family is all right.'

'If you hadn't thought of it—or if that doctor hadn't taken you seriously—'

'I always take her seriously,' Daniel drawled from the doorway, a gleam in his eyes as he glanced briefly at Stella. 'Diane, I've spoken to my colleagues and I'm transferring you for some special treatment, and the others, too.'

Stella helped with the arrangements and once Diane had been transferred, she went back to the room to clear up.

'Well done. You just made someone's Christmas.' Daniel stood in the doorway and her heart danced an uneven rhythm because the way he was looking at her was achingly familiar.

'I'm just glad it turned out all right.' She pushed the ECG machine to the end of the cubicle, reminding herself to keep it professional. If they just talked about work, it would be fine. 'How are the children? Ellie said they should be fine.'

'Their COHb levels were quite high, but hopefully they won't suffer any long-term problems. The fire brigade wore breathing apparatus when they went in. Apparently the gas fire was lethal. Blocked flue or something.' He strolled into the room, his eyes on hers. 'Good job, Stella. I've missed working with you.' His gruff male tones melted her bones to liquid.

'I've missed working with you, too,' she breathed, her

hands tightening around the side of the trolley. 'You're a good doctor.'

There was a painful silence and Stella stood there, so aware of him that he may as well have been touching her.

'Look at me, Stella.' His soft command made her heart skip and she lifted her head and looked at him. And instantly regretted it. With a murmur of confusion, she gave a little shake of her head and his eyes darkened.

'Stella, I—'

'Daniel?' A crisp, female voice came from behind him and they both glanced guiltily towards the door.

A woman stood there. She was slim and businesslike, dressed smartly in a navy suit and a white shirt, and in her right hand she held a briefcase. Her glossy red hair was neatly contained in a professional-looking French plait and her make-up was immaculate.

'Andrea.' Daniel hesitated and then cast a wary glance towards Stella.

And she understood instantly who the woman was.

His lawyer.

'I'll just go and check the waiting room.' Stella intended to slide out of the room, but the woman stopped her.

'Don't run away on my account. I'm due in court in ten minutes so I don't have long. Dan—about tonight. Don't pick me up. I'll meet you there. I'd rather drive myself.' She was all crisp efficiency. 'And I have a breakfast meeting tomorrow, so I won't be staying overnight.'

Stella dug her nails into her palms, horrified by the agonising pain she felt. She was supposed to be over him, wasn't she? *She wasn't supposed to care any more.* So why did it hurt to meet his latest girlfriend? And to hear her talking about 'staying over', as if it was a regular occurrence.

Well, of course it was. What had she expected? Daniel was a red-blooded male. Just because he had no interest in marriage and children, it didn't mean he had no interest in other things.

Shaken by the depth of the pain she felt, Stella mumbled an excuse and slid past the two of them, avoiding eye contact with Daniel.

He had his life and she had hers.

And that was the way she wanted it.

'Caring of Cumbria' was going to be her type, she reminded herself. And he was going to stop her thinking about Daniel.

'What do you know about this guy she's seeing?' Daniel stood in his brother's kitchen, staring across the yard towards the converted stable. A light shone behind a curtain and he assumed that Stella was getting ready to go out for the evening. For some reason that he didn't understand, the thought set his teeth on edge.

'Nothing.' Patrick drained the pasta. 'Posy, sit at the table. Alfie, help your sister. God, I'm tired. I can't remember the last time I spent a whole night in my bed. The labour ward is crazy.'

'You're the boss. You're supposed to delegate.'

'I don't delegate life-and-death situations. Why are so many babies born near Christmas?'

'I don't know.' Daniel leaned forward and stole a piece of pasta. 'You're the obstetrician.'

'Can I have extra cheese on my pasta?' Alfie picked Posy up and sat her on her chair. Then he went to the fridge and pulled out a bottle of milk.

'Not milk,' Patrick said absently, cursing under his breath as the water scalded his fingers. 'Give her water. Otherwise she's too full to eat.'

Daniel felt something pressing on his ankle and looked down to see a kitten looking up at him hopefully. 'About this guy that Stella is seeing…'

'I don't know anything about the guy Stella is seeing.'

'I do.' Alfie replaced the milk and poured water into two cups. 'I know he's not in the mountain rescue team.' He put the cup in front of his sister. 'And I don't think he has muscles. But I know he wants to get married and have kids. That's why she's picked him. I just hope he doesn't turn out to be a real creep. She'll find out tonight. Ellie is going to phone her at nine and if he's really yucky then she's going to pretend there's a crisis at home. I guess that will work. She hasn't given him her address or anything.' He scooped up the kitten that was winding itself around Daniel's legs and sneaked it onto his lap under the table, casting a furtive glance at his father.

Stunned into silence by the volume of information that Alfie had delivered, Daniel gaped at his nephew and then turned to his brother. 'He's ten years old.'

'He inherited his intelligence from me.' Patrick put a bowl of pasta in front of his golden-haired daughter. 'Alfie spends every available minute with Stella. He knows far more about her than I do.'

Daniel turned his attention back to his nephew. 'You've been spending time with her?'

'Why not? She's got this brilliant laptop. It's so cool. And she does this dating thing. You ought to do it, Dad.' Alfie squirted ketchup onto his plate. 'Stella had three hundred and fifty replies. If you had that many they could each come here and cook a meal and you wouldn't have to cook again for a whole year.'

'What's wrong with my cooking? And I know you've brought that kitten to the table again, Alfie. I'm not blind or stupid. Put her on the floor. And don't eat with your fingers, Posy.' Clearly distracted, Patrick put the fork into his daughter's hand. 'Alfie, eat, please. I've got to go back to the hospital in a minute.'

'Dating agency?' Feeling as though he was five steps behind everyone else, Daniel stared at his nephew. 'Stella is using a dating agency?'

'Yup.' Ignoring his father, Alfie kept the kitten on his lap. 'On the internet. It's the only way she's going to meet a decent man. She's been through three hundred and fifty people and she's chosen someone who isn't a bit like you.'

Patrick gave a choked laugh and Daniel glared at him and then pulled out a chair and sat down next to Alfie.

'So she's meeting a complete stranger?'

'Not really. She knows *loads* about him. I think he sounds really boring, but I'm not a girl.' Alfie stuffed a forkful of pasta into his mouth. 'She's really excited. Dad—how long does it take to make a baby?'

A baby?

Daniel had to physically stop himself from sprinting across the courtyard and bolting the stable door from the outside.

There was no way Stella would be intimate with a guy that quickly, he told himself. She wasn't that type of girl, was she? It had been ages before she'd eventually slept with him.

'Nine months,' Patrick said absently. 'Alfie, Mrs Thornton is going to sit with you tonight.'

Alfie groaned. '*Not* Mrs Thornton. She's so old.'

'She isn't old.'

'She smells funny and her mouth is really red. Can't I stay on my own?'

'You're too young. I won't be late.'

'You always say that, but babies are never predictable,' Alfie grumbled. 'They just don't do what you expect them to do. You'll be at the hospital all night, like you always are. If Mrs Thornton is here, can I watch that DVD? She's so short-sighted, she won't know.'

'Which DVD?' Only half listening, Patrick fished his mobile out of his pocket and scrolled through his messages.

'It's a twelve rating.'

'You're ten, so the answer is no.'

'My friends have all seen it.' Alfie wrinkled his nose. 'I don't think it's unsuitable.'

'So why is it a twelve rating?'

'Not sure. It will either be "scenes of a violent nature" or "moderate sex references".' Alfie spooned another pile of cheese over his pasta. 'It doesn't really matter. I fast forward those bits anyway. All that kissing is boring when you're ten.'

Patrick's phone rang and he answered it immediately. 'Buchannan. Yes. How many centimetres dilated is she?' Still listening, he tucked the phone between his cheek and his shoulder and wiped the tomato sauce from his daughter's face. 'No—no, not yet. All right.'

Alfie sighed. 'Wait for it. He's going to have to go to the hospital and sort it out.'

Daniel reached forward and stole a piece of pasta from Alfie's bowl. 'You know everything that's going on around here, don't you?'

'I have eyes and ears. Never underestimate a kid,' Alfie said solemnly, pulling his bowl out of Daniel's reach and wrapping an arm around it protectively. 'I have this whole house wired. I want to be a spy when I grow up. You could stay with me tonight, then Mrs Thornton wouldn't have to drag her creaking joints over here.'

'Creaking joints?' Daniel looked at his brother with disapproval, wondering who he was entrusting with his children. 'How old is this woman you're leaving him with?'

'At least forty-five,' Patrick drawled, sliding his phone into his pocket and removing the cheese from Posy's grasp. 'To Alfie, that's old.'

'She *is* old and she smells strong. And she's always asking about Daddy.'

'She covers herself in perfume before she comes round?' Daniel leaned back in his chair and grinned at his brother. 'Sounds as though she's interested in something other than the welfare of the children.'

'Unluckily for me.' Patrick scooped the kitten from Alfie's lap. 'Mary, go to the kitchen.'

'That's Joseph. I don't know how you can do your job if you can't tell the difference between a boy and a girl.' Alfie pushed his bowl away and looked at Daniel. 'Can't you stay with me tonight?'

'I have a hot date.' Glancing at his brother, who was still on the phone, Daniel leaned forward and lowered his voice. 'So, Agent Alfie, you wouldn't happen to know where Stella is meeting this mystery man of hers, would you?'

'Yes.' Alfie picked up his drink. 'I would.'

Daniel lifted an eyebrow. 'And are you going to tell me?'

'I might. But it's going to cost you.'

Daniel gave a disbelieving laugh. 'You think I'd pay you for information?'

'I suppose it depends how important it is to you.' Alfie slid off his chair and took his bowl to the kitchen.

Daniel followed. 'You're a tough negotiator.'

'You don't have to pay if you don't want to know.'

Out of his depth, Daniel took a deep breath and glanced through the door towards his brother, who was now on the phone again, talking to the hospital. 'How much is it going to cost me?'

Alfie set the dishwasher to rinse. 'Two pounds fifty.'

'That's daylight robbery.'

'Fine. Why do you want to know where she's going, anyway?' Alfie frowned. 'You two don't go out together any more. She thinks you're too macho and you're worried because she wants babies. I'm only ten but even I can see that that's going to be a terrible relationship. Kids are a lot of work. I know, because I am one.'

'She thinks I'm too macho?' Daniel ran his hand over the back of his neck, unable to believe that he was having this conversation with a ten-year-old. 'Where do you hear these things?'

'Stella talks to me. That's why I like her. She doesn't treat me like an idiot.'

'Alfie, you're no idiot.' Daniel dug his hand in his pocket and pulled out his wallet. 'Five pounds.'

Alfie's eyes widened. 'I don't have any change.'

'I want to know everything that Stella has told you about this guy.'

'All right.' Alfie folded the money carefully and tucked it in his pocket. 'They're meeting in the Drunken Fox at eight o'clock.'

'How are they going to recognise each other?'

'She's going to wear red.' Alfie pulled a face. 'I hope the guy likes red. She didn't know whether to wear the red one or the black one, but I said red because I thought she looked nicest in that one. Sort of like a girl from the movies.'

Daniel inhaled sharply. 'You should have gone with the black.'

'You don't want her to look nice?'

'Red is…' *The colour she'd always worn for him?* He'd loved her in red. For a moment his brain tortured him with a mini-clip of Stella in red. The soft red jumper she'd worn the first night he'd kissed her, the silky red dress she'd had on when he'd proposed. 'You should have told her to wear black.'

'Why? She looked better in the red.'

Precisely, Daniel thought viciously, searching for an excuse to stride across to the stable, knock on the door and stop her going out.

'Why are you giving my son money?' Patrick ended the phone call and walked into the kitchen, Posy in his arms.

'I'm his uncle.' Daniel walked across and kissed Posy on the top of her head. 'I can give him money if I want to.'

Patrick's eyes narrowed suspiciously but at that moment the doorbell rang. 'That will be Mrs Thornton. Alfie, make sure you're in bed by eight-thirty. No messing around. And don't watch anything unsuitable.'

'Just go, Dad.' Alfie lowered the kitten gently to the floor and handed Posy her doll. 'We'll be fine. If Mrs Thornton dies of old age, I'll call you.'

'Don't be cheeky.'

Daniel walked towards the door. 'I'll catch you later.'

Patrick reached for his coat. 'Lucky you, having a night off. Are you seeing the lawyer?'

'Yes.' And Daniel strode out of the house before his brother could question him further.

For some reason he didn't want to examine too closely, he wasn't prepared to tell Patrick how he planned to spend his evening.

Nodding to the woman on the doorstep, he made for his car.

CHAPTER FOUR

STELLA turned sideways and looked at herself in the mirror. Was she overdressed? Perhaps she should have just worn jeans. On the other hand, if it went well they were going on to a restaurant afterwards, so jeans might not be dressy enough.

She looked fine. It was just that the dress reminded her of Daniel.

He'd always loved her in red and the last time she'd worn this dress they'd—

Remembering what they'd done, Stella yanked the dress over her head and threw it on the bed with the other clothes she'd tried on. It was no good. She couldn't wear it. It just felt wrong. And the pile of clothes on the bed was growing.

Stella stared in the mirror, reminding herself that this was a new relationship. A whole new chapter of her life. And Daniel wasn't in her life any more.

And the fact that she couldn't stop thinking about him made it even more important for her to go out with someone else.

Exasperated with herself, she grabbed the red dress again, relieved that no one was watching her. If anyone had seen how indecisive she was about a stupid dress, they'd fire her from her job.

She zipped it up a final time and then tried to do something with her hair, but there was so much static after all the clothes she'd pulled on and off over her head she just gave up in despair and left it loose.

Realising that she was going to be late if she didn't move fast, she eyed the clothes on the bed and decided she'd have to tidy them up later. Grabbing her favourite pair of black boots, she pulled them on and dragged her coat out of the wardrobe.

By her bed were various bags, filled with the beginnings of her Christmas shopping. Realising how much she still had left to do was enough to induce a panic attack, so she put the thought aside and reminded herself there was plenty of time until Christmas.

Fifteen minutes later she was in the car park of the pub, her heart thumping so hard she felt dizzy.

What if she knew someone in the pub?

She'd intentionally picked somewhere she didn't usually go, but this part of the Lake District was a relatively small community.

What if Alfie was right and Mr 'Caring of Cumbria' was a creep?

Feeling like turning round and driving straight home, it took all of her willpower to step out of the protective cocoon of her little car and walk across the icy car park to the small village pub.

What was the matter with her? It was just a drink, for goodness' sake. A drink and a meal. If it didn't work out, she wouldn't see him again.

As she pushed open the heavy door the warmth hit her and she felt daunted by the throng of people standing shoulder to shoulder at the crowded bar.

Deciding that she'd wait for it to calm down a bit before trying to buy herself a drink, Stella made her way to an empty table by the fire and slid discreetly onto the chair. Aware that everyone in the pub was staring at her, she wished she'd bought herself a drink. At least then she would have had something to do with her hands.

Feeling self-conscious, she removed her coat, but left her scarf round her neck. Staring at the fire, she found herself thinking of Daniel. Then she realised that she didn't want to think about Daniel and gave herself a mental shake. She wasn't *allowed* to think about Daniel. The whole idea of this exercise was *not* to think about Daniel.

The door to the pub opened, letting in a rush of cold air and a flurry of snow. A short man in a pinstripe suit walked cautiously into the pub, snow clinging to his polished shoes. Hovering on the edges of a group of men dressed in thick cable knit jumpers and sturdy boots, he looked as out of place as a ballerina on Mount Everest.

Stella fought a sudden desire to whip off the red scarf she was wearing and slide under the table out of sight. She couldn't do that, could she? It would be rude. After agreeing to meet, the least she could do was have a drink with him.

But the thought of spending an evening with him made her feel so intensely gloomy that she contemplated texting Ellie and asking her to bring her emergency call forward by an hour.

Watching his tentative attempts to reach the bar, Stella couldn't help comparing him to Daniel.

Would this man be bold enough and strong enough to rescue a vulnerable child from a snowy ravine? Would he be cool and decisive enough to make life-and-death decisions, as Daniel did every day in the emergency department?

She turned her head away and stared at the fire, wondering why all the comparisons she was making were against Daniel's good points. Why couldn't she focus on his bad points? The man hovering nervously at the bar probably wouldn't propose to a woman one day and then change his mind a few hours later. The man at the bar was probably extremely patient with people less intelligent than him. He wanted children, and Daniel had made it clear that he had no intention of ever becoming a father. Those were the things she should be thinking about.

So why, knowing all that, was she still thinking of Daniel when she looked at the man at the bar?

The whole situation felt so hopeless that a lump formed in her throat. Getting over someone wasn't as easy as just finding someone else. It didn't work like that.

Stella slid her phone out of her pocket, intending to text Ellie and ask her to bring her call forward. But then a girl emerged from the crush at the bar and kissed the man on the cheek.

Feeling impossibly relieved, Stella put the phone back in her pocket.

All that worry and anxiety and it wasn't even him. But now she had a new worry.

What if he didn't turn up?

The door opened again and she glanced up expectantly.

Daniel stood in the doorway, flakes of snow clinging to his dark hair and broad shoulders, a dangerous look in his eyes.

'Dan.' The barman called out a greeting and Stella frowned slightly because she hadn't realised that he frequented this pub.

He said something that she didn't catch and glanced around the noisy pub.

Stella slid down in her seat and tried to be inconspicuous, but she knew it was hopeless. There was no way he could fail to spot her. He was going to want to know what she was doing here and she was going to have to confess that she was meeting a stranger. How sad was that? Not only had she had to resort to the internet to meet a man, but he hadn't turned up. Her confidence in herself suddenly evaporated.

She was unattractive and she was never going to meet anyone.

'Stella?'

Accepting the inevitable, she looked up at him.

Flakes of snow clung to his sleek dark hair and his jaw was dark with stubble. With the bulk of his shoulders and those long, strong legs, he looked strong, tough and imposing. A man who was afraid of nothing.

Nothing except commitment, Stella reminded herself wearily, producing what she hoped was a decent imitation of a smile. 'Hi, Daniel. This is a surprise. I thought you had a date with your lawyer at eight. You're going to be late. Will she sue you?'

He didn't laugh. In fact, he seemed a long way from laughing. 'What are you doing here on your own?' His ice-blue eyes glittered in the firelight and he pulled out a chair and sat down, nodding his thanks as the landlord discreetly placed a drink in front of him.

Stella fiddled with her scarf. 'They give you free drinks here?'

'His daughter fell in a climbing accident last summer. Nasty head injury. Tricky evacuation.'

'And you rescued her?'

'I was part of the team.'

Despite his concise, factual answer, Stella knew instinctively that he would have been the one to rescue the girl and manage the head injury. 'Have you had many callouts lately?'

'I don't want to talk about the mountain rescue team.' Daniel's eyes were fixed on her face. 'Tell me why you're here.'

That was the other thing about Daniel. He came straight to the point.

'I—I fancied a drink.'

'On your own?'

'No, not on my own. I was supposed to be meeting some-one but he's been…' She licked her lips. 'He's been delayed.'

'Who are you supposed to be meeting? Your new boy-friend?'

Something in his tone made her look at him closely and she saw the tightness of his mouth and the deadly gleam of his eyes under the veil of thick, dark lashes. 'Why does it mat-ter to you?'

'Because I don't think you should meet strange men in pubs.' His tone abrupt and gritty, Daniel lifted his drink and Stella sensed that he knew.

He knew she was seeing someone she'd met on the internet.

Stella wondered why that felt so humiliating. 'Who told you?'

'That doesn't matter.' He put his drink down on the table with a thump. 'What matters is that you've arranged to meet a guy you don't know. Have you no sense of self-preservation?'

Startled by the anger in his voice, Stella looked at him. 'I'm in a crowded pub,' she said reasonably. 'What's going to happen?'

'He'll invite you back to his place and—' Daniel broke off, his eyes on her neckline.

'What?'

'You're wearing your red dress.'

'What's wrong with that?' Exasperated and self-conscious, Stella reached for her coat and pulled it on. 'I like this red dress. And I'm on a date. Go away and leave me alone, Dan-iel.' She'd hoped that the feelings she'd had for him had died, but she was fast discovering that life wasn't as simple as that.

'It isn't the right dress to wear with someone you've never met.'

'I wanted to look nice!'

'You're asking for trouble.'

'Well, it's hard to get into trouble with someone who hasn't even turned up.' Smarting with humiliation and anger, Stella picked up her bag and stood up. 'Thanks for the feedback, Dan.' Furiously angry with him, and with herself for caring what he thought, Stella walked quickly out of the pub.

The cold punched her in the face and she told herself that it was the weather that was making her eyes water as she picked her way across the icy car park towards her car. The temperature had dropped and a bitter wind breathed freezing air over her as she snuggled deeper inside her coat. Her windscreen was opaque with ice and she pulled a scraper out of her bag and attacked the ice, her fingers numb with cold as it showered over her hands. Scraping methodically, she wondered whether every Christmas was destined to be a romantic disaster for her.

Last Christmas she'd been working and the nearest she'd got to romance had been when a ninety-year-old patient had assured her that if he'd been six decades younger he would have married her. The Christmas before that—well, she wasn't even going to think about that one but this one didn't promise to be too much better.

The way the festive season was unfolding it looked as though she was going to need to stock up on comfort food.

As she pulled her car keys from her pocket and turned to unlock the car, her feet slid from under her and she would have fallen if strong hands hadn't caught her.

'Careful. It's icy.' Daniel's rough, masculine voice was next to her ear and she wrenched herself away from him.

'Let me go, Dan.' Terrified that she wasn't going to be able to hold it together, Stella shrugged him off with as much dignity as she could and opened her car door. 'I wish I could say it was nice bumping into you, but it wasn't.'

With a rough curse he turned her to face him, his hard, powerful body pressing her back against the cold metal of the car. 'Why are you meeting men on the internet?'

'Because I don't meet any decent ones in real life!' Her eyes clashed with his and then his hands slid into her hair and his mouth came down on hers.

It was so sudden and unexpected that she had no time to react.

The warmth of his mouth was such a contrast to the ice cold wind brushing her cheeks that she moaned in shock. And then she was responding to the seductive pressure of his kiss, her arms winding around his neck, her body trembling against his solid, masculine strength. His fingers tightened on her face, his kiss demanding and erotic as he created fire and flame with his mouth and tongue.

It was an explosion of pure sensuality, a heated, unfaltering, indulgent expression of passion that neither of them was able to halt.

And then the pub door opened behind them and the sound of laughter penetrated their sensual haze. Daniel tore his mouth from hers, swore fluently and stepped away from her. Raising his hands in a gesture of apology, he shook his head in disbelief, regret visible in his eyes. 'Stella, I didn't mean to—'

'Oh, get away from me, Dan,' she choked, sliding into the car and slamming the door, her body still reeling from that kiss. She didn't know which was worse—the fact that he'd kissed her or that fact that he hadn't meant to do it.

Damn, damn, damn. She should have pushed him away and showed him that she wasn't interested.

Why hadn't she done that?

Why hadn't she slapped his indecently handsome face?

Her hands shaking, she started the engine, crunched the gears, set the wipers going, skidded the car and then swung onto the road, desperate to get away from him.

Oh, God, she was going to have an accident if she carried on like this.

The knowledge that it would probably be Daniel who would patch her up if she was taken to the emergency department was enough of an incentive to make her slow her speed.

Fortunately the roads were deserted and she switched off the wipers that were moving snow across her windscreen and turned the heating as high as it would go.

What a total disaster.

The evening was supposed to have been the first step in her Daniel Recovery Programme, instead of which she'd slipped right back into her old habits. It was like surviving an earthquake only to be trapped in a lethal aftershock.

It was *all* his fault. He was the one who had kissed her. Why couldn't he have just left her alone? Or why hadn't she slapped his face?

Furious with herself and even more furious with him, Stella crunched the gears again, tears blurring her vision as she drove down the narrow, empty roads that led to Patrick's barn.

It had been stupid to come back to the Lake District again. It was all very well having grand ideas about dating other men but the truth was she didn't *want* another man.

She wanted Daniel. She always had. And it didn't matter how unsuitable he was, she still wanted him. Patrick was right—love wasn't something you could switch on and off.

Her vision blurred and as she pulled into the courtyard of the barn, she almost crashed into the back of Patrick's car.

Slamming her brakes on just in time, the car slid to a halt a mere centimetre from his bumper and she switched off the engine and closed her eyes.

What next?

Her car door opened. 'Are you trying to kill yourself or me?' Patrick took one look at her frozen features and leaned across and undid her seat belt. 'Come on. You look as though you need a drink.'

'Actually, I don't need a drink.' Her teeth were chattering. 'I just want to be by myself.'

'No, you don't.' Patrick pulled her gently out of the car. 'Believe me, I've tried that in your situation. It doesn't work. Much better to have company when you're feeling down.'

'You're the wrong company. I need to yell and say bad things about your brother.'

'You can yell and say bad things about my brother. I promise not to defend him.' Patrick locked her car and pushed her towards the stable. 'We'll use your place. Mrs Thornton is staying the night so there's no guarantee of privacy in mine.'

Stella pulled the keys to the stable out of her pocket and promptly dropped them.

With a sigh, Patrick stooped and picked them up. 'Thank goodness you're not working in Resus tonight. I gather "Caring of Cumbria" wasn't what you were hoping for. Was he ugly?'

'I have no idea. He didn't turn up.' Stella pulled off her boots and dropped them by the door. 'Unfortunately, Daniel did.'

'Dan was at the pub?' Patrick closed the door behind them. 'I thought he had a date with the lawyer.'

'Well, apparently he found the time to come and ruin my evening first.' Stella filled the kettle, grateful for the cosy warmth of the stable. 'Patrick, it's really sweet of you to check up on me, but I'd like to be on my own.'

Ignoring her, Patrick slid onto one of the tall stools by the breakfast bar. 'So Daniel turned up—that's interesting.'

'It wasn't interesting.' Stella pulled a mug out of the cupboard. 'It was inconvenient, thoughtless, annoying—since you're determined not to let me have my tantrum on my own, do you want a coffee?'

'Please. Black, no sugar. I need the caffeine—I have a feeling I'm going to be back at the hospital soon.'

Stella made the coffee. 'You work too hard.'

'You sound like my ex-wife.' Patrick gave a wry smile and lifted his hand in a gesture of apology. 'Forget I said that—you're nothing like my ex-wife.'

'Do you hear from her?'

'No, and the only reason I care is for the kids. I can't believe she can just turn her back on her own children.' His tone was hard. 'Do you know what really gets to me? The fact that Alfie is OK about it. He saw so little of her that he's hardly noticed her absence.'

Stella handed him a mug. 'He's a sweet boy.'

'I just hope all of this hasn't put him off relationships. I worry that he'll think marriage isn't a good idea. Like Daniel.'

'Alfie doesn't seem to think that. It always amazes me how much children see. He's pretty wise for ten years old.' Stella passed him a packet of biscuits. 'I keep them for Alfie's visits. Please eat them or I'll eat them all myself. I'm in that sort of mood. Why did Daniel have to turn up at the pub tonight? Just bad luck, I suppose.'

Patrick took a biscuit. 'Bad luck doesn't take you to a pub when you have a date on the other side of town.'

'You don't think it was an accident that he was there?' Stella warmed her cold hands on her mug. 'How could he possibly have known where I was meeting the guy? Even you didn't know.'

'Actually, I did.' Patrick pulled a face. 'Alfie told me.'

Stella groaned. 'Alfie? You think he said something to Daniel?'

'I think he might have done. The two of them were talking earlier. Money changed hands. Sorry, Stella.'

'It isn't Alfie's fault. And to be honest, it wasn't even a secret. I suppose I didn't imagine for a moment Daniel would be interested. And even if he knew where I was going...' Stella put her mug down. 'Why would he bother coming? It doesn't make sense.'

'Doesn't it? If you want my opinion, I think my beloved twin couldn't face the thought of you seeing someone else. It isn't just me he doesn't want you to have a relationship with.' Patrick took a mouthful of coffee. 'It's anyone. What does that tell you?'

'That he's lost his mind,' Stella muttered, rubbing her forehead with her fingers as she tried to make sense of what he was saying. 'He didn't want me.'

'Oh, he wanted you, angel. And he obviously still wants you.'

Did he want her? Stella thought about the kiss and felt her cheeks turn pink. Quickly she picked up her coffee again. 'Even if the chemistry is still there, nothing has changed.' She was saying it to remind herself as much as Patrick. 'We want different things.'

'Yes. I know. That's what makes the whole thing complicated.' Patrick suppressed a yawn. 'So what did he say to you tonight?'

'He basically turned into a macho, chest-thumping, over-protective…' Stella ran out of adjectives. 'He didn't like the idea of me meeting a stranger.'

'Neither do I.'

'You didn't turn up and hang over me.'

'No, but I confess I did ring the landlord and ask him to watch out for you.' Patrick handed her his empty mug. 'I'd better go. I need to check that Alfie isn't watching unsuitable movies.'

'You rang the landlord?' Stella was stunned by that confession but Patrick simply smiled.

'Daniel isn't the only Buchannan brother who can be macho and over-protective.' He leaned forward and kissed her on the cheek. 'Goodnight. I'll leave you to your internet search. Next time make sure you pick someone who is going to show up.'

CHAPTER FIVE

'STELLA, have you seen Daniel?' Ellie hurried into the treat-ment room where Stella was just finishing a dressing. 'The paramedics are bringing in a baby with breathing problems. I need him.'

'I haven't seen him.' *She'd made sure she hadn't seen him.* She didn't want to set eyes on him until she'd calmed down.

The more she thought about what had happened the eve-ning before, the angrier she became.

Stella saw her patient out of the room and Ellie looked at her closely.

'All right, tell me what's wrong. You've been hiding in the treatment room all morning.'

'I'm not hiding.'

'Your evening didn't go so well, did it? When you texted me to say you were at home, I gathered something was up. Was he creepy?'

'He didn't show up.' Neither had he emailed. Stella frowned, finding it a little strange that he hadn't given her some reason for the fact that he hadn't shown up. Mind you, she hadn't given him her mobile number, had she? Apart from ring-ing through to the pub, he'd had no way of contacting her once she'd left the stable for the evening. But there had been no email waiting when she'd arrived home. 'Obviously he changed his mind.'

'So you just sat there for a bit and then left?'

Daniel's dark, handsome features swam in her brain. 'That's right. Early night.' And she felt horribly confused about the whole thing. Too confused even to talk to Ellie.

'You look tired for someone that had an early night.' Ellie leaned forward and gave her a hug. 'Why don't you come over to my house one evening this week? I can get the kids to sleep early and we can open a bottle and watch something romantic.'

'Romance isn't working for me at the moment, but thanks.' Stella hugged her back. 'You need to make the most of your evenings with Ben. You see little enough of him.'

'That's true, but there's something wonderfully soothing about talking to a girlfriend and ranting about the things that men just don't understand.' Ellie glanced at her watch. 'The ambulance will be here in a moment—I'd better go and find Daniel. I don't suppose I could persuade you to work in Paediatric Resus, could I?'

'What's happened to Andrea?'

'She had to transfer a patient to Theatre and she isn't back yet. And on top of that she irritates Daniel because she's slow.'

Knowing that to refuse would raise more questions than she wanted to answer, Stella gave a nod. 'All right. Tell me about this baby.'

'Five months old. Born at thirty-six weeks by Caesarean section—one of Patrick's, I think.' Ellie frowned. 'Anyway, the mum called the emergency services tonight after the baby turned blue and stopped breathing.' They hurried towards the paediatric area of the emergency department and met Daniel heading in the same direction.

It was the first time Stella had seen him since the previous evening—since the kiss—and she felt the colour flare in her cheeks. Despite her best intentions, all she could think about was the way his mouth had felt against hers.

His eyes raked her face, held hers for a disturbing moment and then his jaw tightened and he pushed open the doors to Resus with slightly more force than was necessary. 'What have we got?'

A mess, Stella thought helplessly, thinking of their own situation.

'Five-month-old baby…' Ellie repeated the information she'd given Stella, just as the paramedics arrived with the baby.

A pale-faced woman with no make-up and untidy hair was with them, holding a squirming toddler by the hand. 'Please don't make me go and sit in the waiting room. I can't bear to leave Poppy.'

'You're her mother?' Daniel walked across to the trolley and the woman nodded.

'We've been up all night for three nights and I can't even think straight anymore.' Her eyes filled. 'She stopped breathing.' She broke off as the toddler started to whine and Stella took one look at his exhausted, stressed mother and scooped him up.

'Come and see what's in my magic box,' she whispered into his ear, and the toddler stopped grizzling and looked interested. Stella pulled out the toy box that was hidden away for occasions such as this, and settled the toddler on the floor. 'This is full of exciting things. See if you can find my special blue car. I'm just going to see to your sister. I'll be back in a minute.'

While Daniel was questioning the mother, Stella attached the baby to a cardiac monitor and a pulse oximeter.

'Sats are 92 in air,' she murmured, and Daniel glanced at the monitor.

'Let's give her humidified oxygen and ask the paediatric registrar to come down. Whatever the outcome of my examination, she's going to need to be admitted.' Removing a stethoscope from his pocket, he turned back to the mother. 'You say that you've been up all night for three nights. Was that when she first became ill?'

'I thought she just had a cold. She just had a runny nose and a bit of a temperature. It's that time of year, isn't it? And then suddenly she started coughing—this horrible dry cough. And she stopped feeding.'

'A baby with a respiratory infection can't always take the same amount of food as usual.' Daniel slid the jumper over the baby's head and undid the vest. 'So what happened to make you call the ambulance?'

'I put her down for a nap and when I looked at her she was blue and she stopped breathing for a bit. Honestly, I didn't imagine it.'

'Her respirations are 70,' Stella said, and Daniel gave a nod as he shifted the vest and looked at the baby's chest.

'I'm sure you didn't imagine it.' He glanced at the mother with a smile, everything about him calm and reassuring. 'It isn't uncommon for young babies with bronchiolitis to have pauses in their breathing and I suspect that's what's going on here. I'm going to take a good look at her and then we'll decide how best to treat her.'

'I honestly thought she was going to die.'

'There's nothing more frightening than being on your own at home with a sick baby. It's hard to think straight, especially when you've been up all night.' Daniel watched the baby's chest rise and fall. 'You did the right thing to bring her in. We have an excellent paediatric department here and we won't be sending Poppy home until we're happy with her.'

In response to his sympathetic comments, the mother put her hand to her face and started to cry. 'Sorry—you must think I'm a total nutcase, it's just that I'm *so* tired and I've been so worried.'

'I'm not surprised. Any normal parent would be out of their mind with worry.' Daniel gestured to the chair and then put the stethoscope in his ears. 'Sit down before you drop and I have to treat you, too. Once I have a better idea what's going on, you can get yourself a hot drink in the café down the corridor. You look as though you need one.' Then he turned back to the baby, his hands infinitely gentle as he examined her.

'Poppy sick?' The toddler wandered across to the trolley, clutching a blue car, and Stella admired the toy before turning back to help Daniel.

He was so good with children and that made the whole thing so much worse.

Although she knew he didn't think so himself, Stella knew that Daniel would make a wonderful father.

While he concentrated on his tiny patient, she found herself looking at him. Why couldn't she be indifferent? He was *so* unsuitable. He didn't want what she wanted. So why did she still find him so desperately attractive? She gazed at the strong, bold lines of his bone structure and the dark shadow that emphasised his jaw. And her heart stumbled.

Daniel removed the stethoscope from his ears and met her gaze. He frowned briefly, clearly aware that she was thinking about more than the patient. 'Fine inspiratory crackles,' he said gruffly, 'and she has a high-pitched expiratory wheeze. She has nasal flaring, grunting and her chest is visibly hyperinflated so I think we're looking at a diagnosis of bronchiolitis. Did you ring Paeds?'

Stella pulled herself together. 'Yes. The registrar is just finishing a lumbar puncture and then he'll be down.' She turned her attention back to the baby, telling herself that her relationship with Daniel would become easier over time. It was bound to feel hard at first, wasn't it? It was up to her to move on.

Maybe 'Caring of Cumbria' hadn't worked out—but that didn't mean she wouldn't meet someone else. She wasn't going to give up at the first fence.

'What exactly is bronchiolitis?' The exhausted young mother stood up and stroked her baby's head gently. 'Could I have avoided it somehow?'

'It's a viral infection of the small airway, very common in the winter months, especially in this age group.' Daniel took his pen out of his pocket. 'There's absolutely nothing you could have done.'

'I feel like a terrible mother. I feel like I've let her down. I should have brought her days ago.'

'She wasn't as ill as this days ago, or you would have brought her.' Daniel wrote up some drugs on the notes. 'You haven't let her down. You've done all the right things. You're a brilliant mum.'

The woman flushed. 'I don't feel brilliant. I feel…incoherent. I haven't been to bed for three nights.'

'That's why you're brilliant,' Daniel said easily. 'Some mothers would have just gone back to sleep. You've put yourself through the wringer because you've been watching over your child. That makes you brilliant in my book. How many feeds has Poppy had today in comparison to normal?'

The mother flushed but it was obvious that Daniel's words had bolstered her self-confidence and given her the extra strength she needed to get through the crisis.

Stella studied Daniel's profile, wondering what his own mother had been like. She knew that his childhood had been far from idyllic, but he rarely divulged any details.

He had firm views on mothers, she knew that.

And fathers.

And he didn't think he'd make a good one.

Oblivious to her scrutiny, he was scribbling on the notes. 'How many wet nappies?'

The mother pulled a face. 'I—I don't know. Why is that important?'

'Because it helps us assess how dehydrated she is. We may need to give her some fluid into her vein, but I'm going to leave that to my paediatric colleagues to decide.'

'Can you give her antibiotics or something?'

'It's caused by a virus so antibiotics won't help.' Daniel looked up as the door opened. 'This is Deborah—she's the paediatric doctor.' He outlined the case to Deborah, who immediately arranged for the child to be admitted.

Stella watched the easy smile he gave to the other doctor and wondered whether they'd had a relationship in the past two years.

Gritting her teeth, she gathered up the baby's things. *None of her business,* she reminded herself. She no longer had any interest in Daniel Buchannan's love life.

And that was the way it was going to stay.

As the paediatric team took over care of the baby and transferred her, she expected Daniel to go back to work. Instead, he closed the door of Resus so that the two of them were alone.

'Listen, about last night—'

'Yes, last night.' Her temper exploded, fuelled by all the confusing feelings he'd released inside her. 'Don't you *ever* kiss me again, Daniel Buchannan. Do you hear me?'

'You kissed me, too.'

'Yes, I did. And it was a mistake!' She glared at him. 'I didn't come back here to get involved with you again. What do you think I am? Stupid? Some sort of masochist? You think I want to put myself through that pain again?'

His eyes narrowed. 'Stella—'

'Kiss me again and I'll injure you!' She stabbed her finger towards him. 'If you want a woman, I'm sure your lawyer will oblige.'

His expression was defensive. 'You have no reason to be jealous of her.'

'I'm not jealous. I'm angry. I'm angry that you can be so— so...' She stumbled over the words. '*Careless* about my feelings.'

'I'm not careless,' Daniel said roughly. 'It's because I care that I broke off our engagement. I knew I couldn't give you what you wanted. I couldn't be what you wanted me to be. If I'd married you, I would have made you miserable.'

'Well, breaking off our engagement didn't exactly make my day, either!' Furious with herself and with him, Stella turned away and started clearing up the equipment from the trolley with more clatter and energy than was entirely necessary. 'We can work together, Daniel, because we're both professionals. As for the rest of it—I want you to stay away from me.' *Because she didn't trust herself...*

With a soft curse, Daniel strode towards her, his eyes glittering dangerously as he moved her away from the trolley and backed her against the wall. 'Enough of this,' he growled, planting his arms either side of her so that she was trapped. 'Are you trying to pretend you don't feel anything?'

'No, I'm not. But I don't *want* to feel anything, can't you understand that?' Her legs were shaking and her insides were as hot and fluid as molten lava. 'You *hurt* me, Daniel.'

'You think I don't know that?' He put his hand under her chin and forced her to look at him. 'You think I don't know exactly what I did two years ago? Believe me, I know.'

'So why did you kiss me again?' She tried to ignore his tantalising male scent and those blue eyes, programmed to drive a woman wild. 'You want to put me through it all a second time?'

'No.' His gaze dropped to her mouth and lingered there. 'I kissed you because I can't be that close to you and not want to kiss you. That's how it's always been. Most of the time I manage to control it but last night—last night, I didn't. I was angry that you were meeting a stranger. Angry that you wore the red dress.' The expression in his eyes was personal—*intimate*—and Stella felt the breath jam in her throat.

'What I wear isn't any of your business.' His face was close to hers, just a breath away from touching.

'Why did you come back, Stella?'

She gave a low moan and closed her eyes, struggling against instincts that were stronger than her. 'I've told you why. Because this is my home.' Her heart was thumping dangerously hard and her body yearned to melt into his. 'Are you suggesting this is all my fault?' *Oh, God, of course it was her fault. She'd overestimated the strength of her willpower, hadn't she?*

'You knew I was here, but you chose to come back. You knew what would happen when we were alone together. Look at me.' His fingers tightened on her chin, demanding—*possessive*. 'Admit it, Stella. This was always going to be difficult.'

She looked at him and immediately wished she hadn't because eye contact simply intensified the chemistry. 'Why would it be difficult?! You didn't want me—'

'That isn't true. You know that isn't true.' His mouth was dangerously close to hers. 'I won't make a good husband or a good father, but that deficiency in my make-up has no effect on my skills as a lover.'

A delicious shiver ran through her body. 'Dan, please—'

'I've always wanted you,' he breathed huskily. 'I've wanted you from the very first day I saw you.'

'Stop it!' Stella twisted her head away, trying to free herself from temptation. '*You're* the one making this difficult.'

'No. It's difficult because our relationship didn't really end. I told you that I didn't want marriage and children, but I never once told you that I didn't want you.'

Stella pushed at his chest and struggled to find willpower. 'You wanted sex with no commitment.'

'I made a commitment,' he said roughly. 'I was with you. There was no one else for me.'

Thinking about their relationship was bitter-sweet. She'd been so excited about the future, in love for the first time in her life...

'It wasn't enough, Daniel. I want more than that. I'm old-fashioned. I want a man to love me enough to marry me.' Her voice broke because it seemed impossible to imagine ever loving a man as much as she loved Daniel. 'Why are we going over this again? Leave me alone, Daniel. I'm trying to build a new life.'

'Is that why you're meeting strange men in pubs? Is that the "new life" you want?' The sudden hardness of his tone slashed like the blade of a knife and her chin lifted.

'That's none of your business.'

'I'm just worried about you, that's all.'

'You don't need to worry. I'm not your problem Daniel.' Unsettled by her own feelings as much as the look in his eyes, Stella ducked under his arm and walked towards the door, her legs shaking so badly she could hardly walk. 'Neither am I your responsibility. If I choose to meet a stranger in a pub, that's my decision.'

'It's a lousy decision.' His blue eyes glittered dangerously as he watched her retreat. 'Why are you meeting men over the internet?'

'Why not?' She held his gaze and for a moment they just looked at each other.

'It isn't safe to meet strangers,' he said roughly. 'You could get hurt.'

'*You* hurt me, Daniel. *You hurt me.*' Stella turned away, confused and frustrated. Was he asking her not to meet anyone? Was he suggesting that they resurrect their relationship? Part of her was appalled at the thought, but another tiny part of her was desperately hopeful and she *hated* the fact that she could still feel that way.

'I know I hurt you.' His voice was low and impossibly sexy. 'I know I can't be what you want me to be.' He broke off and muttered something under his breath, his shoulders visibly tense. 'Just be careful, that's all I ask. If you want to meet a man, go to the Christmas party. At least it's a safe environment. You know lots of the people and you're less likely to get hurt.'

Her fantasies shattered like glass on concrete.

He was encouraging her to meet someone else.

'You can just as easily get hurt by the people you love as by strangers,' Stella said pointedly, turning and looking him in the eye. 'And when I need your help or advice to meet a man, I'll ask.' Without giving him time to reply, she stalked out of the room and let the door swing shut behind her, wishing for the first time in her life that she'd never met Daniel Buchannan.

Stretched out in a chair in his office, exhausted after eleven hours with no break, Daniel stared blankly at the computer screen, his mind full of the night before.

He never should have kissed her.

What had possessed him to do such an utterly stupid thing?

As if things hadn't been hard enough *before* that.

He still didn't understand exactly why he'd lost control.

One moment he'd been furiously angry, the next he'd been kissing her. Usually with women he choreographed every move—he was *always* in control. He made sure of it. He knew when he was going to ask them out, he knew where he was going to take them—control was part of the way he protected himself.

Only with Stella there was no control. And there never had been.

Sliding his hand over his face, he muttered a black oath.

Nothing had changed between them. Except that they were no longer together.

Dwelling on that uncomfortable truth, Daniel glanced up to see his brother standing in the doorway. 'What are you doing here? Is someone giving birth in my department?'

'No. I have some news. And I need a favour.' Patrick frowned at him. 'You look as though you're in a filthy mood. What's wrong?'

'Nothing.' Somehow Daniel couldn't bring himself to confess his thoughts about Stella. He waited while his brother sprawled in the only armchair in his office. 'You don't look so good yourself.'

'Tired.' Patrick closed his eyes and Daniel frowned slightly.

'Is it the job or the kids?' Out of the corner of his eye, Daniel surveyed his desk, barely visible beneath the piles of files and papers that people wanted him to read. For a brief moment he wondered what would happen if he just tipped the lot into the bin. Would anyone notice? He didn't have time to deal with any of it all anyway, so it may as well be in the bin. His computer was telling him that he had seventy-two new messages in his inbox and he stifled the temptation to just switch the thing off at the mains. 'What's the problem?' *Apart from the fact your wife left you with two little kids.*

'I'm knackered.' His brother opened his eyes briefly. 'If the labour ward rings, you haven't seen me.'

'That bad, huh?' Daniel gave a sympathetic grin and transferred the files on his desk to the floor. 'Busy night?'

'Not particularly.' His brother's eyes drifted shut again. 'But I didn't get any sleep, thanks to a certain woman in my life.'

Daniel gave a slow smile of masculine approval. 'Now, that *is* good news. I've been telling you for months that it's time for you to get out there again. Tell me that she was incredible in bed, cooks like an angel and is dying to take on a single dad with two small children who spends most of his waking hours working.'

Patrick opened his eyes. 'What are you talking about?'

'The woman you spent last night with—I want the details. Blonde? Brunette? Redhead? God, I love redheads. My lawyer is a redhead.'

'You always preferred blondes.'

'Well, now I prefer redheads. Very dominant and assertive.' Omitting to mention that he couldn't help comparing every blonde to Stella, Daniel noticed more emails fly into his inbox and swivelled the chair so that he could no longer see the screen. 'And we were talking about you, not me. Why don't we grab a beer after work and you can give me the details?'

'Can't. I need to get home. And there isn't a woman. At least, not the sort that you mean.' Patrick ran a hand over his face. 'It was Posy who kept me awake. I was talking about Posy.'

The smile left Daniel's face. 'You're exhausted because of your three-year-old daughter?'

'That's right.' Patrick's eyes closed again and his head

dropped back against the chair. 'I don't know whether she's teething or whether she has a cold coming but she's really fractious at the moment. In the end she slept in my bed and it was hell. She always lies horizontally so her feet are in my—'

'You know what?' Daniel lifted a hand as he interrupted him. 'This is too much detail. I honestly don't need to know about the sleeping patterns of a three-year-old.'

Patrick was silent for a moment and then he opened his eyes and looked straight at his brother. 'You're very fond of Posy. And of Alfie.'

'Of course I am.' Daniel waved a hand. 'I'm a doting uncle. The job description for doting uncle is that I smother them with extravagant gifts on various important dates like birthdays and Christmas and as they grow up I take them on the odd climbing expedition and for rides in my fast sports car to impress their friends.'

Patrick was silent for a moment and it seemed to Daniel that his twin brother looked more exhausted than he'd ever seen him.

'You need some time away.'

Patrick gave a nod. 'That's what I'm planning.'

'You are? Without the kids? Perfect. What's the plan?'

'Do you remember that lecture I gave in Chicago? Well, they've offered me a job. Part clinical–part academic. It would give me more time at home with the kids—'

'A job in Chicago?' Daniel frowned slightly, unsure how he felt about his brother relocating to the States. 'You're considering that?'

'I thought it was worth a look. They want me to come across and meet them. Look around, interview…' Patrick shrugged. 'You know the score.'

'Great. Go for it. Fresh start. Well, at least go and talk to them.'

'I'd like to. And that brings me to the favour I need.'

'Of course. I know your sweet ex-wife cost you a fortune. I don't know how you've coped.' Even when Patrick's petulant, moody wife had finally stopped having tantrums and left him *and* the children, his brother had just gritted his teeth and got on with his life. He'd shifted his workload so that he could continue in his role as obs and gynae consultant and still spend time at home with the children. Daniel reached for his chequebook. 'How much?'

'I don't need money. Money isn't my problem. I need a different sort of favour.'

'Name it.' Daniel thought of the hell that his brother had been through since his wife had left and waved a hand expressively. 'Anything. What do you need? A lift to the airport?'

'I need you to look after the kids.'

'What?' Daniel stared at him with undisguised horror. 'You have to be kidding. No. Absolutely no.'

'You said anything.'

'Anything *but that.*' Daniel launched himself out of his chair, knocking pens and papers onto the floor. 'Why would you even ask me that? I'm the last person in the world that any sane person would want looking after their kids. I'm terrible with kids. That's why I don't have any of my own.'

'You're my family. And you're their family.'

'That's no reason to punish them! Or me.' Daniel felt panic mingle with guilt. 'Don't ask me to do this, Ric.'

'I'm asking. And it isn't a punishment for the kids. They love you. You've been a constant in their lives since they were born.'

Nervous now, Daniel paced around his office. 'From a

distance. I told you, I do the fun stuff. I don't do any of the nitty-gritty practical stuff. I wouldn't know how. What if they can't sleep, or they fall over—well, actually the falling over bit would be about the only thing I'd be qualified to deal with, but...' Daniel felt the prickle of sweat on his brow and ran a hand over his face. 'Can't you just take them with you?'

'Posy is too little and I don't want Alfie to miss school. And who would look after them while I'm looking around the hospital and talking to people? I don't want some stranger caring for my kids. You'll be fine. It's another week until the Christmas holidays start.'

'Why can't Mrs Thornton do it?'

'I can't give her sole responsibility for the children.'

'Stella?'

'I can't ask her to look after two kids that aren't hers.'

'You're asking me—'

'Because you're my brother.' Patrick sank his hands into his hair. 'Do you honestly think I'd be asking you if I had a choice? I know you'll hate every minute, but I also know the kids will be safe with you.'

Daniel's heart was pounding. 'Ask me anything else,' he said hoarsely. 'A horse for Posy. Anything. But don't ask me to look after them.'

'Posy is too young to need a horse.'

'See?' Daniel spread his hands. 'I don't even know that. I don't know what children do at what age. I wouldn't be safe with them. You're mad even to ask me.'

'You won't have to do much,' Patrick said wearily. 'Just give them breakfast and get Alfie to school. Then you bring Posy here and drop her into the hospital crèche on your way to work.'

'I can't fit the kids in my sports car.'

'We'll swap cars. I'll take the Porsche and you can use my four-wheel drive.'

Daniel lifted an eyebrow. 'If that's supposed to be an incentive, you don't know me very well,' he drawled. 'Listen. I'm the last person in the world that anyone would want looking after their kids. I don't know anything about kids.'

'You work in A and E. You know a great deal about kids.'

'I know how to fix them when they're broken!' Daniel glared at him. 'And I'm assuming you don't want yours broken, which they will be if I look after them!' He felt something close to panic rise inside him and then he looked at his brother—saw the dark shadows in his eyes.

'You're my brother,' Patrick said softly. 'That makes you suitable. You're the only person I trust.'

Daniel lifted his hand to his throat, feeling as though he was being strangled. 'All right, I'll do it.' His mouth was moving even while his brain was still trying to refuse. 'But you have to leave me some textbooks or something.'

'They're just kids, Dan.' Patrick looked amused. 'You don't need books. They'll tell you what they want.'

'Posy is so little. How am I going to know what she wants?'

'She'll tell you. Alfie is good with her. He'll help.' Patrick glanced at the clock. 'I'd better get back. Thanks. And stop worrying. It's only for four days, Dan. What can possibly go wrong?'

'I assume you don't want me to answer that.' Daniel strode back to his desk and delved under a pile of papers for his mobile. 'The first thing I'm doing is calling Andrea.'

'Your frosty lawyer? How's that going?'

'We've both been too busy for me to thaw her out,' Daniel muttered. 'One of the disadvantages of dating a career-woman is that they're too involved in their career to see you.

And when she's available, I'm not. This place is death on a re-lationship, you know that.' Seeing his brother's face, he closed his eyes briefly. 'Sorry.'

'It's all right. Carly didn't leave because of the job—that was just her excuse. She left because she was Carly.' Patrick rose to his feet. 'Why would you call Andrea?'

'Because she's a woman. She'll know what to do with a ten-year-old and a three-year-old.'

'I wouldn't be too sure about that.'

'Well, she's going to know more than me.' Daniel dialled the number. 'When are you leaving?'

'Saturday.'

'That gives me four days to bring in reinforcements.'

'If you get stuck, you can always bang on the stable door and ask Stella to help. The kids love her.'

Daniel thought about the kiss and gritted his teeth. Stella had made it clear she didn't want him anywhere near her, and he was in agreement.

If last night had taught him anything, it was that the chem-istry between them was still alive and well. And that could only lead to trouble.

No way would he be banging on the stable door.

CHAPTER SIX

IT SNOWED for the next four days and they were so busy in the emergency department that when she finally had a day off, Stella slept late.

Relishing the thought of a whole weekend ahead of her, she decided to check whether Patrick needed any help preparing for his trip.

Dressing in warm clothes, she picked her way gingerly across the snow-covered yard and banged on the door.

Daniel yanked it open. One of the kittens shot past him and out of the door and Stella stooped and caught it. She was so shocked to see Daniel there that she was glad of a reason to hide her scarlet face.

'Where do you think you're going?' She cuddled the kitten close and then looked at Daniel, trying to keep her expression neutral. 'I didn't know you were here. I was going to talk to Patrick...' Her voice tailed off as she saw the red streak on his cheek. 'What happened to you? Are you bleeding?'

Daniel lifted a hand and scrubbed at the mark. 'It's probably paint. Posy is painting. She doesn't appear to have a very good sense of direction with the brush. Thanks for catching the kitten. I keep forgetting I'm not supposed to open the door.'

'Right.' The situation felt horribly awkward. 'Is Patrick around?'

'He's gone into town to get a few things for his trip. I'm having a practice run with the children.'

Stella looked at the paint on his cheek. 'And how's that going?'

'Both kids were still alive last time I looked.' His lazy drawl was a contrast to the tension she saw in his eyes.

'You'll be fine.' Stella's eye caught movement behind him. 'That red paint you mentioned—Posy appears to be painting on the wall. Is that what you had planned?'

Daniel turned swiftly, growled deep in his throat and made a dive for Posy. 'How did she get there? I left her safely occupied at the table.'

'Three-year-olds don't always stay where you put them.' It was impossible not to laugh. 'How are your decorating skills?'

'About the same as my childminding skills.' Daniel prised the paintbrush out of Posy's chubby hand. 'On the paper, Posy, not on the wall. The *paper.*'

Posy's lip wobbled and Daniel scooped her up in his arms. 'Don't cry. No one cries on my shift. Understand?'

In response to that rough command, Posy plopped her head on his shoulder, her blonde curls a stark contrast to Daniel's dark masculinity. As the child curled her arm round his neck, Stella saw his mouth tighten and a muscle work in his lean, hard jaw. But his hand came up to steady her and he rubbed the child's back awkwardly.

'I don't deserve that cuddle,' he said gruffly, and Stella suddenly found it impossible to swallow. Emotion stung her eyes and pricked at her throat and she found herself thinking things she didn't want to be thinking.

Her thoughts were already dominated by Daniel the doctor and Daniel the lover—the last thing she needed was to be thinking of Daniel the father.

He didn't want to be a father, she reminded herself. *He didn't want that.*

The fact that little Posy was clinging to him adoringly didn't change anything.

'I'll try and catch Patrick later.' Her mind in turmoil, she backed away, still holding the kitten. 'I just wanted to wish him luck. What time is his flight?'

'He leaves for the airport just after lunch.'

'Stella!' Alfie walked across the yard, another two kittens in his arms. 'Is Daddy back yet?' His voice had a distinct wobble in it and Stella dropped into a crouch next to him.

'What's wrong?'

'Mary and Joseph escaped. I'm worried they've caught a cold.'

Stella stooped and examined the kittens. 'They seem happy enough.'

'They've been outside in the snow.'

'Well, take them back into the house and we'll watch them.'

'Why does Dad have to go?' Alfie looked miserable. 'What if the kittens are poorly when he's gone?'

'Then I'll fix it,' Daniel said firmly, still holding Posy.

Alfie looked at him doubtfully. 'You don't know anything about kids or kittens. I heard you telling Dad.'

'Well, I...' Daniel cleared his throat, 'I don't know much, that's true, but I'm learning fast. In the last five minutes I've learned not to turn my back on Posy when she has a paint-brush in her hand.'

'I could have told you that.' Alfie looked at his sister. 'And you can't turn your back on her in the bath because she likes to splash all the water onto the floor.'

'I'm expected to bath you?' Daniel's handsome face lost some of its colour. 'That sounds complicated. Maybe we could skip that bit.'

Alfie held the kittens against his chest. 'Dad's away for four days. We'll be smelly.'

'Smelly, but in one piece,' Daniel muttered under his breath. 'All right. Fine. I can lead a trauma team. I'm sure I can manage to bath two kids.'

'I can bath myself. It's just Posy that needs help.'

'That's what's worrying me.' But his hand was still stroking Posy's back and his eyes were fixed on Alfie's face. 'How am I doing so far? Have I forgotten anything? Done anything wrong?'

'You're doing OK. For a beginner. You didn't cook the pasta for long enough but I don't mind it chewy.' Alfie shrugged, but his eyes were just a little too bright. 'Is Dad going to say goodbye before he goes?'

'Of course he is.' Daniel watched his nephew. 'Are you worried about him going?'

'No. I'm not a baby.' Alfie's tone was fierce. 'It just feels a bit—weird, him leaving this close to Christmas. There's stuff we should be doing. Stuff he should be here for.'

'Stuff.' Daniel looked out of his depth and cast a helpless glance at Stella. 'What stuff?'

'Christmas stuff.' Alfie held onto the wriggling kittens. 'Don't worry about it. You don't have to do it. I know you didn't do much at Christmas when you were kids. Dad told me it was always a pretty rough time for you.'

Stella hid her surprise. She knew that Daniel's childhood hadn't been happy, but she hadn't known that Christmas had been particularly bad.

The sudden tension in Daniel's shoulders made Stella want to question exactly what Daniel's Christmases had been like as a child. In all the time they'd been together, he had never mentioned Christmas to her. In fact, he'd said very little about his childhood, except to intimate that his parents' relationship had been grim. Whenever she'd tried to probe, he'd changed the subject.

'This "stuff" you're talking about...' Daniel held Posy close '...we can do some of that while your dad is away, if you want to. You just have to tell me what you want to do.'

'You mean that?' Alfie's face brightened. 'Can we go and buy the tree? Dad was going to take us to the forest this afternoon but then he didn't have enough time and he said it would have to wait.'

Daniel nodded. 'We can go and get a tree.' He gave Stella a faint smile. 'Might be easier to be outdoors than indoors with these two.'

'Don't you believe it,' she murmured under her breath, but Alfie was already fizzing with excitement.

'The forest will be so cool after all that snow. Can Stella come with us?'

Daniel looked at Stella and she knew he was thinking the same thing that she was thinking. That neither of them wanted to go on a trip together. And neither of them wanted to disappoint Alfie.

Daniel gave a lopsided smile. 'Will you come?'

She ought to say no. After what had happened between them this week, they needed to spend as little time together as possible.

'Pleeease,' Alfie begged, his eyes wide with hope and his arms full of kittens. 'Please come, Stella. It won't be any fun if you don't come.'

'How can I say no?' Stella gave a weak smile and the tiny kitten she was holding climbed up her jumper and rubbed itself against her face. 'It sounds like fun.' If one's definition of fun was spending an afternoon doing something guaranteed to cause significant mental anguish.

'Great. Then you can spend the rest of the day with us and help us decorate it.' Alfie was looking much more cheerful. 'We can toast marshmallows and watch a Christmas movie on the television, like we did two Christmases ago.'

Two Christmases ago when her heart had been breaking and she'd cuddled Alfie, wondering why she'd had to choose between the man she wanted and the family she longed for.

Stella swallowed. Could she spend the day with Daniel? She felt as though someone was tying ropes around her, preventing her escaping from a situation that was becoming more and more difficult. 'We'll see.'

'Don't say "We'll see". That always means "No".' Alfie looked at her pleadingly. 'Promise you'll come and help us decorate it afterwards.'

Stella's mouth moved without any intervention from her brain. 'I promise.'

'Great.' Bouncing with excitement, Alfie turned back to the house. 'I'll just put Mary and Joseph inside, then I'll take Gabriel from you.'

Stella looked down at the kitten in her arms. 'This is Gabriel?'

'Yes. You can tell because of the black splodge on his ear.' Alfie darted inside the house and Stella was suddenly painfully conscious of Daniel watching her.

Perhaps she should have said no. She should have made some excuse. Choosing a Christmas tree with Daniel and two gorgeous children was going to be something close to torture.

But it was illogical to think about what might have been when she knew it never would have been. That was why they'd parted, wasn't it? Because they both wanted different things.

He was looking after Patrick's children because he was fiercely loyal to his brother, not because he had a secret wish to be a father.

'Sorry.' His tone was rough and apologetic. 'I didn't intend you to be roped into helping.'

'I love the children.' The conversation was stilted. Polite and formal. They were behaving like strangers, not two people who had been lovers. *Two people who had shared everything.*

'I thought if I took them to buy a tree, it might take their minds off their dad leaving. And I think I'm probably better at doing outdoor stuff than indoor stuff.' Daniel gave a rueful glance at the red marks on the wall and Stella smiled.

'That will come off with a good scrub. And I think it's a great idea to take them to the forest to get the tree. Once you've decorated the house, they'll be too excited about Christmas to think too much about Patrick. Christmas routines always do that.' She saw something flicker in his eyes and remembered what Alfie had said about Daniel's experience of Christmas.

But she had no idea what that was, and she had no opportunity to ask because Alfie reappeared and Patrick pulled up in the car.

Stella hugged him, wished him luck on his trip and then retreated to the stable to dress in something suitable for an excursion to the forest in winter.

Part of her wanted to back out of the trip, but she knew that if she did that Alfie would be disappointed and she didn't want that to happen. She'd chosen to come back, she reminded herself. Patrick and the children were part of her life and Daniel was a part of *their* lives. If the only way she could cope with not being with him was to avoid him, she wasn't doing very well, was she?

The forest was like a winter playground and the children soon forgot about Patrick's absence, enchanted by the volume of snow.

'We haven't had snow like this for years. No, Posy—don't take your boots off.' Daniel bent down and scooped her up, shaking his head in frustration. 'You can't walk in the snow in bare feet.'

'You remembered boots and a coat.' Stella retrieved the boots. 'I'm impressed.'

'Posy hates her boots,' Alfie told them, scooping snow into a ball. Then he gave an impish smile and lobbed the snow straight at Daniel.

Shaking snow out of his hair, Daniel carefully handed a startled Posy to Stella and then turned on his nephew. Alfie gave a squeal of delighted anticipation and sprinted up the snowy path, slipping and sliding until Daniel caught up with him. They both tumbled in the snow, rolling and play-fighting until both of them were covered in clumps of freezing white powder.

'Me, too.' Posy wriggled in her arms and Stella deftly slid the child's feet back into her boots and let her run towards the others.

For a moment Stella just stood still, enjoying the peace of her surroundings. The air was crisp and cold and she could smell wood smoke.

It was a perfect winter day.

A couple walked past her, smiling towards Daniel and Alfie

who were still rolling. 'That's how a father is supposed to behave.' The woman laughed and Stella managed a smile.

'Yes.' She wondered what Daniel would say if he'd heard that comment.

That the last thing in the world he wanted was commitment and the responsibility of children.

But he was taking his responsibility seriously, wasn't he?

Correctly assuming that the children would be unsettled by their father leaving, he'd immediately arranged a trip.

Stella watched, suddenly confused. It wasn't that he didn't love the children, because he did. And it wasn't that he wasn't good with them, because he was.

He didn't feel he'd be a good father. But why?

'You're looking very serious.' Daniel was standing in front of her and she hadn't even noticed. She was about to reply when she saw the wicked gleam in his eyes and then gasped as he lifted a huge lump of snow and stuffed it down the neck of her jumper.

'Oh! You…' Gasping at the sudden cold and trying to shake the snow out of her jumper, Stella shot him a warning glare. 'I'll get my own back.'

'I can't wait.' He spread his arms wide, inviting her retaliation, and Stella gave him a slow smile.

'It's going to come when you least expect it.'

'Sweetheart, I'm shivering with terror.' He was teasing her now and the combination of laughing blue eyes and rough, dark jaw made him impossibly sexy.

'You will be shivering, Daniel,' Stella promised, shaking the last of the snow from the inside of her jumper and trying to subdue the shivers in her own body. *Shivers that had nothing to do with the cold.* 'Trust me. By the time I've finished, you'll be shivering.'

Alfie danced on the spot, laughing and jumping to keep warm. 'Can we go and choose our tree now?'

They walked along the path until they reached the clearing. A fire was burning in the centre and trees of various sizes had been piled together.

'This one?' Daniel strode up to the nearest tree but Alfie looked horrified.

'Too small.' He sprinted to the far end of the clearing and waved his arms madly. 'This one.'

Daniel heaved it upright and stared at the top in disbelief. 'This tree will never fit indoors.'

'It's perfect.' Alfie caught his arm. 'Can we have it, Uncle Daniel? *Pleeease?*'

Stella watched with amusement as Daniel made a valiant effort to resist Alfie's superior persuasive technique.

'Alfie, this is just too large for your house. It's—'

'If I can have this tree I'll be so good,' Alfie coaxed. His cheeks were pink with the cold and he was so excited he could barely stand still. 'I'll go to bed when you say, I'll help with Posy and if you make any mistakes I won't tell Dad.'

'Done. That's an offer too good to turn down.' A smile in his eyes, Daniel dug his wallet out of his pocket. 'Where do I pay?'

'That man over there—but you have to carry the tree to the car.'

'But that's miles away. Don't they deliver? I don't suppose my brother wants his four-wheel drive full of pine needles.'

'That's the best bit,' Alfie said happily. 'The car smells like Christmas for months. Dad is always complaining.'

'In that case, let's go for it. Anything that winds my brother up is fine by me. And if I discover that he put a dent in my

Porsche on the way to the airport, I'll volunteer to transport everyone's Christmas trees in his vehicle.'

Alfie giggled. 'Dad would go demented.'

'That's the general idea.' Daniel blew on his hands to warm them. 'Come on, let's get this tree home before we all freeze.'

How had he managed to land the job of decorating the house for Christmas?

What did he know about a family Christmas? Nothing.

Daniel manoeuvred the tree through the front door of Patrick's barn and shifted it upright in the corner of the huge living room. 'Here?'

He looked at the excitement in both the children's faces and felt something shift inside him.

He'd blocked out almost all his memories of childhood Christmases, but he was entirely sure that his face had never looked as bright and happy as Alfie's.

Christmas had been a battlefield, with carnage strewn where there should have been presents and goodwill.

'Uncle Daniel? You're looking all funny.' Alfie peered at him through the folds of his brightly coloured scarf. 'Are you OK?'

'I'm OK.' Daniel cleared his throat and pushed his way through the black thoughts that rolled across his brain like menacing stormclouds. 'Let's get this tree sorted out. Is this a good place for it?'

Alfie dropped the scarf on the floor and nodded his approval. 'It looks good.'

'It looks *big*.' Stella was laughing as she removed Posy's hat and coat and Daniel glanced towards her and found he couldn't look away. Her blonde hair slid in a smooth, shiny sheet over her coat and her cheeks were flushed from the cold.

He looked at her lips and knew that if he kissed them now, they'd be cold. And he also knew they wouldn't stay cold for long. The heat the two of them managed to generate would melt the polar icecap.

Her gaze met his and he saw her smile falter as her thoughts slid in the same direction as his.

'Dad got the decorations out for us.' Alfie dragged a huge box across the room. 'You have to do the lights first. Stella? You're not concentrating!' His excitement was infectious and Stella turned back to him, her cheeks even pinker than they'd been a few moments earlier.

'I hope these lights work.' She helped him unravel the lights, chatting easily about what he'd been doing at school and his part in the nativity play. Posy was popping bubble wrap and giggling with delight.

Daniel had a strange feeling of detachment—as if he were watching them from the other side of a pane of glass.

Was this how Christmas was supposed to feel?

Aware that Stella was looking at him, he forced a smile. 'Are all those bulbs working?'

'Yes.' Stella stood up. Her cheerful red skirt had ridden up her thighs, exposing a mouthwatering length of leg encased in shimmering black.

Devoured by lust, Daniel made a frustrated sound in his throat and turned away. 'Where do you want me to put these lights?'

'All the way round the tree.' Alfie was dancing with excitement. 'Start at the top.'

Stella handed him the end of the lights and their hands brushed.

'Did you get a shock or something, Uncle Dan?' Alfie was concerned. 'You sort of jumped.'

Putting a safe distance between himself and Stella, Daniel started winding the lights around the tree. 'I didn't get a shock.'

'But you jumped. I saw you.'

'I didn't jump.'

'But—'

Daniel sent him an exasperated look. 'Are these lights where you want them?'

Alfie stepped back a few paces, crunching a bauble underfoot. 'Oops.' He looked down guiltily. 'I've broken it.'

'I'll clean it up. Make sure Posy doesn't go near it.' Stella hurried towards the kitchen and Daniel had a feeling she'd been glad of the excuse to leave.

His instincts were confirmed when she carefully brushed up the broken pieces of bauble and then made her excuses.

'Now you've got the tree in place, I really ought to go.' Her tone was bright and cheerful, but Daniel wasn't fooled. She was finding this as difficult as he was.

'No!' Alfie was appalled by that suggestion. 'You can't go now. You promised you'd help decorate the tree. You have to stay for marshmallows and we're going to watch *The Grinch*.'

'Sounds like fun.' Stella stooped and hugged the child and Daniel watched her pretty face soften into a smile as Alfie hugged her back.

If ever a woman was born to be a mother, it was Stella.

Which was why he'd broken it off, he reminded himself grimly. Because Stella was a woman who needed children around her and being with him would have robbed her of that chance.

'Please stay,' Alfie mumbled, his face buried in her jumper, but Stella shifted him away from her and shook her head.

'It's sweet of you to invite me but I have a million and one things to do. I'm going to be a bit busy over the next few days, but if you need anything, you can bang on my door. That tree looks fantastic. Keep up the good work. And make sure Posy doesn't go near those baubles.' Without looking at Daniel, she hurried out of the room and he heard the door slam shut.

Stella curled up in the stable, watching a Christmas movie and sipping hot chocolate, but somehow the evening didn't have any of the pleasure that it should have had.

She kept thinking of the children, decorating the tree. Of the fun of making Christmas special for them. *Of Daniel.*

Angry with herself, she flicked through the channels, trying to find something that would hold her attention.

If she'd stayed there it just would have made things worse. It was bad enough still being in love with Daniel, without having the extra torture of playing house with him.

Finding nothing to interest her on television, she opened her laptop and accessed the internet. She'd finish her Christmas shopping. At least that would be another job done.

Checking the list she'd made earlier, she pulled her credit card out of her purse.

The great thing about internet shopping, she thought to herself as she clicked away, was that you didn't have to battle for a parking space and elbow your way through crowds.

Halfway through the evening her mother rang, full of excitement and stories about her world cruise.

As she listened, Stella felt a lump building in her throat. Her parents had been happily married for fifty years and yet her mother had managed to pick herself up after her father's sudden death and build a new life for herself. She hadn't sat at home feeling sorry for herself.

In fact, she'd sold the house, bought herself a little flat in a retirement complex and used the rest of the money to travel.

Feeling humbled by her mother's drive and determination, Stella hung up and promised herself that she was going to stop being so pathetic.

She was going to enjoy this Christmas, no matter what it took.

By the following day, Daniel was stressed, exhausted and feeling inadequate for the first time in his life.

Posy had woken five times during the night and ended up in his bed where she'd wriggled restlessly, ensuring that he had no sleep at all. At five o'clock he'd given up trying, and had left her in the bed while he went to put the kettle on.

It was dark outside as Daniel flicked on the kettle and leaned on the Aga to warm himself.

The kitchen looked as though it had taken a direct hit from a rocket launcher. There were streaks of red on the wall from Posy's artistic explorations and the remains of the previous night's pasta dinner were still stuck to the saucepan in the sink.

'Want Daddy.' Posy was standing in the doorway, her thumb in her mouth, her other hand clutching the blanket she always slept with.

Daniel glanced at his watch through eyes blurred with sleep. It was barely five-thirty. 'This is worse than being a junior doctor,' he muttered. 'Don't you ever sleep?'

'Want Daddy.' Her face crumpled and Daniel put down his coffee and crossed the kitchen.

'Honestly? So do I. But we're going to have to make do, baby girl. So what is it you normally do at this time of the morning? Draw on the walls? Throw food?' It was a wonder his brother managed to function, he thought to himself as he scooped Posy up and carried her into the sitting room.

Her curls tickled his chin and as her arms wound trustingly round his neck, Daniel tightened his grip on her protectively. 'You wouldn't be so trusting if you knew how inadequate I feel,' he murmured, nudging a pile of toys to one side with his bare foot.

How did Patrick keep the place looking so cosy?

Despite the Christmas tree dominating the beautiful living room, the barn felt cheerless and morose so early in the morning. As if the family living there had moved out.

And that was his fault, wasn't it? He had no idea how to inject sparkle into Christmas. Neither did he have any idea what to do with a three-year-old at five-thirty in the morning.

Feeling bleak, Daniel bent down and switched on the Christmas-tree lights and decided that it was an improvement. 'Enough light for atmosphere, but not enough to illuminate the mess.'

'Thirsty.' Still clinging to him, Posy cuddled the velvet comforter she carried everywhere.

Daniel looked at her blankly. 'What do you drink at this time of the morning? Not tea or coffee, I presume. Milk? Juice?'

'Juice peese.'

Daniel walked back to the kitchen, filled a beaker with juice and gave it to Posy. Glancing idly out of the window, he looked towards the stable, wondering what Stella was doing.

Then he gave a hollow laugh. Stella would be asleep, snuggled under a warm duvet, and one thing he knew for certain—she wouldn't be dreaming of him. Not unless she was having a nightmare.

Moving back to the living room, he rummaged through

the pile of DVDs that Alfie had left strewn on the floor, found one with a cartoon on the cover and slid that into the player. Then he settled himself on the sofa in the darkness, with Posy half dozing on his lap.

At seven, Alfie appeared, yawning.

'Dad never lets her get up this early.' He curled up on the sofa next to Daniel, his hair ruffled and his feet bare. 'He makes her stay in her bed and play with her toys if she wakes up.'

'I'd like to know how he makes her do that,' Daniel muttered, his eyes closing again. 'Your sister is a woman who knows her own mind.' He felt exhausted. The house was a mess and he honestly had no idea how he was going to occupy two small children for one entire day, let alone four.

As if to increase his feelings of inadequacy Posy grabbed her juice and the lid flew off. Orange liquid poured over the sofa.

'Posy, no!' Daniel made an abortive grab at the beaker and watched in horror as an orange stain settled into the fabric. 'Oh, for—'

'Don't say it,' Alfie urged. 'She'll copy you. She's like a parrot at the moment. She's more effective than my spy toys. I can plant her in a room and get an exact reply of everything that was said.'

'How am I going to get the orange out?' Daniel dabbed ineffectually at the stain while Alfie offered advice.

'She's supposed to have milk in the morning, not juice.'

'She asked for juice.'

'Dad only bought that sofa in the summer.'

'Thanks for reminding me of that, Alfie.'

'He doesn't let us bring drinks in here in case we spill them.'

'Right.' Daniel gritted his teeth. 'Anything else?'

'My pyjamas are wet.' Resigned, Alfie slid off the sofa. 'I'll go and get dressed.' His body language was so forlorn that Daniel felt a pang of guilt.

'Alfie—what do you want to do when you come back down?'

Alfie looked at him hopefully. 'Can you make pancakes?'

His confidence at rock bottom on the domestic front, Daniel seriously doubted it, but he didn't want to disappoint Alfie any more than he already had. He could perform the most technically challenging procedures in the emergency department—surely he could make pancakes?

'I can make pancakes.'

Alfie cheered up. 'I can do the mixture if you can cook them.'

'Deal.'

But after the fifth pancake had turned to a scrambled mess in the pan, Daniel wished he'd stuck to cereal.

'It doesn't look like that when Mrs Thornton makes them. Maybe the pan isn't hot enough.' Alfie dragged a chair up to the cooker, clambered up and reached for the pan. '*Ow!* Ow, the handle was hot.' Bursting into tears, he jumped off the chair, sobbing and holding his hand.

Daniel felt a white-hot flash of panic and for a moment he couldn't think.

'Cold water,' he muttered, scooping the child up and sprinting to the tap. 'Hold it under cold water. Is it bad? How bad is it? God, I'm sorry, Alfie. That was my fault. I shouldn't have let you touch that pan.'

'It was my fault,' Alfie sobbed, trying to pull his hand away from the stream of water. 'Can we stop this now? It's so *cold*.'

'It's meant to be cold. It will help the burn,' Daniel said through gritted teeth, discovering that his own hands were shaking. 'Just hold it there a bit longer. Good boy.'

Posy started crying and Daniel felt his head pound.

This was hopeless. He just wasn't the right person for this job.

Switching off the tap, he examined Alfie's fingers. 'I think they're all right.' Relief rushed through him and he made a mental note not to let either child anywhere near the kitchen again. Somehow he had to occupy the pair of them without any more mishaps. 'Can you sit on the chair for a minute while I see to Posy?'

An hour later he was at the end of his tether and he picked up the phone and dialled Andrea's number.

She arrived an hour later, dressed in a slinky wool dress and suede boots that weren't designed for snow or outdoor life. 'I wasn't expecting a lunch date today. Quite romantic.' Her eyes slid to his shoulders. 'You look good in that jumper. Macho. Sexy. But I thought you were supposed to be looking after the kids. Who's babysitting?'

'Babysitting?' Exhausted and exasperated, Daniel looked at her, wondering why he didn't feel the same rush of lust that he did when he looked at Stella. 'We're babysitting. And we're cooking lunch here. You're going to help me amuse the kids. It will be fun. We can do Christmas things.' *Whatever they were…*

Andrea gave a disbelieving laugh, as if he'd suggested she strip naked and indulge in a food fight. 'Dan, I agreed to see you today because I thought you wanted to spend some time together. I allow myself one day off a week and I don't intend to spend it sweating in front of a stove and playing Monopoly with kids who aren't even mine. You said yes to this, not me. And for the record, I don't think you should have said yes. You're too soft.'

'Those "kids" are my niece and nephew,' Daniel said thinly, 'and I said yes because my brother needed my help.'

'Why didn't he just pay someone to do it?'

'Because he wanted family.' Daniel looked at her red hair and her perfectly made-up face and tried to feel something other than disappointment. 'Would you really have said no in my position?'

'Absolutely.' Her tone was devoid of sympathy. 'You make choices in life, Daniel, and you have to live with those choices. Your brother chose to have kids. They're his problem, not yours.'

'Actually, I don't see them as a problem.'

'Really?' One sculpted eyebrow lifted. 'You don't exactly look as though you're having the time of your life.'

'Uncle Daniel, Posy's just been sick on the floor.' Alfie appeared next to him, Mary and Joseph playing around his ankles.

'I'm coming,' Daniel said gruffly, his eyes on Andrea's face. 'Spend the day. I'm not asking you to have babies, just to muck in with me for one day. We could have fun.'

'Fun is a weekend in Paris or a Michelin-starred restaurant.' One wary eye on the kittens, Andrea backed towards the door. 'Keep those things away from my suede boots. Dan, if you can get a babysitter, call me. Otherwise I'll speak to you when this is over. And next time Patrick asks you, just say no.'

'Patrick is my brother,' Daniel intercepted the kittens before they could escape through the open door. 'And I love his kids.' He just didn't love the complexities that went with the children. It made him feel hugely inadequate.

Andrea looked at him for a moment, a strange smile playing around her glossy red mouth. 'For a guy who doesn't want kids, you look pretty comfortable with those kittens in your arms. Maybe you ought to stop kidding yourself.'

Daniel watched her walk back to her shiny red sports car,

waiting to feel regret. Andrea was perfect for him, wasn't she? She was intelligent, strong, and she wasn't embarrassed to admit that she didn't want children. She was just like him, in fact.

So why wasn't he running after her?

CHAPTER SEVEN

HE'D invited the lawyer over.

Telling herself that she didn't care who Daniel saw, Stella curled up in front of the wood-burning stove, sipping her second mug of coffee and staring at the mountains. The Sunday papers were strewn in front of her and she had the prospect of a lazy day doing nothing.

Despite the fact she'd had a terrible night, she should have felt relaxed and happy.

Instead, her head was full of images of Daniel and his redhaired beauty, playing with the children and having fun.

Infuriated with herself, she switched on her laptop. Another forty men had left their details and she wondered why she couldn't be more enthusiastic.

The prospect of dating anyone had lost its appeal.

Forcing herself to concentrate, she identified two that sounded interesting.

'Stella?' Alfie burst through the door, bringing snow and mud with him.

'Whoa!' Stella sprang from the sofa and caught him in her arms before his muddy boots made contact with the cream rug. 'What's the rush?' Through the open door she couldn't help noticing that the lawyer's car was gone.

Why hadn't she stayed?

Was she coming back later?

'I just wanted to see you.' Alfie's shrug was a little too casual and he clung to her more tightly than usual. 'I thought we could hang out, you know?'

Stella focused on his face, sensing that he was close to tears. 'That would be nice.' She helped him pull off his boots. 'Do you want to help me on the computer?'

'Yeah, why not? Maybe I could email Dad.'

Hearing the wobble in his voice, Stella pulled up a chair. 'Good idea. Let's do that. He'll be back very soon. How are you getting on over there?'

'It just doesn't feel like it should.' Alfie typed with one finger. 'It doesn't feel like—like Christmas.'

'Daniel bought you a wonderful tree yesterday.'

Alfie pressed 'send', staring at the screen as his email flew into cyberspace. 'The tree's great. It isn't the tree. It's everything else. I don't know.' He drooped slightly and Stella slid her arm round his shoulder.

'There's a problem?'

'There are lots of problems. Uncle Daniel just doesn't do it right.'

'But he's trying,' Stella said softly, smoothing his hair away from his face. 'He's there with you, trying his best. Isn't that what counts?'

'I suppose.' Alfie thought about that. 'I thought it would be cool being able to do what we liked, but it isn't cool. The sofa's wet, my favourite DVD is scratched and just now he trod on my remote-control car.'

Stella hugged him. 'All those things can be sorted out.'

'The worst thing is that Uncle Daniel can only do one thing at a time, so I'm not going to get any lunch because he can't take his eye off Posy. And I didn't get breakfast because the pancakes were scrambled.' Suddenly he looked very tired and very young. 'Do you think Dad will be back soon? How long can a person be without food before they starve to death? And Uncle Daniel rang the newspaper last night and advertised the kittens.' He burst into tears and Stella rocked him gently, knowing that he was just tired and disturbed by the change in his routine.

'Shh,' she soothed. 'You know you can't keep all the kittens, Alfie.'

'I wish I could keep Gabriel, too.' He wiped his face on her jumper. 'Dad's going to be so mad with me when he comes home.'

'Why is he going to be mad with you?'

'Because I've done something,' Alfie muttered, and Stella eased him away from her and looked at him.

'What have you done?'

'I'm not telling you. Then you can't be blamed. I expect Dad will blame Uncle Dan, because he was in charge.'

Stella wondered what the little boy had done and made a mental note to mention it to Daniel when she next saw him.

Then she realised that this whole situation was ridiculous. She was lonely and Daniel was struggling.

'Come on. I'm going to spend the day with you, if Daniel doesn't mind.' Stella stood up decisively, took his hand and walked to the door. 'Put your boots back on.'

'Really? You're going to spend the day?' Alfie's face lit up like the Christmas tree and Stella smiled.

'Really.'

It was pathetic, she told herself, *staying away because she couldn't cope with seeing him. Was she five or twenty-five?* 'Come on. Let's go and see if Daniel needs some help.'

'Of course he needs help.' Alfie tugged on his boots. 'That's why he rang that woman.'

'What woman?'

'The scary one with the sharp face who doesn't like animals or kids.'

The lawyer. Stella reached for her own boots. 'I saw her car.'

'Don't be upset about it. She was *useless.*' Alfie's tone was disparaging. 'She almost jumped on the chair when she saw the kittens. What a wimp. Uncle Daniel asked her to spend the day with us and she said no—which is a good thing because there was no *way* I wanted to spend my day with *her.* I want to go to the park and I bet she hates monkey bars.'

'You're hard to please, Alfie Buchannan.'

'Yes, well, Uncle Daniel was *not* impressed.'

Trying not to feel pleased about that, Stella bit her lip. 'So what's he doing at the moment?'

'When I left he was clearing up Posy's sick.'

'Seriously?'

'Why are you surprised? He's a doctor. He's used to gross stuff.' Alfie shuddered. 'Anyway, I thought if I hung out with you I might actually get to eat something when it's lunchtime. Any chance of those gingerbread men you made the other day?'

'Maybe.' Stella opened the front door and Alfie frowned at her.

'Are you sure about this? I thought you guys found it difficult being around each other?'

Stella found herself speechless. 'I—er...'

'That's why you went home yesterday, isn't it? He looks at you—you look at him. Then you go pink.' Alfie sighed. 'I may only be ten, but I'm not stupid. I have eyes. I can see he wants to kiss you. And I can see you want to kiss him. I know about sex.'

'Alfie!'

'I guess it's hard because you don't want to end up getting

divorced.' He looked wise. 'I understand that. Divorce is no picnic.'

Suspecting that his parents' divorce had affected him far more deeply than anyone would imagine, Stella pulled him into her arms and hugged him tightly. 'You're a sweet boy, have I told you that lately?'

'I'm not sweet. Sweet is for babies and I'm grown up. I'm cool,' he muttered. 'So—are you going to come and cook something?'

'Stella?' Daniel's voice came from behind her, sharp with anxiety. 'Have you seen Alfie?'

'He's right here. Alfie? Didn't you tell Daniel you were coming to see me?' Stella stood to one side so that he could see the child and Daniel closed his eyes briefly, some of the colour returning to his cheeks.

'Don't do that again, Alfie,' he snapped. 'Do you have any idea how worried I've been? I've been looking everywhere for you. I thought—' He broke off and let out a long breath.

'Don't yell at me! I wanted to see Stella.' Alfie glared at him, a sheen of tears in his eyes. 'This isn't like Christmas! It doesn't even feel like home. I want Dad to come back.' His voice broke and Stella was about to intervene when Daniel dropped to his haunches and hauled the boy into his arms.

'Alfie, I'm sorry,' he muttered, holding him tightly, 'I'm really sorry. I'm sorry I shouted, but I was worried. Not that that's a decent excuse. I'm sorry I'm useless at making it like Christmas.' He released the child slightly so that he could look at him. For a moment he was silent and then he gave a sigh, as if resigning himself to talking about something he hated talking about. 'My parents didn't really do Christmas when I was young so it isn't something I'm good at. We didn't have all those routines and rituals that you do.' He pushed his fin-

gers through Alfie's hair, a lopsided smile on his face. 'You
didn't use a comb this morning.'

'Couldn't find one.'

'I'll try and find one for you.' Daniel paused for a moment,
clearly choosing his words carefully. 'Why don't we go back
home, make ourselves a drink and you can tell me how you'd
like to spend your day.'

'I like making stuff. Cards. Paper chains. Robins.' Alfie
peeped up at him. 'It gets pretty messy. It means lots of glue
and glitter and—'

'Where does your dad let you do that?'

'On the kitchen table. Or on newspaper on the living-
room floor.'

'Sounds good to me.' Daniel nodded enthusiastically. 'Do
we have everything you need in the house or do we need to
go shopping?'

'I can take a look and let you know.'

'Good. Let's do that.' Daniel took the boy's face in his
hands, his eyes gentle. 'I'm sorry about the wet pyjamas, the
scratched DVD and the broken car. And I'm *really* sorry about
your hand.' He glanced up at Stella, who was standing there
stunned by this side of Daniel she'd never seen before.

Daniel Buchannan humble? Apologetic?

She'd only ever seen him self-assured and confident.

'Sounds like you've had quite a morning so far.'

'You have no idea,' Daniel muttered, standing up. 'Alfie?
Can we try again? And this time I'll get it right.'

'It's OK.' Alfie sniffed. 'No one's perfect.'

'Promise me that from now on if you leave the house, you
tell me where you're going.' Daniel's voice was rough and he
curved his hands over the child's shoulders in a protective
gesture. 'Promise?'

'I promise. As long as you promise to look where you're putting your feet.'

'It's a deal.' Daniel looked at Stella and gave a faint smile. 'I'll pay you a million pounds to come and cook some lunch for the kids. Something edible that isn't burned or stuck to the pan.'

She tried not to laugh. 'A million pounds? It's lower than my usual rate—but I expect we can come to some agreement. I was about to suggest that I come and help. I'm pretty bored on my own in the stable. It would be fun to make Christmas stuff. We can decorate the house, make some Christmas cards—'

'Food? Your job is to do some food.' Alfie tugged himself away from Daniel's grip and Stella nearly slipped on the icy surface of the yard.

'Definitely food.' She regained her balance. 'You can help me.'

'Daniel said I'm not to go in the kitchen any more.' Alfie held up his bandaged finger. 'I touched a pan. My fault.'

'No, *my* fault,' Daniel said gruffly, 'and it isn't going to happen again.'

'I'm a kid,' Alfie said patiently. 'I have accidents. You need to chill.'

'I've never felt less chilled in my life.' Daniel ran his hand over the back of his neck and gave Stella a faint smile. 'If you could take over the kitchen bit, that would probably be safer.'

'Where's Posy?'

'Asleep, I hope.' Then he caught her glance and anxiety flared in his dark eyes. 'Don't look at me like that! She's in her room with a stairgate across the door so that she can't escape when my back is turned. Are you telling me she's probably fetched a ladder and is climbing out of the window right now?'

'I'm sure she hasn't.' Stella locked the door of the stable and walked back across the yard with them, noticing that he kept Alfie's hand in his. It didn't matter that he'd made mistakes. What mattered was that he was trying. *That he cared.*

And that was a good thing, she reminded herself.

It was just that it made everything harder for her.

Making the most of Patrick's well-equipped kitchen, Stella occupied Alfie with some cooking. While he was covering himself in flour, she swiftly cleared up the mess, scrubbed the remains of burnt pancakes from the bottom of the pan, and loaded the dishwasher. When every surface was gleaming, she made gingerbread men with Alfie.

He pressed the cutter through the biscuit dough. 'Can we dip them in chocolate when they're cooked?'

'Good idea.' While he was decorating gingerbread men, Stella made a casserole for their supper and then went and examined the stain on the sofa.

'That's a loose cover. It should wash. If I do it on low, hopefully it won't shrink.'

'I'd forgotten how good you are at all this house stuff,' Daniel said gruffly, nursing his coffee in one hand while he fished through a box for glitter and glue. 'You love it, don't you?'

Stella programmed the washing machine, wondering how she was supposed to answer that. 'Well, I can't say I'm in love with the washing machine but, yes, I love the whole house-and-home thing. You know I do.' It was a reminder of why they were no longer together and Daniel was silent for a moment. She knew he was thinking of their relationship and when she glanced towards him, his eyes were fixed on her face.

For a moment they stared at each other and then Stella turned her attention back to the kitchen, determined not to read anything into the moment. She wasn't going to go there. She wasn't going to hurt herself by thinking of things she couldn't have. Neither was she going to delude herself by pretending there might be a happy ever after. She'd done that for long enough.

There would never be happy ever after with Daniel.

She was going to follow her mother's example and move on with her life.

'Can we make paper chains?' Alfie bit the head off a gingerbread man that Stella had laid out to cool. 'These are delicious.'

'Don't eat too many, you'll be sick,' Stella said absently. 'Talking of which, what's the matter with Posy?'

'I don't know.' Daniel frowned as he pulled out a pad of coloured paper. 'I think she's starting a cold. It's winter. I'll go and check on her in a minute. How long does she normally sleep, Alfie?'

'A whole film.'

'How long is a whole film?' Daniel looked at Stella. 'An hour and a half? She's had about that.'

'I'll go and look. You make the paper chains with Alfie.'

She took the stairs to Posy's pretty pink bedroom, opened the stairgate and stared down at the sleeping toddler. Her cheeks were flushed and her breathing was noisy. Frowning, Stella rested her hand against the child's forehead. 'You're burning up,' she murmured softly, removing the covers and smoothing Posy's damp curls away from her face.

She felt a flash of exasperation with life. Why did Posy have to become ill when her dad was away? Daniel was already struggling.

Careful not to wake the sleeping child, she sat down on the pretty little window seat and stared out at the snow-covered trees and the white carpet that now covered the lawn. The children's swing was covered in several inches of snow and Alfie's tractor had been abandoned under one of the apple trees.

Family life, Stella thought with a pang, wondering if she'd ever have that. It was the simple things that were so precious. The simple things that so many people took for granted. When she'd been growing up, she'd always taken for granted that she'd marry and have children. That she'd give her own children the life she'd enjoyed as a child. It was what she'd wanted. It hadn't occurred to her that she'd fall in love with a man who wouldn't want all that.

But life didn't always hand out what you wanted, did it? And she wasn't the sort of woman who would have children without a man she loved.

Old-fashioned, she thought to herself, picking up a couple of stuffed toys that were lying abandoned on the floor. She was old-fashioned. She wanted a man who loved her and she wanted to have his children.

But not any man.

She wanted Daniel. And she wanted Daniel's children.

Cross with herself, Stella put the toys into the basket along with others. It was time to be realistic. She needed to be proactive. She needed to get out there and date other men and stop comparing them to Daniel.

'How is she?' He stood in the doorway, a frown in his eyes as he looked at the little girl. 'Her breathing is noisy.'

'She has a temperature. When she wakes up, we'll give her something.'

Daniel rubbed his fingers over his temple. 'If she's ill, she's going to want her dad.'

'She'll be fine with you.'

'No, she won't.' His jaw was tight. 'I have no idea how to comfort a sick child.'

'Daniel, you do it every day of your working life.'

'No. I sort out the medical problems. I don't know anything about the other stuff. You obviously haven't seen how many mistakes I've made today.'

Stella looked at his taut, handsome face. 'What I've seen is a man doing his best in difficult circumstances.'

'My paper chain just came unglued.'

'But you made it,' Stella said softly. 'That's what's important. And if Posy is ill, you're the man to care for her. I've seen you in the department with kids. You're good. Very reassuring.'

He ran his hand over the back of his neck. 'That's because I know what I'm doing,' he gritted, 'not because I'm any good with kids. What if Patrick comes back and both of them are traumatised?'

'Is that what happened to you?' She asked the question without thinking and immediately regretted it because his shoulders tensed and his ice-blue eyes were shuttered.

'When Posy wakes up, call me,' he said tersely. 'I don't know anything about cooking pancakes or preparing for Christmas but you're right—I do know how to examine a sick child.'

Without giving her time to reply, he turned and walked away, leaving her question hanging in the air between them.

Posy grew worse as the day progressed. She was fractious, her nose was streaming and she developed a dry, barking cough.

'Croup,' Daniel muttered as he held her on his lap along with the velvet comforter. 'Poor mite.'

Wondering how he could possibly think he was no good at comforting kids, Stella carried on helping Alfie make Christmas cards.

They were lying on the rug in the living room, everything they needed spread out in front of them.

'Just one more,' Alfie said, carefully writing a name on an

envelope, 'for my teacher. Do you think she'd prefer the reindeer or the snowman?'

'Reindeer.' Stella passed him the glitter. 'Not too much—Oops…' She watched as a shower of silver covered the living-room floor.

'We could leave it there,' Alfie suggested. 'It sparkles.'

'I'll clean it up later. Don't worry. Those paper chains look nice.'

'Daniel put some in my bedroom. And we put some in Dad's room, ready for when he comes back.'

Posy started to cough again, and this time the cough was much worse.

With a frown, Daniel lifted her little pink T-shirt and looked at her chest. 'I need my stethoscope.'

Alfie sprang to his feet, sending glitter flying everywhere. 'I'll fetch it—tell me where it is.'

'In the spare room. In the black bag by the bed.'

Alfie flew out of the room and Daniel watched him go. 'He's a good kid.'

'He's fantastic.' Stella was looking at Posy. 'You're worried about her, aren't you?'

'As a doctor? No, not yet. But I'm watching her. As a man with responsibility for his brother's kids—yes, I'm terrified.' He gave a hollow laugh. 'It's hard to be detached when you know what's at stake. And it's pretty daunting, having that much responsibility. I'm counting the hours until he's back. As long as they're both still alive, I'll consider that I've done well.'

'If I had a sick child, there's no one I'd rather trust him with. Patrick felt the same way, or he wouldn't have left them with you.'

His eyes met hers. 'Maybe that was a mistake.'

'It wasn't a mistake.' Stella looked at Posy, curled up against his chest. 'She doesn't exactly look traumatised. She couldn't be in better hands.' Thinking how much she'd like to swap places with Posy, Stella started to clear up glitter.

'I noticed that you managed to remove the stain from the sofa cushion. And the marks from the walls.' Daniel gave a tired laugh. 'You're a genius.'

Alfie hurried back with Daniel's stethoscope. 'Can you teach me how to do it?'

'Yes, but let me listen first.' Daniel slipped the stethoscope into his ears, murmured something reassuring to Posy and then listened to her chest. 'She has good air entry but she had some stridor earlier when she was upset. I think some moist air would help. I'll take her into the shower room in my bedroom. It's a fairly small room. If I turn the shower to hot, it should create some steam fairly quickly.' He caught Stella's questioning glance and gave a wry smile of understanding. 'Yes, as a doctor I know that the data shows no clinical benefit for steam. As a worried uncle, I need to do something. And at least standing in a steamy bathroom is doing something. If that doesn't work, I'll take her out into the cold air.'

'You're going to put her in the snow? Won't that give her frostbite?' Alfie contemplated that possibility with a mixture of fascination and excitement. 'I learned about frostbite in school. Your toes can go black and then they drop off.'

'Why are little boys so gruesome?' Daniel stood up, still holding Posy. 'Cold air can help reduce the inflammation in her airways. I can promise you I'm not going to put her in the snow and I can also promise you that no bits of her are going to drop off.' Rolling his eyes towards Stella, he carried Posy out of the room.

Stella tidied up the remains of the glitter and stacked Alfie's cards into a neat pile. Once or twice she glanced towards the door but there was no sign of Daniel. 'You can write your cards now,' she said absently, 'and then there's a Christmas film on TV. Why don't you curl up and watch it? I'll go and check on Posy.'

She was concerned that Daniel hadn't brought the child back downstairs. Hoping that the little girl wasn't worse, she walked up the stairs and along the wide, airy landing. The door to one of the spare rooms was ajar, and she heard the sound of the shower running as she walked inside.

The door to the bathroom was closed, but that didn't surprise her because she knew Daniel would be trying to create as much steam in the atmosphere as possible.

Wanting to help, Stella opened the door and slid inside, closing the door quickly behind her so that she didn't let the steam out.

Then she gave a gasp of shock.

Daniel was naked except for a pair of black boxer shorts, his soaked clothes in a heap on the floor. 'Don't even ask,' he warned darkly, and Stella gave a weak smile, wishing she'd knocked before she'd walked into the bathroom.

He was a study in masculinity, his shoulders wide and powerful, his stomach flat and muscular.

Telling herself that it was the steam that was turning her cheeks pink, Stella stooped and retrieved his damp clothes. Her legs were wobbly and she was suddenly horribly aware of every female part of her body. 'I'll sort these out for you.' Flustered and cross with herself, she started to retreat, but Daniel reached out and caught her arm.

'Wait—'

She stopped because she had no choice, but she didn't look at him. She *couldn't* look at him.

His fingers tightened on her arm. 'It hasn't gone away, has it?'

She didn't pretend to misunderstand him. 'No.' The only noise in the room was the hiss of the shower. 'It hasn't gone away.'

His fingers tightened on her arm. 'We're a very bad match.'

'Terrible.' Her throat felt dry. 'The worst.'

'So if we're such a bad match, why does this feel so difficult?'

'I suppose because it *is* difficult,' she mumbled. 'No one ever said that the right decision is always the easy one.'

Whether it was the intimacy of the enclosed space, his half-undressed state or the topic of conversation, Stella didn't know, but something had shifted between them. They were balancing on the narrow ledge of reason and common sense, with instinct and temptation reaching out to grab them.

And then Posy started coughing again and Daniel released Stella's arm so that he could rub the child's back. His hand was gentle and his voice soothing as he murmured soft words of reassurance. Posy's eyes closed again but her breathing was still noisy.

Stella stood in silence, aware of how close they'd come to doing something that they'd undoubtedly both regret.

It wasn't possible to be in the same room as him and not want him, she thought desperately, wishing she'd never volunteered to help.

'She's hot.' Making no reference to what had passed between them, Daniel put his hand on the child's forehead. 'The problem with being in this hot, steamy room is that I'm raising her temperature. She's probably had enough of this. I'll dress her in a T-shirt and nappy and have her on my lap downstairs. Remind me to be more sympathetic next time a mother brings a child with croup into the ED.'

It was as if the moment of intimacy had never happened

and Stella knew she should be grateful for that. The last thing either of them needed was a rerun of their old relationship.

It was a good job they had the children to focus on, Stella thought weakly, leaving the bathroom and closing her eyes for a moment in an attempt to erase the disturbing image of Daniel almost naked. Her body still hummed with awareness and she forced herself to think back to Christmas two years previously, when he'd broken off their engagement. *Forced herself to remember the misery.*

Did she really want to put herself through that again?

No, she didn't.

It was hard, yes. Mostly because Daniel Buchannan was more of a man than any man she'd ever met. Not because he was insanely handsome, but because his qualities ran so much deeper than the glossy dark hair and sexy blue eyes.

Gritting her teeth, Stella walked back into the living room and sat down next to Alfie who was glued to one of the *Home Alone* films.

'Daniel scratched *The Grinch* so I can't watch that.'

'The rental shop have a machine that can fix that.' Stella sat down on the sofa next to him. 'I'll take it over there tomorrow.'

She was here to help Daniel with the children, she reminded herself. And that was what she was going to do.

Daniel lay sprawled in the chair, watching Posy as she slept in her bed.

In the room along the landing Stella was reading a bedtime story to Alfie. Her voice altered as she spoke the lines of each character and Daniel smiled. That was typical of her, turning a bedtime story into a whole dramatic experience. He could imagine Alfie, too excited by what was coming to let her stop.

It was another half an hour before she appeared in the doorway. 'Alfie's light is out. He should be all right now. Two of the kittens are asleep in his bedroom but I've decided to overlook that. Are you going to go downstairs?'

Daniel looked at Posy. Her little hand was clutching a teddy bear and her eyes were closed. She looked utterly defenceless. 'I'll stay here. In case she needs anything.'

Stella frowned. 'Daniel, you can't spend the night in the chair. You're too tall. You won't sleep and then you'll be exhausted tomorrow.'

'I'm not leaving her. She could get worse in the night.' And Patrick had entrusted them to his care.

'Do you think she will?'

'I think she might.' His voice was soft as he looked at the child. 'She isn't well, that's for sure. I checked her breathing again just before she went to sleep and she's doing all right, but if she gets any worse I'm going to take her in to the department and give her some humidified oxygen.'

'You don't think you're overreacting?'

'Maybe, but she's my responsibility and I'm not taking any chances with her.'

'Why don't I stay?' Flushing in response to his astonished glance, she continued. 'I mean, Patrick has two spare rooms. I can sleep in one of them and if Posy does get worse, you can just sort her out without having to worry about Alfie.'

Daniel wondered whether he needed to remind her of the incident in the shower room earlier. It had been hard to distinguish what had generated the most steam—the hot water or the chemistry between them.

Was she really seriously considering spending the night?

'I'm not sure that's a good idea.'

Her eyes slid to his and he knew that her mind was in the

same place as his. 'This isn't about us, Daniel. We have to get past this thing between us.'

'Any suggestions how?'

She bit her lip. 'We just ignore it. This is about the children. You might need help in the night.'

Daniel wanted to ask if she had any suggestions as to how he could ignore it. He was so aware of her—*so aroused*—that his body had reached screaming pitch.

But he could also see the sense of her staying. If Posy's condition did deteriorate, it would be helpful to have her close.

'All right. If you're sure that's all right with you.'

The connection between them was as powerful as ever. The only thing keeping them apart was a fundamental difference in what they wanted out of life. And the way he was feeling at the moment, that armour felt pretty insubstantial.

And then he had an uncomfortable memory of Stella's face two years earlier—*the devastation in her eyes when he'd told her that he'd made a mistake.*

Even though he knew he'd done the right thing and that her pain would have been a million times more agonising if he'd continued with the relationship, Daniel was in no doubt as to how much he'd hurt her.

And he had no intention of repeating his mistake.

He had to keep reminding himself of those differences.

Stella wanted all this. She wanted marriage, kids and all the chaotic ups and downs that went with it. And she deserved it.

'You must be starving,' Stella murmured. 'I'll go and make some food while you settle her down. Switch the baby alarm on and then we'll hear her if she starts coughing.'

CHAPTER EIGHT

STELLA arranged some cheeses on a plate, added some grapes and walnuts and a basket of bread fresh from the Aga. Then she picked up a bottle of red wine and two glasses and carried the lot into the living room.

The moment she walked in, she knew she'd made a mistake by staying.

Daniel had lit the fire. The lights twinkled on the Christmas tree and the room glowed with warmth, the atmosphere both intimate and festive.

Stella suddenly wished the barn had harsh overhead lighting, but Patrick had gone for ambience and the setting was uncomfortably romantic. She glanced towards Daniel, wondering if he was as aware of her as she was of him.

After his soaking in the shower he'd changed into black jeans and a comfortable checked shirt and he was now sprawled on the sofa, deleting emails with apparent disregard for the contents.

Stella watched him helplessly, feeling the relentless ache of desire, wondering why on earth she'd offered to stay and torture herself. Was she trying to make life as hard as possible? Was she trying to prove something? All she'd proved was that she was a hopeless case when it came to Daniel Buchannan.

Looking at him now, she wondered how she'd ever thought she'd be able to forget a man so unforgettable.

He was everything male, from the way his shirt clung to

the hard contours of his muscular body to the dark shadow that emphasised his strong jaw.

'Is she asleep?' Trying to sound brisk and practical, Stella placed the tray down on the low coffee table. 'Poor little thing.'

'Yes. Patrick called while you were across at the stable.' Daniel reached for the bottle of wine. 'Everything is going well. I took the phone to Alfie so that he could say hello— he wasn't asleep.'

'Did you tell Patrick that Posy isn't well?'

'I told him she had a cold.' Daniel poured wine into the two glasses and passed her one. 'I didn't see the point in worrying him when there's nothing he can do. And anyway, she'll be fine. I'll check her again in a minute. Thanks for making the food. It looks delicious.'

'It isn't very exciting.' She was too physically aware of him to risk sitting next to him, so instead she sat on the floor and put some cheese on a plate for him.

'You don't have to sit on a hard floor, Stella.' His tone dry, Daniel took the plate from her. 'There's room on the sofa and I promise to behave myself.'

That wasn't the problem. The problem was her thoughts.

Playing it safe, Stella stayed on the floor. 'Did Patrick say how he was getting on? Does the job sound interesting?'

'Chicago is freezing but the hospital is very impressive. He likes the people and it looks as though the post would allow him more time with the children.' His tone was even but something about him made her look closer.

'And how do you feel about that?'

'Pleased for him.' Daniel sliced some cheese. 'He deserves a break. It's hard for him here, managing job, house and kids.'

'But you'd miss him.'

He cut a piece of cheese. Studied it. 'I'd survive.'

'Oh, for goodness' sake!' Exasperated, Stella put her wine down on the table. 'Why do you men find it so hard to express their emotions? What's wrong with admitting that you'd miss your brother if he took this job?'

Daniel was silent for a moment. 'I suppose I don't want to think about it.' He drew his hand over his face, his expression suddenly weary. 'That's my way of dealing with it. And it works for me.'

And suddenly she knew how upset he was about the prospect of his brother relocating.

'Do you think it's the right thing for him to do? It seems like a long way.'

He gave a lopsided smile. 'Maybe I'll follow his example. I'm sure they need emergency doctors in Chicago.'

Stella's heart dived and she was appalled by how sick she felt at the thought of Daniel moving to America.

They weren't together, she reminded herself furiously, so what difference did it make? In fact, it would probably be a good thing. It would force her to make the break she obviously found so hard to do herself.

On the other hand, the thought of him living so far away left a gaping hole in her insides.

'Do you have everything ready for Alfie tomorrow?' Swiftly, she changed the subject.

'His school bag is by the door. He finished his maths homework. Did I miss anything?'

Stella smiled. 'I don't think you've missed anything. You've done a great job.'

'If by that you mean that the house is still standing and the kids are alive, then I suppose you're right. We'll ignore the significant casualties along the way.' He frowned as one of the kittens jumped onto the sofa. 'At least I haven't trodden on one of those yet.'

'The kittens are so gorgeous.' Stella scooped the animal into her hands and made a fuss of it. 'Don't you think they're cute?' She placed the kitten carefully in her lap and stroked it gently. 'This is the feisty one. He was trying to attack the Christmas tree earlier. The other two are sleeping in Alfie's bed.'

Daniel yawned. 'I probably should have banned that.'

'He's happy and the kittens are happy.' She fussed over the kitten, wishing that Daniel had less of an impact on her. 'It's only another three days to go before Patrick comes back.'

'Posy won't be well enough to go to the crèche tomorrow.'

'Are you going to ask Mrs Thornton to sit with her?'

'No.' He leaned forward and put his plate down on the table. 'I've rung the hospital—pulled some strings. I'm going to take the next few days off.'

Her hand resting on the kitten's soft fur, Stella gave a disbelieving laugh. 'How did you manage that? It's the middle of winter—the department is busier than ever.'

'Ben agreed to swap with me.'

'That was kind of him. He's a nice guy. Ellie is a lucky girl.' Stella felt a stab of envy, thinking of Ellie with her gorgeous husband and her two lovely children. 'And what do you have to do in return?'

'I'm working Christmas.'

'You're working Christmas Day instead of Ben?'

'He has a family.' Daniel leaned back against the sofa and stretched out his legs. 'Christmas is important to him.'

Whereas, to Daniel, it didn't seem to matter at all. Suddenly she wanted to know. She *needed* to know. 'You really hate Christmas, don't you?'

'It isn't my favourite time of year, that's true.' An ironic smile touched his mouth. 'I'm pretty sure it isn't yours, either, after what I did to you two years ago.'

'I love Christmas,' Stella said simply. 'What happened between us didn't change that.'

Daniel's eyes glittered in the firelight. 'I'm glad I didn't ruin it for you.'

'Until I heard you talking to Alfie, I didn't realise that you found Christmas so hard.' Stella broached the subject hesitantly. 'You obviously don't have very good memories.' She knew she was touching a nerve and, for a moment, she thought he wasn't going to respond.

He stared into the fire, a blank expression in his eyes. And then he stirred. 'I don't have a single happy memory of Christmas and I'm sure that if you asked Patrick, he'd say the same thing.'

The kitten squirmed on Stella's lap and she stroked it, wanting to know more but cautious about saying the wrong thing. 'Did your parents not celebrate?'

'They didn't see being trapped in the house together over the festive season as something to celebrate. It just made the battle all the more intense,' Daniel drawled softly. 'Hand-to-hand combat instead of long-range missiles. The rest of the year my father spent as much time at work as possible. It minimised the opportunities for conflict. At Christmas, there was no opportunity for escape. They were trapped together. And we were trapped with them.' He gave a humourless laugh. 'Patrick and I used to pretend that we were prisoners of war.'

Stella thought about her own Christmases as a child. *About being wrapped in love and laughter.* Decorating the tree, playing games, the carol service in the village church, cooking with her mother...

'If they were so unhappy, why didn't they divorce?'

'The official line was that they stayed together for the sake of the children.' Daniel's voice was loaded with irony. 'But it was more for the sake of neighbours and friends. Divorce was failure.'

'And they didn't do anything to make Christmas special? No tree? No decorations?' Stella lifted the kitten against her chest, finding its warmth comforting. 'No silly games of charades?'

'No. My father tried to lose himself in the television but that annoyed my mother so much she actually broke it one year.' Daniel laughed, but the sound was hard and devoid of any humour. 'I remember inviting a friend over and my mother was hysterical. Vicious. Yelling at my father. After that, I didn't invite anyone again. It was too embarrassing. To begin with I used to try and wangle invitations to other people's houses, but that was hard, too. Seeing happy families just makes you feel even more isolated when yours is a dysfunctional mess.'

'Daniel, that's so sad.' Appalled, Stella reached out to touch his arm and he turned to her with a mocking smile.

'Don't touch me, babe,' he said softly, 'not unless you're willing to go with the consequences. And we both know that isn't a good idea. I can't give you what you want.'

Stella swallowed and removed her hand. But her insides were jumping and fluttering. 'Relationships don't have to be like the one your parents had. Patrick still believes in love.'

'My brother is a fool. Carly walked out on him on Christmas Eve. The only reason those children aren't basket cases is because Patrick is a fantastic dad.'

'Yes. And you have all the qualities he has.'

Daniel lifted an eyebrow. 'Try telling that to Alfie. So far today I've burned his hand, wrecked his favourite DVD, ruined the sofa, burned his dinner and broken his favourite car.'

'You were doing your best.'

He closed his eyes, a faint smile playing around his hard mouth. 'Well, my best isn't good enough and it never will be. I haven't got what it takes to be a good father. I have no experience. I see Patrick and I think, *I'm not like that.*'

'No, you're different.' *And that was why she loved him.* 'No two fathers are the same. There isn't only one right way to be a parent.'

'Maybe not. But there are a million wrong ways and I know far more about those than I do the other.' His tone unusually cold, Daniel stood up and scooped up the tray, his body language announcing that the conversation was at an end. 'I'll take these to the kitchen. Do you want coffee or anything?'

'No, thanks. It will keep me awake.' Feeling pushed out and strangely isolated, Stella transferred the sleeping kitten to the sofa and stood up, too. 'I'll go up and check on Posy. Then I'll go to bed. An early night would do me good.'

'With any luck you won't be disturbed. Sleep well.'

They were stiff—formal—as if their conversation hadn't been deeply personal. *As if they hadn't once been lovers.*

Stella looked at his hard, handsome face and knew he was hurting. And suddenly she desperately wanted to say something that would make everything all right. She wanted to fix things. *She wanted to hug him.*

But life really wasn't that simple, was it?

The past couldn't be undone. Experiences couldn't always be forgotten. And a hug would lead to something that would complicate an already complicated situation.

Feeling tired and low, Stella picked up the small bag she'd packed. 'I'll sleep in the room with the sloping roof. Call me if you need me. Goodnight, Daniel.'

Putting the bag on the bed, she nipped across the landing to check on Posy and found her sleeping peacefully, her breathing calm and even.

Relieved, Stella returned to her room. She had a long, lazy bath, changed into her nightdress and then slid under the duvet and switched on her laptop.

'All right, Mr handsome hunk, shall we meet up before Christmas?' Determined to push forward in her quest to meet someone else, she scrolled through the messages people had left her.

After an hour of staring at the screen and not really seeing anything that was going on, Stella gave up and closed the computer. None of them was Daniel.

And that was a good thing, wasn't it?

She'd ended their relationship because they didn't want the same thing. She didn't want or need another Daniel!

Perhaps she would go to the hospital Christmas party after all. Try and meet someone the old-fashioned way.

She heard Daniel's footsteps on the landing and froze, wondering if he'd tap on her door. *Hoping?* When the footsteps moved past, she found that she'd been holding her breath.

Exasperated with herself, she flicked off the light and slunk under the duvet. She was a sad, sad case. Maybe it would be a good thing if he did move to Chicago. Maybe that would force her to get on with her life instead of staying in this state of romantic limbo, comparing everyone to Daniel.

'How is Daniel coping?' Ellie locked the drug cupboard and slipped the keys back into her pocket. 'When is Patrick due back?'

'Tonight. And Daniel was still alive last time I looked. Just.'

'Posy's better?'

'Yes, fortunately. But Daniel didn't want her to go back into the crèche.'

Ellie gave her a curious look. 'So he's spent three days with her? I thought he was allergic to children.'

'It's not as simple as that.' Stella found it a relief to talk to someone. 'It's more that he thinks he's going to mess them up.'

'Is he good with her?'

'Oh, yes, but he can't see it. He's been painting with her. The entire house is covered in artwork.' Stella walked with her towards the reception area where the board was flashing up a waiting time of two hours. 'And this morning he was making her a papier mâché snowman because there wasn't enough snow outside to build a real one.'

'Oh...' Ellie's eyes filled with tears and she covered her mouth with her hand. 'That's so gorgeous.'

'Posy thought so. She was covered in glue and bits of newspaper and I doubt her fairy pyjamas will survive the experience, but I've never seen a child so happy.'

Ellie sighed. 'There's something about a big strong man looking after a little child that turns me to jelly. Are you the same?'

'Everything about Daniel turns me to jelly,' Stella said gloomily. 'That's the problem. It doesn't matter that he's totally wrong for me. I still want him. I'm thinking of seeing a counsellor. I need a twelve-step programme or whatever they're called.'

'You don't think that caring for the kids might have changed his mind about having them?'

'No.' Stella lifted a set of notes from the pile. 'If anything, it seems to have convinced him that he's made the right choice.'

'Why?' Ellie ducked under a bunch of mistletoe and walked

into the reception area. 'It sounds as though he's done a brilliant job.'

'He doesn't think so.' With a resigned shrug, Stella waved
the notes. 'I'd better get on. That road traffic accident this
morning has increased the waiting time. Everyone is slipping and sliding on those pavements doing their last-minute
shopping.'

'Wait just a minute.' Ellie reached into a drawer and handed
her a slip of paper. 'Secret Santa.'

'What about it?'

'Everyone has to buy a present for someone. Just £5. Chocolates. Bottle of wine. Joke book. Whatever, but if that's my
name on that piece of paper make sure it's chocolates.' Ellie
grinned. 'We're going to put all the presents under the tree
in the staffroom and have a grand opening. Which reminds
me—are you going to the Christmas party? They need to
know numbers by tomorrow.'

Stella hesitated. 'I don't know…'

'You must go,' Ellie urged, handing her another piece of
paper. 'It's at the outdoor ice rink that they've set up by the
lake. Little twinkly lights everywhere, Christmas carols and
mulled wine. So romantic.'

Stella decided not to point out that she didn't have anyone
to be romantic with. 'I'll think about it.' But that noncom-
mittal remark wasn't enough for Ellie.

'Oh, *please* go. You're a fantastic skater, I remember you taking a bunch of us a few years ago. If nothing else, you have an
evening out, get some exercise and impress the men with your
triple salco toe loops or whatever they're called. We can have a
lovely girly bonding session on the ice. There's no chance I'll
catch Ben skating—you know what men are like. He'll be at
the bar with the guys. I need someone to peel me off the ice.'

Stella laughed. 'I'll think about it.'

'And you're sure you don't mind working Christmas Day?'

Stella shrugged. 'It's fine.' Given the option of working or sitting in the stable on her own, she was going to choose to work, even if working meant that she'd be shoulder to shoulder with Daniel. 'Are you and Ben going away?'

'No. Family Christmas at home, everyone welcome. Which basically means disorganised chaos. We'd love you to come over after you finish here. There'll be loads to eat.'

Stella smiled, touched by Ellie's generosity. 'Thanks. But I'll probably be so tired I'll be glad to get home and be on my own.'

'Stella, you can't be on your own on Christmas Day! It's a time to be with people! If you don't sit there grinding your teeth, desperate to get away from everyone, it just doesn't feel like Christmas! And what about turkey? Crackers? Presents? Silly hats? Too much champagne?' Ellie sounded appalled and Stella managed a smile.

'If that's a description of your typical Christmas then I might come after all.'

'I hope you do.' Ellie gave Stella a quick hug and Stella felt a lump in her throat.

She had lovely friends, she reminded herself. People who cared about her.

Maybe she didn't have a family of her own, but life wasn't all about finding that one special person you wanted to be with.

But, for the first time ever, she wasn't looking forward to Christmas.

Patrick's arrival home was accompanied by a flurry of excitement and an even larger flurry of snow.

'If I'd waited twenty-four hours I wouldn't have had to

struggle with that papier mâché snowman,' Daniel observed
as he sutured a laceration on a girl's leg while Stella helped.
'We could have made the real thing.'

'You still can. And I'm willing to bet that papier mâché
snowman will still be in Posy's life in five years' time.' Stella
gave the girl a tetanus injection. 'I'm sure she's missing you.'

'Probably in the same way Alfie is missing all the toys that
I managed to damage,' Daniel drawled, tying off the final
stitch and then applying a dressing. He smiled at the girl on
the trolley. 'That was a dramatic end to a Christmas party.
How are you getting home?'

'Is that an offer?' Still tipsy, the girl looked at him flirta-
tiously and Daniel gave a faint smile.

'It was a concerned question. I can see you've been drinking. Not a good end to the office party, spending an hour in
here.'

'Actually, it was a great improvement on the office party.
For a start, you're five times better looking than anyone I work
with. And if I wasn't here, I'd still be there, which would
mean dodging my hideous boss who was dressed as Santa.'
The girl swung her legs over the side of the trolley and stood
up shakily. 'He was going "Ho, ho, ho" and pinching all the
girls' bottoms. That's why I cut my leg. I dived to one side
and slipped on someone's abandoned sausage roll.'

Stella giggled. 'Sounds like a great party.'

'It's one of those parties where you know if you don't watch
yourself, you're going to end up losing your job.' The girl
looked down at herself gloomily. 'This outfit is ruined. I wish
I hadn't drunk anything. I feel dizzy.'

Stella frowned, concerned. 'Is there someone at home for
you?'

'My flatmate. I suppose I'd better call a taxi. I don't want to lose my licence on top of everything else. Thanks for stitching me up, you delicious doc.' She gave Daniel a sultry smile and scribbled her phone number on a scrap of paper. 'Any time you want to play doctors and nurses—call me.'

Daniel lifted a hand and refused the paper that she was thrusting at him. 'Thanks, but I don't want to be struck off just yet.'

The girl gave a good-natured smile and stuffed the paper into her pocket. 'Oh, well, you can't blame me for trying.' She slid her arms into her coat. 'Have a good Christmas. Whenever I watch those medical soaps on TV, I think it always looks really exciting. There's usually some sort of major accident or something, isn't there? Drama, drama, drama. Someone held at gunpoint, or a train crash.'

'That's TV. They're competing for viewers. In real life we're hoping for a really uneventful Christmas,' Stella said hastily, handing her an information sheet and urging her towards the door. 'I want to eat mince pies, not spend the day sticking people back together.'

But she had a feeling that she was going to spend Christmas Day avoiding Daniel.

Since looking after Patrick's children, everything seemed worse. Up until then Daniel had managed to convince her that he'd be a terrible father, but she knew now that it wasn't the case. He'd be a *wonderful* father. The best.

That precious time they'd spent together had given her a tantalising glimpse of a future more perfect than anything in her dreams. And that glimpse had left her impossibly sad because Daniel still didn't see it the way she did.

CHAPTER NINE

STELLA sat in the back of the taxi, having a moment of doubt.

She shouldn't have come.

It was a Christmas party, for goodness' sake, and she wasn't very good company.

She frowned crossly. Who was she kidding? The reason she didn't want to go was because Daniel was going to be there.

'Are you going to sit there all night, love?' The taxi driver was watching her in his rear-view mirror. 'What's wrong?'

'Can you take me back home again?' Stella slid down slightly in the seat, hoping that no one would see her. 'I've changed my mind.'

The taxi driver looked at her thoughtfully. 'Man trouble?'

'Sort of.' Stella didn't want to admit that she was still in love with a man who had broken off their engagement two years previously. That made her nothing more than stupid, didn't it?

'Take some advice from me—if it's a choice between sitting indoors feeling sorry for yourself or going out and meeting people, always go out.' His voice was gruff. 'I remember after my Lydia died, I didn't want to go anywhere. Didn't want to do anything. But my mates dragged me out all the time. And eventually I started to enjoy myself. And I met Beth. Life moves on, love. But it isn't going to move on if you're on your own on the sofa.'

Stella blinked. 'Well, I—'

'What's the worst that's going to happen? You're going to

talk to a few people and be bored. Maybe you'll slip on the ice and break something.' He shrugged as if that was a matter of no consequence. 'Either way, it's got to be a step up from sitting on the sofa feeling sorry for yourself.'

Stella laughed. 'Breaking something is a step up from watching TV?'

'You can't be lonely in hospital, and you might meet a gorgeous doctor.'

Stella didn't tell him that it was the prospect of meeting one gorgeous doctor in particular that was putting her off. 'I'll bear that in mind.' She pulled her purse out of her bag and handed him a note. 'Merry Christmas. And thanks for the advice.'

He was right, she thought to herself as she stepped out of the car onto the icy ground. A night spent alone in front of the television feeling sorry for herself was the coward's way out. All right, so it was hard not being with Daniel. But life *was* hard. She needed to get a grip.

If her mother could manage a world cruise at her age, then she could manage a hospital Christmas party.

'Stella!' Ellie slithered over to her, her hand in Ben's. 'Isn't it a perfect evening?'

Ben looked at his wife with incredulity. 'El, it's below freezing and it's starting to snow.'

'Precisely,' Ellie said happily. 'Perfect for skating. We almost don't need a rink. Come on. We're already late. If we don't get a move on, they'll have drunk all the mulled wine.'

Stella tucked her arm through Ellie's and walked under the pretty arch that had been created from fairy-lights. A few brave people were already venturing onto the rink, holding the side and moving forward gingerly to the accompaniment of raucous shouts of encouragement from the outdoor bar.

'Isn't that Alan Hardman, the anaesthetist?' Stella stared at the man wobbling on the ice and Ellie giggled.

'It *is* Alan Hardman. I thought he was far too serious to try ice skating but rumour has it that he's very much in love with Alison Waterman from Radiology and she's the one wobbling next to him like Bambi. Oh, my goodness!' Ellie dug her nails into Stella's arm as the couple lost their balance and crashed heavily. 'That *had* to hurt.'

'And I thought this was going to be a night off for us, Ben,' Daniel drawled, strolling up to them, two steaming mugs of mulled wine in his hands. 'Obviously not. Get the traction ready.'

Stella felt her heart rate double as she looked at him.

Wearing a thick jumper with black jeans, Daniel looked nothing like a respectable emergency specialist.

He handed her and Ellie a drink and then pushed his hands into the pockets of his jeans, watching the skaters with amusement. 'Which idiot thought that this was a good venue for a party? If everyone breaks a bone, there'll be no one left in the hospital to look after the patients.'

'Stella won't break anything.' Ellie curved her hands around her hot drink. 'She skated as a child and she's awesome.'

Aware of Daniel's curious glance, Stella blushed. 'I always loved dancing. Ice skating was an opportunity to release my inner ballerina.'

'Ben?' Daniel lifted an eyebrow. 'Do you fancy a spin on the ice to release your inner ballerina?'

'I think Alan Hardman is releasing his inner elephant,' Ellie observed, giggling as the anaesthetist crashed to the ice again.

Daniel winced. 'Somebody ought to drag him off before he ends the evening in our department.'

Ben grinned. 'You'll have the chance to release your inner orthopaedic surgeon.'

'Aren't you guys drinking?' Stella sipped the spiced wine and Daniel shook his head.

'If I'm going to have to deal with major trauma, I'd rather be sober. It's hard to align bones when you're seeing double.'

'I can't drink. I can't take the morning headache.' Ben adjusted Ellie's woolly hat, an affectionate look in his eyes. 'I'm on early baby duty tomorrow. It's Ellie's turn for the lie-in. That means getting up at six in the morning ready to rock and roll.'

Daniel gave a sympathetic smile. 'Until I looked after Patrick's kids, that comment wouldn't have meant anything to me. After experiencing Posy's idea of a lie-in, you have my deepest sympathies.'

Remembering the special time they'd spent together with the children, suddenly Stella felt a desperate need to get away.

They were standing here, talking, and the only thing on her mind was Daniel.

Suddenly she wished she'd argued with the taxi driver. She should have paid him double to take her home and drop the lecture.

'So this is where the action is.' Patrick strolled up to them and everyone bombarded him with questions about Chicago.

'Did you take the job?' Ellie looked anxious and he smiled at her.

'Why are you so worried? Are you pregnant again?'

Ben turned a shade paler. 'Ellie?'

'Not yet.' Ellie gave him a saucy look and Stella felt a pang of envy.

To distract herself, she spoke to Patrick. 'Did you enjoy yourself in Chicago?'

'Yes.' He took a mouthful of beer. 'Actually, I did. Thanks for holding the fort. I gather I have you to thank for the fact that my barn is still inhabitable.'

Something in his expression made her look at him more closely. 'There's something different about you,' she murmured, a frown in her eyes as she looked up at him. And then realisation dawned and she gave a little gasp. 'Patrick? Did you meet someone?'

He hesitated for a few seconds. 'No.'

'Patrick!' Excited for him, Stella drew him away from the others. 'You did, didn't you? You met someone! Tell me about it.'

'Nothing to tell.' He removed a flake of snow from her hair. 'Let's just say I enjoyed myself.'

'Is she American? Are you going to see her again?'

'I have two children and a job here.' With a rueful smile, Patrick drained his drink. 'It was good while it lasted, but not every relationship has a happy ending, as you well know.'

Stella looked towards Daniel and met his hot, intense gaze. 'Yes,' she said softly. 'I do know. I'm sorry it didn't work out for you. You deserve to meet someone lovely.'

'Stella.' A sandy-haired paediatrician she knew vaguely walked over to her. 'Do you skate?'

'Actually, I do,' Stella said quickly, dragging her gaze away from Daniel. Maybe on the ice she'd forget. Muttering her excuses to Patrick, she handed her mulled wine to Ellie and opened the bag on her shoulder.

'Whoa—are those your own skates I see coming out of that bag?' Ben teased her, but Stella ignored him and laced her feet into the skates.

Then she removed her coat and the three men stood in stunned silence.

Ellie was the first to speak. 'Wow,' she said faintly. '*Gorgeous* skirt. And those red tights are stunning.'

'I thought they were festive.'

'You look like a very sexy helper of Father Christmas.'

The paediatrician obviously approved because he took her hand gallantly and the last thing Stella saw before he led her onto the ice were Daniel's blue eyes glinting dangerously.

He had no right to be possessive, she thought miserably, gliding onto the ice without even thinking about it. *Just as she had no right to want him.*

Harry, the paediatrician, flailed along next to her, skating in straight lines and stopping by crashing straight into the side of the rink. Clutching the side for support, he looked helplessly at Stella. 'You've obviously done this before. Any tips?'

'The trick is not to fall over.'

'Very funny.'

Stella prised his fingers away from the side. 'You need to relax.'

He clutched her hand, wobbled and crashed to the ice, taking her with him. 'Sorry. That was a bit too relaxed.'

Laughing, Stella unravelled herself and stood up, deciding that it was possible to have fun after all. And then she turned her head and her eyes clashed with Daniel's ice-cold gaze, and that single look withered her newborn happiness.

This wasn't going to work, she thought desperately. They weren't going to be able to pick up the threads of their life while they were working and living in the same community.

She was going to have to leave this little part of England that she loved so much. She was going to have to move away from her friends—leave Patrick and the children...

That sobering thought helped her to achieve her balance and she reached out a hand and pulled Harry to his feet. 'Copy

me. Watch…' Delaying the moment when she'd have to return to her friends, Stella showed him how to move, how to
balance, and then took his hand and guided him across the ice.

He was slowly gaining in confidence when a dark figure
glided up to them.

'My dance, I think.' Daniel stood in front of them. To the
casual observer he was relaxed and confident, but Stella sensed
the simmering tension in his powerful frame.

Apparently unaware of any dangerous undercurrents, Harry
raised his hands in a gesture of surrender. 'If you can skate into
the middle of the rink with no one holding your hand, you're
a better man than me, Buchannan. You win the lady's hand.'

Clearly unaware of their previous relationship, Harry gave
a good-natured smile and skated carefully off the ice.

Stella was left facing Daniel.

Without speaking, he took her hand and pulled her against
him, his eyes on hers as he glided backwards, taking her with
him. It didn't surprise her that he was competent on the ice.
Daniel was a natural athlete, physically fit and well co-ordinated. She doubted there was any sport that he wouldn't excel
at if he tried.

Feeling the dangerous throb of tension, she tried to lighten
the mood. 'I assume you're releasing your inner ballerina.'

'Actually, I'm releasing my inner caveman.' His sardonic
smile made her heart beat faster.

'I can't see why you'd be possessive.'

'Can't you?'

All the air seemed to have been sucked out of the atmosphere and suddenly she couldn't breathe. It was no longer
about skating and Christmas—it was about her and Daniel.
'Who I skate with is none of your business.' Frustrated, angry
and confused, she tried to pull away from him but he held

her fast. 'I can skate with who I like. I can go home with who I like.'

'Yes.' But the cold glitter in his eyes told her that her reckless remark had turned the situation from tense to dangerous. 'Is that what you wanted? To go home with him?'

'No, of course not. You know I'm not like that. And you're not making sense, Daniel.'

His hold on her didn't slacken. 'I'm just telling you how I feel. I didn't say any of it made sense.'

'In two days' time it's Christmas Eve. It's the two-year anniversary of the night you proposed to me.'

He inhaled sharply. 'I know what day it is.'

Her cheeks stung from the cold. 'And it's the second anniversary of the day you broke off our engagement.'

'I know that, too. But I still don't find it easy watching you flirt with another man.' His hand brought her into direct contact with his body and, because they were moving fast, she couldn't resist.

'I wasn't flirting, but even if I was, it's none of your business. I can flirt with who I like.' Her fingers tightened on the hard muscle of his shoulders. 'Why would you even care?'

Daniel spun her round, his mouth next to her ear. 'I care, Stella.' His voice was rough and male. 'You know I care.' He'd stopped in the centre of the rink, cleverly avoiding the rest of the revellers who were playing it safe around the edges. 'There was never any question of not caring.'

'Is that supposed to make it better? Because it doesn't.' Stella looked up at him, angry with him because it would almost have been easier if he *didn't* care. Her heart was pumping as though she'd run a race and she felt a flash of desperation because the chemistry between them was as powerful as ever. 'I care, too, you know I do. But I haven't changed, Dan. And neither have you. I don't want to spend my life as someone's girlfriend. I want to make that commitment to someone and I want them to make that commitment to me.'

Someone.

Not just someone, she thought desperately, her arms locked around his neck as they stood motionless in the centre of the ice.

Daniel. She wanted Daniel. That had never changed and it was starting to look as though it never would.

The loudspeakers were playing Christmas carols and, as snow floated silently down and covered the skaters, Stella felt his hold on her tighten.

She closed her eyes, the sexual attraction so intense that she could hardly breathe. A stab of awareness shot through her body, spreading heat across her pelvis and making her legs tremble.

It was a feeling she'd only ever experienced with Daniel. *Wanting a man like this.*

Her desperately tempted body responded dramatically to the subtle pressure of his. She knew he was equally aroused and that knowledge heightened her own response.

'Let's get out of here,' Daniel growled, drawing her towards the side and dragging off his skates.

Stella did the same thing, her hair sliding forward in a silvery sheet as she bent to pull her feet out of the skates.

Part of her knew she ought to go back out into the middle of the ice and stay there until Daniel left, but another part of her knew that wherever he was going to take her, she was going to follow.

Another mistake?

Without a doubt.

If she was going to be safe and sensible, she ought to rejoin a crowd of her colleagues—there was protection in numbers, wasn't there? But a reckless part of her drove her forward and she rescued her coat and bag from Ellie who was deep in conversation with one of the other nurses from the emergency department.

Ellie said nothing—simply gave her the coat and a worried look.

Without explaining himself to anyone, Daniel took her hand and led her away from the ice rink through the dark shadowy trees made ghostly by a frosting of snow and along the frozen, rutted path towards the lake. As they moved away from the noise and lights, he fished into his pocket and removed a torch.

'Prepared for every eventuality,' Stella said lightly, but her heart was bumping erratically and she was so conscious of him that every nerve ending in her body was crackling. 'I don't know why I'm coming with you.'

His hand tightened on hers. 'Sometimes it's good to do something just because it feels right. We need to talk and we can't do that with everyone watching and listening.'

Their footsteps were muffled by the snow and Stella shivered and wrapped her coat more tightly around her.

'Cold?' His arm came around her and he drew her against him, the warmth of his body pressing through the fabric of her coat.

They continued to walk and she didn't bother asking where they were going. Their destination had no relevance. The only thing that mattered was that she was with him. And she savoured the moment.

As they reached the water's edge she heard the soft lap of the water. Behind them, in the distance, they could hear muted laughter and music but here, by the pebbled shore, they had privacy.

The intimacy of the setting stole her breath. It was just her, Daniel and the darkness.

She turned to him, intending to speak, but the words never left her lips because he scooped her face into his hands and lowered his mouth to hers. His kiss was fierce and demanding, the contrast between the cold of his fingers and the warmth of his mouth somehow increasing her excitement.

Afterwards, looking back on this moment, she decided that she'd never stood a chance.

From the moment he kissed her, the end had been inevitable because their passion had never been a half-hearted beast. What they shared had never burned itself out, diluted itself or run out of steam. His touch melted her, as it always had, and when he urged her back against the solid trunk of a tree, she didn't resist.

Excitement engulfed her and she wrapped her arms around his neck, unresisting as he closed his hands over her bottom and brought her into contact with the hard thrust of his arousal.

'Daniel...' The heavy ache in her pelvis was almost too much to bear and even while he teased her with his mouth, she wanted more. 'I want you.' Her broken admission came out as a sob. 'I know it's crazy and I know I'll regret it but I want you.' Her hand reached down and covered him and she heard the sudden change in his breathing.

It had been so long...

'I want you, too.' His hands were under her jumper and she gasped as his skilled fingers grazed the sensitive peaks of her breasts. Thick, treacly pleasure poured through her and when he threw his coat onto the ground and lowered her onto it, she didn't resist.

The ground was hard and cold through the wool of his coat, but all she was aware of was heat. The heat of his mouth. The heat of his hands. The heat of her body as the fire built. The flick of his tongue over her nipple drew a gasp from her and when he drew the hard peak into his mouth she moaned and arched against him. Sensation shot from her breast to her belly, the ache in her pelvis building and building until she could no longer stay still.

When his hand moved lower she arched her hips to help him, and when his fingers touched her intimately she dug her nails in his shoulder, feeling the hard swell of muscle through the thickness of his jumper.

The cold air licked at her exposed flesh but she didn't notice, her body devoured by the sensation created by his skilled, clever fingers.

When he shifted over her she murmured his name, the feel of him against her so intolerably exciting that she couldn't breathe the air into her lungs. He was silk, velvet and steel and his initial thrust drew a shocked gasp from her that quickly turned to a moan of ecstasy.

He surged into her and erotic sensation engulfed her body. His hand slid under her bottom, lifting her, and he drove himself deep, his breathing uneven as he established a slow, sensual rhythm.

Stella stroked her hands down his back, found male flesh under the wool jumper, felt the play of muscle as he moved. Her body was a mass of screaming desire, her need for him so great that it eclipsed anything she'd ever experienced before.

'I love you.' She mouthed the words against his neck, a part of her still sufficiently aware to prevent herself making that

admission aloud. But perhaps he felt it because he paused for a moment and looked down at her, his handsome features blurred by the darkness.

She thought he was going to say something but he didn't.

Instead, he lowered his mouth to hers and thrust deeper, shifting the angle so that the pleasure intensified to a level that bordered on painful. Without warning she smashed into a climax so intense that she couldn't breathe or make a sound.

Daniel muttered something under his breath and she was dimly aware that he was struggling to hold himself back, but he lost the fight and, as her body splintered apart, she felt Daniel's hands tighten and his mouth came down on hers.

Pleasure tore through her, thick sublime and beyond anything she'd experienced before, intensified by every movement Daniel made. Shower after shower of excitement held her trapped, but it had to end and eventually her body calmed, the madness slowly fading and leaving in its place a delicious warmth and a bitter sense of loss.

Stella gradually became aware of her surroundings—the rough ground digging through the silk lining of his coat, the cold bite of the night air and the strength of Daniel's body. She closed her eyes for a moment, knowing that she'd never forget this moment.

Regret? Later, perhaps, she'd feel regret.

Now her emotions were so confused that she couldn't untangle them. Neither did she want to. She just wanted to live for the moment.

All she knew for sure was that her belief that she could live and work alongside Daniel and still move on in her life was a delusion. She'd never move on while this man was part of her life because no other man would ever match up to him.

'I didn't use protection,' Daniel murmured, and Stella gave

a painful smile because of all the issues he could have tackled that, of course, was the one that was worrying him.

He didn't want a child, did he?

He didn't want to be a father.

'It's all right.' Wondering how she could behave so normally in a situation that was so far from normal, she lifted her hand and touched his face. 'It's the wrong time of the month.'

'You're not taking the Pill?'

'I didn't have any need to,' she said quietly. 'There hasn't been any man but you.' She was still trapped underneath him, conscious of the weight of his body above hers.

'I thought you were meeting men over the internet.'

She gave a shiver as the cold licked areas of her exposed flesh. 'That didn't exactly get off the ground.'

'You're cold. I'm sorry. I don't know what I was thinking.' Daniel rolled away from her and swiftly adjusted her clothing. Then he pulled her to her feet and draped his coat around her shoulders. For some reason that she didn't understand, the protective gesture made her want to cry.

She was woman enough and romantic enough to want this to have a happy ending.

She wanted to hear 'I love you.' She wanted to hear 'I can't live without you.' But she knew that she wasn't going to hear those words from Daniel's lips.

'I'll call a taxi,' she muttered, grateful that the semi-darkness managed to help her retain her dignity. 'Is there a way back to the car park that avoids the ice rink?'

'Yes.'

'Great. Show me the way.'

'Stella—'

'I just want to go home, Daniel.' Knowing that whatever he wanted to say, it wouldn't be what she wanted to hear, Stella glanced through the trees towards the sparkling lights, wondering how she was going to face everyone in the morning.

They'd guess what had happened. And her friends were going to think she was mad.

And perhaps she was. Perhaps, later, when she lay in bed, thinking about all this, she'd reach that conclusion herself.

'If you want to go home, I'll drive you,' Daniel said gruffly, taking her hand and leading her along a path that she hadn't known existed. He opened a gate and suddenly they were back in the car park.

'I can ring for a taxi.'

'Don't be ridiculous.' He unlocked the doors of his low, sleek sports car and she slid into leather and luxury, grateful not to have to talk to anyone.

'I hope people don't think we're unsociable.' As she made polite conversation, she was painfully conscious of his strong, hard body next to hers and her own body hummed with the memory of what they'd shared.

'It's a Christmas party. Half the hospital is there.' Daniel reversed out of his parking space and the car growled its way out of the car park. 'No one is interested in us.'

He drove down the dark lanes towards Patrick's barn, his eyes fixed on the road ahead.

Stella felt numb.

Christmas Eve was just a couple of days away. The two-year anniversary of the day Daniel had proposed.

Whatever had possessed her to think she could come back here and feel all right about it all? Her love for Daniel wasn't something superficial that could be swept away like debris after a storm. Her love for Daniel had roots. Deep roots that would always be part of her.

And it was becoming obvious to her that the only way to build a life without him was to live that life nowhere near him.

'Stella?' It was only when he spoke her name that she realised that he'd turned off the engine and that they were sitting outside the stable.

'Oh.' She grabbed her bag, her gloves and the rest of her things. 'Thanks, Daniel.' It felt as though she should say something more. It felt as though the moment was important. But she really had no idea what to say.

And he said nothing, either.

Wondering why that should disappoint her, she reached for the doorhandle.

'Wait.' His voice was a hoarse rasp and his hand closed over her leg, preventing her from leaving the car. 'Invite me in, Stella.'

The words were like the sharp edge of a knife pressed against sensitive flesh. 'I don't think that's a good idea, do you?'

For a moment he didn't respond and then he pulled his hand away. 'Maybe you're right. I'll just hurt you again, and I honestly don't want to do that. Are you going to Patrick's on Christmas Day when we finish work?' When Stella hesitated, he gave a bitter laugh. 'I guess the answer to that is "not if you're there". Am I right?'

'I'm not going to Patrick's,' she said quickly. 'I'm going to Ellie's. *You* should be at Patrick's. It's where you belong.'

Daniel rubbed his fingers over his forehead. 'I'm not feeling particularly sociable. If I ever manage to get away from the consequences of people who have drunk too much alcohol and undercooked their turkeys, I'll probably go for a walk.' Letting his hand drop, he stared through the windscreen at the swirling snow and Christmas lights that Patrick had hung from the barn. 'I might just lose myself in the mountains.'

'You should go to Patrick's,' Stella said softly. 'He's your family. He'll need you around. And the children would be disappointed if you weren't there.'

'I'll break their Christmas presents.'

'You'll make it special for them, Daniel.' And suddenly just thinking about him playing with the children was too much for her. If he'd hated kids, or shown no interest in playing with them, maybe this whole thing would have been easier.

As it was, it felt like the hardest thing she'd ever done in her life.

Even harder than the first time because then, when she'd walked away, she'd been angry with him and that anger had sustained her through the long, lonely months of isolation in London.

But that anger had burned itself out and now she just felt sad. Sad because she'd seen what sort of father he'd make.

'Goodnight, Daniel.' She slid out of the car and this time he didn't stop her.

'Goodnight.'

The exchange had a depressing finality and, as she walked the few steps to the front door of the stable, Stella knew that what they'd shared hadn't been a mistake.

It had been a goodbye.

CHAPTER TEN

ON THE morning of Christmas Eve Daniel found himself sitting in Patrick's kitchen, helping Posy mix chocolate brownies.

She waved the spoon in the air. 'Lick the bowl?'

'There's nothing left to lick. At least half this mixture is stuck to your jumper, Posy Buchannan,' Daniel muttered, prising the spoon out of her hand. 'And the other half is around your mouth.'

'Are you going to tell me what happened to you at the Christmas party?' Patrick was scribbling Christmas cards on the small section of the table that wasn't covered in chocolate. 'One minute you and Stella were melting the ice, and the next you'd vanished into the forest, never to be seen again.'

Daniel ignored the sudden flash of heat that warmed his body. 'Why are you writing Christmas cards? They're going to arrive after Christmas.'

'At least they'll arrive.' Patrick scribbled an address on an envelope. 'I was up delivering a baby all night. These people are lucky to have a card from me at all. Why are you avoiding my question?'

'Because there's nothing to say.'

'Are you going to hurt her again?'

Daniel helped Posy scrape the mixture into the tin just as Alfie shot into the room. 'I *hate* you, Uncle Daniel,' he sobbed, the breath tearing in his throat. *'I hate you!'*

'Alfie!' Patrick frowned and put down his pen. 'Don't speak like that.'

'Well, it's true.' Alfie scrubbed his hand over his face to remove the tears. 'I *do* hate him. He's made her go away.'

'Who is going away? Why is this family one big drama?' With a sigh, Patrick stood up and walked towards Alfie but Daniel was there before him.

'Alfie.' He dropped into a crouch and closed his hands over the boy's shoulders. 'Why do you hate me? What have I done?' He wanted to think that this was about the scratched DVD or the ruined remote control, but a cold premonition seeped through his body. 'Who is going away?'

'Stella.' Alfie thumped his fist into Daniel's chest. 'And it's *all* your fault. *I hate you!*'

'I guess I have the answer to my question,' Patrick muttered. 'Alfie, watch your manners.'

'Leave it,' Daniel said softly, lifting a hand to his brother. 'Alfie, what exactly did Stella say?'

'She didn't say anything. I went over there to just hang out, like we always do...' Alfie sniffed and wiped his nose on his sleeve '...and then I saw all this job stuff all over the table. And she was filling out forms. And she looked really sad. When she opened the door her eyes were all red and funny and I knew she'd been crying, but she said she was fine.'

'Then what happened?'

'She made me hot chocolate with marshmallows and cream.'

'No, I mean...' It was a struggle to keep his voice calm. 'How did you find out she was thinking of leaving? Did she say something?'

'I asked her about the job and she said she couldn't stay here and I said why not, don't you love us, and she said, yes, that was the point, she loved us too much and it was all too hard or something weird like that.' Alfie sucked in a breath. 'And I said she ought to marry you, Uncle Daniel. And then her face went all funny and she said that you didn't want to marry anyone and you don't want kids and she does.' His face crumpled. 'Why don't you want kids? Is it our fault? Were we bad? Don't you like us any more?' He started to sob and Daniel tugged the boy into his arms.

'I love you, Alfie,' he said gruffly. 'You know I do. And you weren't bad. You were fantastic.'

'So why don't you want any of your own? Don't you love Stella?'

Patrick sighed. 'OK, enough. Alfie, this stuff is compli-cated and it's private. It's between Stella and Daniel—you can't interfere. I know you think you understand but, believe me, you don't.'

'But she's sad and I want to help.' Alfie wriggled out of Daniel's arms. 'That's what friends do, right?'

'Yes,' Daniel said gruffly. 'That's what friends do.'

Stella was taking another job? She was leaving?

'If you loved us, you'd marry Stella so that she wouldn't have to go away and then we'd all be together.' Alfie stared at him accusingly and Patrick intervened again.

'I said enough. Alfie, you have to let Daniel and Stella sort it out by themselves.'

'But Stella is going to go away, and she loves Daniel.' Alfie stared up at Daniel accusingly. 'Why don't you want kids? Did you hate looking after us?'

'No. I didn't hate it.' Daniel ran his hand over the back of his neck. 'But it was a big responsibility and I got to hand you back after four days.' Sensing that his relationship with Alfie was going to be seriously damaged if he didn't give a proper explanation, he chose his words carefully. 'It isn't about not wanting kids, Alfie. But having kids is a huge thing. It's an important job—the most important job. If you get it wrong, you can really mess up someone's life. Do you understand?'

Alfie shook his head. 'No. I know your mum and dad always argued. And they didn't do any of the fun stuff at Christmas. Dad told me. But you're not like them. You and Stella are great. And if you have kids, it wouldn't be like that. You'd be a great dad.'

Out of his depth, Daniel looked at Patrick. 'Say something.'

'What?' Patrick folded his arms, his expression implacable. 'I happen to think that my son is talking sense. You *would* be a great dad.'

Realising that he wasn't going to get any help from his brother, Daniel let out a breath. 'I'm afraid that if I have children, I'll mess them up,' he confessed in a raw tone. 'I'm scared that I'll get it all wrong. Like I did when I looked after you and Posy.'

Alfie frowned. 'You didn't get it wrong.'

'I scratched your favourite DVD, I broke your toy car, I let Posy have juice on the sofa.' Daniel waved his hand. 'The list is endless. Do I really need to carry on?'

'That's the first I've heard about the juice,' Patrick muttered, but Daniel and Alfie ignored him.

'Kids don't care about that sort of thing.' Alfie's eyes were wide as he stared up at Daniel. 'Grown-ups don't have to be perfect. We don't need grown-ups to be perfect—we just need them to always be there and not go away. And you were there. When Posy was sick, you were there. You took time off work to watch cartoons with her and I know how boring that is because she only likes baby stuff. And when you broke things, you tried to fix them. And when it all went wrong and it was hard work, you were still here. You didn't go away when it got too much.' His voice wobbled slightly. 'Not like Mum did.'

Patrick made a sound but Alfie was looking at Daniel. 'And you *hate* cooking, but you did it anyway.'

Stunned by Alfie's passionate speech, Daniel gave a crooked smile. 'I burned your hand and I almost poisoned you.'

'Don't worry. I've bought you a cookery book for Christmas.' Alfie scuffed his foot on the floor. 'I'm sorry I shouted.'

'And I'm sorry I upset you,' Daniel said gruffly, pulling him into another hug. 'I'm sorry.'

'Are you going to fix things with Stella?'

'That's enough, Alfie.' This time Patrick did intervene. 'Daniel and Posy have been making brownies.'

Alfie walked over to the table and stuck his finger into the mixture. 'When are these going to be ready?'

'When I put them in the oven,' Daniel said roughly, 'but don't raise your hopes. You know I'm useless at cooking. They'll come out burnt.' He felt strange. As if Alfie had taken everything inside him, thrown it into the air and it had come down in a different pattern.

His mind racing, he sank down onto the nearest chair, trying to make sense of his thoughts. *Of what Alfie had said.*

Alfie reached across the table for the rest of the chocolate bar, spreading fingerprints over Patrick's half-written cards. 'Are you OK, Uncle Dan? You look weird.'

'I feel weird,' Daniel croaked, looking at his nephew.

'You probably ate too much brownie mixture. That makes me feel weird, too. If Dad ever goes away again, you can look after me. That would be cool. What do you think, Posy?'

'Want a cuddle,' Posy mumbled, sliding off the chair and pressing her chocolaty face into Daniel's trousers.

Staring down at the tangle of golden curls, Daniel felt humbled.

The children wanted him to look after them again?

After everything he'd done—and everything he hadn't done—they still wanted him?

A lump in his throat, Daniel scooped Posy onto his lap just as the phone rang.

Patrick hunted for the receiver and answered it. 'Yes—yes, that's right. Two—a boy and a girl. They're really sweet.' He gave a thumbs-up sign to Daniel. 'No trouble at all. It doesn't matter that you're ringing on Christmas Eve. No, I don't think it's weird at all. I'll give you the address...'

When he put the phone down, he punched the air. 'Yes-s-s. Someone is interested in the kittens. She's coming round later.' He slammed his hand against his forehead. 'Can you believe I forgot to ask her name?'

Daniel just happened to be watching Alfie, otherwise he wouldn't have seen his reaction.

The little boy froze and then slid off the chair, his cheeks pink and a look of guilt in his eyes. 'I'm just going to go and squash my presents.'

Seeing that Patrick was distracted, gathering stuff together for the kittens, Daniel lowered Posy to the floor and followed Alfie into the living room.

'All right, sport, tell me the truth—what's going on?'

'Nothing.' Alfie kept his head down, dragging presents from under the tree. 'Everything's fine.'

'I lived with you for four days. That was long enough for me to know when you're lying.'

Alfie looked at him, anxiety in his eyes. 'If Dad gets really, really mad with me and throws me out, can I come and live with you? I know your flat is very flashy with lots of glass, but I promise not to touch anything.'

'Why would he get mad with you and throw you out?'

'Because I've done something.'

'I thought so.' Daniel pushed his hands into his pockets and narrowed his eyes. 'Tell me.'

'That woman on the phone…'

'The one phoning about the kittens?'

'She wasn't phoning about the kittens. Dad misunderstood.' Alfie spoke in a small voice. 'I sort of arranged something. For Dad. Only now I'm wondering if he's going to be too mad to enjoy it. If he gets really, really mad, do you think he'll take away my presents?'

Daniel grinned. 'I don't know. You still haven't told me what you've done.'

'It's bad.'

Daniel shrugged. 'As you keep telling me, no one is perfect.' And that realisation somehow made him feel light-headed. Had he been putting too much pressure on himself? Had he created this image of perfection that didn't exist? 'You'd better tell me what you've done so that I can protect you.'

And then he was going for a long walk to think about what Alfie had said.

'Why are we so busy? Christmas morning is supposed to be quiet.' Feeling numb and exhausted after another night with no sleep, Stella picked up another set of notes. 'Everyone is supposed to be at home with their families, enjoying themselves.'

'It's the "enjoying themselves" bit that's causing the problem,' Daniel drawled, checking a blood alcohol level and frowning in disbelief. 'How can anyone start drinking at eleven in the morning?'

'It's probably left over from the night before.'

'If this is left over from the night before, I'm going to be transferring the guy to the mortuary.' Daniel strode away to see the patient and Stella stared after him, wondering when to tell him that she was applying for jobs back in London.

Or maybe she shouldn't tell him at all. Maybe she should just quietly melt away.

She tried to focus on her work, smiling automatically at patients who wished her merry Christmas, trying not to let her low mood infect anyone else.

'Stella?' Towards lunchtime, the receptionist walked towards her, a pair of red antlers swaying on top of her head. 'There's a mother out there with a child who has stuck a Christmas decoration up his nose.'

'It must either be a large nose or a small Christmas decoration.' Daniel appeared from nowhere. 'Put them in one of the cubicles. I'll see the child.'

'Great, thanks. After that, we're going to gather in the staffroom and do the Secret Santa. We've got mince pies and champagne. No reason to starve ourselves just because we're working.'

'That's just what we need,' Daniel murmured to Stella. 'Drunk staff handling drunk patients. The day is getting better and better.'

She managed to smile, but part of her felt hurt that he seemed to be in such a good mood.

Clearly what they'd shared the night of the Christmas party hadn't affected him. He hadn't been round to see her and at work he'd acted as if nothing had happened.

Which basically meant that nothing *had* happened, as far as he was concerned.

Just a bit of hot sex in the snow.

Trying not to think about it, Stella called the mother and child into the cubicle.

'Honestly, I can't believe this has happened.' The mother was pink in the face and flustered. 'I'm in the middle of cooking a turkey and I've got twelve for lunch—it's such chaos in the house, no one noticed that the bead garland on the tree had broken. My father-in-law almost broke his hip, sliding across the floor, and we were all fussing about him when I realised that Oliver had pushed one of the beads up his nose.'

'Dangerous things, Christmas trees.' Daniel strode back into the room and crouched down beside the little boy. 'Hello, Oliver. I'm Dan.'

The little boy looked at him. 'I've got a bead up my nose.'

'So I gather. I don't suppose this was how you planned to spend Christmas morning. Have you opened your presents yet?'

'My main one.'

Daniel pulled on a pair of gloves. 'And what was that?'

'A remote-control tyrannosaurus.'

'That sounds pretty cool. Look up for me.' Daniel adjusted the light. 'There's a chance we might be able to remove it here in the department, if it's in the right position.'

'We could always try the nose-blowing technique,' Stella suggested, and Daniel looked at Oliver.

'That's not a bad idea. Are you any good at blowing your nose?'

Oliver shook his head and his mother rolled her eyes.

'Usually he just wipes it on his sleeve. He holds the tissue, but he hasn't got the hang of the blowing part. What are the other options?'

Daniel looked at Stella. 'I could try a nasal speculum—or we could use gentle suction.'

Stella knew what he was thinking—that he didn't want

to send this child down to Theatre to have it removed under general anaesthetic on Christmas Day.

'Let's not abandon the nose-blowing idea,' she said, kneeling down in front of Oliver. 'Oliver, here's what we're going to do. You are going to keep your mouth closed and no matter what happens, you don't open it. I'm going to press on the side of your nose and you are going to blow as if you're a dragon making fire. Got that?'

'A dragon making fire.' Daniel lifted an eyebrow. 'That's a new one. What do you think, Oliver? Are you feeling dragon-like this morning?'

Oliver looked doubtful. 'I don't know.'

'Imagine that you are going to blow the biggest, hottest fire.' Stella stood up quickly and, using a tissue, pressed on the side of his nose that wasn't obstructed. 'Now, breathe in deeply and when I say go, you blow as hard as you can through your nose. OK. Go!'

Oliver blew until his face turned scarlet and the bead flew out of his nose and landed on the floor.

Daniel grinned. 'For someone who doesn't know how to blow his nose, that was pretty impressive. You no longer have any excuse for using your sleeve.'

The boy's mother breathed a sigh of relief. 'Thank you so much. I was terrified that we might actually have to stay in hospital and my husband couldn't cook a turkey if his life depended on it.' Still muttering profuse thanks, she ushered Oliver out of the room and Daniel looked at Stella.

'I didn't know that you were an expert on dragons.'

Was it her imagination or did his eyes seem bluer this morning? And his smile sexier? It was just because she knew that, in a few more weeks, she wasn't going to be seeing him again. Her brain was storing all the details. 'I don't know much about dragons,' she confessed, 'but I'm well trained in useful children's skills, like nose-blowing.'

'Yes...' He was watching her with a curious expression in his eyes. 'When it comes to handling children, you're a pretty useful person to have around.'

And that was how he saw her now, wasn't it?

As a colleague.

'Hey, you two.' The receptionist stuck her head round the door. 'Everything is set up in the coffee room. Secret Santa time.'

Secret Santa?

Stella's heart plummeted.

Oh, God, she was supposed to be cheerful and festive and all she wanted to do was slink home and hide under the duvet.

'Secret Santa. The moment we've all been waiting for.' Daniel was so good humoured that Stella felt even worse. Normally he was dour and bleak at Christmas. It was a difficult time of year for him. But today—today was different.

He seemed light-hearted.

As if everything had changed in his life.

Perhaps he'd heard that she was thinking of leaving and was relieved.

She was astonished by how much that possibility upset her.

Suddenly the challenge of looking as though she was enjoying herself seemed like too much, but she knew that if she didn't join in there would be questions. And she'd spoil other people's fun and she had no wish to do that.

Hoping that she could keep up the act long enough not to disgrace herself, Stella joined the rest of the staff in the coffee room, which was dominated by a ridiculously large tree.

Her low mood seemed to be in direct contrast to everyone

else's happiness. She tried not to think about the fact that everyone else had families waiting for them at home.

She tried not to think about Daniel.

There was much laughter as presents were exchanged and Stella dutifully handed hers over to the radiographer whose name had been on the piece of paper that Ellie had handed her.

Not wanting to draw attention to herself, she helped herself to a mince pie and nibbled one side, trying to look as though she was enjoying herself. And then she glanced towards Daniel and caught him looking at her.

For a moment they just stared at each other, allowing the conversation to wash over and around them. And then finally Daniel dragged his eyes from hers and focused on the nurse who was talking to him.

As everyone lifted a glass of orange juice in a toast, Stella mumbled, 'Merry Christmas,' and the sudden stinging in the back of her throat caught her by surprise.

So this was it, then.

The end.

She'd thought she had her feelings under control, but watching Daniel laughing with the rest of the staff was incredibly painful.

Next year he'd still be here, raising a glass with the staff.

Where would she be?

She didn't know. All she knew was that it had to be somewhere far from Daniel but the thought of that made her feel sick.

How was she going to live without him?

How was she going to get through each day if he wasn't part of her world?

She'd tried that before, hadn't she, and her life had been flat and colourless. And it was no good telling herself that she'd meet someone else one day because she knew she wouldn't. What she felt for Daniel was a once-in-a-lifetime thing. It was *real*. For her there never would be anyone else, she knew that now.

Horrified by that realisation, Stella melted out of the room and hurried down the corridor, frantically blinking back tears—refusing to let them fall. She knew that if they started to fall, they might not stop.

But holding back the tears required an almost inhuman effort because she knew that no matter how much she tried to convince herself otherwise, she never would meet anyone else. How could she? After Daniel, any man she met could only be second best. And because she wasn't willing to settle for second best, she knew that she was going to always be on her own. No family. No children.

Alone.

The corridor blurred, and Stella pushed open the door to the tiny room where they kept all the sterile packs. Shutting herself in, she leaned back against the door and drew in several deep breaths, trying to compose herself.

She'd never cried at work before. Never. It was so unprofessional of her.

And she didn't understand the awful feeling of finality that was hanging over her like a death sentence.

All right, so Daniel obviously wasn't feeling the way she was feeling, but that shouldn't matter. She'd already made up her mind that the only way to move forward was to leave and, in a way, his reaction just confirmed that her decision was the right one. She couldn't work alongside him any more.

She knew that. So why was she so upset?

The door behind her back was pushed open and she gave a little gasp and held it closed, horrified to think that someone might see her like this. 'Just a minute.' But the door kept opening and she had no choice but to step back and let whoever it was enter the room. Instinctively she rubbed her fingers over her face and smoothed her hair, trying to eradicate the evidence of her loss of control.

'Why are you hiding in a cupboard?' It was Daniel. He closed the door behind him, his eyes searching her face. 'You sprinted off before I could give you your Secret Santa.'

The fact that he'd come looking for her was horrifying.

Given her current state of emotional meltdown, he was the last person in the world she wanted to see.

He'd know it was about him.

Cringing with embarrassment, she tried to look as though nothing was wrong. *As though it was normal to take refuge in a cupboard.* 'You drew my name?' She turned to take something from one of the shelves, trying to hide her expression. 'That's a coincidence.'

'Stella, put the dressing packs down. I can't talk to you while you're clutching dressing packs.'

'Daniel, go back to the staffroom and I'll be there in a minute.'

'Actually, I don't really want to give you your Secret Santa in front of everyone.' He turned her to face him and frowned. 'You've been crying.'

Dear God, could he see that?

'I'm not crying.'

'Don't lie to me, Stella. We've never lied to each other.'

'No. We never have.' Stella focused on his shirt and decided that there was no reason not to be honest. Their whole relationship was such a mess, what was a bit more carnage? 'I made a mistake coming back, Daniel. I thought that two years was long enough for me to have moved on. I was wrong.'

'Yes. It hasn't been easy.'

'I've decided that I can't do this any more.'

His hands tightened on her shoulders. 'I feel the same way.'

'Oh.' Even though she'd already come to that conclusion herself, it still hurt to hear him say it. 'Well—in that case you'll be relieved to know that I contacted my old hospital in London and they've said that I can have my job back. I'm going to leave in the New Year.'

'Leave?' His tone was sharp, as if she'd said something surprising. 'Why would you leave?'

'Because I can't work alongside you any more! It's just too hard.' Her voice betrayed her and he muttered something under his breath and pulled her against him.

'Don't cry,' he said hoarsely. 'Please don't cry, angel. I promised myself that this Christmas I wasn't going to make you cry.'

'You haven't. It isn't you, it's me.' Her voice was muffled against his chest and she knew she ought to pull away but she couldn't bring herself to. If this was going to be the last time he held her then she wanted to make the most of it. 'I just want too much. And seeing you with Patrick's children was— it made it all worse. I'm going to leave, Daniel, then maybe both of us can get on with our lives.'

He eased her away from him gently and took her face in his hands. 'Before you say anything else, can I give you my Secret Santa?'

Stella looked up at him, depressed that he could still be thinking about the trivia of Christmas when their relationship was ending for the final time. 'Fine,' she croaked, 'give me my Secret Santa. Thank you.' Braced for the usual box of chocolates or bottle of wine, she was surprised when he dug his hand into his pocket and pulled out a tiny parcel. She frowned. It was definitely too small for chocolates. 'What is it?'

'Open it, and you'll find out.'

'I might save it until I get home.'

'Stella, open it.'

Too emotionally drained to argue, Stella slid her finger into the wrapping and pulled out a small silver box. Still frowning, she flipped it open and stared in stunned silence at the beautiful diamond ring sparkling against a bed of midnight-blue velvet.

'Say something,' Daniel muttered, and Stella gulped back a gasp of shock.

'There's no way that cost £5.'

With a soft laugh, Daniel took the box from her numb fingers, removed the ring and took her hand. 'Will you marry me?' His own hands sure and confident, he slid the ring onto her finger and lifted her hand to his lips. 'I can't carry on like this, either. I love you, sweetheart. I want to be with you. Always.'

He was proposing?

Stella's legs shook and she felt suddenly dizzy. 'Daniel...' Then she remembered that he'd done this to her once before and the emotional trauma caused from plunging from high to low in such a short space of time was still with her. 'You— No. No, I can't. You know I can't. You gave me a ring once before. Nothing has changed.' How could she say yes after what had happened last time?

'Everything has changed. You said you thought I'd be a good father.'

'Yes, but what I didn't understand was that you don't *want* to be a father. Until we spent that time with Patrick's children, I didn't really understand what your childhood had been like. I couldn't understand why a man like you wouldn't want marriage and a family. But during those four days I learned a lot about you.' Her voice cracked. 'I do understand and I ache for you and I'm angry with your parents for being so selfish and putting their own feelings before yours, and for not having any idea of the impact their behaviour had on you.'

'I don't want to talk about my parents. Stella, I'm asking you to marry me.'

'I know you are.' Stella pulled away from him and forced herself to do the hardest thing she'd ever done in her life. Refusing him. *Removing his ring from her finger.* 'And this time I'm saying no. Which is what I should have said the first time. I won't marry you. I *know* you, Daniel. I know what you want and what you don't want. And you don't want this.'

'You love me.'

'Oh, yes.' She smiled through her tears, no longer trying to hold them back. 'I do love you. And I believe that you love me, but that isn't a good enough reason for you to do something you don't want to do. That just leads to resentment. I'm not one of those women who just think, He'll be fine once he's married and he'll fall in love with a child if we have one. What if you don't, Daniel? What if all you feel is resentment? Resentment isn't a good foundation for a marriage.'

'Stella, look at me.' His voice hoarse, Daniel reached out a hand and caught her chin, turning her face to his. 'Look at me and listen. You say that looking after Patrick's children taught you something about me. Well, looking after those children taught me something about myself, too. It wasn't that I didn't want children—it was just that I was terrified of failing them. Of getting it wrong. Of messing them up.'

'Daniel, I know that. I—'

'Let me finish.' His hands cupped her face, his eyes holding hers. 'I won't blame you if you won't take a chance on me again, but at least let me tell you what I'm thinking. This time it's different, Stella. When I proposed to you two years ago, I was in love with you. I wanted you. I thought I could get over my phobia about marriage and children—and then Patrick's wife walked out. At Christmas, leaving a trail of emotional devastation behind her. Up until that point I'd always believed it would have been better if my parents had just divorced. And then I realised that staying and going can be equally agonising for the children.' His tone was suddenly harsh. 'And I thought to myself, *I never want to hurt a child like that.* I won't do it. And that's why I broke it off. Not because I didn't love you, but because I wasn't sure I could be the man you wanted me to be. I didn't think I could give you what you wanted.'

'I know that, too, and—'

'I was terrified by the responsibility of parenting. I suppose in my head I'd spun this image of a perfect happy family. I was afraid I could never match that image.'

'I don't suppose anyone does.'

'No. But then I realised that plenty of people get it right, even when circumstances aren't perfect. Even though he's single, Patrick is a wonderful father. Alfie and Posy are happy and confident. And someone told me recently that a good parent doesn't have to be perfect.' He gave a crooked smile. 'They told me that DVDs can get scratched and toys can be broken, and a family can still work. None of those things mess a child up. A perfect family is a family that loves each other and is always there for each other.'

Stella swallowed. 'Who told you that?'

'Alfie. And he's something of an expert.' Daniel's voice was suddenly soft and his gaze was disturbingly intense. 'He also told me that what children really need is to be loved and to know that they're loved. And our children are going to know that, Stella.'

Their children?

Stella felt the lump in her throat return. 'Daniel, we really can't—'

'We can. We can, Stella.' He lowered his mouth to hers and kissed her gently. 'I know I'm asking a lot. You're standing there thinking, It's Christmas Day and he's going to break my heart a second time. But I promise you that this time you're wrong. Make a family with me, Stella. If you're there, I know we'll do it right.'

He sounded so sincere that Stella had to rein in the urge to just yell, *Yes, yes, yes!* 'You want a family?'

'That's what I'm telling you.'

'You really want to marry me?'

Daniel lifted her hand so that the diamond twinkled under the lights. 'You think this is a joke?'

Despite the tears misting her eyes, Stella smiled. 'I think it's a really nice ring for £5. What would have happened if you hadn't picked out my name in the Secret Santa?'

'I didn't pick your name. I had to persuade Ellie to fix it for me.'

'You're shameless.' But she was smiling through her tears and suddenly Christmas was starting to feel the way it was supposed to feel.

'I can't believe you've changed your mind. I never thought that was going to happen. I'd given up hoping.'

'But Christmas is a time for hope, and I wanted Christmas to be perfect for you this year,' Daniel said softly. 'And perfect for me. Are you going to make it perfect, angel? Are you going to give me another chance? Say yes.'

Yes.

Did she dare?

Feeling suddenly light-headed, Stella glanced around her. 'Talking of situations not being perfect, I'm intrigued as to what motivated your decision to propose to me in a cupboard?' She felt ridiculously happy and if there'd been more room, she would have danced around the dressing packs.

'You were the one who chose the cupboard,' Daniel drawled, a gleam of humour in his blue eyes. 'I just wanted an intimate conversation without an audience. I thoroughly approve of teamwork in the emergency department but this is one situation in which I don't need anyone's help.' He pulled her hard against him. 'I'm still waiting for your answer. But if you say no, I have to warn you that I'm not going to listen.'

There was a sudden banging on the door and one of the nurses called out, 'Daniel? Are you in there? Ambulance Control just called. They're bringing in a Santa who fell off his sleigh. Possible Colles' fracture. They think he's been drinking.'

Daniel rolled his eyes. 'Don't any fantasies remain intact? Santa drinking in charge of a sleigh? Unbelievable,' he breathed, and then he tilted Stella's face to his. 'You'd better decide quickly before we have a department full of elves and reindeer. Your answer?'

Stella smiled, tears blurring her vision. 'Yes,' she whispered. 'My answer is yes. Of course. I love you. I always have. I always will. You're the only man I've ever wanted.'

Daniel lowered his head to hers, everything he felt for her communicated in that one devastating kiss.

'Thank you,' he murmured against her mouth. 'Thank you for trusting me. Thank you for saying yes a second time. I promise I won't let you down.'

The thumping on the door interrupted them. 'Daniel?'

Daniel lifted his head reluctantly. 'We'd better go and see Santa,' he drawled, his arm still around her waist as he reached for the doorhandle. 'When we've finished patching him up, you can tell him what you want for Christmas.'

'I already have everything I want for Christmas.' Stella slid her arms round his neck, her happiness so great she just wanted to smile and smile. 'I have you. And you're the only present I've ever wanted.'

★ ★ ★ ★ ★

CHRISTMAS EVE: DOORSTEP DELIVERY

PROLOGUE

PATRICK strode through the doors of the labour ward, his bleep and his phone buzzing simultaneously. Pushing open the doors of the delivery room, he walked straight into an atmosphere of palpable tension.

His eyes met those of a white-faced midwife. Despite the soothing words she was muttering to the panicking mother, there was no missing the strain in her expression and her relief at seeing him.

'Cord prolapse, Patrick. The trace has shown persistent variable decelerations and prolonged bradychardia. I've put her in the knee-elbow position, they're preparing Theatre and I've emergency-bleeped the anaesthetist. I'm so sorry to drag you out of your meeting. I know the chief exec gets furious when you go running off.'

'It's not a problem.' Patrick shrugged off the jacket of his suit, slung it over the back of the nearest chair and unbuttoned his shirtsleeves. 'Ed?' He turned to his registrar and noticed that he looked unusually stressed.

'She needs a crash section,' his colleague muttered in an undertone. 'After I called you, I put a line in and infused 50 mils of saline into her bladder, as you instructed. Did I miss anything?'

'Did you do an ultrasound?'

'Yes. There's good blood flow through the cord.'

'All right. Good job. So we've bought ourselves some time.'

Patrick rolled up the sleeves of his shirt. 'You say she isn't suitable for a general anaesthetic?'

'That's right.' The registrar handed him the notes but Patrick gave a brief shake of his head and walked to the head of the bed.

'Hello, Katherine. I'm Patrick Buchannan, one of the obstetric consultants.'

'I know what you're going to say and I don't want a Caesarean section,' the mother wailed. 'I want to have this baby naturally. That's why I only came into hospital half an hour ago. I knew this would happen. I knew if I came in earlier, you'd muck about with me.' She was kneeling face down on the trolley, her bottom in the air in an attempt to prevent the cord being compressed between the pelvis and the baby's head. 'I feel ridiculous in this position. It's so undignified.'

'This position is saving your baby's life.' Patrick squatted down next to her so that he could have a proper conversation and build a connection with the labouring woman. 'Do you understand what is happening, Katherine?'

'Yes. You're going to cut me open instead of letting me have the baby the way nature intended!' The woman was sobbing now, her head on her arms. 'I hate you. I hate you all. Oh, God, why did this have to happen?'

'You're very tired, Katherine.' Patrick spoke gently. 'From what I've been told, you were in labour for a long time at home before you came to us.'

'I didn't want to come to you at all! I just want to have the baby naturally.'

Seeing how terrified she was, Patrick felt his heart twist in sympathy. 'You can't have this baby naturally, sweetheart. It's too much of a risk. The cord is prolapsed—that means that it's dropped down below the baby's head. That's why you're lying in this undignified position. The cord is your baby's blood supply—if that blood supply is obstructed, the baby could die.'

Katherine gave a low moan and turned her blotched, tear-streaked face to him. 'Don't say that! *Don't say that!*'

'It's the truth. And I won't lie to you.'

'You're putting pressure on me to have the one thing I don't want!'

'I'm putting pressure on you, that's true—but because this is a medical emergency, not for any other reason.'

'You're a surgeon. You'd much rather intervene than let women do it by themselves.'

'I'm the last person in the world to intervene surgically when there is another option.' Patrick spoke quietly, holding up his hand to silence his registrar, who had drawn breath to speak. 'Katherine, if I thought you could deliver this baby yourself, I'd let you do it.'

Katherine sniffed, but she kept her eyes on his, desperate for reassurance and guarantees. 'How do I know you don't just want to get home in time for Christmas?'

Patrick smiled. 'Because it isn't Christmas Eve until tomorrow. I've done all my shopping, the turkey is in the fridge and my kids don't want me home until they've "secretly" wrapped my presents. If I turn up now, I'll be in trouble.'

Katherine's breath was jerky from crying. 'I can't have a general anaesthetic.'

'So I understand. Don't worry. I know the whole thing sounds scary and you feel out of control.' Patrick rubbed his hand over her shoulder to reassure her. 'I'm going to ask you to trust me to do what's best for you. Can you do that? I promise you that everything I do will be for you and the baby. Not for me.'

'If I can't have an anaesthetic—'

'We'll give you a spinal. You won't feel any pain, I promise.'

'Is that like an epidural?'

'Similar.' Keeping his hand on her shoulder Patrick stood up, his gaze flickering to the senior midwife in the room. 'Is the anaesthetist on his way?'

'He's meeting us in Theatre,' the registrar said, and then lowered his voice. 'Can he put in a spinal when she's in the Trendelenberg position?'

'Who is the anaesthetist?'

'Gary Clarke.'

Patrick gave a faint smile. 'Gary could put in a spinal if she was hanging from the ceiling. I'm going to go and scrub. I'll see you in there.'

Katherine gave a little moan. 'It's going to go wrong. I know it is.'

'No, it isn't.' Maggie, the senior midwife, took over the role of offering moral support. 'Patrick is the best there is. He'll have your baby safely delivered in less time than it takes you to make a cup of tea. Come on, now, love. I know it isn't what you planned, but you have to think of the baby.'

'Kathy.' Her husband added his pleas, 'I know you're scared but you have to do this.'

Katherine looked at Maggie, panic in her eyes. 'Would you let him deliver your baby?'

'Patrick *did* deliver my baby,' Maggie said gruffly. 'I had a condition called placenta praevia, which is when the placenta is lying across the cervix. Patrick did my Caesarean section. And that was seven years ago when he was still a registrar. He was brilliant even then, and he's had tons of practice since.'

Katherine gave a choked laugh. 'Perhaps you should start a fan club for him.'

'I'm too late. If you go on the internet you'll find loads of threads devoted to chatting about how brilliant he is. We get women coming up from London just to see him because he's an expert in premature labour. You see? He can even teach those London doctors a thing or two.'

Katherine groaned. 'It's just that I hate needles, I hate operations.' She hiccoughed. 'I hate—'

Knowing that he couldn't proceed until the anaesthetist arrived, Patrick turned his attention back to the labouring woman. 'It's difficult when things don't go the way you planned. I understand that. When my daughter was born the whole thing was a nightmare from beginning to end, and I'm an obstetrician. Nothing went the way I wanted it to go.'

He didn't add that his wife had blamed him.

Ex-wife, he reminded himself wearily. She was his ex-wife.

Katherine's face was discoloured from crying, her eyes tired after a long labour. 'I wanted to have this baby at home.'

'And having a baby at home can be a wonderful experience, but there are certain times when that just isn't safe,' Patrick said softly, 'and this is one of them.'

She gave a strangled laugh. 'I thought you'd lecture me for staying at home for so long.'

It wasn't the time to tell her she should have come into hospital hours ago. What was the point in adding to her guilt and worry? What he really needed to do was gain her confidence. 'I'm a great supporter of home birth, providing the circumstances are right. This isn't one of those circumstances.'

Katherine looked at him, exhausted, confused and wrung out by the whole physical and emotional experience of childbirth. 'I don't want anything to happen to the baby.'

'I know you don't.' Patrick watched as the foetal heart monitor showed another dip. 'The baby isn't happy, Katherine. We need to do this, and we need to do it now. Maggie, can you bleep Gary again? Tell him I want him up here any time in the next two seconds. The rest of you—transfer her into Theatre while I go and scrub. Move.'

Patrick changed quickly and then started to scrub, allowing the hot soapy water to drain down his arms.

'She's ready.' Another the midwife hurried up to him. 'We've taken blood for cross-matching and she's breathing 100 per cent oxygen. Gary is doing a spinal. He says can you please start soon because he's getting bored.'

Patrick gave a smile of appreciation and moments later he was gloved and gowned, scalpel in hand. 'If you need any advice, Gary, just let me know,' he said smoothly, exchanging a glance with his colleague. 'Katherine, if you feel anything at any point, you just tell me. Are you all ready for Christmas?' He chatted easily, the words requiring no concentration, all his focus on the technical operation he was performing. Even though the foetal heart was stable, he knew that time wasn't on his side.

He also knew that he didn't intend to lose this baby.

'I've bought the presents.' Katherine's voice was wobbly with nerves. 'I'm supposed to be picking up the turkey tomorrow.'

The staff draped sterile cloths in such a way that Katherine couldn't see what was happening.

'Someone else can do that for you—it will be good practice for your husband.' Patrick held out his gloved hand and the midwife assisting him passed him the instrument he needed. 'Any tips on cooking turkey are gratefully received. Last year it was a disaster, I ended up cooking cranberry omelette. My children have never forgiven me.' His gloved fingers widened the incision he'd made and he glanced at the clock. Three minutes.

The door to Theatre opened and the paediatrician hurried into the room, ready to take the baby.

'Good timing. Come on, little fellow.' Patrick eased the baby out and there was a collective sigh of relief when the child started to bawl loudly. 'You have a son, Katherine. Merry Christmas.' He allowed the mother to see and touch the baby briefly before handing the boy to the hovering paediatrician. 'Nothing to worry about. We just need to check him over, Katherine.'

Leaving the baby in the hands of his colleague, Patrick turned his attention back to his own job. Delivering the placenta and then closing. He worked quickly and quietly, aware of Katherine and her husband in the background talking in low, excited voices.

'That was fast, even for you.' Watching him close, Maggie opened another suture for him. 'A new record. I think you could just be a genius.'

Patrick grinned. 'I do love a bit of hero-worship. Does all this admiration mean you're willing to perform that traditional midwifery task of making me a cup of tea when I've finished here?'

'Don't push your luck, handsome. I didn't train for all those years to make you tea.' Maggie handed him a swab. 'And, anyway, you won't have time to drink it.'

'That's probably true.'

'I don't know why you're complaining. You have Christmas off.'

Patrick's fingers worked swiftly and skilfully. 'This will be my first Christmas at home with my kids in years.'

'Want me to come and cook that turkey for you?' Maggie winked saucily and Patrick smiled.

'You're happily married. Behave yourself.'

Watching what he was doing, she opened a sterile dressing. 'Tom Hunter is on call over Christmas. If his wife delivers, you might have to come in anyway. He doesn't trust anyone else. He's going to have a nervous breakdown if you're not here.'

'I saw Sally in clinic today. She won't deliver until Boxing Day at the earliest.' Patrick secured the dressing. 'This year, I'm going to eat my turkey in peace. That's if I manage to work out how to cook the damn thing. Katherine. I'm done here.' He smiled at the patient. 'I'm going to get cleaned up, we'll transfer you to the ward and then I'll come and see you.'

The woman's eyes were misted with tears of gratitude and euphoria. 'Thank you. Thank you for saving my baby—and thank you for making the whole thing so unscary. I'm sorry I was so pathetic. You are a fantastic doctor and your wife is a lucky woman.'

There was sudden tension in the operating theatre and several of the staff exchanged embarrassed glances, but Patrick simply smiled.

'Unfortunately my now ex-wife would have disagreed with you,' he drawled, stepping back from the operating table and ripping off his gloves. 'She would have been the first to tell you that fantastic doctors make lousy husbands. I'll see you later, Katherine. I'll be in my office if anyone needs me.'

He stayed longer in the shower than he should have done, feeling the hot water sluice over his bare flesh while he tried to shut down his thinking.

Lousy husband.

That was what he'd been to Carly, wasn't it?

Feeling the familiar stab of guilt, he turned off the water and cursed softly.

He'd already promised himself that he wasn't going to spend

another Christmas brooding over Carly. What was the point of going over it again? *Of asking himself if he could have done more?*

He dressed quickly and walked down the corridor of the bustling maternity unit to his office, frowning when he saw the stack of paperwork on his desk. Picking up the first file, he sat down just as the door opened and Maggie slunk into the room, an anxious look on her face and a box of chocolates in her hand.

'These arrived from the woman we delivered yesterday. You'd better have one before they all go.' Scrutinising him closely, she closed the door behind her and walked across the room. 'Katherine has just gone to the ward. Paeds are happy with the baby which, by the way, is now named Patrick Gary.'

Reflecting on how his friend and colleague would greet that news, Patrick smiled. 'As long as it isn't Gary Patrick.'

Maggie rolled her eyes. 'You two are ridiculously competitive. I don't know how you managed to be in the mountain rescue team together and not push each other off a cliff.' She stuck the box of chocolates on his desk and sighed. 'All right. I'll come straight to the point. Are you OK? You didn't have to answer that woman's question about your wife. She's really worried she upset you. We're *all* worried about you.'

'She didn't upset me.' Patrick signed a document that had been left out for his attention. 'I'm fine, Maggie.' *And the last thing he wanted to talk about was his ex-wife.*

But Maggie showed no sign of shifting. 'I know you *hate* this time of year—have you heard from her? Has she been in touch?'

'No.' Resigned to having the conversation he didn't want to have, Patrick put his pen down. 'She sent a card and a cheque for me to choose something for the kids.' The anger rushed through him but he controlled it, as he always did.

He'd trained himself to be civilised about the whole thing for the sake of the children. He didn't want them to feel like tennis balls being thumped between two players. 'She said I was more likely to know what they wanted than she was.'

Margaret's mouth tightened with disapproval and Patrick knew what she was thinking. The same thing he'd been think-ing—*that Carly should have known exactly what to buy her own children for Christmas.*

'It's been two years since she walked out, Patrick. It's time you found someone else. Let's face it, it isn't going to be hard.'

Patrick gave a faint smile of mockery. 'Not hard at all to find someone you want to spend your life with and trust with your children's happiness.'

'All right, all right—it's hard.' Maggie pushed the box of chocolates towards him. 'The kids are lucky to have you. You're such an amazing dad.'

Patrick's jaw tensed. *If he was so amazing, why were his chil-dren living without their mother?*

'Maggie, I appreciate your concern but you don't need to worry about me. The children and I are fine. Goodness knows, my life is complicated enough without adding in a relation-ship.' He helped himself to a chocolate. 'Does this have nuts in it? I hate nuts. You midwives always know the chocolates by heart.'

'That's because we eat too many of them. That one's cara-mel. And relationships don't have to be complicated, Patrick.'

'Mine always seem to be.'

'That's because you picked the wrong woman last time. Next time choose a nice, kind, motherly girl who would love those gorgeous children of yours and be proud to be with a high-flying doctor.'

'I don't want a nice, kind, motherly girl.' Patrick unwrapped the chocolate and ate it. 'I want a raving nymphomaniac with the gymnastic skills of an Olympic athlete.'

Margaret choked with laughter. 'And there was me thinking you need someone intelligent you can have a conversation with. I never knew you were so shallow. Or are you just trying to shock me?'

'I'm trying to shock you.' *And move her off the subject of his ex-wife.*

'What about that girl you met when you were in Chicago?'

Patrick sighed. 'Remind me why I told you about that?'

'I caught you in a weak moment.' Smiling, Maggie settled herself on the edge of his desk. 'You *really* liked her, didn't you?'

'I spent twenty-four hours with her, Mags,' Patrick said carefully, pushing aside the memory of a girl with long legs and an endless smile—*and a night that would stay with him for ever.* 'Hardly a recipe for happy ever after.'

'You should have taken her number.'

'She didn't give me her number.' Patrick sat back in his chair, a wry smile on his face. 'Clearly she didn't want to repeat the experience.'

Maggie started to laugh. 'Is that really what you think? It's far more likely that she felt awkward at having spent the night with you and slunk out of your room before you woke up.'

Not having considered that possibility, Patrick frowned. 'She seemed pretty confident.'

'Was that before or after you'd removed her clothes?'

'Does it make a difference?'

'Of course it does! Confident women are often full of insecurities when they're naked. That's why we prefer to keep the lights off.'

They'd kept the lights on. *All night.*

'Enough!' Patrick aimed the chocolate wrapper towards the bin in the corner of the room. 'You and I may have been colleagues for years but there are limits.'

'I'm just saying that maybe she didn't want you to see her in daylight.'

'She showed me around the hospital in daylight.'

'But presumably she was wearing clothes at that point.' Maggie dipped her hand into the box and pulled out a chocolate. 'Trust me, it's different. If I ever went to bed with you, I'd want the lights off.'

'If I ever went to bed with you, your husband would kill me.' Patrick emptied the contents of his in-tray into his briefcase. 'Can we drop this conversation? Relationships aren't a priority for me at the moment. And if you ever mention this to anyone else on the unit, I'll drown you in the birthing pool.'

Maggie looked smug. 'You really did like her.'

'Yes.' Exasperated, Patrick reached for his coat. 'Yes, I liked her. Satisfied?'

'You liked her a lot.'

'Yes, I liked her a lot.'

'Was she pretty?'

'Very.'

'Did she make you laugh?'

Patrick thought about the day they'd spent together. 'Yes. She was fun. She smiled all the time.' *Which had been a refreshing change after Carly's endless moaning.*

'And you didn't take her number?' Maggie rolled her eyes. 'I thought you were supposed to be clever.'

'Clever enough to spot when a relationship isn't going to work.' Patrick put his coat on. 'If she'd wanted me to have her details, she would have left her number. And even if she'd left her number, it would have been somewhere in Chicago because that's where she lives.' He snapped his briefcase shut. 'I, on the other hand, live in a small corner of England. Even if she hadn't made her feelings clear by slinking out of my bedroom, I wouldn't get in touch with her. It would never have worked and I don't need another romantic disaster.'

'So that's it, then?'

'That's it. It was just one night and the only reason you even know about it is because you have an uncanny ability to prise information from the innocent.'

'I care about you. You deserve to be with someone special.'

'My kids are special. I'm with them.' Patrick walked towards the door. 'Any luck finding an extra midwife willing to work over Christmas?'

'No. So far that particular miracle hasn't happened. I'm just hoping that no one has contractions on Christmas Day because there's definitely no room at this inn.'

'You can call me if you're desperate. I can always bring the children in with me. They can sit in the staffroom with the chocolates.'

'We'd love to see them. I haven't seen Posy for a few months. But I don't want to call you in over Christmas. You deserve the break.' Maggie walked to the door. 'I'm glad you didn't take the job in Chicago. I would have resigned and gone with you. Tell me honestly—were you tempted?'

Yes. Because if he'd taken the job, he would have seen the girl again.

He'd even picked up the phone once, but had put it down again before it could ring. What would he have said? *Hi, you know that night of hot sex we shared? Any chance you could give up your job and your life in the States and come and live over here so that we can do it again?*

Patrick sighed. He didn't even have to say it aloud to know it sounded ridiculous.

He'd already wrecked one woman's life. He wasn't going to do the same thing a second time.

'I wasn't tempted.' Reminding himself that he had two young children depending on him, he glanced at the clock. 'I'm off home. It's Christmas Eve tomorrow. I've promised to spend it with my children. This raving nymphomaniac you're finding me...' He gave Maggie a slow smile. 'Just make sure she has a passion for sexy underwear.' He regretted the words immediately.

She had worn the sexiest, classiest underwear he'd ever seen. Just thinking about the provocative silky knickers he'd found on the floor of his room the next morning made him glad he was wearing his coat.

'Go home and do battle with that turkey,' Maggie said cheerfully. 'I'll see you in three days.'

Discovering that there was nothing like the thought of cooking a turkey to cure a man of an attack of lust, Patrick groaned. 'I'd forgotten about the turkey. I'd rather deliver triplets than cook a turkey.'

Maggie gave a choked laugh. 'Welcome to the festive season. Merry Christmas, Patrick.'

'Merry Christmas.' Patrick felt exhausted as he thought of the challenge ahead of him. 'Yet another family Christmas that I'll mess up. Alfie still hasn't let me forget last year's turkey disaster. I need a miracle.'

CHAPTER ONE

HAYLEY climbed out of the taxi, slipped on the ice and landed hard on her bottom in the snow.

'Are you all right, love?' The taxi driver peered at her and she gave a weak smile as she slithered and slid her way back onto her feet, clutching the door for support and mentally itemising the damage.

'I'm fine,' she lied, trying not to picture the bruise that was going to appear later. 'Fortunately my bottom is big enough to provide a decent cushion. Which is useful because I'm not that great at walking on ice. Actually, I'm not that great at walking on pavements either. I'm the only person I know who can trip on a flat surface.'

The taxi driver chuckled sympathetically. 'Uncoordinated, are you? I have a sister like that. Always falling over, she is.' He flicked on the windscreen wipers to clear the snow. 'It's been great chatting to you, Hayley. Cheered up my Christmas Eve, you have. Feel as though I've known you for years.'

Remembering just how frank she'd been, Hayley squirmed with embarrassment. She'd said *far* too much. As usual. He knew everything about her except her bra size. Come to think of it, he probably knew that, too, because she *had* mentioned that she always felt nervous in strapless dresses. In her head she could hear her stepbrother's mocking voice saying, *Hayley doesn't have an 'off' switch.* But what was she supposed to do? She'd been in the car for twenty minutes and it would have been rude not to speak. 'I'm glad you were the one who picked me up from the station, Jack. And I hope you get that hip of yours sorted out soon.'

'I'm sure I will. The doctors are very clever around here. Good with their hands, you know?' He gave her a knowing wink and Hayley blushed, wondering what had possessed her to confess *that* particular bit of her life history.

'How much do I owe you, Jack?'

'Nothing. Haven't enjoyed a fare so much all year. You made me laugh so hard I almost had the car off the road at that last corner,' he said cheerfully, setting his meter to zero. 'And if you really want my opinion, I think your family should be ashamed of themselves. If my daughter were a midwife I'd be proud as punch—I wouldn't be telling her she was wasting her talents and should have been a lawyer. Where would the world be if we all picked our jobs on the basis of how much they pay? No wonder you wanted to come up here and escape. Now, forget about the lot of them and have a good time. I hope the romance works out for you. With any luck he'll propose by New Year and then you can invite me to your wedding.'

Wedding?

Had she actually confessed that bit of her fantasy?

'If there's a wedding, you'll be there. I'll need someone rooting for me on my side of the church,' Hayley said weakly, holding onto the door and wishing she hadn't revealed *quite* so much to someone she'd known for twenty minutes. It wasn't so bad to have told him why she wasn't going home to her family for Christmas, but it was probably a mistake to have told him about *that night*.

But she was excited! And happy! And it was all because of a man.

At least now she was in the same country as him, she

thought dreamily. The thought that he might be within miles of her made her want to sing and dance. It was only the knowledge that dancing might leave her with two broken ankles that stopped her from twirling in the snow.

That and the fact that she didn't want to make a bad impression on her new employer.

Brushing the snow from her coat, she thought to herself that for once—*just once*—it would be nice to be a naturally elegant and dignified person. She would have liked to arrive at her new job as housekeeper looking like one of those women you saw in magazines—long black coat, elegant boots, lipstick...

'You've got snow in your hair, love,' the taxi driver said helpfully, and then nodded at the house behind her. 'Well, this is it. High Fell Barn. Nice place. Smart. Like something from one of those fancy architect designed home programmes you see on the TV. I know you haven't met the family but I can tell you from looking at this that they're loaded. I wouldn't mind spending Christmas here myself. Starting to think you might be right to ditch the whole family thing.'

'Oh, no, I think family is wonderful,' Hayley said hastily, dragging snow out of her hair with her fingers. 'Just not *my* family. And they'd probably be all right if I was different. They're all scarily clever and co-ordinated and have really well-paid jobs and apartments with big windows and glass— you know the sort of thing. I was the runt of the litter. Well, actually I came from a different litter because they're my stepsiblings. My mum married their dad and they never forgave me for that.' *She was doing it again, talking, talking, talking.* 'Anyway, enough of that,' she said lamely, and Jack smiled at her.

'Stepfamilies can be complicated. Everyone knows that. Lots of jealousy there.'

'I don't think my stepsiblings are jealous,' Hayley said humbly. 'More embarrassed to be officially associated with me, I think.'

Whoops—here comes Hayley. How many babies has she dropped this year?

Not for the first time Hayley indulged in a swift fantasy about her acid-tongued stepbrother choking on a chicken bone and her saving his life with a skilfully performed Heimlich manoeuvre. Of course, he'd be blubbering with gratitude, her whole family open-mouthed with awe at her hidden talents, begging her forgiveness for having so grossly underestimated her.

We had no idea, Hayley.

Trying not to dwell on how inadequate her family made her feel, Hayley stared at the huge glass windows and the snow-covered roof of the barn. Despite the size of the place, it was the most welcoming building she'd ever seen. Lights twinkled along the front of the barn and through the window she could see a haphazardly decorated Christmas tree standing guard over piles of brightly wrapped parcels.

To the side of the barn was a wide stream in full flow, the winter silence disturbed by the roar and rush of white water as it frothed down from the top of the icy fells.

'That's the beck.' The taxi driver nodded. 'That's what we call it in these parts. In summer it's no more than a trickle of water but now, with the snow melting...'

'It's fantastic.' After the urban chaos of Chicago, Hayley savoured the sound of the water smashing over the rocks on its way down the mountain.

Behind the barn stretched acres of fields, sparkling white with snow, and beyond that the forest and the mountains. Pine trees stood tall and straight as sentries either side of the barn, tiny twinkling lights twisted through their branches.

It was like something from a Christmas card. She half expected to see Santa and a team of reindeer hauling a large sack towards the gently smoking chimney.

'It's enough to lift your spirits, isn't it?' The taxi driver grinned at her. 'Talking of which, it's time I went home and lifted spirits with the wife. Brandy is her tipple. You never know—I might get lucky. Hope you do, too.'

'I don't know—I'm starting to think this might have been a mistake,' Hayley confessed, cautiously letting go of the car door and pushing her hands into her coat pockets for extra warmth. 'I don't even know where the guy lives. I just know it's the Lake District.'

'But you know he works at the hospital so he should be easy to track down once Christmas is over.'

Desperate for reassurance, she bit her lip. 'Do you think it's crazy to have come all this way to find a guy I've only met once?'

'I think it's brave.'

'Brave as in stupid or brave as in courageous?'

'If you hadn't done it, you would have spent the rest of your life thinking, What if he was the one? And what if he was? You'd have thrown it all away. What's the worst that can happen? He can reject you and you'll be a bit embarrassed. So what?'

Feeling her nerve seep out of her like air from a punctured tyre, Hayley decided that if she was going to find the courage to carry out this plan, she needed to end this conversation. 'Thanks for the lift, Jack. Merry Christmas.'

'Merry Christmas to you.' His eyes twinkled. 'Will you make it to the door without slipping?'

'Probably not, but don't worry—bruises suit me. I look good in blue and purple.' Hayley smoothed her hair, even though she knew that without a pair of straighteners and half an hour in front of a mirror her attempts to look groomed wouldn't make an impact.

With a final wave and toot of his horn, Jack drove away and Hayley was left staring at the house.

A pair of child's red Wellington boots were tipped over in the snow, and a tiny shovel had been discarded on the path, as if the owner hadn't been able to wait to run back inside this wonderful house and prepare for Christmas.

It wasn't a house, Hayley thought wistfully. It was a home. *A dream home.*

And inside was a family who needed her—a family who wasn't going to spend the whole festive season treating her as the entertainment.

So why was she suddenly nervous?

Well, because she was always the same about decisions. Right thing, wrong thing? This or that? Invariably she jumped in with both feet and then realised that the other way was the better way. In fact, she'd spent most of her life unravelling the consequences of decisions she'd made.

When she'd been miles away in Chicago, Christmas with a bunch of strangers had seemed like a brilliant idea. Suddenly she wasn't so sure.

She was about to take a job with a family she'd never even met, in a part of the country she didn't know. And all so that she could avoid her own agonising family Christmas and track down a gorgeous stranger she'd spent one night with.

When she'd come up with the plan it had seemed bold and proactive.

A plan worthy of a competent, twenty-first-century woman.

Hayley swallowed. She didn't need her stepsiblings to point

out that she wasn't really a competent, twenty-first-century woman.

If she *were* a competent, twenty-first-century woman she wouldn't have slunk out of an impossibly sexy man's swanky hotel room before he'd woken up, neither would she have been wearing the previous night's dress and a scarlet face that announced her sins to anyone who happened to be looking. And she definitely wouldn't have left her knickers on his bedroom floor! A twenty-first-century woman would certainly have been able to find her knickers in the dark. Except that a twenty-first-century woman wouldn't have needed to. She would have woken up next to the impossibly sexy man, calmly ordered room service and then handed him her phone number or left with her head held high.

She had slunk out like a criminal, ensuring that there was no chance he would ever call her, because *he didn't have her number.*

All he had was her knickers.

At least Cinderella had had the sense to make it a shoe, Hayley thought gloomily as she picked her way through the snow to the front door. Losing a shoe made you seem slightly dippy and a little romantic—although it made it difficult to walk, of course. But losing knickers…

She didn't even want to think about how losing a pair of knickers made you look.

Prince Charming would never have roamed his kingdom looking for the bottom that fitted the knickers, would he?

Cross with herself, she kicked a lump of snow and watched it scatter. She'd met the man of her dreams *and then she'd walked out!* What an idiot. Her stepsiblings would have laughed themselves sick. *Soppy, romantic Hayley, always dreaming of marriage and happy endings.*

Hayley sighed. She wasn't *that* old-fashioned. She *had* spent the night with him—although her embarrassingly quick surrender had had more to do with his superior seduction technique than her impressive decision-making abilities.

But she wasn't going to think about that now. She wasn't going to think about his skilled hands, or his clever mouth or the way he knew exactly where to touch and how…

Oh, God, please, please, don't let him reject her. Please let him be dreaming of her right now. And most of all please let him have spent the past few weeks frantically calling detective agencies trying to track her down. *All I know about her is that she has great taste in underwear.*

Surely he was going to be pleased to see her?

Imagining his reaction to her unexpected arrival brought a smile to her face. Perhaps she'd better make sure that their first meeting took place in private in case he just hauled her into his arms and proposed on the spot.

She wondered what her stepsister would say when she met him.

How did our Hayley ever get herself a man like that?

Smiling at her own fantasies, she reached towards the doorbell.

Patrick pushed the haphazardly wrapped presents under the tree and looked at his ten-year-old son. 'Alfie, why are you looking at the clock?'

Alfie gave a guilty start. 'I don't keep looking at the clock.'

'Yes, you do.'

'Well, it's Christmas Eve. I—I'm excited.' Alfie's gaze slid furtively to the door. 'Daddy, don't you wish you had someone to help cook the turkey?'

'I can cook a turkey.' Patrick added a strip of sticky tape to a parcel that was bursting out of its wrapping.

'Last year you said if you ever saw a turkey again it would be too soon.'

Patrick winced. *Was Christmas ever going to run smoothly?* 'That was last year. I've studied a cookery book. I don't foresee any complications.' He tried to look confident. He could perform a Caesarean section in less than four minutes if the need arose. Why did he struggle to cook a turkey?

'If you had a wife, she could cook the turkey.'

'That isn't a reason to get married. These days, women don't always like doing that sort of thing.' Patrick extracted himself from under the tree, his wide shoulders dragging through the branches and sending a shower of needles over the pale wooden floor. 'Why are you talking about wives? We're going to have a great Christmas. You, Posy and me.'

'And the kittens.'

'And the kittens.' Remembering the kittens, Patrick frowned. 'That woman who phoned earlier is coming to look at them any moment now. With any luck she'll fall in love with them and that will solve one of our problems.'

'The kittens aren't a problem!'

'Having four of them is a problem.' Seeing the forlorn look on Alfie's face, Patrick felt a flash of guilt and squatted down in front of his son. 'Alfie, we cannot keep four kittens.'

Alfie fiddled with a bauble on the tree. 'What if the woman gets here and she doesn't want the kittens?'

'Why wouldn't she want the kittens? That's why she's coming.' Patrick scooped up a pile of discarded books and stood up. 'Take this lot up to your bedroom, will you? We need to make room for all the new mess you're going to make on Christmas Day.'

Alfie looked up at him, a flash of desperation in his eyes. 'Do you promise that whatever happens you won't be angry?'

Patrick frowned. 'Alfie, what is going on?' He forced himself to ask the question that always niggled at the back of his mind. 'Are you missing Mum? Is that what this is about?'

Alfie rubbed his foot along the groove in the floor. 'Do *you* miss her?'

How did you tell a child that divorce had come as a blessing?

'Your mum and I made a mistake when we got married,' Patrick said gruffly. 'It happens. It has nothing to do with you. We both love you.'

'But you didn't really love each other.'

Abandoning the books, Patrick squatted back down in front of his son. 'No,' he said quietly. 'We didn't. Not enough to make marriage work. We'd only known each other a month when we decided to get married.' He didn't add that Carly had become pregnant on purpose. 'We didn't know each other well enough and it's important to take the time to get to know someone. I didn't make your mum happy.'

'Is that why she was always yelling at you?'

'She didn't always yell,' Patrick said tactfully, but Alfie interrupted him.

'She yelled all the time. And that day she left—two Christmases ago—she shouted at you because you went to deliver those triplets when she had lunch on the table.'

Patrick knew from experience that there was no point in lying. 'That's right, she did. She was upset.'

'She said she was thinking of getting pregnant again because that way she might at least get to see you in the damn antenatal clinic.'

Patrick pressed his fingers into the bridge of his nose, knowing that this wasn't the time to lecture on language. He was just relieved that neither of his children appeared to have inherited his ex-wife's filthy temper. 'She was very angry with me,' he said evenly. 'She'd made plans for a special Christmas, but I was on call at the hospital and I—well, in my job, I can't always plan.' Not for a moment would he tell the child that his mother had liked the idea of being married to a wealthy obstetrician, but not the reality. 'Why are we talking about this now?'

'I don't know.' Alfie shrugged. 'Because it's Christmas and Mum left at Christmas.'

'Christmas can be a difficult time for lots of families,' Patrick said roughly, watching his son's face. 'Is it full of bad memories for you?'

'No. I like being with you,' Alfie said honestly. 'I like the fact that there's no shouting because you never shout. Does it make me bad that I don't miss her?'

Was that what had been worrying the child? *Guilt that he didn't miss his mother?* 'It doesn't make you bad.' Anger towards his ex-wife shot through him like white heat and Patrick hugged the boy tightly, feeling his heart split in two.

Alfie gave a croak of protest. 'Daddy, you're squeezing me!'

'Sorry.' His tone gruff, he released his hold. 'I love you. You know that, don't you?' The words came easily, driven by a burning determination to be a better father to his son than his own father had been to him. *To feel, and to express those feelings without embarrassment.*

'And I love you.' Alfie was openly affectionate. 'And you're the best doctor in the world, everyone says so. If you have to go to the hospital this Christmas, I'll come with you. We're a team. Team Buchannan. Do you think they'll have chocolates?'

Touched by the hero-worship, Patrick smiled. 'Stacks of

them. Maggie is saving you the best. And, Alfie, I'm not the best doctor in the world.'

'You are. You're *so* cool. You saved Matt's little sister's life when she was born—she would have died if it hadn't been for you. And Jenna's mum says she'd marry you if you asked her.'

Startled, Patrick lifted his eyebrows. 'You heard her say that?'

'Yes. I heard her talking to another mum on the phone. She said you were really hot. But I don't see how she could have known what temperature you were because you weren't there and, anyway, it had just snowed. You made me wear a vest. How could you have been hot?'

Patrick let out a long breath and made a mental note to keep his distance from Jenna's mum. 'Well—I—'

'Do you want to get married again, Dad?'

Patrick felt the conversation spiralling out of control. 'Marriage is a big thing,' he said carefully, 'and when you've been wrong once, it makes you wary about doing it again. But maybe one day. If I know someone really, really well.' He wouldn't be making the same mistake he'd made with Carly. *No more whirlwind relationships.* Trying not to think about the girl he'd met in Chicago, he concentrated on his son. 'Do *you* want me to get married again?'

'It would be nice to have someone on our team who can cook.'

'I can cook.' Patrick picked up the books again. 'Just wait until tomorrow.'

Alfie looked unconvinced. 'Will you poison us? Uncle Daniel said the emergency department is always full on Christmas Day of people being poisoned with salmon—something, but I don't get how a turkey can turn into a fish.'

'Salmonella. It's a bacterium. And I'm not going to poison

you.' Patrick dropped a kiss on his son's head. 'Time to wake Posy from her nap.' He lifted his head as the doorbell sounded. 'Ah—that will be the lady who wants the kittens.'

Alfie gulped and the guilt was suddenly back in his eyes. 'I'll get the door. You get Posy.'

Hayley stood on the doorstep, trying to look the way a competent housekeeper was supposed to look.

Fingering the advert in her pocket, she suddenly felt nervous. *Must like children and be able to cook turkey.* What exactly was this family expecting? A cross between Mary Poppins and a celebrity chef?

Thumps and childish shrieks came from behind the door and suddenly it was tugged open and a young boy stood there. There was a large blob of chocolate on his sweatshirt.

'Hi.' He gave her a tentative smile and then glanced nervously over his shoulder. 'You've come about the advert?'

'Yes.' Hayley took an instant liking to him. 'You must be Alfie. You look exactly the way you sounded on the phone.' Sweet, bright, bouncy, straightforward—nervous?

'I wasn't sure you'd come.'

Hayley wondered why he was nervous. Was he scared his new housekeeper was a dragon? 'I've been dying to meet you.' She gave him a friendly smile. 'I spoke to your dad briefly— is he in?'

The anxiety in the child's eyes bordered on panic. 'Yes. But there's something I need to—'

'Alfie?' A deep male voice came from behind him and a man strolled towards the door, a little girl in his arms. 'Is it the lady who rang about the advert?'

'Sort of.' Throwing Hayley a desperate look, Alfie shrank

to one side and Hayley frowned slightly, disturbed that he seemed to be afraid of his father.

Hoping that she wasn't about to spend Christmas with a family even more dysfunctional than her own, she turned to introduce herself and gave a gasp of shock.

It was *him!*

Here. And every bit as good looking as she remembered in a rough, male I-can-kill-a-lion-with-my-bare-hands sort of way.

The smile started inside her and spread to her lips. What a fantastic coincidence! She wouldn't even have to take the trouble to track him down. He lived right here, in this beautiful barn with two beautiful children, and—

Her thoughts came crashing to a halt.

He lived with two beautiful children?

His two beautiful children?

Oh, God, he had children.

He wasn't an indecently handsome sex god, he was a faithless rat.

The shock was like a fist punching her hard in the stomach. Hayley gave a whimper of disbelief. Please let it be a mistake. *Please.* Don't let them be his children. Let him be looking after them for someone else.

No, no no…

But even as she stared in horror at her fantasy man, the little girl burrowed sleepily into his shoulder.

'Want to go back inside, Daddy,' she mumbled, and Hayley felt her happiness evaporate in an instant.

All that was left of her bright, shiny new life was the bitter, grey sludge of melted dreams.

So much for her fantasy man.

So much for imagining that he'd been thinking about her.

No wonder he hadn't contacted her.

He had another life. A family.

What now? How on earth was she going to get out of this mess she'd made for herself?

Hi, there, I came to find you but you're not the man I thought you were, so I'm going home now. And, by the way, I hope you trip and bash your head on something really hard.

A cold sweat of panic drenched her skin. What if his wife was in the house? Dear God, how was she going to face the woman? There was no way she'd ever threaten anyone's family.

Horrified, Hayley started to back away but her feet shot in different directions and she ended up flat on her back in the snow.

'Ow.' Pain mingled with humiliation as she stared up at the grey winter sky. And then she was being hauled to her feet— easily, as if she weighed nothing, the strength in his muscular grip making her feel light and feminine.

'Hayley?' His tone was guarded and his sexy blue eyes held a glimmer of disbelief. 'What are you doing?'

'Well, obviously it isn't that easy to walk in the snow,' she said defensively, and he frowned slightly.

'I meant—what are you doing *here?*' he said gently, and Hayley realised that he hadn't yet worked out that she was the one who had answered his advert for a housekeeper.

What a nightmare.

How was he going to react when he discovered that his dirty little secret was supposed to be spending Christmas with them?

Looking at the two vulnerable children clinging to him, she felt a flicker of anger. It would serve him right to have a moment of panic. It might make him think twice before he did the same thing again.

He reached out a hand and touched her hair and all her violent thoughts faded away. Hayley gazed up at him for a moment, completely disorientated by his touch, oblivious to the snow that had managed to find its way inside her clothes. 'What are you doing?'

'Removing a pine cone from your hair.' He held up the small brown cone that was dusted with snow. 'I thought it might be uncomfortable.'

Nowhere near as uncomfortable as realising that your dream of the future had just crashed and burned.

'Dad? What's going on?' Alfie's puzzled enquiry drew nothing more than a lift of an eyebrow from his father.

He showed no sign of guilt. His handsome face wasn't shifting into a sheepish look. He wasn't sending her silent messages. He was as relaxed as if he'd just opened the door to a carol singer.

Maybe he had affairs all the time. Maybe that was why he'd been so good at it—lots of practice.

The thought made her want to stuff a handful of freezing snow down the front of his trousers. She was sure that Diana, her stepsister, would have slapped his face at this point and then turned and stalked away. But Hayley had never hit anyone in her life and really effective stalking required good balance so that was out of the question.

But the thing that was really keeping her rooted to the spot were the two children hovering close to Patrick—*was that his name or had he lied about that, too?* It wasn't *their* fault that their father was fuelled by high-octane testosterone levels and a superstud sex drive. They shouldn't have to suffer. She wasn't going to be responsible for breaking two little hearts on Christmas Eve. And if he had any sort of decency he'd help her find a polite excuse and leave, otherwise she had a fairly good idea of what she was going to do with the carving knife and her plan didn't require a turkey.

'I told your dad my name on the phone.' Proud of her improvisation, she locked gazes with Patrick, giving him her best I-know-what-you're-up-to-but-I'm-not-going-to-drop-you-in-it-yet look but his features remained impassive.

She envied his composure. His face revealed nothing. Nothing. Not a glimmer. *Definitely not the sort of man who would reveal his bra size to a taxi driver.*

'You're the woman who phoned? It was you?'

'Yes.' And she was wondering why she hadn't recognised his voice. Presumably because she hadn't expected to hear it. It hadn't occurred to her that he had anything to do with the advert she'd answered.

The coincidence was ridiculously unfair.

It couldn't happen to anyone but her.

And now she had to work out a way to unravel the mess, but she couldn't concentrate on anything while he was staring at her. Those deep blue eyes made her mouth dry and her heart bumped against her chest. At one point during their fantasy night she'd even felt pleased that he'd left the light on because it had meant she could stare at him and marvel that such an indecently handsome man was in bed with *her*.

She should have known it was too good to be true.

Realising how naive she'd been, Hayley wanted to hide herself in a hole.

Why hadn't it occurred to her that he might be married?

She was stupid, stupid, stupid.

Of *course* a man as gorgeous as him was going to be married.

She'd chased all the way from Chicago to follow a dream that didn't even exist. It was too embarrassing for words.

For him it had just been a one-night stand. Hot sex. This

was the twenty-first century—the divorce rate was higher than ever and people's priorities had changed. Her friends had short, meaningless relationships, didn't they? Some even boasted about it—as if the ability to have sex without feeling was something to be proud of. A sign of the times. Progression. People did it all the time.

Other people.

Not her. She was out of step. And that was the reason she was here, instead of just filing the night away in her memory.

Alfie was looking at her anxiously. 'You came because of the advert.'

'That's right.' And she'd been excited by the prospect of spending Christmas with a family other than hers.

'You answered the advert?' Patrick gave a faint frown, as if he found that surprising. Then he gave a little shrug. 'In that case, why are we all standing on the doorstep? Let's show you the kittens.'

'Kittens?' It was Hayley's turn to look confused. 'What kittens?'

'Our kittens. The kittens in the advert.' Patrick pushed the sleeves of his jumper up his forearms in a casual gesture that made her stomach curl with desire.

How could a man's arms be sexy? Those dark hairs were like a declaration of his masculinity. And why did he have to have such a good body? She'd spent an entire night exploring every muscular curve of his powerful physique.

Reminding herself that his wife probably did the same thing all the time, Hayley dragged her eyes away from his arms and his body and focused on the tumbled blonde curls of his daughter. His *daughter*. If looking at her didn't kill her libido, nothing would. He wasn't available. He'd never been available. Even for that one special night, he hadn't been hers.

'I don't know anything about kittens.' If he was making up some story to satisfy his son, she wished he'd at least make it plausible.

'You said you answered the advert,' he said patiently, and Hayley wondered why he was trying to make her look stupid.

'I did. The advert asked for a live-in housekeeper over Christmas. Someone to cook a turkey.'

'I didn't advertise for a housekeeper.'

'I spoke to you a few hours ago.' *How could a man look so good dressed in faded jeans and a black jumper?* 'I asked you about the children. You told me that you had two—a boy and a girl.' He'd look good in anything, she decided. And nothing.

His eyes were narrow and assessing. 'We were talking about the kittens,' he breathed. 'We have kittens that need a good home. A boy and a girl—which is what I put in the advert. No mention of a housekeeper. Nothing about turkeys.'

He was going to pretend he didn't know?

Hayley dug in her pocket and pulled out the crumpled advert. 'Here.' She pushed it into his hand, noticing that the little girl had inherited her father's killer blue eyes. '*Someone who knows how to cook a turkey*—that's what it says.'

'Can I see that?' His fingers brushed against hers and that touch was sufficient to ignite the same powerful chemistry that had made her forget morals, common sense and her own rules and spend the night with a stranger.

Determined to look as indifferent as he did, Hayley yanked her hand away and pushed it into the pocket of her coat. If her hands were in her coat then she couldn't give way to the temptation and touch him, could she?

'I don't know anything about this advert.' He scanned it swiftly, a puzzled frown on his face. 'It's our phone number, but—' His voice tailed off and he slowly turned his head and looked at his son, his blue eyes suddenly dark with suspicion. 'Is this the reason you've been so jumpy all day?'

Pinned by his father's sharp, questioning gaze, Alfie shrank against the door. 'I can explain...'

Patrick was ominously still. 'I'm waiting.'

Alfie fiddled with his sweatshirt and gave an audible gulp. 'Uncle Dan was placing that advert for the kittens when you were away having that interview in Chicago and he was looking after us. He kept saying, "Problem solved," and I thought if we got ourselves a housekeeper, that would be another problem solved.'

'Are you saying that Uncle Daniel placed this advert for a housekeeper?'

Alfie stared up at his father in silence, apparently frozen to the spot. 'No.' His denial was a tiny squeak. 'That was me. I did it. It wasn't Uncle Dan.'

Hayley wondered why the child's mother couldn't cook the turkey. Was she hopeless in the kitchen? Or maybe super-stud kept her too busy in the bedroom, she thought miserably. Or perhaps his wife thought cooking was beneath her, like her stepsister did.

Hayley watched as Patrick gradually coaxed the truth from his son. She sensed that he was angry—he *had* to be angry—and she braced herself for him to yell.

Suddenly she couldn't bear it.

The little boy was so sweet, he didn't deserve to be yelled at by a father who couldn't keep his trousers zipped.

But Patrick didn't yell. Instead, he hunkered down in front of his son. 'You advertised for a housekeeper over Christmas?'

'We need someone, Dad,' the boy blurted out. 'You're good with babies, but you're hopeless with turkeys. And the rest of the Christmas stuff. And you're bound to be called to the hospital because you always are and then you'll call Mrs Thornton—and I *hate* Mrs Thornton. Her lips are too red. It's like she's drunk *blood* or something.' The child glanced at Hayley and she gave a sympathetic shrug.

'That can happen with red lipstick,' she muttered. 'You have to be really careful with the shade. I once had one that made me look as though I'd been punched in the face. Hopeless.'

Alfie gave a delighted laugh while Patrick looked at her with incredulous disbelief.

Hayley stiffened defensively. 'What?' She was fed up with him looking at her as though she was from another planet. 'I happen to agree with Alfie. Red is a very dodgy shade. And, anyway, whoever wears red lipstick for babysitting?'

'She wears it because she fancies my dad,' Alfie told her, and Hayley rolled her eyes.

Another one?

The man was even having sex with the babysitter. Had he no shame?

'Can we get back to the subject?' His voice slightly tighter than it had been a few moments earlier, Patrick ran his hand over the back of his neck and turned his attention back to his son.

'Where did you get the money for the advert?'

He would have made a good interrogator, Hayley thought moodily, remembering how much information she'd given him during their day and night together. Every time he'd looked at her with those sexy blue eyes, she'd divulged another personal detail.

Alfie's face was scarlet. It was obvious that he *hated* being in the wrong.

Hayley knew that feeling.

'Uncle Dan left his credit card by the phone,' the child mumbled, and Patrick's mouth tightened.

'And you took it?'

'If he was careless enough to leave it lying around then he can't complain if it was abused,' Hayley said firmly, glaring at Patrick as he sent her a slow, fulminating look. Really, he was hardly in a position to be self-righteous, was he?

He turned back to Alfie, who was gazing at Hayley as though she were a lifebelt and his father was a giant wave. 'I'll pay him back, Dad. I promise. I'll clear snow or something and earn some money.'

'How could you place an advert? Didn't the newspaper know you were a child?'

'They asked me how old I was and I made a joke of it. I said my dad had no idea how to cook a turkey and I needed an expert.'

'So if she rightly insisted on checking with a grown-up, how did this advert…' Patrick waved the cutting slowly '…end up in the paper?'

'Uncle Daniel walked back into the room and I told him he needed to just say that the advert was all fine.' Alfie swallowed. 'And he did that. He wasn't concentrating. Posy was coughing really badly. He thought he was confirming the kitten advert.'

Patrick scanned the crumpled, torn newspaper in his hand. 'Instead of which he confirmed an advert for a housekeeper to come and spend Christmas with us.'

'I thought if it worked out all right, you'd be pleased,' Alfie confessed in a small voice. 'And then when I woke up today, I wasn't so sure. I thought you might be angry. Are you really angry, Dad?' Alfie looked so forlorn that Hayley's spine stiffened at the injustice of it.

Poor Alfie.

She glared at the back of Patrick's head, determined not to notice his cropped dark hair. Who cared if he looked macho? And good shoulders weren't everything, were they? He was a snake. How *dared* he give his son that you've-disappointed-me-with-your-behaviour look, while betraying his marriage vows in every empty bed he could find, *and* with a woman who had no taste in lipstick.

Hayley was about to leap passionately to Alfie's defence when Patrick tugged the boy into his arms.

'How can I be angry when it's my fault for being so lousy at cooking Christmas dinner?' His tone gruff, he released his son and ruffled his hair. 'I like the fact you saw a problem and tried to solve it. And I'm proud that you used your initiative.' He spoke quietly, keeping the conversation between him and his son. 'I also like the fact that you've been honest with me and not tried to duck out of it. But it *was* wrong of you to use Uncle Daniel's credit card, Alfie. That was stealing. We'll need to talk about that later.'

Hayley subsided slightly, although she was still simmering at his devoted dad act. Devoted dads didn't take advantage of their sex appeal, did they? Devoted dads weren't supposed to turn into sex gods in their spare time.

Patrick straightened and looked her directly in the eye and Hayley glared back, hoping he couldn't read her mind and wishing she could look as cool and unflustered as he did.

'There's been a mistake.' As his eyes flickered to her mouth she wondered exactly which mistake he was referring to—the advert, or the night they'd spent together.

'I can see that. You obviously don't want a housekeeper so I'll leave you to cook your own turkey and I hope you find a good home for the kittens.' Trying to maintain her dignity, she picked up her bags and smiled at Alfie. 'You have a lovely Christmas. I hope Santa brings you everything you want.'

Proud of the way she'd handled herself so far, Hayley knew that what she needed to do next was turn and walk away, but walking on snow hadn't been a great success so far, had it? And, anyway, where was she supposed to walk to? They were in the middle of the countryside with snow-capped mountains behind them and the stream in full flood only a few steps away. If she stalked off here, her body would be discovered frozen in the morning encased in a layer of ice and very possibly washed into the next valley. And dignity and hypothermia were definitely incompatible. 'Go back inside. It's freezing. I'll call a taxi.' *Hopefully before his wife emerged to see what was going on.*

At least he didn't know she'd come here specifically to see *him.*

That was one small consolation.

'You can't go!' Alfie sounded horrified. 'And we *do* need a housekeeper. Dad can't cook a turkey, honestly. And if you leave, you won't be able to surprise your friend. Remember? You told me that on the phone. You said you were coming over to surprise a special friend and you needed somewhere to live while you tracked him down.'

Oh, no. No, no, no.

Feeling Patrick's gaze on her face, Hayley wanted to throw herself into the stream. Her impetuous nature had got her into some embarrassing situations in the past, but none quite so embarrassing as this one.

It was almost as bad as that day at school when she'd discovered that her stepbrother had planted a camera in the girls' showers.

All she needed now was for Patrick to produce her knickers from his pocket and her humiliation would be complete.

He leaned against the doorframe, watching her. 'You came here to look for...someone?' His pause was significant and Hayley felt her face fire up to a shade that probably matched the dreadful Mrs Thornton's vampire lipstick.

How dared he look amused? *Obviously* he was a sadist as well as being hugely insensitive. And an adulterer. This situation was about as amusing as discovering you were the only one in fancy dress and everyone else was in black tie. As the list of his crimes grew longer, Hayley grew more affronted.

'I'm not looking for anyone. I mean—I might have been, originally, yes...' She knew she was babbling incoherently, but all hope of a smooth response had deserted her. 'My friend let me down.' She looked at him pointedly and saw his eyes narrow slightly. 'So I won't be looking for him.'

'Is that right?' His soft drawl was as annoying as his blank expression and Hayley wondered whether falling face down in the snow would put out the fire in her cheeks.

Deciding that she needed to make her exit no matter how undignified, Hayley started to back away but Alfie grabbed her arm.

'No, I won't let you go! Dad, tell her she has to stay! I know you didn't put the advert in, but she's here now and think how great it would be to have someone helping over Christmas. Dad? *Say* something.'

CHAPTER TWO

SHE had the sexiest mouth he'd ever kissed.

Not beautiful—her mouth was too wide to qualify for beautiful—but soft, full and with a slight pout that made a man think the most basic, primitive thoughts. And then there was the tiny dimple in the corner that was so deliciously feminine. Suddenly Patrick wished life wasn't so complicated. All he wanted to do was throw her over his shoulder and carry her up to his bed.

The fact that she was flustered, embarrassed and visibly angry with him did nothing to cool his libido. Far from it. It just reminded him how refreshingly open she was with people. He'd seen that from the first moment they'd met—been intrigued by just how much she'd divulged about herself as she'd shown him around the hospital.

He even found her slightly ungainly battle with the ice appealing. The fact that she didn't seem fully in control of her legs simply reminded him that she had incredible legs. Incredibly *long* legs.

A vivid image of exactly how long her legs were brought a groan to his lips but he managed to stifle it. Why did everything about her make him think of sex?

He remembered the moment when she'd landed flat on her back in the snow. For an unsettling moment, the contrast between her dark hair and the white powder had reminded him of how she'd looked against the sheets in his hotel room and he'd been on the verge of lowering himself on top of her and doing what he was burning to do when Alfie had disturbed his red-hot daydream.

And now his son was looking at him, waiting for an answer.

Dragging his mind away from sex, Patrick tried to remember the question.

But what did you say to a woman with whom you'd been intimate but hadn't expected to see again?

Hi, there—what are you doing on my doorstep?

Patrick stood in silence, the reality of his life squashing the fantasy. He felt the children looking at him and he knew that, no matter what he said next, someone was going to be hurt. If he told her that they didn't need a housekeeper then she'd be hurt and so would Alfie. If she stayed—

He dismissed the thought impatiently.

How could she possibly stay?

They always said that the past would catch up with you, but he hadn't expected it to catch up with him this quickly—*hadn't thought his children would find out about what had happened in Chicago.*

On the other hand, there had to be a reason why she was here. And only one reason came to mind.

She was pregnant.

She *had* to be pregnant. It was the only explanation for the fact that she was standing on his doorstep on Christmas Eve. She'd travelled over six thousand miles to talk to him.

Patrick closed his eyes briefly, forcing himself to stay calm and think clearly.

He still didn't understand how her visit to the UK had somehow become entangled with Alfie's innocent advert for a housekeeper. All he knew was that his private moment of self-indulgence was no longer private. And the fact that she was pregnant...

Biting back a word he tried never to say in front of his children, Patrick ran his hand over the back of his neck and concentrated on her face. If he looked at his kids he'd just feel guilty and lose his thread, and that wasn't going to help anyone.

They were going to be hurt. That was inevitable.

It was up to him to try and minimise the damage.

'Dad?' Alfie was throwing strange looks at him. 'Say something. She can cook, Dad,' he urged. 'I know she's a stranger, but why wouldn't you want her to stay?'

Because she wasn't a stranger.

But he wasn't ready to confess as much to Alfie. Not yet. Not until he'd worked out the best way of handling the situation. For now he needed to pretend that this was the first time he'd met her.

Patrick's eyes lingered on her long, dark hair. It was damp from the snow and curled softly over her shoulders, the rich colour emphasising the pallor of her skin.

Her eyes met his briefly and then she turned to Alfie.

'Don't worry.' Despite her obvious agitation, she gave the child a soft, reassuring smile. 'I can see there's been a mix-up.'

The icy wind blew a flurry of snow around her ankles and Patrick noticed that the bottoms of her jeans were as wet as her coat.

'You're wet—shivering.' The doctor in him suddenly felt concern but she shrugged it off.

'I'm fine.' Avoiding his gaze, she dug her hand into her pocket and pulled out a shiny pink phone. 'Go back in the warm. I'm sorry I can't help you out with those kittens. I'll just call a cab and I'll be out of your way.'

She thought he was just going to let her go?

Did she think he was the sort of man who would let a pregnant woman walk away in the depth of winter?

Feeling the familiar weight of responsibility, Patrick decided that the first thing he needed to do was get her inside quickly, before she became any colder.

Hypothermia wasn't a good state for anyone, let alone a pregnant woman.

'Dad?' Alfie nudged him. 'It's really bad manners to keep someone on the doorstep! You taught me that.'

'Yes. Hayley, please come inside.' Without giving her the opportunity to object, he stepped forward and picked up her small suitcase. 'We can talk about it in the warm. It's freezing out here and it's snowing again. And you're wet.'

'I'm only a little damp.' Her teeth were chattering. 'Nothing that won't dry.'

'Nothing is going to dry out here.' He watched with mounting exasperation as fresh snowflakes settled on her hair. 'Come in. Please.' He could see her backing off and his mouth tightened. Doubtless, now that the moment was here, she was dreading having to tell him her news.

'I'll call a taxi.'

'Hayley, it's Christmas Eve. You're in the Lake District, not London. There won't be that many taxis around, and they won't be driving out here.'

'Jack only dropped me twenty minutes ago. I'm sure he'll be happy to turn round and pick me up again.'

'Jack?' Her suitcase still in his hand, Patrick frowned. 'Who is Jack?'

'The taxi driver.'

'You're on first-name terms with the taxi driver?'

'He was a nice guy.'

'Right.' He'd forgotten how friendly she was. And yet hadn't it been her warmth and humanity that had attracted him to her that day at the hospital in Chicago? She'd had a smile and a greeting for every person they'd passed. 'Well, Jack has probably gone home to his family by now. Come inside, at least while we decide what to do.'

He didn't blame her for being wary of him. He'd hardly given her a warm welcome, had he?

'Please.' Alfie slipped his hand into hers. 'Come and see my kittens. And I can show you the presents under the tree.'

Hayley murmured another refusal but Alfie gave her hand a determined tug and she stepped over the threshold of the barn, as cautious as a deer sensing danger. 'Just for a moment. Then I'm calling a cab.'

Patrick put her cases down and closed the door on the cold. 'I'll make a hot drink while we decide what to do. Tea? Coffee? Hot chocolate?' *Was she nauseous? No, she couldn't possibly be nauseous. It was too early.*

'Tea, please.' Her tone was polite and she seemed to be making a point of not looking at him. 'Tea was the thing I missed most. It just doesn't taste the same in America.'

'You've come from America?' Alfie's eyes were round. 'My dad went to America a few weeks ago. He had an interview for a job, but he didn't like it.'

Patrick closed his eyes briefly. This was her chance to drop him in it but she merely smiled at Alfie, her cheeks dimpling prettily.

'Is that right? Well, you live in a beautiful place and I can quite see why he wouldn't want to leave it. After all, he has family here.' Her eyes slid to Patrick's and he saw the accusation in her gaze. 'A lovely family.'

Alfie opened the cake tin and helped himself to a brownie,

oblivious to the sudden tension between the two adults. 'Are you American?'

'No.' Her smile didn't slip. 'I'm English.'

'Then why were you working in America?'

Her hesitation was so brief it was barely noticeable. 'I wanted a change. A fresh start. So a year ago I took a job there.'

'Why did you need a change?'

'Alfie!' Patrick's tone was sharp and he turned away to fill the kettle, still trying to work out how he was going to engineer privacy so that they could have the necessary grown-up conversation. 'It's rude to ask so many questions.'

'It's all right. I'm not big on secrets.' Her swift, pointed glance in his direction was another accusation. 'I wanted to do something completely different, Alfie, to prove to myself that I could. Sometimes when people have knocked your confidence, you start to see yourself the way they see you. Then it's good to get away from everyone and see what you can do when you haven't got people waiting for you to make a mistake.'

'Someone was waiting for you to make a mistake?' Alfie's horrified expression reflected Patrick's own thoughts.

'Who?' He barked the question angrily and then saw Alfie's startled look and frowned. 'What?'

'Dad, you look *really* mad.'

'I'm not mad,' he lied. 'I just…' He gestured with his hand. 'I mean, Alfie and I would both—we'd like to know who undermined your confidence.'

Hayley was looking at him as if he was slightly mad and he didn't blame her. The strength of his reaction had shocked him, too.

'That doesn't really matter,' she said faintly, turning her attention back to Alfie. 'Anyway, as I was saying, I wanted to prove myself so I took a job in this big, fantastic hospital in Chicago.'

Alfie nodded. 'I've seen Chicago on television.'

'Right. Well, I'd never even been to America before. I didn't know anyone and at first it was hard—strange...' She frowned slightly. 'But then I settled down and it felt good. I love midwifery.'

'You're a midwife?' Alfie gave a gasp. 'Dad, did you hear that? Hayley is a midwife!'

Patrick ran his hand over the back of his neck. Alfie was a bright boy and any moment now he was going to put two and two together. And there was absolutely nothing wrong with his son's maths. 'That's...great.'

'My dad's an obstetrician,' Alfie said proudly. 'You guys can talk about babies if you like. I don't mind.'

Patrick winced. He had a feeling that the subject of babies was going to be right at the top of their list of conversation topics.

What were her plans?

Was she upset about being pregnant?

Was that why she kept sending him angry looks?

'Tell her she has to stay, Dad.'

Patrick made two mugs of tea. *If she was pregnant then she'd be staying a long time.* Was that what she wanted? Was that what *he* wanted?

No. Definitely not. A baby was *not* a reason to get married. He'd learned that the hard way. There were other ways of being responsible. 'Hayley and I need to talk in private, Alfie.' He decided that there was no point in postponing the inevitable. 'I'd like you to take Posy and go and watch a cartoon or something.'

'I've seen all the cartoons on television.' Alfie didn't budge.

'It's Christmas Eve. And Hayley doesn't have anywhere else to go because she thought she was going to be living here. We've got plenty of space—I don't understand why you want her to go.'

Because he felt suffocated, trapped—back in the same place he'd been before. Patrick looked at his son—*the son he was going to hurt*—his mind already racing forward, planning how he was going to break the news that there was going to be another child in their family. 'It's complicated, Alfie.'

'You're making me feel bad because this is all my fault!' The child's eyes shone with tears. 'I didn't know it was going to turn out like this. I thought you'd be really grateful that you didn't have to cook the turkey by yourself. I was just trying to help!' Bursting into tears, he stormed out of the room and Posy ran after him, trailing her velvet comforter behind her.

Hayley made a distressed sound. 'Go after him.' Troubled, she turned to Patrick. 'Just go after him. I'll call myself a taxi and sort something out. I shouldn't have come.' Her phone was in her hand again and Patrick walked over to her.

'Wait—put the phone away, Hayley...' The scent of her hair wound itself around his senses and his eyes dropped to her mouth, everything he'd been intending to say evaporating from his mind. A rush of heat poured through his body and he knew he had to get to the point before he did something that complicated matters even further. 'Tell me why you're here.'

'Because everyone does stupid things at least once in their life and this was my moment,' she muttered. 'Don't worry about it. Go to your child, Patrick.'

Don't worry about it?

'Alfie will be all right for a minute,' he said roughly. 'We have things to talk about.' Even while his brain was warning him that this was a *big* mistake, his body was reacting to her presence. He wanted to slide his hands into her damp, silky hair—*he wanted to press his mouth to those rosy lips.*

Reminding himself that those impulses were the reason he was in his current mess, Patrick ruthlessly reined in his baser instincts. 'You came over here to see me, and… I know it's difficult, but just tell me the truth. Tell me whatever it is you came to tell me.'

She must be dreading telling him—afraid of his reaction.

And he braced himself not to overreact, reminding himself that this must have been hard for her. *She must be worried sick.*

But even while he was acknowledging her emotions, he was even more acutely aware of his own. He was angry with himself. And frustrated. And fiercely determined that this time he was going to do the right thing. And that was not going to include marriage.

'I didn't come here to tell you anything. I just thought it was time for a change and I might as well…' Her voice tailed off and she blushed scarlet. 'All right, yes. I came to find you. Could you stop looking at me like that? This is embarrassing enough without you studying me as though you're a prosecution lawyer or something.' Her whole body was shivering and Patrick sighed and grabbed his heavy coat from the back of the door. He peeled off her damp coat in a decisive movement and placed the dry one around her shoulders. It swamped her, of course, because she was so much smaller than he was, and that evidence of her vulnerability pricked his conscience.

'I understand that this is difficult—' he fought back the urge to just demand the truth '—but you obviously have something to say to me and I really think it would be better for both of us if you just came right out and said it.'

He wanted to know what he was dealing with. They needed

to talk dates, make plans—preferably before his children lost interest in television.

'All right. I'll say it.' She looked up at him, her dark hair falling in damp curls over his coat, a spark in her eyes. 'I think you're quite possibly the biggest snake and the most *horribly* insensitive man I've ever met.'

Stunned, Patrick stared at her. 'Sorry?'

'I said you're a snake. And horribly insensitive. And you're a hypocrite, of course.' She seemed to gain confidence as she talked. 'And two-faced because you're pretending to be such a great father but you're obviously sleeping with every woman who takes your fancy even if her lipstick is hideous, which means you also don't have much taste and that makes it even worse—'

'Hayley—'

'And you may be seriously good-looking and have a fit body—a very fit body, actually...' her eyes slid to his shoulders before she looked away quickly '...and be super-intelligent, and obviously quite staggeringly talented in bed, but that doesn't mean you can just abandon morals and common decency and—'

'Hayley—'

'And I don't think a rampant sex drive is an excuse, and the worse thing is you're a liar because you didn't *once* mention your children or the fact that you're married, and—'

'Hayley, I'm divorced.'

'If you really didn't—' She broke off and stared at him. 'What did you say?'

'I'm divorced.' Patrick spoke the words quietly. 'My wife and I separated two years ago. I haven't seen her since then. And you need to breathe before you pass out.'

'You— I...' Her voice cracked. 'You're *divorced*?'

'Yes.'

'Well, why didn't you say so? Why didn't you tell me that night?'

'It didn't seem relevant.'

Hayley rolled her eyes. 'Only a *man* would think that wasn't relevant. Of *course* it's relevant! What about your children? Did you forget about them, or were they irrelevant, too?'

'My children had nothing to do with the night we spent together.'

Her mouth fell open. 'You see? That's what I mean. You come across as this really caring guy—a bit macho perhaps, but basically caring—and then you go and deny your children!'

'I'm not denying my children,' Patrick said patiently. 'I'm saying they had no relevance to the night we spent together.'

'You mean you conveniently forgot them.' Her breathing rapid, she stroked her hair away from her face. 'Well, at least you're divorced. That's one thing to be grateful for.' Realising what she'd said, she blushed scarlet and shrank slightly. 'Sorry, sorry. That came out wrong. What I meant to say was—*ob-viously* it's not good that you're divorced, but I'm relieved to know you're not married.'

Patrick stilled, his radar on full alert and screaming a warning. 'Why would you be relieved?' His tone was several shades cooler as he contemplated the gulf between her expectations and his. 'Because now you know I'm available?'

She looked at him as though he was mentally incapacitated. 'No. Because I don't have affairs with married men, of course.'

'Right. Of course.' She sounded so affronted that he wanted to smile, and it occurred to him that this woman continually surprised him. He was trying to adjust his expectations when he realised that she was glaring at him.

'Are you laughing at me?'

'Absolutely not.'

'Good, because I don't see anything to laugh about.'

'Me neither.' Reminded of the reason she was here, Patrick's desire to smile faded instantly. 'Can I talk now?'

She stood stiffly. 'Of course. Go ahead.'

Patrick rested his hips against the kitchen table, wishing he could switch off the urge to take her straight to bed. 'First— I'm sorry if I was insensitive. It was a shock to see you on the doorstep and I accept that I probably didn't handle that as well as I could have done.'

'If you'd—'

He leaned forwards and pressed his fingers against her lips. 'It's my turn to talk, Hayley,' he drawled softly, watching as her eyes widened. Her lips softened and parted against his fingers and he removed his hand, wishing he'd found some other less erotic way of silencing her. 'Let me finish.'

The tip of her tongue traced her lips where his fingers had been a moment before and it took Patrick a moment to re-member what he'd been planning to say.

'I'm not a hypocrite. I try and be a good father, although I'm sure I fall short of that ambition fairly frequently, and, despite the evidence to the contrary, which I admit in your case is incontrovertible, I am not sleeping with every woman who crosses my path. And while I'm flattered that you think I'm good-looking and you like my body—'

'I didn't exactly mean to say that bit out loud,' she muttered, and Patrick gave a faint smile and continued.

'I can assure you that I have not abandoned morals and common decency.' He watched as her smooth cheeks turned a delicious shade of pink. 'Neither have I ever lied to you.'

'Maybe not directly. But you didn't mention your children.' She looked tired, disillusioned and younger than he remembered, and for some reason she reminded Patrick of the young single mothers he sometimes saw in the antenatal clinic. Occasionally they were excited, but often they were overwhelmed and daunted by the enormity of it all.

He felt a twinge of guilt.

She was probably worrying about being alone and pregnant and she had no idea how to bring up the subject.

Instinctively he took charge of the situation.

'Hayley, I didn't mention the children because we had other things on our minds. Which brings us neatly to the reason for your visit.' Deciding to make it as easy as possible for her, he turned briefly to make sure the kitchen door was shut. 'I'm sure you're feeling really mixed up about the whole thing. I'm sure it's come as a shock. I'm sure you're scared.' *Were there any other emotions he'd missed?* She'd called him insensitive and he was doing his best to be as sensitive as possible. 'But I don't want you to be scared. I take full responsibility. It was my fault. To be honest, I don't understand how it happened because I thought I'd protected you, but we'll work something out, I promise you that. You're not on your own.'

'Protected me?'

In the circumstances he couldn't blame her for sounding stunned. He *hadn't* protected her, had he? Clearly something had failed that night. And she blamed him. She had every right to be angry.

'As I said, I take full responsibility. But we need to talk about this calmly. We need to work out a solution together.'

'What are you taking responsibility for? It was my decision to come here. You had nothing to do with it.'

'But I'm glad you came.'

'Are you?' Her voice faltered and she looked at him carefully. '*Really?* I thought I'd made things awkward for you by coming.'

'Well, obviously it's a shock.' He wasn't going to tell her just how much of a shock. She obviously needed reassurance that he wasn't going to overreact. 'But we'll work something out. Let's start with the practicalities. You're sure you're pregnant? It's pretty early on. There's no mistake about that?'

'*Pregnant?*' The word seemed to echo around the kitchen and Patrick winced, hoping that Alfie wasn't listening outside the door.

'Hayley, could you please try not to—?'

'You think I'm *pregnant!*' She backed away from him, so agitated that her breath came in uneven jerks. 'Is that why you think I'm here? Because I'm pregnant?'

How many times did she have to say the word?

'Yes, of course. Why else…?' His voice tailed off as he registered the shock on her face.

'*Why would you think I was pregnant?*' Her tone made it obvious that he'd made the wrong assumption and Patrick pressed his fingers to the bridge of his nose, wishing he'd broached the subject differently.

'It was a shock to see you on my doorstep. I just assumed—'

'I didn't know it was your doorstep! And what did you assume? That the only reason I'd come to find you is because I was *pregnant?*' She made a distressed sound and started to pace around his kitchen, breathing so rapidly that Patrick eyed her with concern.

'You're hyperventilating, Hayley, and—'

'I am *not* hyperventilating,' she gasped, her hand pressed to her chest. 'I'm trying to control my emotions. It's all down to the breathing.'

'Right.' He watched her carefully, sure that she must be

making herself dizzy. 'But you're breathing a bit fast. I'm a doctor, and I can see that you—'

'Oh, shut up, Patrick!' She groaned his name and turned away, digging her fingers into her hair and shaking her head in disbelief. Then she took a long deep breath and let her hands drop, as if she'd come to a decision. 'All right, I'm going to make a really big effort to think the way you seem to think. So—the sequence of events goes like this. Boy meets girl, boy sleeps with girl who conveniently lives in a foreign country so boy is never going to see her again, girl turns up on doorstep—girl must be pregnant.' She looked at him. 'That's what you're thinking?'

Given that that was *exactly* what he was thinking, Patrick didn't utter a denial and she made a faint sound in her throat.

'So, still thinking like you—although I have to confess that's a challenge—presumably the next demand I'm going to make is for money, is that right? Or marriage. Oh, God, *now* I understand your remark about married men being unable to give me what I want. Is that why you think I'm here? Because I'm looking for a *meal ticket?* God, that's truly awful.' She plopped back down on the nearest chair, as if her legs couldn't be trusted to hold her. 'You'd get on really well with my stepbrothers. They think life is all about money and using people, too.'

Feeling the situation spinning out of control, Patrick intervened. 'Judging from your reaction, I assume I'm wrong.'

Her breathing still far too rapid, she stared sightlessly at a spot on his kitchen floor. 'Yes,' she snapped. 'You're wrong. Of *course* you're wrong. I haven't even missed a period, for goodness' sake.' She broke off, her face scarlet, and Patrick sighed.

'You don't have to be embarrassed,' he said quietly. 'I'm an obstetrician.'

'I know you're an obstetrician!' She squirmed in her seat, the look she flung him suggesting she wished he was in a different profession. 'Is that why your mind went off on that track? Because you're obsessed with babies?'

He took a deep breath, thinking of what had happened with Carly. 'It just seemed…possible. But obviously I was wrong.'

'Yes. You're wrong. And so was I. About a lot of things.'

He wasn't sure he wanted to explore that final cryptic remark, sensing that he might find the translation more than a little uncomfortable to hear.

The fact that she *wasn't* pregnant should have filled him with relief but instead he felt nothing but concern. She looked shocked and *horribly* pale and the bulk of his coat made her seem even more fragile.

Patrick suddenly realised that this was the first time he'd seen her without a smile on her face. In the short time they'd spent together, she'd smiled constantly. In fact, it had been her warm, engaging smile that had attracted him to her in the first place. He'd wanted to press his mouth to that smile and taste the happiness she exuded.

But her smile had gone and he knew that he was the reason the light had gone out inside her. She was right. He *was* insensitive.

'Hayley—I owe you an apology.' He tried to redeem himself. 'Can we start this conversation again?'

'I don't think so. It was bad enough the first time.' She gave a tiny, hysterical laugh. 'Now I know why other people have one-night stands—so that they can maintain the illusion about the person they were with.' Her hand shaking, she dragged her phone out of her pocket. 'I'm leaving now and I don't want you to stop me. The children aren't watching so you don't have to be polite.'

Patrick's analytical mind was computing the data at his disposal. 'But if you're not pregnant—'

'If you say that word again, I might just punch you.' She dialled a number, her fingers shaking. Then she lifted the phone to her ear.

'I just want to know why you came here.' Suddenly it was imperative to find that out. 'I want to understand why you came to see me.'

Her disparaging glance suggested that the answer was obvious. 'Because we had an amazing night, and the way you kiss might just possibly be the best thing that's ever happened to me and you seem to know more about my body than I do and although I actually did leave my knickers in your bedroom that night I— Hello, Jack?' She turned scarlet. 'No, no. It's me, Hayley— No, I didn't leave anything in the cab, that isn't what I meant— Well, I'm wearing them. I was talking to someone else— Well, no, not really.'

Resisting the impulse to smile, Patrick leaned forward and removed the phone from her hand. 'She just rang to wish you Merry Christmas, Jack,' he said smoothly, holding the phone to his ear. 'Thanks for delivering her safely. Great.' He held the phone out of reach as Hayley made a grab for it. 'Yes, and you, too.' He snapped the phone shut, his eyes on her face. 'Where were we? Oh, yes, you'd left your knickers in my bedroom and you were telling me that I'm an amazing kisser and that I seem to know more about your body than you do...'

'Don't get big-headed,' she warned darkly. 'I've realised that the reason you know more about my body than I do is because you've been *trained*—so it isn't a special skill. Actually, it's more like cheating.'

Still keeping the phone out of her reach, Patrick raised an eyebrow. 'It's cheating to know what turns you on?'

'Yes, because you sort of have an unfair advantage.' She eyed the phone in his hand. 'You spend your days with women.'

'Delivering their babies,' Patrick pointed out mildly, sliding the phone into his back pocket. 'And I can assure you that when I'm delivering babies, I'm not thinking about sex.'

'Well, you obviously know everything there is to know about...' Her face hot, she shifted in her chair. 'Oh, never mind. It's my fault for getting involved with an obstetrician. I can't believe we're actually having this conversation. I should never have come in, but I didn't want to upset your sweet, lovely son who, by the way, is far too nice to have a disreputable father like you.'

Smiling, Patrick reached down and hauled her to her feet, tightening his grip on her arms when she tried to wriggle away. After a few seconds he sucked in a breath. 'Actually, Hayley...' His voice was tight. 'You'd better not do that.'

'Do what?'

'Wriggle.'

'Well don't hold me, then.'

'I have to hold you,' he gritted, 'or you'll make it worse.'

'Make what worse?'

'My—er, problem.' His eyes dropped to her mouth and lingered. 'I have a rampant sex drive, remember? And you're... very attractive. And moving against certain parts of me...'

She froze like a child playing musical statues. 'Give me my phone back.'

'You can move your lips,' Patrick said dryly. 'That isn't the part of you that's causing me a problem.'

Her eyes threatened him. 'My phone.'

'No.' He gently removed the coat from her shoulders and dropped it over the chair. Then he stroked her hair away from her face.

She tensed like a cat. '*What* do you think you're doing?'

He gave a slow smile. 'You said that kissing me was the best experience of your life.'

'That was before I knew the truth about you.' But her breathing quickened and he felt the chemistry flash between them.

'I didn't deceive you, Hayley. There was nothing dishonest about that night we spent together. I want to clear up that misunderstanding right now.'

Outside his kitchen the snow fell, dusting the window with soft white flakes.

Inside, the only sound was the slow jerk of her breathing and his own heartbeat as he struggled to control his shockingly powerful reaction.

Still not moving a muscle, her eyes were locked with his. 'You didn't tell me about your children. *How could you not mention your children?*'

'As I said, because that night was about you and me,' he said softly, sliding his fingers slowly through her hair. 'No one else.'

She closed her eyes and swayed slightly. 'Stop it. Stop touching me like that.'

'No.' His eyes slid to a shiny curl that had wrapped itself around his fingers. 'You're beautiful, Hayley.'

'You can't talk your way out of this, Patrick,' she whispered, and he lowered his head slowly.

'All right.' He murmured the words against her mouth, his body on fire. 'No talking. But that rule has to include you, too. And just to help you out...'

She gave a low moan and her lips parted against his. It was like being burned at the stake and Patrick's mind went blank.

And then she gave him a hard shove.

'No!' She backed away, her expression one of self-disgust,

one hand raised, warning him to keep his distance. 'And you're *not* to do that again without warning me!'

Shaken by the erotic ache in his loins, Patrick hooked his thumbs into his front pockets to ease the pressure on his jeans. 'You want me to warn you when I'm intending to kiss you?'

'Yes. I need to prepare myself.'

Sensing that if he smiled he'd be in even greater trouble, he kept his expression deadpan. 'How much warning do you need? I mean, just so that I know. Are we talking seconds? Minutes?'

'Actually, forget it.' Visibly flustered, she pressed her fingers to her forehead. 'Just *don't* kiss me again, all right? Not unless you can learn to do it badly.'

'Could you define "badly"?' Patrick, who was feeling *extremely* bad, suspected he might have already qualified.

'Bad as in yucky.' Her glance was exasperated. 'The sort of kiss that makes you shudder and reach for a hairdryer. You know the sort!'

'I don't think I do.'

'Are you laughing at me again?'

'Absolutely not.'

'You *are* laughing at me!'

'All right, maybe,' he conceded, 'but in a good way.'

'There is no good way to mock someone.'

His amusement faded. 'I'm not mocking you. I'm complimenting you. You...surprise me. I've never met anyone quite like you before.'

'An embarrassing disaster, you mean? You don't need to point out that you're used to women who are far more sophisticated,' she mumbled, 'but you're not perfect either. Well, apart from the whole kissing thing, which you're actually pretty good at. And the...' She waved a hand. 'Well, you know. But there's plenty wrong with you. The worst of it being your very suspicious nature and your tendency towards the negative. I still can't believe you assumed I was pregnant. I mean, that has to be the most unromantic thing I've ever heard. What on *earth* would make you think that?'

'Hayley...' Trying to think cold thoughts to relieve the throbbing ache in his body, Patrick tried to focus on the conversation and not her mouth. 'It's Christmas Eve. I assumed that only the direst emergency would bring you to my doorstep in weather like this when everyone is decorating Christmas trees and preparing cranberry sauce.'

'I didn't know this was your doorstep.'

'But you came to Cumbria to find me.' He watched as the colour deepened in her cheeks. 'Unless I misunderstand what's going on here, you took this job because it would give you somewhere to stay over Christmas. And then you planned to track me down.'

'I've already told you, that was before I knew the real you.' Despite the bravado, he noticed that she was careful to keep a safe distance from him. *As if she didn't trust herself.*

'So you came all this way to find me.'

'Could you stop rubbing it in?'

'And now you're planning to leave.'

'Yes.'

'That isn't logical, Hayley.'

'Yes, well, logic doesn't have to be the basis for every decision.'

'Have you given any thought to where you're going to go?'

'No. Somewhere...' She gave a defensive shrug. 'Somewhere nice. With a big Christmas tree. And very possibly a log fire.'

'We have a big tree here. And a log fire.'

'Somewhere with a big tree and a log fire *where you don't live.*'

'Hayley, it's Christmas Eve,' he said gently. '"Somewhere"' generally needs to be booked a good six months in advance.'

'Then I'll take a train down to London or something.'

The thought of her sitting on a lonely, empty railway platform sent a chill down his spine. 'You answered the advert for a housekeeper—'

'That was before I knew this was your house.'

Feeling like a monster, Patrick sighed. 'I know I've made a bad impression but why don't we just start again, Hayley?'

'*Again?* Which part do you want to live through again?' Her expression was horrified. 'The part where I discover you have two children or the part where you assume that the only reason I've tracked you down is because I'm pregnant? Believe me, the whole thing was bad enough the first time. I'm not up for a repeat.'

Despite her flippant tone it was obvious that he'd offended her deeply and he was surprised to discover he felt ashamed. 'Hayley, in my defence, girls don't travel over six thousand miles to see a man they met just once unless—'

'Unless what? Unless they're pregnant and looking for a meal ticket? Was that what you were going to say? Just for the record, if I *had* been pregnant, I probably wouldn't even have told you.'

Patrick felt the sudden tension in his spine. 'You wouldn't?'

'I don't know.' Her voice rose. 'Maybe. Maybe not. Don't think I'm against marriage, because I'm not. But I think getting married just because you're having a baby is decidedly dodgy. Frankly I wish my mum *hadn't* married my stepdad. I often think we would have been happier just the two of us. The thing is, you never really know, do you?' The information spilled from her like water from a fountain. 'I mean, if pregnancy was the reason for marriage, how would you ever know if that person loved you enough? You'd always wonder.'

As someone who had found himself in exactly that position, Patrick stared at her, unable to think of a suitable response.

'What's wrong now?' Her expression was exasperated. 'Did I say something wrong?'

'No. I'm just…surprised, again.' Patrick looked at her curiously, envying her ability to reveal intimate details of her life so unselfconsciously. 'You don't have any difficulty talking about private things, do you?'

'The reason most people don't talk about private things is because they're afraid of looking foolish or being judged, but I'm used to looking foolish *and* being judged.' She gave a little shrug that told him a great deal about her self-esteem. *Or lack of it.*

'Hayley—'

'You thought I was tracking you down because I needed money, didn't you?' She recoiled slightly. 'Why does everyone think that life has to be about money? Give me my phone.' Catching him off guard, she reached out and snatched the phone from his back pocket, her face scarlet as she stuffed it in her bag. 'I'll call a taxi from the road. A different taxi, *obviously,* given that Jack now knows everything there is to know about my sex life and even I don't feel comfortable getting in a cab with a stranger who knows that I once left my knickers in a man's bedroom. Go back to your children, Patrick, and have a good Christmas.' Sliding her bag onto her shoulder, she walked towards the door, but Patrick was before her, blocking the door, feeling as though he'd failed a test he hadn't even known he'd been taking.

She'd come all this way to see him again.

'Hayley.' His hand closed around her wrist and he felt the instant charge of electricity that had connected them from the first moment—*felt the pulse thrumming under her fingers.* 'Wait. You left your job in the States to track me down?'

People didn't do that, did they? *They didn't throw away a life they had for a life that they might have.*

She stilled, blinked several times and for a moment he thought she wasn't going to answer. 'Yes.' Her voice was thick. Clogged. 'That's what I did. It's called being impulsive. Or stupid. Can I ask you something?'

'Go on.'

'What would you have done if I hadn't left that morning?'

Patrick stared down at her, the tension throbbing between them. Then he gave a slow smile, watching with masculine satisfaction as the colour in her cheeks darkened. 'Yes,' he admitted. 'I would have done that.'

'I meant—would you have wanted to see me again?'

He sensed that it took her a lot of courage to ask the question. 'Yes. But it wasn't an option. I didn't want the job in Chicago and I wouldn't have asked you to come to Cumbria. As far as I could see, our relationship had no future.' He inhaled sharply. 'OK, I'm giving you a ten-second warning.'

'About what?'

'Five seconds.' His head lowered towards hers. 'Stay, Hayley. You answered an advert for a housekeeper. I need a housekeeper.'

And he wasn't going to let her leave.

'You didn't advertise for a housekeeper.'

'I would have done if I'd thought of it.' He pressed her up against the door, his mouth only a breath away from hers, 'I know you're angry with me. I know I've upset you. But that doesn't change what happened. There was nothing false about the night we spent together. Nothing.' He saw her breathing quicken, saw her gaze flicker briefly to his as the charge between them heated to dangerous levels. And then she looked away, as if it was the only way she could keep her sanity.

'As you keep telling me, it was a one-night stand.' Her eyes were fixed on one of Posy's childish drawings, haphazardly stuck to the kitchen wall. 'I should have left it at that.'

'I'm glad you didn't.'

She looked at him cautiously. 'I've never had a one-night stand before.'

'I know. I could tell.' Seeing her eyes widen, he gave a faint smile. 'That was why you ran off in the morning—you were embarrassed. And panicking. And thinking, *What have I done? I wish I'd woken up. I would have stopped you.*'

'Why didn't you mention your children, Patrick?' Even though they were alone in the room, she whispered the words. 'It isn't as if you didn't have the chance. We had dinner together. We *talked*.'

The chemistry between them was so intense he could taste it. 'Because for one night of my life I wasn't someone's father, or someone's doctor, or someone's boss,' Patrick said huskily. 'I was a man, enjoying the company of a beautiful woman. It was about you and me, Hayley. Nothing else. No one else. And now it's my turn. If I ask you something, will you answer me honestly?' He slid his hand behind her head, his eyes locked with hers.

'What?'

He gave a slow smile. 'Can you really cook a turkey?'

She stared up at him and then gave a reluctant laugh. 'That's what you want to ask me? Can I cook a turkey?'

'It's very important to me,' Patrick murmured, his eyes

dropping to her mouth. 'You have no idea how appallingly untalented I am in the kitchen.'

'Don't worry about it. You're good in other rooms of the house.' Although her tone was mocking, the humour was back in her eyes.

'But that isn't going to help cook a turkey—unless we use a hairdryer. Stay, Hayley.'

She laughed but then gave a little shake of her head. 'I can't. We both know that would not be a good idea.' But he sensed her indecision and jumped on it with ruthless determination.

'If you'd ever tasted my Christmas dinner, you'd know it's an excellent idea.'

'I'm talking about the rest of it. I came here looking for the man I spent that night with but...' she took a breath '...you're not that man, Patrick. You have children. Responsibilities.'

Her opinion of him had clearly plummeted and he couldn't blame her for that. So far he'd made a mess of their meeting. 'I won't hurt my children, Hayley, that's true. They've been through enough because of me.'

'And that's a good enough reason for me not to stay, Patrick. It would be unfair on them. You obviously don't want them to know about us and I understand that.'

'This house has five large bedrooms, each with its own bathroom. You'd have space and privacy, somewhere warm and cosy to spend Christmas. A large tree and a log fire. Isn't that what you wanted?' It hadn't escaped him that she'd taken a job with a family. 'Alfie is so excited about you being here. He thinks Christmas lunch might be edible for once.'

'But—'

'Please, Hayley.' His voice was smooth and persuasive. 'I know I've made a mess of this and I know I've upset you. Yes, I was shocked to see you at first but...I really want you to stay. No strings. My son put an advert in the paper and you accepted the job. The job is yours. No more, no less. As for the rest of it, well...' He was standing so close to her that he could smell the floral fragrance of her shampoo mingling with the rose of her perfume. His senses communicated her scent to his libido and he was just deciding whether his previous warning counted when the door moved.

Reacting quickly, Patrick shifted Hayley out of range and stepped back just as Alfie came charging into the kitchen, almost knocking into both of them.

'Dad, Posy's had an accident and the delivery van from the supermarket is at the door.'

CHAPTER THREE

HAYLEY held a packet of frozen peas against the little girl's leg, watching as Patrick soothed the child.

He was calm and concerned, his fingers gentle as he checked the joint. 'She's all right, Alfie—no permanent damage.'

Alfie was hovering anxiously. 'She banged herself *really* hard, Dad.'

'I'm sure she'll have a bruise, but nothing more.'

Hayley wondered whether she should borrow the frozen peas for her own bruises. Not the external ones—those would heal by themselves—but the internal ones. The ones caused by the realisation that their steamy night had been nothing more than sex for him.

It hadn't been a romantic encounter.

It hadn't been special, or earth-shattering.

It had simply been an opportunity for him to do what any red-blooded male would do in the same circumstances.

What had he said?

For one night I was a man, not a father.

But now he was a father again. And you didn't need a degree in psychology to see that his role as a parent was his first priority.

Hayley was trying really hard to hate him but it was impossible. How did you hate a man who clearly cared for his children so much? She found herself wondering exactly what had happened with his wife. If *she* were lucky enough to be

married to a man like Patrick, she would have found a way
to make the marriage work.

'How's that leg, Posy?' He stroked his daughter's hair gently
and she buried her face in his chest.

'Uncle Daniel fix it.'

Patrick gave an amused smile. 'There isn't anything for him
to fix. You'll be fine.' Catching Hayley's questioning look,
he offered an explanation. 'My twin brother is a consultant
in the accident and emergency department.'

'You have a twin? Identical?'

'We look similar but that's where the resemblance ends.'

'That's not true.' Alfie dived in. 'You both have big muscles.
And you were both in the mountain rescue team.'

Patrick shifted Posy slightly. 'That's right. We were.'

'You could still do it.' Alfie picked up Posy's velvet comforter and sneaked it into his sister's hand. 'We wouldn't mind,
would we, Pose? We'd be OK here. I'm almost old enough
to look after you.'

Posy grinned at her brother but showed no sign of relin-
quishing her grip on her dad. There was something about the
sight of the young child clinging to her father that brought a
lump to Hayley's throat.

Oh, great.

She was going to embarrass herself yet again.

And just because the guy was patient and kind to his daughter. Really, she needed to get out more.

So he was good with kids—*so what?*

Plenty of men were good with kids.

It was just that Patrick managed to do it in a way that
didn't diminish his masculinity. His hands were firm. Sure.
He had a quiet confidence that soothed the child as much as
his calm voice.

'I can imagine you in the mountain rescue team,' Hayley muttered, and then wished she hadn't when he lifted an eyebrow in question. 'I mean, you just look the outdoor type,' she said lamely. 'What exactly do you do? You go out into the mountains and find people?' *And slide down ropes, and save lives and generally behave like a hero.*

Nothing particularly attractive about that, she told herself firmly. He was just doing a job.

'People often find themselves in trouble in the fells.'

'Fells?'

'In the Lake District we call the mountains fells.' He checked Posy's knee again. 'People often underestimate the peaks here. They go out wearing the wrong footgear and with the wrong equipment. And that makes plenty of work for the mountain rescue team. I did it for a few years—my brother still does it. He doesn't have kids so he can take off at short notice and come back eight hours later without having to worry.'

'Do you miss it?'

His eyes narrowed, as if he hadn't asked himself that question. 'No.' His gaze slid to Alfie and Hayley sensed that he was protecting his son's feelings.

Being a single dad had obviously demanded some big sacrifices.

He'd given up something he loved so that he could spend more time with his children.

Her cheeks pink, Hayley looked away from him, telling herself that he wasn't *that* attractive. All right, so he could kiss, but just because he had a particular skill in that area, it didn't make him a good person.

There was certainly no reason for her stomach to feel as though it had been left on the fast spin cycle of the washing machine.

'Dad, is there any chocolate in those shopping bags?' Alfie was looking hopefully at the supermarket bags that had been heaped by the door ready to be unpacked. 'Did you order something to go on the Christmas tree?'

'Let's go and take a look.' Patrick tried to ease the little girl off his lap but she clung to him, her thumb in her mouth, her fist locked in his thick jumper. 'Sweetheart, Daddy has to spend some time in the kitchen or Christmas isn't going to happen.' He bent his head and kissed his daughter's blonde head, the contrast between strong and vulnerable so vivid that Hayley sighed. Just the sight of Posy's sweet red stockings against the hard muscle of his thighs was enough to make her tummy tumble.

Oh, help, she didn't want to feel this way.

This man was no saint.

He'd had sex with her. He hadn't told her he had children.

'I'll sort out the shopping.' Desperate to look at something other than his unshaven jaw and the tempting line of his lips, Hayley scrambled to her feet, the peas still in her hand. 'Have you finished with these?'

His gaze searching, Patrick nodded. 'Yes. Her leg is fine. But I don't expect you to unload the shopping, Hayley.'

'It's fine. Really.' Decisions, decisions. She really *hated* making decisions and she was going to have to make one now. Stay or go. Stay or go. Go, *obviously.* After what had happened, it would be just too embarrassing to stay here, wouldn't it?

On the other hand, where was she going to go, this late on Christmas Eve?

It would be more sensible to stay. More practical. The last thing she needed was to find herself with nowhere to go. Yes, she'd stay. But *not* because of Patrick. Her decision had nothing to do with the fact that this man knew how to turn a woman from a solid to a liquid.

She gave a careless shrug, hoping that she looked suitably casual. 'You haven't given me a job description, but I presume that unloading shopping is the responsibility of the house-keeper.'

Alfie gave a squeal of delight. 'You're staying? Yay! We'll have a proper Christmas lunch.' He leapt over to the bags and hugged Hayley, and she hugged him back, a lump in her throat. Over the top of his head, she met Patrick's steady gaze.

'You're staying?'

'Yes.' She gave an awkward shrug. 'And let's just hope it doesn't prove to be the second biggest mistake of my life.'

'The first one being?'

Hayley gave him a meaningful look and guided Alfie towards the bags. 'Come and show me where everything goes, Alfie.' She needed to keep busy to stop her brain from working overtime. So far it hadn't done a good job. Her over-active mind had taken her down routes that had brought her nothing but embarrassment.

Next time she saw a happy ending on the horizon she was going to reprogramme her internal sat nav.

'There's chocolate in those bags.' Alfie bounded over the bags with all the energy of an over-excited puppy. 'When do we put the turkey in the oven?'

'Not until the morning.' Hayley smiled at him. 'Actually, I think you can cook it overnight in the Aga, but we're not going to do that. We'll cook it tomorrow.'

As she unloaded bags and found her way around Patrick's state-of-the-art kitchen, Hayley couldn't help wondering if she'd done the wrong thing by staying.

Patrick knew exactly how she felt about him—how could

he not? She'd crossed an ocean to find him. Cringing with embarrassment, she put a net of sprouts on the table ready to be prepared. Patrick, on the other hand, had given away nothing.

Frowning slightly, Hayley tipped a container of fresh cranberries into a pan and reached for an orange.

What had he told her about himself?

Precisely nothing.

The only information she had about him was the obvious stuff—like his two children.

He had told her he was divorced, but he hadn't told her anything else, had he?

She added the zest and juice of an orange to the simmering cranberries.

He hadn't told her why his relationship had fallen apart. He hadn't told her why his wife wasn't spending Christmas with them.

Leaving the cranberries to simmer, she dug around in the fridge, searching for the ingredients for stuffing, her heart rate doubling as Patrick walked into the kitchen, Posy in his arms. 'Do you have any pork?'

Patrick looked at her blankly and sat Posy on the nearest chair. 'Pork? As in a joint of pork? I thought we were having turkey.'

'I need pork for the stuffing,' Hayley said patiently, and Patrick gave a lopsided smile.

'I'm lucky if I can get the thing in the oven, let alone stuff it.'

'It just helps the flavour. Don't worry,' Hayley muttered, 'I'll see what you have in your fridge.' She returned to the fridge, found some sausages and parsley and helped herself to an egg. 'This will do. I don't suppose you have any chestnuts?'

'I think there's a box in the larder, but they're probably past their sell-by date.' He produced them and Hayley checked the date and emptied them onto her chopping board.

'They're fine. Alfie, can you pass me an apple from the bowl?'

'I don't like apples.' He wrinkled his nose in disgust and she smiled.

'It's going in our stuffing. You won't taste it.' As she chopped, stirred and cooked, Alfie buzzed around her, helping.

'What's that you're doing now?'

'Bread sauce.' She infused the milk with an onion and cloves. 'It's delicious. If I do it now, it will be one less thing to worry about tomorrow.'

Alfie was watching, wide-eyed with admiration. 'Who taught you how to do all this stuff?'

'I taught myself. I had to. No one else in my family can cook.' She took the milk off the heat. 'Well, they probably could cook if they tried. Everyone can cook if they try.'

'My dad can't.' Alfie stood on a chair, slowly stirring cranberry sauce, his lower lip locked between his teeth. 'And he *has* tried. His cooking is a disaster.'

'Thanks, Alfie,' Patrick said dryly, and Alfie shrugged.

'Even your pasta is gluey.'

'You're not cooking it in enough water,' Hayley said absently. 'You need a large pan so that it doesn't stick together. That looks done, Alfie. Take the saucepan off the heat and put it on the mat to cool. Good boy.'

'This is so brilliant. Like being in a restaurant or something.' Alfie lifted the pan carefully and put it on the table. 'Now what?'

'We let it cool and then we put it in the fridge.'

Alfie watched, wide-eyed, as she deftly made little stuffing balls. 'Wow. You are so clever at that. If you're here with us, who is cooking Christmas dinner for your family?'

Hopefully someone really inept.

Hayley gave a weak smile. 'They'll probably go to a hotel to eat.'

'I bet they miss you.'

Feeling Patrick's gaze on her face, Hayley tried not to reveal her thoughts. *He saw too much.*

'Yes, I'm sure they miss me.' Like lions missing an antelope. No one to pick on.

Patrick leaned forward and pulled the pan further onto the mat, avoiding disaster. 'You have brothers and sisters?'

'Two stepbrothers. One stepsister.' She kept her tone neutral but knew he wasn't fooled.

'You lived with a stepfamily?'

Oh, God, he wasn't going to let it go, was he? 'My dad left when I was little. My mum married her boss. He already had three children. End of story.' Except it wasn't the end of the story and she had a feeling he knew it.

'My mum left, too.' Alfie said the words casually but Hayley sensed the depth of emotion behind his simple confession and felt as though her heart was being tugged out of her chest.

Out of the corner of her eye she saw Patrick still, but Alfie was looking at her and she knew he was waiting for her to respond.

Suddenly she wished she'd done a degree in child psychology—at least then she would have known just the right thing to say. 'That must have been very difficult for you.'

'It was sort of difficult.' Alfie gave an awkward shrug. 'She went on Christmas Eve. Two years ago.'

'Christmas Eve?' Horrified, Hayley's eyes flew to Patrick but he was watching his son.

'We're doing pretty well, aren't we, Alfie?'

'Brilliantly. We're a team. Team Buchannan, that's us. High five, Dad.' Slapping his palm against his father's, Alfie slid off the chair and walked over to the fridge. 'The only thing wrong is that no one in our team is good at cooking. Sometimes Stella helps us, and that's good. She can make gingerbread men. Can you make gingerbread men, Hayley?'

Still choked at the thought that their mother had left on Christmas Eve, Hayley struggled to answer. 'Yes,' she said huskily, feeling a rush of anger towards a woman she didn't even know. 'I can make gingerbread men. Who is Stella?'

Patrick stirred. 'A friend.'

Friend? Hayley felt a stab of jealousy and then realised how ridiculous it was to feel jealous of this man. They didn't have a relationship, did they?

'Stella used to be engaged to Uncle Daniel but he didn't want to get married because he thinks he won't be a good father.' Alfie pushed the fridge door shut, a yoghurt in his hand. 'Which is rubbish, because he's pretty cool at a lot of things, but he doesn't think so, so he told Stella that he wouldn't marry her. That was the same Christmas Mum left, so Stella came here and cooked lunch and it was brilliant. And she and Dad drank a lot.' He dug a spoon out of the drawer and Hayley's eyes flew to Patrick, who rolled his eyes in apology, his neutral expression revealing nothing about what must have been a hideous time.

Oblivious to his father's discomfort, Alfie dug the spoon into the yoghurt. 'And then Stella went away for ages because she was so upset that Daniel wouldn't marry her, but she still sent me nice presents. Then she came back.' He licked the spoon. 'And then she and Uncle Daniel were trying not to kiss each other all the time, and—'

'Alfie.' Patrick's tone was mild. 'Enough. Eat your yoghurt and stop talking.'

'I'm just telling Hayley about our family.'

'You've told her enough.'

'But I haven't finished.' The spoon still poised in the air, Alfie frowned at his father. 'I haven't told her the best bit.'

'Go on, then,' Patrick said wearily, rubbing his fingertips across his forehead. 'Tell her the best bit. Whatever that is. But make it quick.'

'Uncle Daniel is going to propose to Stella. Tomorrow.'

Patrick made a choked sound and suddenly sat upright. 'He is *what?*'

'He is going to propose to her.' Smug now he had his father's attention, Alfie slowly finished his yoghurt. 'He told me. I saw the ring. He's putting it in her Secret Santa—you know, you buy a present for someone at work, and—'

'I know what Secret Santa is.' Patrick interrupted him impatiently. 'What's this about a ring? Since when has my brother decided to propose and how come you know about it?'

'I helped him decide. He wanted to marry her, really, but Stella wants lots of babies and Uncle Daniel is worried he won't be a good dad. So I sort of helped him out with some tips.' He saw his father's astonished look and shrugged. 'It wasn't that hard. Uncle Daniel was OK when he looked after us when you were in America. Posy and I liked being with him. I just told him that. And he listened.'

Hayley couldn't hold back her laughter. 'So your brother is getting married?'

'So it would seem.' Patrick ran a hand over the back of his neck and looked at his son as though he were a stranger. 'Where do you get all this information?'

'Uncle Daniel and I had a long talk this morning. And,

anyway, I see things.' Alfie dropped the empty yoghurt pot in the bin. 'I know about se— I mean, *you know what.* I can't say the "s" word in front of Posy because she's too young.'

'Quite right,' Patrick said faintly, 'and so are you, frankly.'

'Dad, you're behind the times. Two of the boys in my class have girlfriends.'

Patrick closed his eyes. 'Alfie, you are ten years old. You are *not* having a girlfriend.'

'It's all right,' Alfie said kindly, 'you can stop panicking. All the girls in my class are pretty yucky, to be honest. I wouldn't want to kiss any of them. At the moment I prefer football.'

'I suppose I should be thankful for small mercies,' Patrick muttered under his breath, casting Hayley a look of comical disbelief. 'How did we get onto this subject? I thought we were talking about *your* family?'

'My family is boring by comparison.' She laughed and Alfie looked at her closely.

'But they're the reason you moved to America? Because they made you feel like you couldn't do anything? If you ask me, they're dumb. And anyone who can cook like you shouldn't have to prove anything to anyone.' Having made that announcement, he strolled out of the room, leaving Hayley staring after him.

Patrick cleared his throat. 'I apologise for Alfie. He's always been pretty direct. Probably my fault.'

'I think he's very special.' Hayley rescued the bread sauce, desperately wishing that Alfie hadn't left the room. Without him she was too aware of Patrick.

Oh, God, she shouldn't be here.

She'd taken a risk—*exposed her feelings*—and now she felt like an utter fool because she had nowhere to hide.

He *knew* how she felt about him.

And she knew how he felt about her.

She stirred the bread sauce vigorously to avoid having to look at him.

He'd taken advantage of being away from his children to have some easy sex. And she'd been easy sex. And she was angry and humiliated that she'd allowed her dreamy personality to turn a steamy encounter into something more.

Even though she was trying to be pragmatic about the whole thing, his assumption that her reason for tracking him down must be because she was pregnant had crushed her. His reaction was so far removed from the one she'd expected. She'd honestly thought he'd felt the same way about her as she did about him. Of *course* she had or she would never have travelled all this way and risked making a fool of herself. It hadn't occurred to her that she *was* making a fool of herself.

Alfie bounced back into the room. 'Come and see your room, Hayley. You'll love it. It has a sloping ceiling and a *really* cool bathroom with a drench thing.'

Hayley looked down at him for a long moment and then turned her head to look at Patrick.

He held her gaze and something flickered between them.

Hayley dismissed it as her imagination. She wasn't making that mistake again. *Wasn't assuming there was a connection where there was none.*

'I'd like you to show me my room,' she said to Alfie, and he grinned happily.

'Your room is right next to mine. If you're lonely, you can sleep in my spare bunk.'

Hayley couldn't help smiling. 'That's really generous of you, Alfie. I might just do that.' He was the sweetest, most engaging child she'd ever met. 'Come on, then. Show me the room.'

Relieved to escape from Patrick's brooding gaze for a short

time, Hayley followed Alfie up the beautiful wooden staircase and up to the top floor of the barn. He pushed open a door and Hayley gave a gasp of surprise because nothing had prepared her for the breathtakingly beautiful view from the room.

Floor-to-ceiling windows faced open fields, framing the snow-covered trees and the mountains behind. 'Oh, my goodness,' she said weakly. 'It's stunning.' *Was he a millionaire or something?* The house was *incredible*.

'You should see my dad's bedroom. It's *huge*. So is his bed. Mind you, he needs an enormous bed because Posy often crawls in with him in the middle of the night.' Alfie darted across the bedroom and pushed open another door. 'This is your bathroom. The window goes all the way along so you can still see the view from the bath. You've gone really red—I suppose you're worrying about someone seeing you naked, but they won't. We don't have any neighbours, which is quite useful when Posy is having one of her tantrums.'

Hayley, whose colour had more to do with inappropriate thoughts involving Patrick's bed than modesty, managed a smile. 'Thanks. I'll remember that.'

'I'm just saying that you don't need to worry too much about wandering around with no clothes on.'

'There is absolutely no way I'll be wandering around with no clothes on,' Hayley assured him hastily, shrinking at the thought of bumping into Patrick in anything less than full clothing.

She'd already left one pair of knickers on his bedroom floor. That was more than enough.

From now on she would be making no moves at all, except ones that took her in the opposite direction.

'I thought Dad would be really mad with me for advertising for a housekeeper,' Alfie confided, 'but I think he's pleased now that you're going to be cooking the turkey. He's *hopeless* at it.'

'Well, if we want a delicious lunch without a nervous break-down, we'd better go and finish our preparations.' Hayley held out her hand. 'Are you ready, Chef?'

Alfie grinned. 'Ready.'

Another layer of snow fell overnight and Hayley woke to a world so impossibly beautiful that for a moment she didn't move. Warm and snug under the soft duvet, she lay there, lis-tening to church bells chiming in the distance.

Christmas morning.

And for once she didn't have to brace herself to face her family. *To try and be someone she wasn't.*

There was a tap on the door and Patrick walked in, a mug in his hand. He was wearing a pair of black jeans and his jaw was dark with stubble. 'You wanted to be woken at eight...'

Oh, my, he looked good in the morning—heavy lidded and un-shaven...

'Yes. I want to get the turkey in the oven so that we can eat at a decent time.' Hayley decided it was safer to look at the mug he was holding, rather than him. 'Thanks for the tea.'

'I thought it might help you wake up. I'm guessing you're jet-lagged. What time did you get to sleep?'

'Oh—not sure,' Hayley mumbled, pulling the duvet up to her chin. 'Late. Still feels like the middle of the night.' She wasn't going to confess that her appallingly disturbed night had had everything to do with him and nothing to do with the time difference. 'Thanks for the tea.'

'The children are going to wait until you're down before they open their presents.'

'They don't have to do that.' Hayley was dying to drink the

tea but she didn't want to expose any part of her body while
he was in the room. It was bad enough being in bed while
he was standing there. It felt intimate. And she was doing her
best to avoid all suggestion of intimacy. 'But I'm not family
or anything. I was going to spend the morning in the kitchen.
Let you get on with it.'

'You're living with us, Hayley,' he said mildly. 'You're one
of the family.'

In her dreams.

She was so aware of him that she was relieved to have the
kitchen as an excuse to hide.

In the end she did join them for present opening, watching
wistfully as the children tore paper off parcels and squealed
with delight.

'I have a present for Hayley.' Alfie vanished and then reappeared, carrying two kittens.

'Oh!' Hayley gasped in delight and Patrick groaned.

'Alfie, you can't—'

'My cat had four kittens…' Alfie placed the kittens in Hayley's lap '…and Dad says I can only keep two. So I'm giving
you the other two. I want them to go to someone nice.'

The kittens snuggled into each other and Hayley stared
down at them with a lump in her throat. 'They're gorgeous.'

'Alfie…' Patrick ran his hand over his jaw '…you can't just
give someone an animal. Hayley doesn't have anywhere to
keep them.'

'Well, they're hers just for Christmas, then,' Alfie said stub-
bornly. 'While she's staying here. I'll let her feed them and
things.'

'I think she's going to be busy enough feeding us,' Patrick muttered, but Hayley shook her head, enchanted by the
kittens.

'They're beautiful, Alfie. And wherever I go after Christmas, I'll make sure it's somewhere I can have kittens. Thank you.'

Later, while Alfie and Posy were playing with their presents and her kittens were curled up on the sofa asleep, Hayley slipped away to the kitchen.

This was the perfect Christmas, wasn't it?

Snow falling outside the window and children laughing in the next room.

She worked steadily and without fuss and when she eventually placed the bronzed turkey in the centre of the table, Alfie gasped and clapped his hands.

'For once it looks the way it always looks in the pictures. Thanks, Hayley. I'm starving.'

Lunch was a noisy, happy affair. Crackers were pulled, jokes were read and paper hats were worn, although Hayley had to make use of a roll of tape in order to stop Posy's from falling down around her neck.

She was just setting light to the Christmas pudding when Patrick's mobile rang.

He fished it out of his pocket, frowning as he saw the number. 'Excuse me—I need to answer this. Tom?' Moving away from the table, he strolled to the other end of the living room and Hayley's gaze lingered on his broad shoulders.

'Hayley, the pudding is going to fall off the plate,' Alfie said helpfully, and she gave a start and concentrated on what she was doing.

'Pudding?' But she could still hear Patrick talking.

'Well, it's her first labour... No, I wouldn't think so... Calm down, will you?'

'Someone is in trouble,' Alfie predicted, pouring brandy

sauce onto his pudding. 'Is this alcoholic? Am I going to get drunk?'

'You're not going to get drunk.'

'Good, because the next thing that's going to happen is that Dad is going to come off the phone and say he has to go to the hospital.'

Patrick slipped the phone back into his pocket and strode back to them. 'I'm really sorry but I'm going to have to go to the hospital.'

'Told you.' Alfie leaned across the table and pushed the candle away from his sister's fingers. 'Don't touch that, Pose, or you'll be going to the hospital, too. In an ambulance. What is it this time, Dad? Twins?'

'No.' Patrick looked distracted. 'Tom Hunter's wife has gone into labour. And he's worried about her.'

'Tom works with Dad,' Alfie told Hayley, and Patrick gave a frown of apology.

'Sorry, Hayley.'

'It's fine. Do you want pudding or are you going straight in? I can stay with the children.'

'It's more complicated than that.' Patrick ran a hand over the back of his neck, and then looked at her thoughtfully. 'You're a midwife.'

Hayley slowly put the pudding down on the table, wondering where this was leading. 'You know I'm a midwife.'

'We're chronically short of midwives at the moment—particularly over the Christmas period. People are being struck down by flu and apparently there isn't an agency midwife to be had north of Birmingham. Tom's worried that Sally won't have continuity of care.'

'I registered with the agency when I arrived in the UK, but I haven't—'

'You're already registered?' Patrick's face cleared. 'Fantastic. In that case, is there any way I can persuade you to come to the hospital with me?'

'No way!' Alfie shot to his feet, his eyes fierce. 'You are *not* leaving us with Mrs Thornton on Christmas Day! I want to stay with Hayley.'

'You can both come to the hospital,' Patrick said immediately, scooping Posy out of her chair. 'Alfie, go and pack a backpack with all her toys and a change of clothes. You can play in my office. Bring some DVDs.'

'Yippee!' Alfie bounced towards the Christmas tree where the presents were still scattered. 'There's always loads of chocolate at the hospital. Will Aunty Mags be there?'

'Yes.'

'W–wait a minute,' Hayley stammered. 'I can't just turn up and work. I'm not sure they'd want me to just—'

'I'll call Human Resources on the way in and they can do whatever it is they need to do.'

'Human Resources?' Hayley gaped at him. 'But it's Christmas Day! They're not working.'

'My dad is really important,' Alfie said proudly as he reappeared, carrying a bulging rucksack. 'If he says someone has to do something, they have to do it.'

Patrick lifted an eyebrow. 'I hadn't noticed that rule applying to you.'

Alfie grinned. 'That's different. I'm your son. I get special treatment.' He grabbed Posy and manoeuvred her into her coat. 'Come on, Pose. We're going to have fun.'

CHAPTER FOUR

'SHE's dilated less than two centimetres in the last four hours but she doesn't want me to intervene,' Tom said in a raw tone, his face pale and tired. 'And I feel helpless. I'm an obstetrician! I've delivered hundreds of women, but I can't think straight.'

'That's because she's your wife.' Patrick switched on the television in his office, pulled up two chairs and settled the children. 'It's different when you're emotionally involved.'

'Well, you know what Sally's like—stubborn. I think the time has come to intervene but she refuses to even consider anything that constitutes aggressive management.'

'I'll take a look at her.' Patrick removed his jacket and slung it over the chair. 'This is Hayley. She's going to be Sally's personal midwife.'

Suddenly the focus of attention, Hayley turned pink. She wanted to open her mouth and protest that he'd never even seen her work, but Patrick was already ushering her along the corridor.

Without pausing, he pushed open the first door he came to and walked into the delivery suite.

Hayley looked around her in surprise. The room was light, bright and homely, with views across the mountains from the large picture window.

A petite woman sat on the bed in the middle of the room, concentrating on her breathing.

'Sal?' His voice gentle, Patrick strode across to the bed,

leaned forward and kissed her on both cheeks. 'You really pick your moments. I haven't eaten my Christmas pudding.'

'You're a lousy obstetrician, Ric,' the woman moaned. 'You told me there was no way this baby would come until Boxing Day.'

'I hate to disillusion you, babe, but it could well be Boxing Day.' Patrick looked at the clock and then at the chart by the bed. 'Not exactly motoring, are you?'

'It's definitely time to intervene,' Tom said gruffly. 'Sally, I really think you should—'

'If you don't shut up, Tom Hunter, I'm never speaking to you again. And I'm certainly not sleeping with you again. Not if this is the outcome.' Sally screwed up her face as another pain hit her and Hayley saw Tom tense helplessly.

'Sally—'

Like a wounded tigress, Sally growled at him. 'Patrick, talk some sense into him. And here's a hint—while you're having that conversation I don't want to hear the words *amniotomy, oxytocin infusion, ventouse* or *forceps*. And I *definitely* don't want to hear *Caesarean section*. Or I am never again cooking you my special crispy duck or my lemon tart. Got that?'

Patrick grinned. 'I think we'll have this conversation outside. That way, at least I'll protect my future dining prospects.' He took Tom's arm and guided him out of the room, leaving Hayley alone with the woman.

Her eyes bright with pain, Sally glanced at her. 'Sorry— I love Tom. Honestly I do, but he's in a state and he's making me worse. We haven't been introduced—' She caught her breath as another pain hit and Hayley hurried across to her, sensing that the other woman was feeling isolated and alone.

'You're not breathing properly,' Hayley murmured, sliding her arm round Sally's narrow shoulders. 'You're talking too much—thinking about everyone else and not yourself.'

'That's because my husband is having a meltdown,' Sally gritted, and Hayley rubbed her back gently.

'Patrick will sort him out. You think about yourself. You're obviously struggling with the pain. Do you want some gas and air?'

'Nothing at the moment.' Sally shifted on the bed. 'God, it hurts. Isn't it typical? I can't believe I'm still only four centimetres. I should have delivered by now. That's what happens when your husband is an obstetrician. You're doomed. Fate intervenes to give you the worst delivery possible.'

'Don't think like that. We just need to have a plan and try and help you relax.' Relieved that she'd had the foresight to grab her bag before she'd left Patrick's barn, Hayley reached inside and pulled out a small bottle. 'See if you like the smell of this.'

She unscrewed the cap and held it under Sally's nose.

'Nice.'

'It is, isn't it? It's an aromatherapy oil I used a lot in America. Perfectly safe in pregnancy and labour. Would you like me to massage your shoulders? I find that sometimes it helps and you really need to relax.'

'At this point I'm willing to try anything,' Sally gasped. 'It really does smell good. Takes your mind off hospitals.'

'Close your eyes and just think about your breathing,' Hayley soothed, lifting Sally's T-shirt just enough to allow her to massage the woman's back.

Sally closed her eyes and breathed out. 'All right—that's better. Actually, it feels unbelievably good. But I think my husband needs it more than me.'

'We're not thinking about your husband right now,' Hayley reminded her, 'we're thinking about you.'

'Oh, yes, I remember.' Sally was silent for a few minutes, only the slight change in her breathing indicating a change in her pain levels. 'You are very clever. Where did Patrick find you? I'm starting to feel a bit better. Just don't let my panicking husband back in here. I've never seen him like this. He's Mr Cool. Every bit as calm as Patrick. And suddenly he's lost it and turned into the worst kind of panicking man.'

'It's because he loves you.' Hayley's hands moved gently, smoothing and soothing. 'Have you thought about using the pool, Sally? I assume they have one here.'

Sally sighed. 'Tom isn't keen. *Don't* ask me why.'

'It's just that I think you might find it relaxing. In my experience women tend to need less pain relief and they just find the whole experience more satisfying. I think it might be perfect for you.'

'Well, I certainly like all your other ideas. I think I might just want to be massaged by you all the way through my labour,' Sally murmured. 'You are so good at that. Another contraction coming...'

'So focus on your breathing.' Hayley coached her quietly and then glanced up to see Patrick and Tom standing by the door. She wondered how long they'd been there. Watching.

'Tom, Hayley thinks I should use the birthing pool and I agree with her.' Sally spoke firmly, as if she was expecting argument. 'I want to give it a try.'

Tom glared at Hayley and then let out a breath and looked at Patrick. 'I don't think it's a good idea. What do you think?'

'I think it's up to Sally. There's no medical reason why she shouldn't.' Calm and relaxed, Patrick walked over to the bed.

'What I'd like to do is examine you properly, check on the baby and then we can make a decision together.'

'I don't need an obstetrician—I need a midwife.'

Tom sighed. 'Please, Sal...'

'Oh, for goodness' sake.' Sally flopped back against the pillows. 'Tom, go and get a cup of coffee.'

'But—'

'If you really want Patrick to examine me, fine, but I don't want you here while he does it. Hayley can chaperone, although I'm sure Patrick isn't exactly having indecent thoughts about me at this point. I'm about as sexy as a whale.'

Patrick laughed and moved over to the sink to wash his hands. 'I'm saying nothing. This is one of those conversations where a man can only ever be wrong. Tom, do me a favour and check on my kids, will you? They're in my office. Maggie was going to get them some chocolate and drinks but I don't want them being sick on the carpet.'

With obvious reluctance Tom left the room and Sally sighed.

'He's worried.'

'Understandably.' Patrick listened to the foetal heart rate. 'But his anxiety is stressing you and you already have enough stress. When I've checked on you, I'm going to go and calm him down.'

'How are you going to do that? Knock him unconscious? What do you think about Hayley's water-birth idea?'

Patrick looked at Hayley, his gaze quizzical. 'Persuade me.'

Was he testing her? 'Stress can lead to reduced uterine activity and dystocia.' Confident in her own skills, Hayley explained her reasoning. 'Which is why I think you should consider water. It can help relaxation and pain relief. I think it's worth a try. If she makes no progress, you can always think again.'

Patrick finished his examination and straightened. 'You're four centimetres, Sally.'

'Is that all?' Sally gave a groan and closed her eyes. 'Tom is going to have a breakdown. And I might have one with him.'

'Why are you lying on the bed?' Hayley sat down next to her, her voice soft. 'I wonder whether you should mobilise for an hour or so. Walk around the department with me—see if we can get you moving a bit faster. Then go for the pool.'

Sally gave her an ironic look. 'You want me to run a marathon?'

Hayley grinned. 'No. I had in mind more of a stroll down the corridor, talking about shoes and similarly frivolous distractions.'

Sally stared at her. 'How do you know I like shoes?'

'Because I've been admiring your shoes since I walked into the room.' Hayley's gaze slid to the pair of silver mules that Sally had tucked under the chair. 'I love them.'

Patrick backed away, shaking his head. 'I'm not qualified to participate in a discussion about shoes. I'll go and handle Tom.' He glanced at Hayley, a smile playing around his mouth. 'I like your plan. You've managed women labouring in water?'

'Yes. All the time.' She had no doubts about her abilities as a midwife but she realised that he knew nothing about that side of her. He hadn't worked with her, had he? Their only professional contact had been when she'd shown him around the department and that hadn't included any clinical work. 'Who do I speak to about the pool?'

'I'll get someone onto it now. You need to change—Maggie has found you a set of scrubs that should fit. You can use my office.' Patrick took a pen out of his pocket and wrote in the notes. 'Get walking, Sally. When it gets too much, try the pool. Hayley can examine you again in four hours.'

Sally grabbed his hand. 'Tom is *seriously* worried.'

'I know that,' Patrick said gently. 'But we're watching you. The baby is happy at the moment. You're the one who isn't happy and we're going to do something about that.'

He was so good with the patients, Hayley thought wistfully as she helped Sally put on her shoes.

'Let's go for that walk. I can change in a minute.' Hayley slid her arm through Sally's and walked with her to the door. 'I don't suppose jeans matter for walking up and down the corridor. I can't imagine anyone in authority is going to be in today.'

'Patrick's the highest authority here anyway.' Sally gritted her teeth and rubbed her abdomen while Hayley looked at her in surprise.

'Really?'

'He runs the unit, didn't you know? He's astonishing—so bright. And really nice with it. He's the only person Tom is likely to listen to.'

Hayley wondered whether Sally knew the details of Patrick's divorce.

She didn't like to ask, but Sally's mind was obviously moving in the same direction because she paused in the corridor and looked at Hayley curiously. 'So how do you know Patrick?'

'Oh.' Hayley made a conscious effort not to spill everything out. 'I applied for a job as his housekeeper over Christmas.'

'He advertised for a housekeeper?'

'Not exactly.' Drawn to Sally's warmth and unable to help herself, Hayley told Sally the story of the advert. She laughed.

'That's brilliant. Good for Alfie. Oops—another contraction coming.' She leaned on Hayley, breathing steadily. After a few moments she straightened. 'Actually, I quite like being upright. Hi, Maggie.' She smiled at a midwife who approached them.

'How are you doing, Sally? And you must be our Christmas miracle.' Smiling warmly, she pushed a set of clean scrubs into Hayley's hands. 'Alfie has told me all about your amazing cooking skills. I'm sorry to interrupt your Christmas Day but I can't tell you how relieved I am to have you helping us out today.'

'I—I'm pleased to help,' Hayley stammered, touched by how generous these strangers were. They didn't even know her, for goodness' sake. 'I *am* a qualified midwife.'

Maggie gave a delighted laugh. 'I'm hoping so—we're trusting you with our consultant's wife so you're going to need more than the ability to baste a turkey.'

The consultant's wife.

Hayley gave Sally a weak smile. 'No pressure, then.'

'You've met my husband,' Sally said dryly. 'There'll be nothing but pressure. If Patrick doesn't keep him busy he'll be hanging over you, watching everything you're doing.'

'That doesn't bother me.' Hayley rubbed Sally's back gently. 'I've been working in America—everyone watches everything there. It's the land of litigation.'

Maggie looked curious. 'Ah, yes—Alfie mentioned that you've been working in America. What a coincidence—our Patrick was in America just a few weeks ago, interviewing for a job.'

'Really?' Hayley squeaked the word, searching for ways of extracting herself from what was fast developing into a conversation she didn't want to have.

'Oh—that hurts.' With a gasp, Sally clutched her. 'Could we go back to the room, Hayley?'

'Of course.' Concerned, Hayley slipped her arm round her

new friend, sending Maggie a look of apology. 'Thanks for the scrubs. I'll change in a minute.'

'No hurry. We owe you.' Maggie watched them walk slowly down the corridor. 'And the birthing pool will be ready whenever you are.'

Hayley pushed open the door to Sally's room and helped her inside.

The other woman immediately straightened and gave her a look. 'All right, I rescued you from the inquisition—my price is that you tell me the truth.'

Hayley stared at her. 'You weren't having a contraction?'

'No, but I will be in another minute so could you get to the juicy part fairly quickly?' Sally lumbered over to the bed. 'And the more detail the better, please. Good sex is a thing of the past for me. Whoever said that women always feel sexy in pregnancy had never put on this much weight. I can't imagine why Tom would want to touch me, looking like this.'

'You look gorgeous, Sally.'

'No, it's my shoes that look gorgeous.' Sally eased herself onto the edge of the bed. 'I just look fat. Oh…' She screwed up her face and started to breath steadily, trying to work through the contraction.

Hayley put her hand on Sally's abdomen, feeling the strength of the contraction and looking at the clock. 'They seem to be coming more frequently, Sally. How do you feel about that pool?'

'Let's go for it. But not until you've told me about Patrick. You met him in America, had sex and it was completely amazing and that's why you're here.'

Hayley's eyes widened. 'Are you clairvoyant?'

'No, I'm a woman.' Sally reached for her bag. 'Patrick is unreasonably sexy. If I'd met him when I was single, I would have slept with him, too. But don't tell Tom that. I need Patrick conscious until this baby is born. On the other hand, he might be the one to floor my Tom—he's strong enough. Mmm…' She gave Hayley a wicked look. 'So—I haven't actually seen him naked but it's got to be a good sight. Am I right?'

Hayley was laughing, her face scarlet. 'Sally, for goodness' sake…'

'Oh, please indulge me, Hayley. I feel like a whale and I'm in pain and scared. I need distraction.'

Hayley saw something flicker in Sally's eyes and she leaned forward and hugged her impulsively. 'Don't be scared,' she said huskily. 'You're going to be fine. We're going to do it together.' Wondering whether she'd overstepped the mark, she pulled away, but Sally yanked her back again.

'Don't stop. You have no idea how good it feels to be hugged. Tom is so stressed he's forgotten to hug me. But don't think that's going to get you off the hook. I still want to know everything. We've all been longing for Patrick to find someone.'

Hayley straightened. 'Don't get the wrong idea.' Hayley reached for the set of scrubs that Maggie had given her. 'It really isn't like that.'

Sally's eyes narrowed. 'But you'd like it to be, obviously. And he couldn't stop looking at you when he was in here earlier.'

'Really?' Startled by that piece of information, Hayley felt her stomach curl and then she shook her head. 'I don't know what to think. He wasn't that thrilled to see me.'

'Hold that thought—contraction coming.' While Sally breathed steadily, Hayley struggled to hold back the sudden surge of happiness that engulfed her like a cloak. Had he been looking at her? Really?

Now that the shock of her arrival had faded—*now that he knew she wasn't pregnant*—was he pleased she was here?

'Hey, no dreaming unless it's out loud.' Sally poked her in the arm and gave a faint smile. 'You're depriving me of a vicarious sex life, I can feel it. Tell me every little detail. You know you want to.'

And Hayley discovered that she *did* want to. So she told Sally everything.

'And you just left his room? You didn't even wake him up?' Sally clutched her arm. 'I think I might be ready for the water.'

'Let's get you over there now.'

'Wait a minute.' Sally winced. 'Has he given you your knickers back?'

Hayley blushed. 'He hasn't mentioned them.'

'Probably too much of a gentleman.'

Hayley thought about the way he kissed. 'I don't think he's that much of a gentleman.'

'Ooh, don't tell me that—you're making me all hot.' Sally laughed, reaching for her bag.

'I'll carry that.' Hayley took it from her and together they walked across the corridor to the room where the birthing pool had been prepared. 'Don't say anything to him, will you?'

'And risk upsetting him? You're kidding, aren't you?' Sally eyed the pool. 'That sexy man of yours is the only thing that's standing between me and a Caesarean section. I don't know what's wrong with Tom. He doesn't usually intervene so readily. With me he just wants to yank it out and get it over with. I suppose it's the whole control thing.'

Hayley helped Sally change into a swimsuit and step into the bath. 'How's the water?'

'Perfect, thanks. I wonder what Patrick has done with my husband?'

'I think he knew you needed time to calm yourself down, without having to worry about him.'

'Possibly.' Sally slid into the bath. 'Oh, my goodness, that feels fantastic. I should have overruled Tom ages ago when he said he didn't want me in water.'

'Why doesn't he want you in water?' Hayley checked Sally's temperature and recorded it in the notes. 'Has he had a bad experience or something?'

'He's fine with other pregnant women using the pool.' Sally closed her eyes and leaned back against the side of the pool. 'Just not me. As I said, he just wants to get this baby out as fast as possible. Poor man. I don't think this is going to be fast. Which brings me to another issue—you're not even supposed to be working, and neither is Patrick.'

'I don't mind.' Hayley poured Sally a drink. 'Here. You have to drink plenty while you're in there—I don't want you getting dehydrated.'

'It's Christmas Day. You could at least have provided champagne.'

'That comes after you've delivered the baby.' Hayley saw Sally's expression change. 'You're having another contraction?' She waited for the contraction to end and then listened to the foetal heart with the aqua Doppler.

'That sounds loud and strong.' Patrick strolled into the room, with Tom hovering behind him. 'Do you mind me in here, Sally? I have seen you in a swimming costume before.'

'Please don't tell my husband that.'

Tom dropped into a crouch by the pool, his expression contrite. 'I'm sorry I've been an idiot.'

'It's all right.' Sally leaned forward and kissed him, her eyes soft with love. 'I'll find a way to make you pay, you handsome thing.'

Tom looked up at Patrick. 'You won't give her systemic opioids while she's in the pool, will you?'

Patrick rolled his eyes. 'Do I look stupid?'

Tom ran his hand over the back of his neck. 'Sorry.'

'I thought I'd calmed you down,' Patrick said wearily, and his colleague gave a sheepish smile.

'I'm not going to be calm until this child is at university. Probably not even then.'

'In that case, I want a divorce,' Sally said, and Hayley tensed, wondering whether Patrick would be sensitive about that comment, but he was busy checking the notes she'd made.

'This looks good.' He flicked through the pages and glanced at her. 'You're thorough, aren't you?'

'She's amazing,' Sally murmured, holding onto Tom's shoulders as another contraction ripped through her. 'I'm so glad you brought her in, Patrick. She's the best Christmas present you could have given me.'

Tom scowled, but his hand was gentle as he smoothed Sally's damp hair away from her face. 'Since when has my colleague bought you Christmas presents?'

'Since he was my colleague, too.' Sally groaned and leaned her head against his shoulder. 'I worked with him until six months ago, don't forget. That was when you were still sane, by the way.'

'You worked here?' Startled, Hayley put down the aqua Doppler that she'd been using to check the baby's heart rate. 'Are you a doctor?' *Please don't say she'd been giving advice to a doctor for the past few hours.*

'Sally is a midwife.' Tom looked at her and Hayley gave a whimper of embarrassment.

'You're a midwife? Why didn't anyone tell me? I had no idea.'

'I'm not a midwife at the moment,' Sally murmured. 'I'm a pregnant woman and, believe me, it's entirely different. You can see that just by looking at my husband. Normally he's a cool, calm professional but today he's turned into a psycho freak father-to-be.'

'Thanks,' Tom said dryly, offering his wife another sip of water. 'It's just because I care about you.'

'Please don't get sentimental.' Patrick gave a mock shudder. 'I prefer it when the pair of you row.'

'No. No rowing.' Sally gritted her teeth again and dug her nails into Tom's arm. 'It was a row that put me in this position.'

'Actually, it wasn't so much the row as the making up,' Tom drawled, and Patrick backed towards the door, shaking his head.

'Enough! Hayley and I will leave you to be romantic for a few minutes.'

Agreeing that the couple needed some private time, Hayley checked the foetal heart once more before following Patrick. But before she left the room she cast a final glance towards Sally. 'Everything is fine. I'll be back in ten minutes but if you're worried, press the buzzer.'

Patrick pushed coins into the vending machine and bought two cups of hot chocolate. 'I'm not asking you what you want.' He handed one to Hayley. 'You'll just have to trust me when I say that the tea tastes like dishwater and the coffee tastes like battery acid. Hot chocolate is the only option.'

'Hot chocolate is good.'

'You must be exhausted—let's go and sit in my office for five minutes.'

She followed him into the room and looked around. 'Where are the children?'

'They've gone down to the play area outside the children's ward. Posy likes the rocking horse.' Patrick gestured towards the armchairs. 'Collapse for a minute, I'm sure you need it. I can't thank you enough for everything you're doing for Sally.'

'Oh...' She blushed and sipped her chocolate. 'It's my job.'

Her job.

Patrick lounged in his chair, realising that he'd never given any thought to Hayley in her professional capacity. In fact, he was embarrassed to admit that most of his thoughts about her had been of a much shallower nature. 'You're a fantastic midwife. Tom isn't easy to deal with but you stood your ground with him and you calmed Sally down. And she isn't easy. She's very exacting.'

'There's nothing wrong with being exacting.'

'That's why she's so relaxed with you—your attention to detail is incredible.' He looked at her curiously. 'You don't know this department but in no time at all and with no apparent fuss you've located every piece of equipment you need, every request form and observation chart—it's all done. Perfect. I could stand up in a court of law and produce evidence of perfect care.'

Hayley looked alarmed. 'I hope you won't have to stand up in a court of law because of anything I've done. In my experience that sort of thing only happens when there's a breakdown in communication.'

Patrick grinned. 'And that's another thing you excel at—communication. The aromatherapy was a good idea. Who taught you to do that?'

'I went on a course. I think relaxation is important for a pregnant woman. I used to run relaxation classes in Chicago and I often used aromatherapy on the unit.' She blew gently on her drink to cool it. 'I don't believe childbirth is all about following the textbook. It's about doing what works for the individual, isn't it? That might not be aromatherapy or massage. A few weeks ago I had a woman who couldn't bear to be touched so massage was out of the question.'

'So what did you do with her?'

'I found out what she usually did to relax.' Hayley took another sip of her chocolate. 'Turned out she liked listening to story tapes. So that's what we did. Instead of playing music, we listened to an actor reading Charles Dickens. I quite enjoyed it, actually. Made a nice change.'

Patrick lifted his eyebrow. 'You got to the end of the book?'

'It was a long labour,' Hayley said cheerfully, and Patrick looked at her with new respect, realising how little he knew about her.

Away from the work environment she was funny and self-deprecating, but here she was pure professional. 'Did you always want to be a midwife?'

'It was that or paediatric nursing but I found that too upsetting,' she admitted. 'Midwifery is a happy job.'

Patrick laughed. 'A *happy* job?'

'Yes.' She gave a self-conscious shrug. 'You get to spend time with people in their happiest moment and I think that's very special. There is no feeling as good as handing someone their child, is there? Of course, sometimes it goes wrong and that's dreadful.' She paused for a moment and he sensed there had been plenty of moments in her career that hadn't been 'happy'.

'And then there's the long hours.' Patrick thought about the moans of the midwives he worked with. 'Missing weekends.'

'But that's because, generally speaking, you're staying with a woman right the way through her labour, and that's wonderful.' Hayley put her cup on the floor. 'The alternative would be handing over care to someone else halfway through labour. I think that's unfair on the woman and stressful. You have a short time in which to build a relationship of trust—you can't go home halfway through and expect that woman to just bond with someone else.'

'So you're not tired of midwifery?'

'Tired of it? Gosh, no. Never. I love it. Perhaps I haven't done it for long enough to become disenchanted.'

Patrick watched her curiously. It was so unusual to hear someone saying how much they loved their job. But Hayley was so enthusiastic he could imagine she'd lift the spirits of any colleagues she worked with. And he couldn't imagine her becoming disenchanted with anything. 'You must love it,' he drawled softly, 'or you wouldn't be here on Christmas Day.'

'You gave me no choice.' But her smile said otherwise. 'What about you? Don't you love it?'

'Yes. Although occasionally I worry about my children. Inevitably I'm called out more than I'd like to be.'

'How do you cope with child care? I would have thought you'd have a live-in nanny.'

'I didn't want someone living in our home,' Patrick said quietly. 'I wanted it to be just us. A family. But it's harder that way—requires more planning. Posy comes to the nursery in the hospital—that's easy. Alfie goes to school. And I use Mrs Thornton before and after school. And she stays the night occasionally if she has to.'

Hayley grinned. 'This is the same Mrs Thornton who wears scary red lipstick and fancies you?'

Captivated by her smile, Patrick had to force himself to concentrate. 'That's the one. She's actually very good with the children. And she's relatively local, which helps. Although clearly I have to make sure I'm not alone in a room with her.'

Hayley looked at him. 'Well, I'm sure it's hard, juggling work with children, but you obviously thrive on it. You look very happy for a man who's working on Christmas Day.'

Did he?

Patrick gave a start. He *was* happy, he realised. *Very happy.* Just being around her made him want to smile. That realisation unsettled him. 'It's Christmas Day,' he said blandly, standing up and throwing his cup in the bin. 'And my friends are about to have a baby. Plenty to smile about.'

Hayley stood up, too. 'Christmas babies are always exciting.' Her eyes sparkled and Patrick suddenly wanted to box her up like a present and keep her in his life for ever.

Seriously spooked by his thoughts, he dragged his gaze from hers and pushed open the door. 'Come on. We'd better get back before Tom has a nervous breakdown.'

Over the next few hours, Hayley stayed with Sally, monitoring mother and baby.

'Tell me I'm making progress,' Sally moaned, and Hayley smiled and dimmed the lights slightly.

'You're making excellent progress. I'm proud of you.' As she finished speaking the door opened and Patrick strolled into the room.

'Hi, there. Just checking up on you.' Patrick squatted down next to Sally and touched her arm. 'How are things?'

Hayley's heart was bumping so hard she turned away and concentrated on the charts to give herself a moment to recover.

'I'm never sleeping in the same bed as Tom again if that's what you're asking me.' Sally breathed in deeply. 'And I want Hayley to come and live with me and be my new best friend. Apart from that, everything is fine.'

Realising that if she didn't respond she'd draw attention to herself, Hayley turned with a smile. 'I'll come and live with you. You make me laugh and you have the same size feet as me. I can borrow your shoes.'

Patrick glanced at Tom. 'You're looking tense. What's the matter?'

'I want her out of the water,' Tom muttered, but Sally rolled her eyes and Patrick stood up and took the charts from Hayley.

'This is looking fine.' He scanned them carefully. 'Remind me how long she's been in the water?'

Hayley checked the clock. 'Four hours.' She lifted her eyebrows. 'That went quickly.'

'It's because we were talking about the three S's.' Sally tightened her grip on the side of the pool. 'Shoes, shopping and sex.'

'Sex?' Patrick's eyes narrowed and he turned to look at Hayley, a question in his eyes.

She tried to look innocent but felt her cheeks growing hotter and hotter under his sharp blue gaze.

He knew. He knew she'd been talking about him.

Oh, help—couldn't Sally have been a little more discreet?

'Nothing like a conversation about sex to remind a girl how she got herself in this mess,' Sally said blithely, and Hayley squirmed.

'I think I'll just get myself a quick drink as the two of you are here.' Desperate to escape, she pushed the aqua Doppler into Patrick's hand and slunk towards the door. 'Back in a minute.'

CHAPTER FIVE

HAYLEY hunted down somewhere to hide her burning face. Why had Sally been so tactless? *What on earth was she going to say to Patrick?* She wished she hadn't been so honest with Sally. Slinking along the corridor, she found a staffroom. Fortunately it was empty, several half-drunk cups of cold coffee abandoned in the middle of the table.

New Year's resolution, she told herself firmly.

No more talking about herself. Ever.

'So whose sex life were you talking about?' Patrick's voice came from behind her and she spun round nervously.

'Oh, I thought you were with Sally.'

'Tom's with Sally. Despite his apparent ineptitude he is, in fact, more than capable of monitoring his own wife for ten minutes.' Patrick's gaze didn't shift from her face. 'So?'

'So, what?' Keeping her tone innocent, Hayley avoided the subject, hoping he'd just give up. 'Sally's lovely, isn't she?'

'Delightful. She's also extremely preoccupied with my love life.'

'She cares about you. Do you want tea? Coffee? No, of course you don't. You want to get back to Sally.' She looked at him pointedly but he didn't move.

'How much did you tell her?'

Hayley looked around desperately, wondering if the staffroom had an emergency exit. She had a feeling she was going to need it. *What had Sally said to him?* She tried to buy herself some time, hoping that his mobile would ring. 'What makes you think I told her anything?'

'Hayley.' Patrick's voice was patient. 'There is a taxi driver a few miles from here who knows everything about you from your bra size down to the colour of your knickers, and you were only in his vehicle for fifteen minutes. You've been with Sally for the best part of six hours so I think it's fair to assume that she has a fairly good grasp of your life story by now.'

'I did *not* tell him the colour of my— That was a total accident because he just happened to pick the phone up when I was talking to you and that was *absolutely* not my fault.' Affronted, Hayley looked at him but still his gaze didn't shift from hers and she scowled. 'Did you ever think about being a lawyer? You should be a lawyer. You have a way of looking at people that makes them want to confess to things they didn't do. Could you stop looking at me like that?'

Patrick's brows lifted, but there was a glimmer of humour in his eyes. 'How am I looking at you?'

'Like I'm an idiot,' Hayley mumbled, and the humour faded.

'Hayley, I do not think you're an idiot. Far from it. On the contrary, I think you're an exceptional midwife. *Really* exceptional. Sally isn't an easy patient and you've got her eating out of your hand.'

'That's different.' Hayley stopped the pretence of making tea. 'That's my job. But the rest of it—I feel guilty,' she admitted hopelessly. 'And, yes, I feel like an idiot because I should have been able to find some way of smoothly deflecting her questions, instead of which I just blurted everything out like I always do.' She gave him a look of helpless apology. 'Why do I always do that? Why can't I just be discreet and enigmatic?'

'I'm not sure if that was a rhetorical question but if you really want an answer then I suspect it has something to do with the fact that you're incurably honest.'

'Well, whatever it is I am, I wish I was something different.' Frustrated with herself, Hayley flopped down onto the chair and buried her face in her hands. 'I'm *so* sorry. I messed up. I admit it. I didn't *want* to say anything, I didn't want to embarrass you, but Sally sort of wormed it out of me and if I hadn't answered I would have looked rude. She's a patient and a consultant's wife and anyway she sort of guessed and—'

'Hayley, breathe.'

'Sorry?' She glanced up at him and saw that the humour was back in his eyes.

'As usual, you're forgetting to breathe. You're going to pass out.'

'I never pass out. I've never fainted in my life.'

'Then let's not make today the first time.'

'Look, I feel really guilty, OK? I mean, this is where you work.' Nervous under his steady gaze, she pulled the clips out of her hair, twisted it and pinned it up again. 'And I can understand that you don't want people gossiping about you. I'm *really* sorry I told her.'

'In the interests of consistency, what exactly did you tell her?'

'The truth, of course.'

Patrick studied her for a moment, a strange look in his eyes. 'How much of the truth?'

'Enough. I mean, I didn't tell her absolutely *everything*—' Hayley frowned, trying to remember exactly what she *had* said. 'I definitely missed out the part where you thought I was pregnant and I skirted over the bit where you kissed me in the kitchen.' Her face burned at the memory. 'But I might have mentioned one or two things about that night in Chicago.'

His face was poker straight. 'Did you tell her that you left your knickers on my bedroom floor?'

Hayley squirmed. 'Maybe. Possibly. It might have been mentioned.'

The corner of his mouth flickered. 'It sounds to me as though you've been the soul of discretion.'

'You're laughing at me again.'

'I'm not laughing. Hayley, you're so sensitive—'

'Because I know I keep saying the wrong things at the wrong time! I just can't stop myself. My mouth is constantly getting me into trouble.' She heard him draw in a breath and saw his gaze drop to her mouth and linger there as if he was thinking about…

And so was she.

She was thinking about nothing else. *Sex, sex, sex.* That was the only thing on her mind when she looked at Patrick.

Hayley jumped up and hurried over to the water cooler, wondering whether she could fit her burning body inside it. She'd made a decision that she wasn't going to think about him in *that way.* And now she was doing it again. One look, and she was willing to forget all her promises to herself. Really, she needed to do something about herself. Something serious.

'So you're not mad with me, then?' Keeping her tone light, she poured herself a glass of water that she didn't want.

'I'm not mad. But I did want to check exactly what you've told her so that we give her the same story.' Patrick joined her at the water cooler and gently removed the cup from her hand, his fingers brushing against hers. 'Do you mind if I drink that, given that you don't want it?'

'How do you know I don't want it?' Her voice was a squeak and his eyes gleamed with gentle mockery.

'Because you're easy to read.' His eyes rested on hers for a moment and then he sighed. 'I think perhaps it's time I took you home.'

Hayley's heart pounded like the drum in an orchestra.

He wanted to take her home? Oh, God, yes. Right now. She wanted to try out his enormous bed with the view over the forest. She wanted to see if he could repeat the magic he'd created that night in Chicago.

Staring up at him, her legs wobbled. *His eyes were so blue,* she thought dreamily—so blue it was like staring into the Caribbean ocean. Lost in a fantasy that involved herself and Patrick on a white sandy beach, it came as a shock when he frowned urgently.

'Hayley? You need to decide. Is it yes or no? No one is going to judge you. I'll take you if you want me to.'

She felt a thrill of shock at his unapologetically direct approach.

He wanted her that badly?

'Gosh, Patrick, I— You make it really hard for a girl to stick with her decisions, I'll give you that.' But the fact that he was so desperate for her he just wanted to take her home *right now* sent excitement pouring through her body. Flustered, she tried to disengage her eyes from his. How was she supposed to think when he was staring down at her with unflinching concentration, as if she was the only thing in his world? 'I mean it is flattering, obviously, that you feel this way. And I'm not pretending I'm not really tempted—I mean you *know* I am because I already left one pair of knickers in your room.' She fiddled with her hair. 'But the sensible side of me is saying that we ought to give this a bit more thought this time. I suppose what I'm saying is that frankly I'm surprised you even want to take me straight home given what happened last time.

I mean, you didn't contact me, I contacted you. And then you thought I was pregnant—'

He looked taken aback. 'Hayley—'

'I know, I know.' She lifted a hand to silence him. 'That was all a misunderstanding, but still I think it should remind us both that we have to think about this. Not jump in with both feet. Yes, there's chemistry. I'm not denying that. But that doesn't mean that we have to do something about it.' *Who was she kidding?* If they didn't do something about it soon she was going to go screaming mad. Her body was melting, her pelvis was on fire and all she wanted him to do was kiss her the way only he could kiss. 'I'm just saying I think it might be a mistake. Not that I'm not flattered that you asked, of course—'

'Hayley.' His expression hovering somewhere between stunned and incredulous, Patrick ran his hand over his jaw. 'I was asking whether you wanted to go home.'

'I know, I heard you, and I still think that—'

'Because it's late. I thought you might be very tired.' He spoke the words slowly, emphasising each one as if she were a small child. 'You're jet-lagged. I thought you'd need some rest.'

Rest?

He was suggesting that she go home to *rest?*

Facing the onset of massive embarrassment, Hayley looked at him stupidly. 'You want me to— You were suggesting— Oh.'

There was a shimmer of amusement in his eyes, but also a flicker of sympathy. 'Hayley, listen, don't for one moment think that I don't—'

'If you laugh now, Patrick Buchannan, you will never be able to deliver a baby again,' she warned huskily, 'let alone make another one of your own. If you laugh, you will never again have to ask a woman if she's pregnant.'

'I'm not laughing.'

'Good.' She lifted her chin, trying to hold onto the last shreds of her dignity, trying to look as though this situation was entirely normal and that she didn't really want to die on the spot. But she saw immediately that this whole misunderstanding was her fault. Because she'd been thinking about nothing but sex, she'd assumed he'd be the same.

'Right. So you were, in fact, asking whether I want to go home and sleep.' Hayley cleared her throat and tried to make her voice sound casual. As if she had conversations about sex every day of the week. As if she were a twenty-first-century woman. 'Of course. That's fine.' *This was even more embarrassing than realising she'd left her knickers on his bedroom floor.*

'Hayley—'

'It's kind of you to offer, but actually I'm not particularly tired.' She felt like a stripper who had accidentally turned up at a children's party. 'I don't need to go back to the house now.' She was never going back to his house again. As soon as the shift was over she was going to change her identity and leave the country. Maybe she'd become a nun—at least that way she wouldn't have the opportunity to proposition men.

'You've done us a favour, coming in,' Patrick said cautiously, watching her closely as if he was afraid she might flip at any moment. 'You've calmed Sally down, it's probably because of you that she's progressed. But none of us are forgetting it's Christmas Day and you weren't supposed to be working. The night staff will be here soon.'

'Sally is only eight centimetres dilated. I won't leave until she has the baby.' And that would mean staying near to Patrick. *Oh, Hayley, torture yourself, why don't you?* Still, if things got too bad she could always drown herself in the birthing pool. 'I'll stay.'

'You're sure?'

'Oh, yes. I'm very good at decisions. Once I've made a decision…' Hayley snapped her fingers '…that's it. Done. I never change my mind.' *Well, only about three thousand, two hundred and fifty-four times.*

'That's very generous of you. Sally will be relieved—and so will Tom. He rates you, and that's a compliment coming from Tom.'

Now he was flattering her to make her feel better, Hayley thought gloomily, remembering the sympathy in his eyes. He must think she was a sad, desperate woman. Not wanting to dwell on that, she changed the subject. 'What are you going to do about the children? It must be Posy's bedtime.'

'It is. If you're sure you're willing to stay for Sally, I'll send the kids home with my brother. They won't complain—they adore Daniel.'

'So you're not going to ring the babysitter with the vampire lipstick?'

A sardonic smile flickered across his handsome face. 'I think we might give her a miss this time. I think spending Christmas night with a vampire might be a little unfair on the kids. Although I have asked her to pop in and check on the kittens.' His eyes gleamed with irony. 'Yours and mine.'

'I love the kittens.' Why did he have to be so good-looking? It wasn't fair. Things would have been much easier if he'd been small, earnest and academic. Reminding herself that if he'd been small, earnest and academic, she wouldn't have left her knickers on his bedroom floor, Hayley smoothed her scrub suit and tried to look professional. *As if she hadn't just made it obvious that her feelings about him were anything but professional.* 'I'd better get back before Tom has a breakdown. You go and sort out the kids.'

'Alfie advertised for a housekeeper? And he used my credit card?'

'Yes, but that will teach you to leave it lying around.' Patrick handed his brother a large bag. 'This is everything they're going to need for the night. You know, it might be easier if you just stayed in our house—'

'No.' Daniel gave a strange smile. 'Today I asked Stella to marry me—'

'I know.'

Daniel's brows rose. '*How* do you know?'

'You're forgetting I have Alfie. He knows everything that goes on around here,' Patrick said wearily. 'So, did Stella say yes?'

'Of course she said yes.'

'Then she's a brave woman.'

'She is brave. Brave and beautiful.' A strange look crossed Daniel's face. 'I never thought I'd feel this way, to be honest. Never thought I'd have the courage—never thought I'd feel this way about a woman.'

Patrick opened his mouth to deliver the usual onslaught of brotherly banter but the words wouldn't come. Instead, he found himself thinking of Hayley. 'I'm pleased for you,' he said gruffly. 'And I'm sorry I'm giving you the children tonight. You must be looking forward to romance.'

'Stella is thrilled to be having the children,' Daniel said dryly. 'You know what she's like.'

'Yes. You're lucky.'

At that moment Stella bounced through the doors, her eyes shining. 'Patrick! Has he told you our news?'

'Alfie told him our news,' Daniel drawled, and Stella giggled. She was about to speak when the door opened and Hayley entered.

'Oh—I'm sorry. I didn't know you had anyone with you.' She coloured prettily and would have left but Patrick beckoned her into the room.

'Hayley, this is my brother, Daniel, and Stella—his wife-to-be. The children are going to stay the night with them. Guys, this is Hayley—she's Alfie's housekeeper. And she just happens to be a midwife, too.'

'She worked in America, isn't that a coincidence?' Alfie was bouncy and cheerful. 'You should taste her turkey, Uncle Dan. I want Dad to keep her for ever. No more gluey pasta. No more burnt everything.'

Hayley's face grew scarlet and she busied herself retrieving Posy's toys from the floor. 'I'm just here for two weeks, Alfie.'

Patrick's eyes lingered on the curve of her bottom as she stooped. Then he started thinking about the tiny pair of silk knickers he'd found on the floor of his hotel bedroom...

Dragging his gaze from her curves, he discovered his brother watching him with amusement.

'You look hot and bothered, Ric.' Daniel's eyes gleamed wickedly. 'Something wrong?'

'It's always difficult juggling kids and work,' Patrick said smoothly, and Daniel's grin widened.

'Well, we're taking the kids off your hands for a night, so that should make things easier for you.'

Apparently oblivious to the byplay, Hayley zipped up the bag and Alfie hugged her.

'Tomorrow can we play Monopoly? I want you to stay longer than two weeks, Hayley. Promise you will.'

'Well, no...' Flustered, Hayley hugged him back. 'I can't do that, Alfie, but—'

'I know.' Alfie looked crestfallen. 'You have to track down the friend you met when you were in America.'

Seeing Hayley's stricken expression, Patrick intervened. *She'd had enough embarrassment for one day.* 'Alfie, get your things together. Posy needs to get to bed.'

'It's Christmas night, Dad. It doesn't matter if she's late.'

'If she's late she'll be cranky in the morning.'

Patrick felt Stella's eyes on his face, questioning. Clearly Alfie's unguarded comment hadn't passed unnoticed.

Damn. He wasn't ready to field her questions—*didn't know what his answers would be.*

'So...' He took the bag that Hayley had packed and thrust it towards Daniel. 'I'm sure you want to go home and I have to get back to work.'

'You were supposed to be off over Christmas,' Stella murmured, and Patrick shrugged.

'Sally went into labour.'

Stella gasped. 'No. Really? I must go and see her for a minute. Which room is she in?'

'She's in the water.'

'That's what I came to talk to you about.' Hayley pushed her hair behind her ears. 'Tom wants her out of the water, but she's refusing.'

Patrick wondered if she knew she always played with her hair when she was nervous. 'I don't want her to deliver in the water either. I'm with Tom on that.'

Stella rolled her eyes. 'Obstetricians unite. What do you think, Hayley?'

The door opened again and Tom stood there, panic on his

face. 'She wants to push, Hayley. And I can't get her out of the water.'

Patrick noticed that his colleague immediately turned to Hayley. She'd gained his trust over the hours she'd been with them. And that didn't surprise him. She'd gained his trust, too. There was no doubt in his mind that she was an exceptional midwife. Even now she didn't panic. She kissed Alfie briefly, congratulated Daniel and Stella again and then walked briskly back along the corridor with Tom, talking quietly and calmly.

'I've got to go.' Patrick thrust slapped his brother on the shoulder and kissed Stella. 'Thanks, guys.'

Having hugged his children, he followed Hayley and Tom along the corridor. When he opened the door he sensed the change in the atmosphere. Tom was beside himself and Sally was pushing. In the water.

'Please, angel.' Tom was white-faced. 'Out of the water.'

'If you move me now, I'll kill you,' Sally gritted, screwing up her face as another contraction hit her. 'Oh, God, Tom, how could you do this to me? It's agony!'

Tom looked stricken and Hayley touched his shoulder gently. 'This is part of labour,' she said softly. 'Don't take it to heart.'

Patrick had entered the room, prepared to find ways of persuading Sally out of the water, but, watching Hayley, he held back.

'What do you want me to do?'

'Nothing.' She gave Sally another sip of water. 'You can stay around and give Tom some support.'

Patrick caught his friend's desperate look. 'There's no reason why she shouldn't deliver in the water, Tom—'

'We don't do that.'

'Not normally,' Patrick agreed. 'But Hayley has delivered

babies in the water, and it's what Sally wants. And to be honest, it's too late to get her out. Let's go with it. I'll be right here all the time. If there's a problem, I'll intervene.'

'Thanks for being so positive,' Sally groaned, and Patrick grinned.

'I'm an obstetrician. What do you expect?'

'Oh, go and get a coffee or something.' Sally grabbed Hayley's hand. 'I don't want this to be unsafe and I'm not thinking clearly. What do I have to do? I want you to tell me everything. I don't want you to assume I know anything.'

'You're doing fine.' Hayley waited for another contraction to come and go and then checked the foetal heart. 'The baby is fine, too. Don't push, Sally, not unless you have the urge.'

'Just get the baby out,' Tom muttered, but Hayley ignored him, all her focus on Sally.

'You're doing so well. The head is nearly out, Sally. So now we've come this far, the baby needs to be born under the water. And I'm going to be as hands-off as possible because that's best for both of you.'

Tom looked as though he was going to pass out, but Patrick was fascinated.

He watched as Hayley calmly soothed Sally, offering encouragement and guidance but in such a low-key way that it appeared that she wasn't helping in any way. But Patrick saw the skill in what she was doing.

'I want to push,' Sally groaned, and Hayley nodded.

'Push, then.'

Realising how rarely he saw calm, normal deliveries, Patrick felt a lump build in his throat as Sally and Tom's baby was born into the water with a minimum of fuss.

Hayley brought her gently to the surface and into Sally's arms.

'Congratulations. You have a daughter.' The baby gave a

little wail and then Sally was crying and when Patrick looked at Tom he saw that his colleague's face was wet.

'Congratulations,' he said huskily, and Tom pressed his fingers to his eyes and then bent to hug his wife.

'You clever, clever girl.'

Smug and proud of herself, Sally glanced up from admiring her daughter. 'You see? Sisterhood. We women can do it without you.'

Hayley grinned. 'Actually, we could do with their help to get you out of the pool now, Sally. Then we can clamp the cord and cut it.' She reached for a towel and gently dried the baby. 'We need to keep her warm.'

As Hayley calmly checked the baby's Apgar score and finished the delivery, Patrick found himself watching her work.

'I've never witnessed such a calm delivery,' he said softly, and she smiled as she tucked the baby up warmly against Sally's breast.

'It's the way it's supposed to be.'

'Only *without* the water,' Tom muttered, and Sally grinned.

'I told you I wasn't going to get out of the water.'

'I thought you were joking. If I'd known you were serious I would have made you give birth in the middle of a desert.'

'Everything looks fine, Sally,' Patrick said quietly, 'but, given that you delivered under the water, I'd like a paediatrician to check the baby.'

'I'd like that, too.' Sally smiled at him. 'Thank you for letting me do it. Thank you for not panicking and thinking about your legal position.' She turned to Hayley, her eyes misting. 'And thank you for making it all so special. When I have my next baby, I want you there.'

'Next?' Tom was incredulous, his expression comical as he

dragged his hands through his already untidy hair. 'Sal, a moment ago you were saying never again.'

'That was then and this was now.' Sally's happiness was infectious. 'I want lots of babies, Tom.'

Patrick grinned. 'And she wants them all underwater.'

CHAPTER SIX

IN THE car on the way home, Hayley shut her mouth tightly and kept it shut. Once or twice she felt Patrick glance towards her but she kept her eyes straight ahead, staring at the snow that swirled across his headlights.

He seemed unconcerned by the horrendous weather conditions, his hands firm and confident on the wheel as he negotiated the snow and ice. 'You were amazing with Sally.'

'Mmm.'

'Is that all you're going to say? "Mmm"?' His tone was amused and she sneaked a look at him and then immediately regretted it as her body responded in its usual predictable fashion.

She concentrated her attention back on the snow.

Was it normal to feel like this about a man? After her outburst earlier he was probably terrified to be alone with her. The situation was so embarrassing it made her squirm.

She shifted slightly to the far edge of her seat so that she was as far away from him as possible.

'Hayley, you're worrying me.' He eased the four-wheel drive through the gate and pulled up in front of the barn. 'Are you ill? Tired?'

Actually, she *did* feel tired. Bone-achingly weary, but that was hardly surprising, was it?

'I'm fine.' They were the only words she allowed herself but he gave a sigh and switched off the engine.

'You're upset about earlier.' With the engine off the cold immediately penetrated the car and he looked at her profile for a moment and then sighed. 'Come on. We can talk inside.'

Hayley Hamilton, you are not talking, she reminded herself fiercely. *You are not saying a word. Nothing.*

She slid out of the car, took a moment to balance herself and then Patrick put his arm round her and guided her to the door. And she couldn't pull away because she knew that any sudden movement was guaranteed to land her flat on her back on the ice.

So she endured the warmth and strength of his arm but still kept her mouth zipped shut.

Even when he closed the door on the cold Christmas night, she didn't move her lips.

Instead, she hurried across to the dining table, which was still covered in empty plates and abandoned crackers.

'What are you doing?' Patrick watched as she noisily stacked plates and scooped up jokes, toys and paper hats. 'Leave that.'

'I'll just take it through to the kitchen,' she said brightly, balancing a stack of plates and walking away from him.

'In that case, I'll help you.' The muscles in his shoulders flexed as he removed his coat. 'It will be quicker if two people do it.'

'I don't want you to help! I'm the housekeeper. This is my job.' She disappeared into the kitchen, hoping that he wouldn't follow. She wanted to be left alone with the washing-up and her humiliation.

But he didn't leave her alone. 'You've also worked all day as a midwife,' he said mildly. 'We'll do it together, Hayley.'

Together.

Why did he have to use that word? She was trying not to think 'together'.

'Fine.' She hurried back to the table, horribly conscious that it was just the two of them in the barn—horribly conscious of the width of his shoulders and the way he kept looking in her direction.

Swiftly she gathered glasses and after several trips to the kitchen the beautiful contemporary dining area was once more clear. Patrick had turned on the Christmas tree lights and chosen a CD. A female with a sexy, smoky voice sang about love and loss and Hayley returned to the kitchen, clattering as loudly as possible to drown out the soulful notes.

'I've never known you so quiet.' He stood in the doorway, a concerned look on his face. 'What's wrong?'

Oh, for goodness' sake! How could he ask her that? *What's wrong?*

Wasn't it obvious?

She gritted her teeth and finished loading the dishwasher. 'Nothing is wrong.'

'Is this about what happened earlier?'

'Of course not. Why would you think that?'

'Hayley, you have no reason to feel embarrassed.'

'Of course, no reason at all.' Hayley crashed the door of the dishwasher shut and set it to rinse. 'It isn't embarrassing to proposition a man at work. It happens to people all the time.'

'You didn't proposition me.' His tone was mild. 'You thought I was propositioning you.'

'Thanks for reminding me of the details. I'm well aware that I misread the situation, but do you mind if we don't talk about this?'

'And I would have been propositioning you if the wife of my closest friend hadn't been on the point of delivering and my children hadn't been across the corridor.'

'I really think we should just—' She broke off and stared at him. 'What? What did you just say?'

'I said I would have been propositioning you. You didn't misread the situation, Hayley. I was worried that you were tired, that's true. I thought you might want to hand Sally's care over to another midwife and get some rest, that's true as well.' His tone was soft. 'But I want you as much as you want me.'

'Oh...'

'And I've already missed the cut-off point for a four-minute warning, so I'm giving you about...' he glanced at his watch '...three seconds.'

'Three sec—' The words vanished under the pressure of his mouth and Hayley moaned as his tongue traced her lips, sending shock waves of excitement through her body. She had no idea how he'd crossed the room so quickly, but as his hands slid into her hair and his mouth grew more urgent on hers, she didn't care.

He powered her back against the table, his hands biting into her thighs as he lifted her up and lowered her onto the surface. A mug toppled and smashed on the kitchen floor, but neither of them noticed. Hayley was incapable of noticing anything except the hot burn of sexual desire in Patrick's eyes. The fact that he wanted her so badly increased her own desperation and she gave a whimper of need and arched her hips, but he was already there, his hands unzipping her jeans and stripping them from her legs.

His breathing was uneven as he brought his mouth back down on hers, his kiss so disturbingly erotic that Hayley's mind blanked. Heat pooled in her pelvis and she tried to shift against him, instinctively trying to relieve the delicious burning that had become her entire focus. The dangerous throb and ache became so intense that she sobbed against his mouth and he muttered something against her lips and then slid his fingers inside the elastic of her panties.

His touch was unerring, his fingers so impossibly skilled that Hayley was left in no doubt that he knew more about her body than she did. Without warning she exploded in a climax that made her cry out in shock, the sound muffled by his mouth, every contraction intensified by the fact that his fingers were deep inside her. His mouth still on hers, he gently removed his hand and Hayley was dimly aware of him altering her position slightly—and then there was a brief pause before she felt the hard probe of his erection against her hot, molten core. He entered her with a smooth, decisive thrust, the strength and power of his body robbing her of breath. And he felt so shockingly good that she arched her hips, responding to the rhythm he set. His mouth stayed hot on hers, his body virile and demanding as he slid his hand under her hips, hauling her closer still, increasing the contact that was already driving both of them wild.

Neither of them spoke—not a word was exchanged—all communication channelled through their bodies and expressed through the ragged drag of their breathing.

When he finally lost control Patrick's hands tightened on her hips. His rhythm altered and that subtle change was sufficient to boost Hayley over the same precipitous edge until both of them were tumbling, spinning, falling through a kaleidoscope of sensations.

Hayley had long since lost track of time but eventually Patrick dragged his mouth from hers and dropped his head to her shoulder, his breath warm against her neck. 'That was...' His voice husky, he struggled to finish his sentence. 'Sublime.'

She lay there, too drugged to move, her body still trem-

bling. It was only when he shifted above her that she felt the
hardness of the kitchen table pressing into her back.

Patrick registered her wince of discomfort with a wry smile
of apology. He hauled her upright in a decisive movement and
scooped her into his arms as if she weighed nothing.

Hayley wound her arms round his neck. 'You'll do yourself
an injury.' Eyeing her jeans on his kitchen floor, she wondered
whether she was destined to leave clothes in every room this
man inhabited.

'You don't weigh anything.' He took the stairs that led to
the bedrooms, pushing open the door that led to his room.
As he laid her down on the bed, Hayley realised that he was
still wearing his coat.

'One of us has the dress code wrong,' she muttered. 'Either
you're wearing too much or I'm wearing too little.'

'We're both wearing too much,' he drawled, his eyes glittering like sapphires as he shrugged off his coat and reached
for the buttons of his casual shirt.

Her mouth dried. 'Patrick—'

'Hayley?' The shirt went the same way as the coat and his
fingers slid to the snap of his jeans.

Her eyes were on his board-flat abdomen and then he was
on the bed beside her. Reaching out, he dimmed the lights
and then pulled the duvet over both of them. 'Now—where
were we?'

Hayley lay still in the darkness, feeling the warmth of his
arms around her. He hadn't bothered to close the blinds in
the bedroom and tiny lights glowed like stars in the fir trees
outside the barn. Through the thickness of the glass she could
hear the dull roar of the beck as it raced down from the fells.

'You're very quiet.' Patrick's voice was low and masculine. 'What's wrong?'

'What makes you think there's anything wrong?'

'Because normally you don't stop talking,' he said dryly, curving her against him in a possessive movement. 'I've learned that when you're quiet, it's time to worry.'

'That isn't true.' She resisted the temptation to snuggle into him and heard him sigh.

'Hayley, I can tell there's something wrong. Do I have to put the lights on and interrogate you?'

'I'm fine, Patrick, really.'

'Why are we whispering? We're on our own in the house. Apart from the kittens, of course, and I don't suppose they're interested in us.'

His words hastened the deflation of her happiness. It was like going from a slow puncture to a blowout, she thought miserably. Her emotions crashed and with it her desperate attempt to keep her feelings to herself.

Hayley shot out of the bed but his arms caught her easily and he pulled her back.

'Leave me alone, Patrick,' she muttered, her voice thickened by tears she desperately didn't want to shed.

'Hayley, now you're really worrying me.' His voice concerned, he flicked on the bedside lamp and shifted above her, his eyes fixed on her face. 'Tell me what's wrong.'

'I just hate myself, that's all.' Hayley turned her face away from the light, aware of the tension in his powerful frame.

'You hate yourself? For spending the night with me?'

'Yes!'

Her confession was followed by a long silence and then she heard his slow, indrawn breath. 'Did I hurt you?'

'No.' Her face was burning and she wished she'd stayed silent or given him a neutral response to his original question. 'It was fine. Can we just forget it?'

His fingers slid around her face and he forced her to look at him. This time there was no trace of humour in his eyes. Just serious intent. 'Hayley, don't avoid this—I thought it was what you wanted. Was I wrong?'

'No, you weren't wrong! Of course I wanted you—that must have been pretty obvious to you from the moment I dropped my knickers on your bedroom floor the first time.' Her voice rose slightly. 'And I wasn't exactly fighting you off tonight, was I? So it's a little unfair of you to rub in the fact I can't say no to you.'

His eyes were wary. 'I didn't want you to say no to me. So what's the problem?'

'The problem is that you only ever do this when your children aren't around—when I turned up yesterday, or the day before yesterday or whenever it was...' She realised that she'd lost track of the time. It must be the early hours of the morning, which meant it was no longer Christmas Day. 'When I turned up, you looked at me with the same enthusiasm you would have shown a tax bill. Almost the first words you say to me are, "When is the baby due?" Then at the hospital you're very remote and distant and suddenly we arrive home and just because the house is empty you turn back into a rampant sex god—' She broke off with a moan as he covered her mouth with his, kissing her slowly and thoroughly until the fire in her pelvis flared to life again.

When he finally lifted his head she was dizzy and disorientated.

'We need to talk,' he said softly, curving his hand around her face. 'You're right—I haven't behaved well where you're concerned. Give me the chance to explain.'

'You don't need to explain.' Hayley tried to wriggle away from him but his weight kept her still. 'Honestly—just forget I said anything. It's my fault, I know. Other women have one-night stands all the time and have no problem with it— I'm just built wrong.'

'You're built perfectly.' There was a sardonic gleam in his eyes as his gaze lingered on her mouth and then drifted lower. 'And I do have things to tell you. Things you deserve to know.' He rolled away from her and sat up. 'Can I get you anything? Are you hungry? We haven't eaten since lunchtime.'

Hayley realised that she was *starving,* but she wanted to hear what he had to tell her. Was it about his ex-wife? 'I'm not hungry.' But her stomach chose that moment to growl in protest and she rolled her eyes as he laughed.

'Not hungry?' Springing from the bed, he strolled into the bathroom and emerged wearing a black robe. 'I'll go and put some food on a tray. I'll be back in a minute. I've put the bath on. I thought your muscles might ache after all that…activity.'

Avoiding the glitter of his eyes, Hayley waited for him to leave the room and then slid out of bed and padded towards the door he'd used.

Seeing his bathroom, she felt ever so slightly faint. It was huge. Huge and super-luxurious in a cool, contemporary style, with a walk-in shower and what seemed like hundreds of tiny lights in the ceiling. But the real luxury was his bath. It was easily big enough for two. Water cascaded into the tub and mixed with the scented bubbles he must have added before he'd left the room.

As the water level rose quickly, Hayley looked at the bath longingly. Maybe a bath was a good idea.

Just a quick one.

She slid into the water and closed her eyes with a moan of pleasure.

'I didn't know what you wanted to eat so I made a few different things.' Patrick's voice came from inside the bathroom and Hayley opened her eyes with a shocked squeak.

'What are you doing in here?' She noticed that the tray he was carrying contained a bottle of champagne as well as a stack of thick-cut sandwiches.

There was a dull popping sound as he removed the cork from the champagne. 'I thought this would be a good place to eat. That way we don't get crumbs in the bed.' He poured champagne into two glasses and handed her one. 'Merry Christmas.'

'Merry Christmas,' Hayley said weakly, watching as he placed the tray next to the bath, discarded his robe and stepped into the water next to her. 'When you suggested a bath, I didn't know you were going to be joining me.'

'Why not?' He gave a slow, sexy smile and drank from his glass. 'Have something to eat. I'm not much of a cook, as you've been told, but I can just about manage sandwiches. Turkey, of course. No surprise there.'

'I love turkey sandwiches,' she said truthfully, reaching for one and biting into it. 'I really am starving.'

'I'm not surprised. It was a long day. Sally and the baby are fine, by the way. I called when I was downstairs.'

'I'm glad.' Hayley was tense with anticipation, wondering what he was going to tell her. 'I love your bathroom. I could move in here for the rest of my life.'

Patrick gave a faint smile. 'My wife hated it.' He glanced around the bathroom. 'She thought it was too modern.'

'Really? I think it's gorgeous. Like being in a smart hotel. I'm waiting for you to give me a bill when I step out of the door.' Hayley lay back against the side of the bath. 'I feel as though I'm in a Hollywood movie.'

'I don't think they usually eat cold turkey sandwiches in Hollywood movies.' Patrick watched with amusement as she devoured another sandwich and she shrugged.

'Jet-lag always makes me hungry.'

He lifted an eyebrow. 'Jet-lag?'

'Well, OK.' She felt her cheeks redden. 'It's entirely possible that the sex had something to do with it—maybe—just a little.' She watched while he put his glass down, sensing that he was deciding exactly what to tell her. 'I wish I could be more like you. I mean, I can see you carefully planning what to say and I just can't do that! I have all these plans to keep my thoughts to myself and then they sort of tumble out of my mouth.'

'I'd noticed.' He smiled at her and lifted the bottle of champagne but she shook her head.

'I'm already tired. If you give me any more I won't wake up until January.' She hesitated. 'You don't trust me enough to tell me, do you?'

'It isn't about trust,' Patrick said evenly. 'It's more about not wanting to relive it, if I'm honest. You already know some of it. You know that my wife—ex-wife—left on Christmas Eve two years ago.'

'Yes.' But she didn't know *why*. And she wanted to know why. 'The poor children. And poor you, of course,' she added quickly, but he shook his head.

'No. Your first reaction was the right one. I'm a grown-up, I can look after myself, but Alfie and Posy…' After a moment's hesitation, he topped up his own champagne glass, watching as the bubbles rose to the surface. 'If Carly had cared more about their feelings, she might have handled the situation differently. But she didn't. She was angry with me and she didn't care that they suffered.'

'Why was she angry?'

'Because I wasn't who she wanted me to be.' Patrick's tone was devoid of emotion, his eyes strangely blank. 'She thought she'd married a high-flying obstetrician. When I was made a consultant her words were, "Now I've made it." At the time I thought she'd made a mistake and what she'd meant to say was, "Now you've made it." But, no, she really did mean that. For her it was all about social status. She pictured herself walking into smart dinner parties with me—the problem is that obstetricians are probably the most unreliable guests on anyone's list.'

'You were always working.'

'Of course. In fact, you could say that there was an inverse correlation between the growth of my career and the decline of my marriage. The more successful I was, the busier I became. I started to see patients from all over the country and because some of the work was challenging, I couldn't always delegate.' Patrick gave a humourless laugh. 'In business, inappropriate delegation leads to lost revenue—in obstetrics it's a dead baby or a dead mother. And that's a no-brainer as far as I'm concerned.'

'Couldn't she understand that?'

'Carly wasn't interested in my work—just in the concept of being married to a successful consultant. But there's not much point in being married to a successful consultant if he's so busy working he can't take you anywhere. She was bored.'

'She had the children.'

Patrick gave a cynical smile. 'As I said, she was bored.'

'Did she have a career of her own?'

'When I met her she was working as a secretary to my colleague—I was a registrar. She didn't want a career. She wanted a successful husband.'

'You fell in love with her?'

'Honestly?' Patrick put his empty glass down. 'No. That wasn't what happened. I thought she was pretty. I asked her out a few times—'

Hayley gave a soft gasp of understanding. 'Oh, no, she became pregnant—and you married her.'

His blue eyes narrowed. 'Astute, aren't you?'

'Not particularly—but it explains why your first thought when you saw me on your doorstep was that I must be pregnant.' She stared down at the bubbles in the bath, absorbing that new information. 'No wonder. No wonder you thought that.'

'The crazy thing was Carly and I didn't even really have a relationship—not a proper one. I'd taken her out to dinner twice and on that last occasion she invited me in for coffee.' Patrick dragged his hand over the back of his neck and shrugged. 'She told me she was taking the Pill and on that one occasion I wasn't careful—'

Hayley remembered how he'd always used condoms with her. *Always been careful.* 'So you married her.'

'And we were happy enough, or so I thought.' Patrick shrugged. 'She wanted a big house—I gave her a big house; when she said Alfie was hard work, I paid for her to have help. I did my best to turn up at dinner parties, although I confess I rarely managed to stay through three courses. There were lots of occasions when I worked through the night—you know what it's like. But we muddled through—and then we had Posy.' He closed his eyes briefly. 'It went downhill from there.'

'Why?'

'Because Carly nearly died in childbirth,' he said hoarsely, 'and she blamed me. I think her exact words were, "*You save every other bloody woman but you're going to let me go because I'm not good enough for you.*"'

Hayley winced. 'What happened?'

'I don't know,' Patrick said wearily. 'I wasn't doing the delivery for obvious reasons—we were having a nightmare in the department, staff off sick, too many difficult deliveries in one night. Carly was in labour, but everything was fine—routine. And then there was a real emergency and I had no choice but to leave Carly and perform an emergency section on this lady. And I was only just in time—we would have lost that baby if I hadn't operated when I did. But while I was gone Carly started to bleed heavily.'

'Oh, Patrick…'

'The midwife was from another hospital and she panicked—I suppose because she knew Carly was the wife of a consultant. There was a delay. By the time I returned to the room it was horrendous. I thought we were going to lose Posy, so in the end I took over charge of the delivery—I couldn't trust anyone else at that point. And I had no choice but to do a Caesarean section.' He pulled a face at the memory. 'If I'd been there all the time—monitored her—I might have been able to do everything differently.'

'And another woman's baby might have died,' Hayley said softly, tears in her eyes. He'd performed an emergency Caesarean section on his own wife—to save the life of his own baby. 'You must have nerves of steel to have been able to do that.'

'I had no choice. To be honest, I blocked it out. I didn't let myself think, This is my wife, my baby.'

'Patrick, that must have been so hard. You had to make decisions that no man should have to make.'

'Carly didn't see it that way,' Patrick said roughly. 'She

thought I'd let her down, and maybe I did—I don't know. I go over it in my head again and again. What didn't I see? What did I miss?'

'You didn't miss anything,' Hayley said quietly. 'I'm sure of that. You're a brilliant obstetrician.'

'But a lousy husband,' Patrick said softly, and Hayley shook her head.

'No. You were put in an impossible position. But I don't understand why Carly was so upset. If she knew the other lady would have lost her baby...'

'I think she just panicked and I wasn't there,' Patrick said wearily. 'And when I was there I was focused on saving her and Posy, not on stroking her arm and telling her I loved her. In fact, I pretty much ignored her emotional trauma at the time—I just didn't want her to bleed to death or Posy to die. But I see now that I made it much, much worse. If Tom or one of the others had been on duty it would have been different, but you can't be an obstetrician and a husband at the same time.'

'That's why you sacrificed your Christmas day to help Tom and Sally.'

Patrick leaned back against the bath and closed his eyes. 'I just know what it's like trying to play both roles—and it's not good. Anyway, Carly was furious about the section—she hated having a scar.'

'Having seen the way you work, I doubt she had much of a scar.'

'It was more than she could cope with.'

'Wasn't she relieved that you'd saved Posy?'

'If anything, she saw that as more evidence that I didn't care for her.' Patrick opened his eyes and looked at her. 'The one thing I didn't tell you was that she got pregnant on purpose that first time—she confessed as much to me after one too many glasses of wine one night. She was shocked it only took once, but thrilled with herself. She said that all she ever wanted was to marry a doctor. But the reality wasn't what she expected and she became more and more unhappy.'

'Did you love her?'

Patrick hesitated. 'I adored the children, and she knew that. She always said I only cared about the children. I used to try and get back from the hospital in time to bath them and put them to bed, and then I'd go back to work again and sometimes stay out all night. It's hardly surprising my marriage collapsed.'

'She has to take responsibility for it, too,' Hayley said stoutly. 'She forced you into that position.'

'I shouldn't have married her, but that was just one of many mistakes I made with Carly, the first being the fact I took her to bed in the first place,' he said wearily. 'My second mistake was trusting her to take care of contraception—I take full responsibility for that. It was carelessly irresponsible of me, but I can't feel too sorry about it because if it hadn't happened, I wouldn't have Alfie.'

And she knew how much he adored his son. 'So what happened two years ago? Why did she suddenly walk out?'

Patrick gave a short laugh. 'It was a pretty memorable Christmas. Daniel proposed to Stella on Christmas Eve and we all opened a bottle of champagne and Carly had made an elaborate celebration lunch. Just as she put it on the table—'

'Your phone went and you had to go to the hospital?'

Patrick gave a faint smile. 'How did you guess? There was no way I could delegate it. This lady was having triplets and I was concerned about them.'

'Triplets? Wow.' Hayley slid closer to him. 'I've never delivered triplets. Sorry, go on.'

'When I arrived back from the hospital there was a taxi in the drive and Carly was waiting by the door with her bags packed. She'd already told the children she couldn't live with me any more.'

'Oh, God, Patrick, no.' Hayley's heart ached at what that must have done to Alfie, who would have been old enough to understand. 'And that was it? What about access? Seeing them?'

'She doesn't see them,' Patrick said coldly. 'Don't ask me why.'

Hayley tried to imagine a woman not wanting to see her children but failed. 'Do you think it's because she loved you so much she just had to make a clean break?'

Patrick gave her an odd look. 'That's the generous interpretation,' he said softly, lowering his head to kiss her gently. 'I don't think that. I think she wanted to start afresh and the children would have held her back. If you want my honest opinion, I'm not sure she ever really wanted children. I think they were just part of the lifestyle package she wanted for herself. An acquisition. Like a new kitchen,' he said wryly, 'only more work.'

Hayley felt a surge of outrage on his behalf. 'So you were left on your own on Christmas Eve—'

'Actually, no.' Patrick turned the hot water on again. 'Daniel was so freaked out that Carly had walked out, he broke off his engagement to Stella and he walked out, too.'

Hayley stared at him in disbelief and Patrick shrugged.

'Daniel and I had a very dysfunctional childhood. It was like living in a war zone most of the time. Dan was always nervous about marriage. In fact, it was an indication of just how much he loved Stella that she even got him to propose—and if Carly hadn't walked out that night they might have stayed together and not have wasted two years.'

'It scared him?'

'It reminded him that relationships are difficult, fragile things. So Stella and I were left on our own, both of us crushed.' He gave a faint smile. 'Unbelievable, really. Anyway, we joined forces that Christmas and put on a giant act, as you do when you have children—and somehow we got through.'

Hayley slid deeper under the warm water. 'So for two years you concentrated on your children and then you met me—and you thought you'd made the same mistake again.'

'No.' Patrick's tone was rough. 'I never thought that. What you and I share is entirely different and it has been from the first moment.'

'But I can see why you must have been so worried. Your children's lives have been shattered and you've just got things back together—and then I arrive. And you thought I was pregnant. You were worried I'd expect you to marry me.'

Patrick sighed. 'I admit I'm a bit sensitive to that issue. I overreacted.'

'And I can understand why.'

Patrick took her face in his hands. 'I'm glad you came, Hayley. I'm glad you stayed. Alfie already adores you. I've never seen him take to anyone so quickly.'

'Thank you for telling me the truth,' Hayley said softly. 'And for what it's worth, I don't think pregnancy is a reason for marriage either. My dad married my mum for the same reason and it was a disaster. There's no love there. Never was. And my stepsiblings really resent me and always have. It hasn't made for a happy family.'

'I can see why you didn't want to spend another Christmas with them.'

'I wanted to find *you*. I wanted to know whether what we'd shared was all in my imagination.'

'It wasn't in your imagination.'

'When you opened the door on Christmas Eve I wanted to die on the spot. All I kept thinking was, *I got this wrong,*' she confessed. 'I wanted to melt into a snowdrift. I realised then that for you it had just been a one-night stand.'

'That wasn't how it was and you didn't get it wrong—although I admit that seeing you on my doorstep was a shock.' Patrick stepped out of the bath and tugged a huge warm towel from the heated rail. 'That night in Chicago took me by surprise. I hadn't been with a woman for a long time. That should tell you something about the way I felt.'

Hayley followed him out of the bath and took the towel he offered her. 'Desperate?'

He made an exasperated sound and brought his mouth down on hers. 'Smitten,' he said against her lips. 'I was smitten, you silly girl.' He scooped her up again. 'But I was desperate, too.' He strode back into the bedroom and tumbled her onto the bed, the damp towels falling onto the floor. As he stroked her hair away from his face, his eyes were suddenly serious. 'I'm glad you came, Hayley. You have no idea how glad.'

'I thought you were panicking.'

'I never panic.' He wiped a droplet of water from her face. 'But I was worried—for all the reasons I just explained.'

'Well, I'm not pregnant, so you can relax.' Hayley stifled a yawn, thinking that she'd never felt so tired in her life.

Patrick pulled her into his arms. 'You poor thing—first jet-lag then a day at work and then—'

'Fantastic sex,' Hayley said sleepily, a grin on her face. 'Don't apologise for that bit.'

She was already drifting off as she felt him pull her into his arms. 'Sleep,' he said quietly. 'And tomorrow we can have some fun with the children.'

CHAPTER SEVEN

'So much for not working over Christmas.' Maggie handed Patrick a thick set of notes. 'What are you doing for New Year? Are you treating yourself to a night off?'

'Maybe. Depends on this place, doesn't it?' Patrick frowned at the list on his computer screen, careful not to reveal his plans for New Year's Eve. He was taking Hayley out. *They were going to have some time on their own.* 'Why is this clinic so busy?'

'Because everyone who was trying not to see you over Christmas now wants to see you.' Maggie was looking at him expectantly and Patrick lifted an eyebrow.

'What?'

Maggie grinned. 'You were right. She's very pretty. And fun.'

'*Who* is very pretty and fun?'

'Hayley, of course.'

'You fancy Hayley?'

'Patrick Buchannan, you are *not* going to change the subject.'

'I wasn't aware that I had.' Resigning himself to the inevitable, Patrick sighed. 'Go on, then. What do you want to know?'

'Is it serious between you?'

'She's my housekeeper, Maggie.'

'I've seen you looking at her, Patrick.'

'Obviously, I look at her.' Patrick kept his tone casual. 'She's worked every shift here for days.'

'It isn't the fact that you look at her it's the way you look at her. You're clearly crazy about her,' Maggie said happily. 'And she *adores* you, anyone can see that. And I just love happy endings.'

Patrick ran his hand over his jaw. 'Maggie, there is no happy ending—it's too soon. We haven't even…' *What?* What hadn't they done?

Spent time together.

Their relationship had been intense and concentrated and he knew better than anyone that sex was no basis for a long-term relationship.

But it wasn't just sex, was it?

The more he discovered about her, the more he liked and admired her.

Maggie folded her arms. 'I've known you for seven years. I knew you when you went through the trauma of Posy. I even made you tea when Carly left you. I deserve to enjoy the good bits with you.'

It was just the reminder he needed. 'Given that my wife walked out two years ago, I'm not likely to jump into another relationship in a hurry.'

'Your relationship with Carly was over a long time ago. And if something is right, it's right,' Maggie said stoutly. 'You don't need decades to know it's right.'

'Hayley arrived a week ago. A week!'

'But you met her a few weeks before that.'

'We spent one night together, that's all.' Patrick dropped his pen on the desk and exhaled sharply. 'Why am I discussing this with you?'

'Because I love you. And because I deserve some excitement in my life. What about Alfie and Posy? The children like her, I'm sure. She's such fun.'

Patrick had a mental image of Hayley playing hide and seek through the barn the day before. Alfie had been Robin Hood, Posy tripping over a long dress as Maid Marion and Hayley had been the wicked Sheriff of Nottingham. He smiled slightly at the memory. 'The children adore her.'

Maggie gave a wistful sigh. 'That's wonderful, Patrick. I'm so pleased for you. At last you've found someone.'

Patrick sent her a warning glance. 'Don't. I'm taking this slowly, all right? I'm not going to make another mistake.' *At least she wasn't pregnant.* That took the urgency out of it. They had no need to make any quick decisions about anything. They had time to let their relationship develop. He was going to take her out. 'If it works, great. If it doesn't, we'll part company.'

'You'd better not part company. She's a fantastic midwife, I can tell you that.' Maggie glanced at her watch. 'We're quiet on the labour ward so I've brought her down here to help you in clinic.'

Patrick greeted that news with mixed feelings. 'You think I'm going to feel romantic in clinic?'

'No, but the only other available midwife is Sandy and she's so in love with you she can't concentrate. Hayley actually seems to manage to be in love with you and still get her work done.'

'Oh, for goodness' sake.' *She was in love with him?* Patrick frowned. No. Of course she wasn't.

'And you care for her, too. I've never seen you as happy as you've been over the past week. Marry her, Patrick,' Maggie advised. 'Don't hesitate.'

'Maggie, I barely know her. She's been over here for less than a week.' *And it had been the most frustrating week of his life.* Apart from Christmas night when they'd been on their own without the children, they'd made a point of staying away from each other. And abstinence was driving Patrick nuts.

'Right. Enough of this.' Striving to hold onto his sanity, he changed the subject. 'Anything going on upstairs that I ought to know about?'

'Katie King's blood pressure went up so she's fed up because she knows you won't be sending her home.'

'She's right. I won't.' Patrick sat back in his chair. 'What else?'

'Vicky Thomas has gone into labour. She came in last night.'

'Vicky? Why didn't anyone call me?'

'Because you deserve the odd evening at home with your family,' Maggie said mildly. 'Tom sorted her out last night. He said he owed you that one. He adjusted her insulin. He said he was going to call you to discuss it.'

'He didn't. No doubt he's in new father mode. All right— I'll go up and see her when I've finished clinic. What about—?' Patrick broke off as someone tapped on the door and opened it.

It was Hayley, wearing the dark blue scrub suit that all the midwives wore, her dark hair fastened haphazardly in a twist at the back of her head. 'I'm sorry to interrupt you—I've just seen a woman who is thirty-six weeks and I'm worried about her. She says she has flu—she's been ill over Christmas.'

'Another one?' Maggie sighed and walked towards the door. 'The Lake District is simmering with germs at the moment. I still have three midwives off sick.'

Patrick was looking at Hayley, trying to keep his mind on the job. 'You're worried?'

'Yes. I don't think it's flu.'

'What are her symptoms?'

'Vomiting, epigastric pain, headache, shivering.'

'Vomiting? Could be norovirus,' Maggie murmured, but Hayley shook her head firmly.

'It could be, but I don't think it is. Her face is swollen, and she looks…' Hayley shrugged. 'I don't know—I just have a bad feeling. I think she could be showing signs of pre-eclampsia.'

Maggie checked the list in her hand. 'What's her name? Who is her consultant?'

'She isn't local. That's the other reason I'm worried. She told me that she was checked in clinic just before Christmas. They told her that a certain amount of swelling is normal, but her ankles are so bad she's having to wear her husband's slippers.'

Patrick stood up. 'She's staying up here?'

'With her family over Christmas. And in the last week she's put on 4.5 kilos.'

'It *is* Christmas,' Maggie said cautiously. 'I haven't dared stand on the scales myself, but I'm willing to bet that—'

'No.' Hayley interrupted her with a brisk shake of her head and Patrick found himself wondering how she could be so confident in her work and so under-confident in the rest of her life.

But that was the impact of her stepsiblings, he thought, knowing only too well what damage family could do.

'I know it's Christmas,' Hayley said, 'but I've questioned her carefully and she hasn't eaten much—she's been feeling too ill.'

Patrick was already by the door. 'Blood pressure?'

'She says it's been "high normal" for the past two months but the hospital didn't seem to think there was any reason to worry. It's 140 over 100.'

'Urine?'

'Trace of protein.'

'I'll take a look at her before I start clinic. Maggie, do we have an antenatal bed should I need one?'

Maggie sighed and pulled her notebook out of her pocket. 'Yes, because Tom is going to discharge his twins lady this morning once Paeds have checked the babies.'

'Good. I'll let you know if I'm going to need it.' Patrick followed Hayley out of the door and into the next room.

'Charlotte, this is Patrick Buchannan, the consultant.' Hayley picked up the notes and handed them to Patrick. 'Charlotte carries her own notes.'

'Which is helpful.' Patrick scanned the notes, picking out the information that he needed. 'Hayley, there's no record of a platelet count from the day assessment unit—could you call them and see if they did one? It might just not have made it into the notes.' He listened as Charlotte outlined what had happened, and by the time she reached the end of her story Hayley was back.

'They only do it on new hypertensives.'

Patrick glanced at the blood-pressure reading in the notes but decided not to worry Charlotte by verbalising his thoughts. 'All right, so we'll start fresh. I want to do an ultrasound now, and then I want to do a full blood count and check liver function and renal function.' While Hayley fetched the ultrasound machine, Patrick turned back to the woman on the bed. 'I agree with Hayley—I don't think this is a virus.'

Charlotte exchanged glances with her husband. 'But I saw my GP in London before I left and he just said there was a lot of it around—everyone is ill.'

'That's true,' Patrick said carefully, 'but in this case it's something different.'

'You think it's the baby?'

'Yes, I do. Have you heard of pre-eclampsia?'

Charlotte shook her head. 'No.'

'It's a condition that occurs only in pregnancy and it causes a number of changes in your body, including high blood pressure and a leakage of protein into your urine.'

'But I felt fine until just before Christmas—surely it's more likely to be a bug?'

'In its early stages it has no symptoms, but as the condition becomes more serious a woman is likely to experience changes—for example, headaches, stomachaches, vomiting, sometimes visual disturbances.'

Charlotte stared at him. 'I saw flashing lights for a short time yesterday evening.'

Patrick kept his expression neutral. 'Right. Well, that might be related. The swelling may also be related.'

'My doctor told me that no one takes any notice of swelling now—that it's normal for pregnant women.'

'It can be normal,' Patrick agreed, preparing the ultrasound machine. 'But it can also be a sign of problems. In fact, all those symptoms I just mentioned can be attributed to other causes, which is why the condition can be missed. I want to start by looking at the baby and the placenta, Charlotte. Has the baby been moving?' As he performed the scan he kept questioning her, his eyes on the screen. 'All right, there's the baby's head—and his heart—and that's the placenta.'

Charlotte peered anxiously at the screen. 'It all looks like a squirmy mess to me. Does the baby seem all right?'

'The baby seems fine.'

Charlotte's husband cleared his throat. 'So how do you treat pre-eclampsia?'

'You can't treat it. You can manage it...' Patrick pushed the ultrasound machine away from the bed '...but basically the condition ends when the baby is delivered.'

'But I have another month to go!'

Patrick sat on the edge of the bed. 'Charlotte, you need to

prepare yourself for the fact we may need to deliver the baby sooner than that. At thirty-six weeks, your baby is well developed and should have no problems at all. We have to balance all the factors.'

'All right. Obviously I want to do what's right for the baby,' Charlotte said nervously. 'So what happens now?'

Patrick stood up. 'I'm going to arrange for you to be transferred to the labour ward. Then I'm going to do a series of tests and when I have the results I'm going to decide what the best course of action is. In the meantime, I'm going to give you something to lower your blood pressure and Hayley is going to stay with you and monitor both you and the baby.'

Charlotte's eyes filled with tears but before Patrick could speak, Hayley slipped her arm round Charlotte's shoulders and gave her a hug. 'You poor thing, this must be such a shock for you,' she said soothingly, 'but it will all be fine. I'm going to take you upstairs and make the room cosy, and we can have a good chat. You can tell me everything about your Christmas.'

She was so tactile, Patrick thought to himself as he stood up and picked up the notes. As sensitive with the patients as she was with his children.

'One of my team is going to come and take some bloods from you,' he told Charlotte, 'and I'll be up to talk to you later. Hayley, let's give her some labetalol.' He scribbled on the drug chart and handed it to Hayley, who followed him out of the room.

'You're worried, too, I can tell. You're treating a borderline blood pressure.'

He gave a faint smile. 'I am. I'm sure my colleagues would frown with disapproval.'

'You think her condition is worse than it appears.'

'Yes, I do,' he said frankly. 'I think her blood pressure is going to rocket.' He heard her sigh with relief at his response and then she stood on tiptoe and impulsively kissed him on the cheek.

'I was afraid you might not take it seriously. That's what I love about you—I mean like,' she amended hastily. '*Obviously* I mean like, not love. What I *like* is that you follow your instincts and don't just rely on tests and machines.' She was delightfully flustered by her slip and Patrick wondered what she'd say if she knew that his instincts were prompting him to behave in a deeply unprofessional way. In fact, if he followed his instincts at the moment there was a strong chance he'd be arrested and struck off simultaneously.

Obstetrician interrupts busy clinic to have steamy session with midwife.

'We'll watch her for the next hour and see how she goes, but I'm ready to deliver that baby if it becomes necessary.' His eyes lingered on her face for a moment. 'You did well. It could easily have been a virus at first glance. What made you suspicious?'

'I'm hyper-sensitive to it. I've looked after a woman with eclampsia before.' Her eyes misted. 'We lost her, Patrick. The only time I've ever lost a patient. And she wasn't our patient—it was similar to this situation. She was visiting her sister in Chicago and she had a fit. It was awful. Truly awful. That poor father, the baby...'

Patrick reached out and touched her shoulder and then wished he hadn't because the chemistry was instantaneous. He stepped back from her at exactly the same moment she stepped back from him. 'Take her upstairs and get her on a monitor,' he said roughly. 'I'm going to start my clinic and once the results are back I'll come and see her. But if there is any change, call me.'

★ ★ ★

Patrick arranged the tests immediately. While they were waiting for the results, Hayley settled Charlotte into the room, trying to make her comfortable.

'I wish Patrick Buchannan was my consultant,' Charlotte said as she flicked through a magazine that Hayley had given her. 'He's very approachable, isn't he? And gorgeous to look at—not that I'm interested in that, of course.'

Hayley smiled as she checked the woman's blood pressure once more. 'I should think you have other things on your mind at this point.'

'Is he married?'

Hayley felt her heart miss a beat. 'No,' she said carefully, 'he isn't.' And that meant he was free to marry *her*. And no matter how hard she tried to rein in her mind, she had an average of a million fantasies an hour, all of which involved her walking down the aisle towards him. He'd be stunned by her beauty, of course, and for once she was going to manage *not* to fall over—

'Hayley?'

'Sorry? What did you say?' Blushing, Hayley pulled the CTG machine closer to the bed. 'I'm going to monitor you for a while, Charlotte, is that all right?' She must stop thinking about marriage! Technically she'd known him for about a week. And that one night, of course. But that probably didn't count because they hadn't done much talking. Either way, it had been a short time. They needed to get to know each other slowly, and maybe then—

'I asked you whether he's the sort of doctor who can't wait to do a Caesarean section.'

'No.' Hayley frowned. 'None of the doctors here are like that.'

Charlotte sighed. 'Back home I never see my actual consultant anyway. Every time I go it's someone else.'

'That happens sometimes.' Hayley didn't add that the 'someone else' who had seen her last time hadn't done their job properly.

'I wouldn't mind being one of Dr Buchannan's patients.'

'Mr Buchannan.' Silencing the wedding bells in her head, Hayley adjusted the machine. 'He's a surgeon, and we call surgeons Mr.'

'Oh—yes, of course. I knew that. I think.' Charlotte shifted slightly on the bed, looking at Hayley anxiously as the sound of the foetal heart pulsed around the room. 'Does that sound all right?'

'Sounds good.' Hayley checked the trace and then Charlotte's blood pressure.

'So how long have you worked here?'

'Actually, I arrived just before Christmas. Before that I was working in the States.'

'Oh. Are you here for good?'

Was she?

She hadn't actually given any thought to the future. Technically her job as their housekeeper was going to come to an end in a few days but no one had mentioned her moving out. And she couldn't imagine living anywhere other than High Fell Barn.

Perhaps the children would slowly just get used to the idea that she lived with them and from there it would be a natural progression for her and Patrick to get together.

Hayley was about to indulge in another brief wedding fantasy when Charlotte suddenly went rigid and started to fit.

'Oh, God, no, don't do this to me,' Hayley muttered, slamming her hand onto the crash button while supporting Charlotte to make sure she didn't fall off the bed.

The door swung open and Maggie ran in. 'What's happened?'

'She's fitting,' Hayley gritted, turning Charlotte onto her left side and reaching for the oxygen. 'Call Patrick and the anaesthetist and I need some mag sulphate.'

'I'll get the trolley.'

Maggie ran out of the room but she was back moments later and Patrick was with her.

Attaching Charlotte to a pulse oximeter, Hayley didn't even question how he'd arrived so fast. 'Her sats are 96.'

'How long has she been fitting?'

'Two minutes.'

'Let's give her a loading dose of 4 grams of mag sulphate. Have we got an infusion pump?'

They worked as a team, slick and professional as they tried to control the seizure.

'Foetal bradychardia,' Maggie said, watching the trace, and Patrick nodded.

'As soon as she's stable I'm going to do a Caesarean section. Gary?'

'Yes.' The anaesthetist was monitoring Charlotte's airway and breathing. 'Let's do it. Who is the next of kin?'

'Her husband, Andrew,' Hayley said. 'But he's just gone to phone his sister. They were staying with her over Christmas.'

'I'll go and sort out consent,' Patrick said, and Gary glanced at him.

'Didn't she show any early signs?'

Patrick checked Charlotte's patellar reflexes. 'Yes, although some of her readings were borderline. Her blood pressure was never quite high enough to ring alarm bells. But they ignored mild proteinurea, which wouldn't have happened in my unit.'

Gary lifted an eyebrow. 'Are you going to call them?'

'Yes.'

Surprised by Patrick's unusually terse tone, Hayley glanced at him and realised that he was really angry.

'Hayley is the hero of the hour,' he said quietly. 'She spotted it in clinic.'

Embarrassed to suddenly be the focus of attention, Hayley blushed and the anaesthetist smiled.

'Can we offer you a permanent job?'

'Oh— Well...' Hayley gave an embarrassed laugh, aware of Patrick's swift glance, but she was spared the trouble of answering by the arrival of Patrick's registrar and the rest of the team.

It was only later—hours after Patrick had safely delivered a baby girl and Charlotte was stable—that she had time to think about that remark.

A permanent job?

Stay here—permanently?

With Patrick. And his gorgeous children...

'Hayley?' One of the other midwives put her head round the staffroom door. 'Mr Buchannan wants you in his office. I don't know what you've done, but you'd better start thinking up your excuses. He looked serious.'

'OK, thanks.' Sure that she'd handed over Charlotte's care without missing anything out, Hayley walked to Patrick's office. Oddly nervous, she tapped on the door and walked in.

'You want me?' Oh, help, why did everything always come out wrong? 'I mean—I was told you wanted to see me?' Her cheeks were hot and he stood up in a fluid movement and strode towards her, slamming the door shut behind her with the flat of his hand.

'You were right the first time. I want you.' His mouth came down on hers and he kissed her with erotic purpose, his lips as skilled as ever as he aroused her to a state of screaming ecstasy in less time than it took her to gasp his name.

Desperate after several days when she hadn't been allowed to touch him, Hayley melted against him, his kiss muffling her gasp of shocked pleasure as his hands slid to her thighs.

'Patrick—' She tried to say that they probably shouldn't be doing this *here* but her mouth refused to do anything except kiss him back.

It was hot, desperate and frantic. When he stripped off the flimsy trousers of her scrub suit Hayley didn't protest, and when she felt him hard and ready against her, she gave a low moan and dropped her hands to his zip.

He entered her with no preliminaries but she was so ready for him it was as if they'd spent hours indulging in foreplay. And perhaps they had, she thought as her vision blurred. They'd been stepping around each other, trying not to do anything that would unsettle the children—trying not to touch.

But they were touching now. Hungrily. Ravenously seeking their fill of each other, their bodies joining in almost animal desperation. Overtaken by sensations so intense they were almost painful, Hayley felt her body reach its peak and he joined her in the same place, his strong fingers digging hard into her thighs, his mouth silencing her cries.

Breathless, her mind blank, Hayley dropped her head against his shoulder, and suddenly became aware of their surroundings. His computer screen flickered on the desk and somewhere in the distance she heard the wail of an ambulance siren.

'I've been wanting to do that all week.' Patrick's voice was low and rough and he scooped her face into his hands and kissed her gently. 'Sorry. It was a bit fast.'

'No problem,' she muttered faintly, her eyes on his mouth. 'Perhaps we can do it slowly, er, next time. When that midwife said you wanted to see me I thought I'd done something.'

'You have done something.' He kissed her again, his mouth lingering on hers. 'You've driven me wild. Living with you and not being able to touch you is starting to have an adverse effect on my mental health. What are the chances of you being able to sneak into my bedroom without the children finding out?'

'Sneaking isn't something I do well,' Hayley confessed as she adjusted her clothing. 'I have a habit of banging into things and falling over, remember? To sneak you have to be stealthy and graceful, and that isn't me.'

'I don't care.'

'Patrick, you do care,' she said gently, glancing towards the door, relieved that no one had needed the consultant in the past fifteen minutes. 'You don't want to hurt or unsettle your children and neither do I.'

'No.' Patrick raked his fingers through his hair. 'So we'll do this slowly. Tomorrow I'm taking you out to dinner. You can wear a dress that I'm not going to remove and we'll have a conversation. I'll book a babysitter for the kids—'

'Can't we have dinner at home? Alfie hates Vampire Lips. I'll cook us something special and you can open a nice bottle of something from your cellar.'

Patrick shook his head. 'No. I want to spend some time with you without the children.'

'I love the children,' Hayley protested, and Patrick lifted his eyebrow.

'You don't want to be alone with me?'

'Of course I do.' She blushed. 'It's just that Posy looked as though she was starting a cold this morning so I don't want to leave her.'

He held her gaze for a long time. 'All right, this is what we'll do. If she's ill, we won't go out. But if she's fine, then I have a surprise for you. And you'll need to dress up.'

Hayley brightened. 'Dress up as in lipstick and heels? That sounds fun.' Happiness bubbled inside her as she reached for the door. It was going to be a lovely evening. He wanted time with her. He *liked* her. Life was perfect.

As she went back to the staffroom to change, she couldn't hold back her excitement. He hadn't mentioned that her contract was almost up. He hadn't suggested that she look for alternative accommodation. Far from it. He was as desperate for her as she was for him. And now he'd asked her to dinner.

Perhaps he was going to suggest that she just carry on living with them. They'd make plans for the future...

'Fabulous restaurant,' Hayley breathed. 'How on earth did you manage to get a seat right by the window? Don't tell me—you delivered the chef's baby.'

'Actually, yes. Have you met the waiter before?' Patrick watched as the blushing member of staff retreated to the kitchen.

'No. Never. But he was very friendly, wasn't he?' Hayley took a sip of champagne and gave a low moan of pleasure. 'Oh, that tastes delicious. What a great idea to get a taxi so that we can have champagne.'

'Given that you're so intimate with our local taxi drivers, I'm surprised you didn't invite him to join us.'

'He wouldn't have wanted to. Jack's popping over to his daughter's for a few hours because she lives near here, but he'll be back to pick us up when we call.' She smiled at the waiter who was back with a basket of warm, freshly baked bread. 'Mmm. They smell good. I'll have the one with poppy seeds, please. Yum.'

The smitten waiter gave her two and Patrick managed not to smile until the man was safely back in the kitchen. 'Jack needs to watch out. I think he has competition. Maybe you shouldn't have worn that dress.'

There was a flash of insecurity in her eyes. 'You don't like the dress?'

'I love the dress,' he drawled. 'And so does every other man in the room.'

Her cheeks dimpled. 'Really?' She glanced down at herself self-consciously. 'Alfie liked it.'

'Alfie likes everything about you.' Patrick reached for his glass. 'To us.'

Hayley tapped her glass against his. 'To us.'

'Thank you for cooking us the best turkey we've eaten in years...' he kept his eyes on hers, unable to look away '...and for giving us such a happy Christmas.'

'I had a happy Christmas, too.'

'You didn't miss being with your family?'

Hayley took a sip of champagne and put her glass down. 'Families aren't always idyllic, are they? I used to hope that things would change as we all grew older but nothing ever did. I even tried changing myself to be more the way they wanted me to be, but it didn't work.'

'Why would you want to change?'

'Because I irritate them.' Hayley sat back as the waiter placed her starter on the table with a flourish. 'That looks delicious, thank you.' She beamed at him and Patrick watched as she picked up her fork.

'How could you possibly irritate them?'

'Just by being me.' She speared a prawn. 'I'm so different from them. They see me as a clumsy idiot who laughs too much and talks too much. And they're probably right. But it's impossible for me to be silent and academic. I've tried. It doesn't work. And it's exhausting trying to be something you're not.'

'Don't put yourself down. The things you tried to change about yourself are the things that make you special.' He studied her across the table and found himself noticing new things about her—like the fact her eyelashes were long and dense and her lower lip was slightly fuller than her top lip. 'Aren't they proud of what you've achieved professionally?'

'They don't think I've achieved anything professionally.' Her voice was matter-of-fact. 'That's the point. They think I've wasted my life. They're always asking me when I'm going to get a "proper" job.'

Patrick felt a rush of anger towards her family. 'I think you've achieved tremendous success in your professional life.'

'It depends on how you define success, doesn't it?' She ate another prawn. 'Is success about making a difference to people's lives, or is it about how much money you accumulate?'

'Money isn't a measure of success so much as an indication of career choice.' Patrick discovered that he'd finished his starter without even noticing that he was eating. 'If you pick a career like nursing or teaching you're never going to be rich, but that doesn't mean you aren't successful.'

She smiled at him. 'And that's why I'm eating dinner with you and not them,' she said lightly. 'Because you don't make me feel as though my entire life has been wasted.'

'Families can be tough.'

'Well, that's true. And from what you've told me, yours was no picnic either.'

They ate and talked and, by the time midnight arrived and the New Year had been toasted, Patrick discovered that he'd told her more about himself than he'd ever told anyone before. Certainly more than Carly.

Studying Hayley's smiling face as she told him a ridiculous story about one of her friends, he realised that comparisons with Carly were inappropriate.

There *was* no comparison.

When had Carly made him laugh like this? Had Carly ever asked if he should check his mobile phone in case there was a message from the hospital?

Aware that the restaurant had emptied and they were the last couple still talking, Patrick retrieved his phone from the pocket of his jacket and called the taxi, feeling nothing but regret that the evening had to end.

He wanted her to keep talking. He wanted to know *everything* about her.

It was the champagne, he told himself as he watched Hayley engage in conversation with the man who fetched them their coats.

She was a beautiful woman and good company.

It was natural to enjoy being with her.

What man wouldn't?

CHAPTER EIGHT

I'M IN love, I'm in love, I'm in love.

Hayley bounced into the antenatal clinic and Maggie looked up from the desk and raised her eyebrows.

'How much?'

'Sorry?'

'How much have you won? I'm assuming from the look on your face you've won the lottery.' Maggie studied her face and started to laugh. 'Only in this case I suspect the jackpot is a six-foot-two, super-sexy obstetrician called Patrick. Am I right?'

'Don't be ridiculous.' But it was impossible to keep her happiness inside her and Hayley virtually danced round the desk to give Maggie a hug. 'Oh, Maggie, I've never felt like this in my life before. I want to smile and smile. And I...actually I can't put it into words.'

Maggie laughed and hugged her back. 'That's probably a good thing because clinic is about to start.'

'That's why I'm here. The labour ward is really quiet and Jenny said you needed some help down here.' Hayley pulled away from her and realised that her hair hadn't survived the hug. With a grin, she pulled the clasp from her hair, scooped it up and fastened it in her usual haphazard fashion. 'I'll be your wing man. Have I wished you happy New Year yet? Happy New Year! Where do you want me to start?'

Maggie picked up a set of notes from the pile. 'You can see Olivia. It should be routine but you know the drill anyway.

Any problems, yell. Patrick's registrar is doing the clinic because the boss is in some meeting or other. But I expect you know that.'

'Actually, I do, because this morning he was wearing one of his gorgeous suits.' Remembering how good he'd looked as he'd left the house, Hayley smiled dreamily and then pulled herself together. 'Sorry. Where is Olivia?'

'Room 3. Good luck.' Maggie gave a wry smile. 'Olivia talks almost as much as you do.'

After five minutes with the young woman, Hayley was forced to agree.

Olivia had regaled her with everything from her disastrous Christmas to the agonies of morning sickness.

'Honestly, you have no idea.' The woman rolled her eyes. 'I didn't know I'd feel this bad. Other women seem to sail through pregnancy, but I feel as though I've picked up some vile bug that doesn't want to shift.'

'It's like that sometimes,' Hayley murmured sympathetically, checking the height of Olivia's uterus and recording it in the notes. She kept thinking about her evening with Patrick. *The way he'd looked at her across the table.* 'Hopefully it will pass soon and you'll start to feel better.'

'I hope so. I think maybe it's my punishment for all the drinks I had before I knew I was pregnant. This whole thing has come as a shock,' Olivia confessed. 'I'm embarrassed to admit this—*I mean, how stupid can a girl be?*—but I didn't even suspect I could be pregnant. It's not as if we were trying or anything. And I'm not the sort that marks my period on a calendar every month, you know? I'm just not obsessed with that sort of thing.'

'I'm the same,' Hayley said absently, recording the blood-pressure reading and comparing it with the time before, her head somewhere else entirely.

He'd said she was special.

'It just sort of hit me one night. I thought to myself, My period is late. And then I worked out when my last one was and I thought, Oh…' The girl used a word that made Hayley start.

'I can imagine it must have been a bit of a shock.'

'You have no idea.' Olivia rolled her eyes heavenwards. 'I keep telling Mick—he's my boyfriend—well, at least I noticed I was pregnant before I actually delivered. You do hear of women who actually deliver the baby before they find out. I wasn't quite as clueless as that.'

'It isn't always straightforward,' Hayley said tactfully. 'Some women do still have a light period for the first few months and that can delay them realising that they're pregnant.'

'Oh, that didn't happen to me.' Olivia slipped her feet back into her shoes and stood up. 'I had no period at all, but I was basically just too busy to notice. If you're not expecting to be pregnant, you're not looking, are you? I bet you're not like that. You midwives must be really up on stuff like that. I bet no midwife has ever had an unplanned baby. I bet you tick off that date in your calendar every month, just to be sure.'

'I don't go that far.' Hayley laughed. 'But I always know when—' When she was due. And…

Oh, God, she'd missed a period.

The realisation hit her along with a wave of almost crippling nausea and panic.

She'd missed a period. She'd missed a period.

'What's the matter?' Olivia stared at her in alarm. 'Is something wrong? You said everything seemed fine. Are you worried about the baby's growth?'

'No. Nothing. I just...' Frantically she searched for some explanation that would satisfy the patient. 'I just remembered that I had to ring the lab about some results. Not yours. Someone else's.'

How could she not have realised?

She'd been so affronted when Patrick had assumed she was pregnant, it hadn't even occurred to her that she *might* be pregnant. She desperately wanted to go through her diary and check the dates, but Olivia was still chatting.

Somehow Hayley managed to finish the conversation and then she hurried to the desk. 'Maggie, I'm sorry but I have to go to the staffroom for a minute.' Panic engulfed her like rolling clouds and she barely registered Maggie's concerned look before she fled from the department, her heart beating and tears stinging the back of her eyes.

Please, no. Please let her be wrong. Let her have miscalculated, missed a week. Please, please...

The staffroom on the labour ward was empty and she rummaged through her bag and found her diary. Her fingers were shaking so badly it took ages to find November and check the date she needed to know. And as soon as she saw it, she dropped the book back into her bag and stared blankly at the chipped paint on the wall. She didn't need to count twenty-eight days to know that her period was now over a week late. She'd lost track.

She didn't even need to do a pregnancy test.

She knew.

And she also knew that her relationship with Patrick was over.

Pregnancy was no basis for a relationship, was it?

He'd made that clear to her.

And she was very definitely pregnant.

★ ★ ★

'What do you mean, she just ran out of clinic?' Patrick frowned. 'Was she feeling ill or something?'

'I don't know. Maybe.' Maggie shrugged helplessly. 'Actually, I think she looked more upset than sick, but she didn't say anything to me.'

'Well, that's unusual,' Patrick drawled, 'because Hayley always tells everyone what's on her mind.'

'That's what I love about her,' Maggie said stoutly, and Patrick gave a faint smile.

'And that's why you can stop worrying. As soon as I track her down, she'll tell me what's wrong and we can fix it. At least with Hayley you know where you are.'

'Yes.' Maggie looked at him doubtfully. 'Yes, you're right. Go and find her, Patrick.'

Patrick glanced at the clock. 'I'm due in Theatre in thirty minutes. I have a gynae list.'

'Thirty minutes is ages…' Maggie pushed him towards the door '…and Hayley talks quickly. Go, Patrick. She really did look upset and I'm worried about her.'

Patrick took the stairs to the labour ward, mentally listing the things that could be wrong with Hayley.

They'd had a wonderful evening the night before, but it had been a late night. Was she tired?

Had a patient been rude to her?

Had a member of staff offended her?

Or maybe she was feeling poorly. There were certainly plenty of people off sick with flu.

Pushing open the door of the staffroom, he saw Sally sitting there, talking to Tom.

'Hi, Patrick.' Sally gave a sheepish smile. 'I was bored with the ward so I came up here for a change. How are you doing?'

'Fine, thanks.' Patrick barely registered her. 'Have either of you seen Hayley?'

'No. Why?' Tom frowned. 'Aren't you supposed to be operating?'

'I'm on my way there now.' Patrick paused, frustrated that he hadn't been able to find her. 'If you see Hayley, will you tell her I was looking for her?'

Sally winked at him. 'We certainly will.'

Hayley sat in the toilet, staring down at the test in her hand. It had taken her less than fifteen minutes to grab her coat, sprint to the nearest chemist and buy the test.

And now she was staring at the irrefutable proof that she was pregnant.

She was having Patrick's baby.

How ironic, she thought numbly, that having his baby would mean the end of their relationship. And she knew that it would. Their relationship was too new, too fragile. And given Patrick's past...

It was the cruellest irony.

She couldn't tell him.

She had to keep it from him or he'd feel obliged to do the same thing he'd done with Carly. He was a responsible guy, wasn't he? He'd want to do 'the right thing'.

Only what *was* the right thing?

Marriage certainly hadn't been right for him.

And it hadn't been right for her mother either.

And what about the children? Alfie, Posy and—Hayley rested a hand low on her abdomen—*her baby.*

She knew better than anyone that stepfamilies could be a disaster. She thought of the resentment that her stepsiblings had felt when she'd arrived in their family. Did she want to do that to three more children? Alfie and Posy liked her, she knew that. But this was something different entirely. This was *huge*.

She had to make a decision. And she *hated* decisions. And of all the decisions she'd ever had to make in her life, this was the hardest.

Should she tell him? Yes, of course she should. He had a right to know. But if she told him, he'd talk her out of going and it would be for all the wrong reasons.

He didn't want her to be pregnant, she knew that.

Remembering his face when he'd opened the door to her on Christmas Eve, Hayley gave a choked sob. He'd braced himself for hearing that she was pregnant and it was impossible to forget his relief when she'd told him she wasn't. So, knowing that, what choice did she have?

Obviously he adored his children, but he'd made it clear that he didn't want another relationship that was held together only by a pregnancy.

So the right thing to do—the only decision—was to leave.

Pretend their relationship just wasn't working.

And she had no idea how she was supposed to do that convincingly.

How was she supposed to pretend to be miserable?

As the tears dripped onto her hand she almost laughed at herself. She *was* miserable. Horribly miserable. She wouldn't have to act at all. She just needed to not tell him the real reason. For once in her life she had to keep her thoughts locked inside her.

Hayley spread icing on the top of the cup cakes and watched with a lump in her throat as Posy carefully pressed a chocolate button into the centre of each one.

'That's great, Posy,' she said huskily, leaning forwards and hugging the little girl tightly. Her blonde curls smelled of shampoo and the thought of leaving her hurt Hayley almost as much as the thought of leaving Patrick.

'Yum.' Alfie reached out a hand and stole a cake. 'Just one more.' He took a large bite out of the cake and stole a look at Hayley. 'Aren't you going to tell me off? Normally you only let me eat one before tea. You're not acting like yourself.'

She wasn't acting like herself? Obviously she needed to concentrate harder on what she'd usually do. If she wasn't even able to fool the children, how was she going to manage with Patrick?

Before she had time to consider that challenge, she heard his key in the door and dipped her head, pretending to help Posy with the cakes, panic racing through her. He was home really early, which was just going to make the evening longer.

She hoped that for once in her life everything she was feeling wasn't written all over her face.

'Hayley, I've been trying to catch up with you all day.' Patrick slung his coat over the back of the chair and strode across to her. 'Where were you?'

'All over the place. In clinic, then on the labour ward.' Implying that her day had been one mad rush, Hayley smiled at him briefly and then turned her attention back to the chocolate buttons. Never had she paid so much attention to decorating a cake. 'You must have just missed me. How was your theatre list? Any dramas?' *Did she sound normal?* Was she doing OK?

'No dramas.' Patrick kissed Posy on the head, his eyes still on Hayley. 'Are you feeling all right? Maggie said you weren't too good earlier.'

'She's definitely *not* herself,' Alfie said firmly, 'because I've eaten five cakes and she hasn't even noticed.'

Hayley bit back a gasp of horror. Five? He'd eaten *five?* 'I assumed you must be hungry,' she said calmly, desperately hoping he wasn't going to be sick. 'And dinner won't be ready for another twenty minutes. Anyway, you're old enough to judge whether or not you're going to spoil your appetite.'

'I'm only a day older than yesterday,' Alfie said with faultless logic, 'and you didn't think I was old enough to judge then.'

'Well, I'm not going to be around for much longer,' Hayley said brightly, 'so it's good for you to learn not to eat too many cakes in one go.'

Her words were greeted by a stunned silence.

'Wh-what do you mean?' Alfie gaped at her in horror. 'What do you mean you're not going to be around for much longer? Why not? Where are you going?'

'You advertised for a housekeeper for two weeks over Christmas and New Year.' Hayley started to put the cakes carefully into the tin. 'The two weeks is up in a few days' time.'

'But that was before we knew you. Now you're here, we don't want you to leave after two weeks. We want you to stay for ever!' Alfie was frantic. 'Tell her, Dad! Tell her we want her to stay for ever.'

Hayley knew she ought to speak but the lump in her throat was so huge she knew she was going to embarrass herself.

'We'd like her to stay,' Patrick said carefully. 'Of course we would. She knows that.' His eyes were on her face and Hayley dug her nails into the palms of her hands, wishing she'd come up with a more solid plan for dealing with their protests. But she honestly hadn't known the children would care so much. And as for Patrick…

He wouldn't want her to stay if he knew the truth.

'It's been fantastic.' Somehow she managed to form the words. 'Really—the best Christmas ever. But it was only ever temporary. And so is the work on the unit. I need to get myself a proper job. And I need to visit my family.'

'But your family are mean to you. That's why you didn't want to go there for Christmas.' Alfie was appalled. 'Why would you want to visit them?'

'Well…' Oh, why on earth hadn't she thought this through? 'Nobody's family is perfect. Now Christmas is over, I ought to see them.'

'You can go and see them and then come straight back.' Alfie looked at his father. 'Dad?'

Patrick stirred. 'Hayley is free to do whatever she wants to do,' he said gruffly, and Alfie gave a choked sob, flung his cake onto the floor and stormed out of the room.

As always, Posy followed, dragging her velvet comforter behind her. 'Alfie sad.'

Hayley stood up immediately, intending to follow, but Patrick took her arm.

'Wait. What's this all about? Why would you want to leave?'

She gave a tiny shrug. 'It was only ever for two weeks and, let's face it, you didn't even want that! It was Alfie's advert.'

'Alfie's advert ceased to be an issue a long time ago. Hayley.' He frowned down at her. 'Tell me what's wrong. Has someone upset you?'

'Gosh, no!' She winced as she heard her falsely bright tone. She wasn't even fooling herself, so how did she hope to fool him? 'Why would you think that? Who could possibly have upset me? Everyone is great. No, I just think it's time to move on. It's been fantastic, Patrick. A fantastic Christmas. This barn is just the perfect place, it's just been—'

'Fantastic. Yes, I got that. You've said it three times already. What I really want to hear is all the things you're *not* saying.'

Patrick's mouth tightened and his eyes were suddenly searching. 'Is this about us?'

'Us?' How was she supposed to respond to that? OK, so definitely *not* like Hayley. She tried to work out what a twenty-first-century woman would say. What would Diane, her stepsister, say? 'It was fun while it lasted, Patrick. But we both knew it wasn't practical in the long term. We both have our own lives to lead. You have the children.'

'I thought you liked the children.' Patrick's tone was cautious. 'I was under the impression you liked them quite a lot.'

'They're gorgeous!' *Rubbish answer, Hayley,* she thought to herself. *You're thinking like yourself, not like Diane.* With a huge effort she forced herself to say words that were so alien it was almost impossible to voice them. 'But I don't know how you do it, Patrick. I mean, you have no time to yourself. No time to chill out. They're always *there!*'

And she loved that. *She really loved that.*

'Yes.' His voice was strangely flat and he released her suddenly. 'They are always there.'

'And I suppose I'm just used to being single. Needing my space.' Oh, God, she was useless at this. Utterly useless. And she needed to get out of here before she blew it totally. 'Well, anyway, talking of space—I must go and take a bath. A long soaky bath. It's been a long day.'

His gaze didn't shift from her face and Hayley was suddenly terrified that she had *Pregnant* written on her forehead.

He was an obstetrician, for goodness' sake, and a skilled one at that. What if he could diagnose pregnancy from a distance?

Why didn't he say something?

She carried on babbling. 'I might not join you this evening if you don't mind.' For a start, she wasn't sure she could make it through the evening without sobbing, and on top of that she needed to start acting like a woman who found children a bit much. 'I'm in the middle of a really good book. I might just sprawl on the bed—you know, veg out, generally relax and do nothing.'

Still he didn't respond and still his gaze didn't shift from her face. It was as if he was looking for something.

'The casserole should be ready by now and I did baked potatoes.' Her voice tailed off under the intensity of his blue gaze. 'So, I'll say goodnight, then, just in case I don't see you later.'

She slunk towards the door, heard Alfie crying and fought a desperate urge to go to him. How could she go to him when she'd just claimed that she wanted a child-free evening? But the fact that she couldn't comfort the little boy—the fact that she was the cause of his tears—made everything even worse.

She was doing it for them, Hayley reminded herself miserably when she eventually slid into the bath and let the tears fall freely.

She was doing it for them.

In the long run, it would be better.

CHAPTER NINE

'SHE's leaving? Why would she leave? *What did you do to her?*'
Maggie stood in front of Patrick's desk like a sergeant major
in a court-martial.

'Maggie.' He dragged his gaze from the computer screen.
'I don't have time for this now.'

'Then make time, Patrick Buchannan, because if you let
that girl leave this unit, I swear I'll resign, too!'

Patrick sighed. 'I know she's a good midwife, but I can't
force her to take a job here.'

'But she's leaving because of you! And I want to know why!'

'I don't know why!' Exploding with tension and frustration, Patrick rose to his feet and paced to the far end of his
office. 'Damn it, Maggie, *I don't know why!*'

Maggie looked startled. 'You don't? I assumed—'

'You assumed what? That we'd had a row?' Patrick gave a
bitter laugh and turned to stare out of the window. The day
was bleak and cold and totally in keeping with his current
mood. 'I wish we had had a row. At least then I would have
known what it was about. But this is—'

'Something happened yesterday in the clinic.' Maggie sat
down in Patrick's chair, a frown on her face. 'She came bouncing in, told me that she was in love with you and then she—'

'Wait a minute.' Patrick turned, his gaze sharp. 'She told
you she was in love with me?'

'Yes. Well, virtually. Yes, definitely. Patrick, she's *crazy* about you. Surely you don't need me to tell you that.'

Patrick considered the evidence. 'Up until last night I would have agreed with you, but...' he shook his head '...she virtually said she'd had enough of living her life around the children. That it was a massive sacrifice.'

'Hayley adores children,' Maggie scoffed, 'and she especially adores yours. She talks about nothing else. All day we have to listen to tales of what Posy has drawn and the funny things Alfie has said. She's worse than you are.'

'Thanks,' Patrick said dryly, and Maggie grinned.

'No offence meant. But what I'm saying is that Hayley is as crazy about your children as she is about you.'

'Maybe, but that doesn't mean that living with them constantly isn't a strain. They're full on, Maggie. They're all over her. In her bed, wrapped around her in the evenings—she can't even go to the bathroom without Posy banging on the door.' Patrick sighed. 'Last night Alfie was crying and she didn't go to him.'

Maggie looked startled. 'She let him cry?'

'Well...' Patrick ran his hand over the back of his neck '...she left the room. Said she needed a bath or something. Wanted to read her book.'

'In other words, she couldn't bear to hear him crying and not comfort him.' Maggie folded her arms. 'If you ask me, Hayley thinks she has to leave and she's doing everything she can to make it seem as though she wants to.'

'What?' Patrick was totally confused. 'Is that female logic? Because if so, could it please come with a translation? I have no idea what you're talking about.'

'For an incredibly intelligent man, you can be very dim.' Maggie stood up and walked across the room until she was standing in front of him. 'Hayley is in love with you. That is a fact. I know you haven't known each other very long, I know it's all been a bit whirlwind, but she is definitely in love with you. She is also in love with your children. If she's talking about leaving then it's because something has happened.' She frowned. 'Or maybe because something hasn't happened. Did you propose to her?'

'Of course I didn't propose to her!' Patrick looked at his colleague in incredulous disbelief. 'Maggie, I can't believe we're having this conversation.'

'Well, you obviously weren't getting anywhere by yourself. Could that be the problem? Have you told her that you love her?'

'I— No, I haven't because I don't even know that I...' Patrick rubbed his fingers across his forehead. 'Maggie, I've been married before—'

'To a woman you didn't love. And that was *entirely* different.'

'I've only known Hayley for a few weeks.'

'And in that time you have more feeling for her than you ever did for your wife.'

Stunned, Patrick let his hand drop. 'How do you know that?'

'Because Christmas is a bad time of year for you, my friend,' Maggie said softly. 'And suddenly, this year, it's all different. You're smiling. You're relaxed. Your children are smiling and relaxed. Ask yourself why, Patrick. And then do something about it. Quickly. Before it's too late.'

'I'll go and prepare the pool for you, Ruth,' Hayley said. 'You might like to take a walk up the corridor and back again. It's good to keep moving at this stage of your labour. I'll only be in the room across the way, but if you need anything, just press the buzzer.'

Feeling exhausted and slightly sick, she took refuge in the empty room opposite.

As she prepared the pool, she pondered on the fact that this was her last shift.

She really ought to ring her mother and warn her that she was coming home tomorrow, but she couldn't face the conversation.

Neither could she face the thought of moving out of Patrick's house.

Of leaving the children.

Tears filled her eyes and she tested the temperature of the water, barely able to see the thermometer. Oh, this was ridiculous! If this was what being pregnant was like, she'd better buy shares in a tissue company.

'Hayley?' Patrick's voice came from the doorway and she realised with a start of horror that she'd been so preoccupied in her own misery that she hadn't even heard the door open.

How long had he been standing there?

Did he know she was crying?

'Just doing the pool, Patrick,' she said brightly. 'Did you want me?'

Oh, for goodness' sake, she'd done it again! Used the wrong words at absolutely the wrong time.

'Yes, I want you.' His tone was firm. Steady. 'I thought we'd already established that. I also thought we'd established that you want me, too.'

Hayley blinked back tears and concentrated on the surface of the pool. 'Patrick, this really isn't a good time. We should—'

'I have something to say to you and I want you to listen.'

Hayley froze. He was probably going to tell her that she'd upset Alfie. 'Honestly, I really don't— Can we talk later?'

'No.' He was right behind her and he drew her to her feet, turning her so that she faced him. 'There are things I want to say to you, and they can't wait. I love you, Hayley.' His voice soft, Patrick took her face in his hands and forced her to look at him. 'I love you, sweetheart.'

No, not that.

He couldn't be saying that to her. Not here. *Not now.*

Before she'd discovered she was pregnant, *I love you* were the words she'd been desperate to hear, but now they were the words she was desperate *not* to hear because hearing them just made everything so much worse.

'Patrick—'

'I haven't finished. There's something else I want to say to you.' He let his hands drop and when he lifted them again he was holding a velvet box. 'I want you to marry me. I want you to be my wife.'

Her hands still wet from the pool water, Hayley stared at the box in stunned silence and then at his face.

She stared into those blue eyes and then back down at the box. 'You— I...'

With a soft laugh he opened the box and removed a ring. A beautiful diamond solitaire. 'Marry me, Hayley.' He took the ring out of the box, slid it onto her finger—and she didn't even stop him.

For a moment—just for a moment—she wanted to know what that ring would look like on her finger. *She wanted to dream.*

And then she remembered that dreams only happened while you were asleep. That was why they were called dreams.

And she was wide awake.

'I can't marry you, Patrick,' she said in a choked voice. 'I can't do that.' She sensed his shock.

'I know it's a bit sudden,' he said carefully. 'I know we haven't known each other that long—but it's right, Hayley. You know it is. Say yes.'

'I can't, Patrick.' She stared down at the ring he'd placed on her finger. It sparkled under the lights, the diamond winking at her, as if taunting her with what she couldn't have. 'I can't marry you, Patrick.'

'Is this because of what I said to you the day you arrived? I know I was tactless and insensitive.' He gave a rueful smile. 'I know I upset you by assuming you must be pregnant—'

'Patrick, I *am* pregnant.' Her voice rose. '*I am pregnant,* OK? I'm pregnant, pregnant, pregnant. I'm having your baby. So *now* do you understand that it's all hopeless? All of it. And it can't ever work.' Tears falling down her cheeks, she tugged at the ring—*the ring that had been on her finger for less than two minutes*—and pushed it blindly into his hand.

She waited for him to say something but he was silent and his silence was like a vicious blow.

What had she expected?

She'd *known* what his reaction would be.

'Please.' She gave up waiting for him to speak. 'Please—do me a favour and don't come back on the labour ward while I'm here. I just can't— I need to pull myself together— I won't be unprofessional.' She wiped her eyes on the back of her hand and made for the door. 'As soon as this shift is over, I'll go home and pack. I'm sorry, Patrick. I'm sorry for all of it.'

Ruth didn't deliver until the early hours of the morning and Hayley stayed with her, offering support, enjoying her moment of happiness, which was even more poignant given how thrilled Ruth's husband was.

Afterwards she drank a cup of tea on her own in the staff-room, wondering what would happen when her time came.

Would she be alone? Or would some kind midwife be willing to sit with her through the night while she laboured?

It was still dark outside when she finally arrived back at Patrick's barn and Hayley crept up to her bedroom, packed her one small suitcase and lay fully clothed on top of the bed until it seemed like a reasonable time to call a taxi.

Maybe she was being cowardly, leaving while everyone was still in bed, but she couldn't face an emotional departure.

She'd written letters to the children and left them on the table in the kitchen. She'd tried to write a letter to Patrick but after about fifty attempts she'd given up.

At some point they'd have to talk, of course. They needed to sort out what they were going to do. He'd want access to his child and she wanted that, too. She didn't want their child growing up not knowing his or her father.

And she'd do the right thing. Make it as easy as she could for everyone—try and get a job close by. Not too local—that would be asking too much—but close enough.

The crunch of tyres in the drive told her that the taxi had arrived and she took a last look around the barn before step-ping out into the snow and closing the door behind her.

Jack, the taxi driver, waved from the car and she waved back, hoping he wasn't going to ask her too many questions. Hayley felt as though she'd lived a whole life since he'd first dropped her here two weeks earlier.

She was four steps down the path when her legs went in different directions.

'Oh, for—' Bracing herself for impact, she screwed up her

face but this time powerful arms caught her, lifting her upright before she hit the ground.

'I don't know how you think you're going to manage without me,' Patrick drawled. 'You can't even walk if I'm not there to catch you.'

Her heart pounding, Hayley clutched at him as he steadied her. 'I didn't know you were awake.'

'I haven't been to sleep. Have you?'

'Well, no.' She doubted she'd ever sleep again. The misery inside her felt so great she had no idea how she was going to cope. 'Patrick, I have to go. Jack is waiting.'

'He's all right for a minute—you're not running away from me, Hayley. Not before we've talked.' Patrick was still holding her, his hands firm on her arms. 'And we have lots to talk about.'

'I know. I *know* we're going to have to talk at some point, but I can't do it now. I need some time—'

'Time for what?'

'Time to think! Time to—I don't know. Time to get over you.'

Patrick inhaled sharply. 'Why would you want to get over me?'

'Because we can't be together.' Her voice was clogged. 'And having your baby is difficult, but it's my problem and I'll sort it out.'

'Problem?' He frowned, his eyes searching hers. 'You haven't told me how you feel about being pregnant. Is it a problem, sweetheart? Is that how you feel?'

Her heart turned over. 'No, of course not. It's just...' *Just because of us,* was what she wanted to say. But what was the point?

'Hayley, I don't want you to "get over" me.' His lean handsome face was unusually pale, his voice ragged. 'I want you to marry me. I told you that yesterday.'

'I *can't* marry you, you know that.'

'I don't know that.' His eyes shimmered with raw intensity. 'I love you and at first I couldn't work out why you would possibly say no when I know you love me, too. I spent the night thinking about it. I spent the night thinking, *Why would she turn me down?*'

'Patrick, you *know* why.'

'When did you discover you were pregnant, Hayley?'

'Yesterday morning in clinic.'

His eyebrows rose. 'And you didn't say anything to anyone? The one time you need some support—the time you needed to talk—you kept it a secret?'

'It was too big to share.'

Patrick muttered something under his breath. '*Nothing* is ever too big for us to share.'

'This was. I didn't know how to tell you,' Hayley said huskily. 'What was the *point* in telling you?'

'I can't believe you just said that.' Patrick's grip didn't ease. 'It took me most of the night to work out why you would turn me down, Hayley. And then I realised that it's my fault. The reason you won't marry me is because of what happened with Carly, isn't it?'

'Yes. Partly.' She didn't deny it. 'A baby isn't a reason to get married, Patrick. You told me that.'

'And I stand by that. It's true. A baby isn't a reason to get married. But the baby isn't the reason I asked you to marry me.'

'Of course it is. You said that—'

'I proposed to you before I knew you were pregnant, Hayley.'

She opened her mouth and closed it again. Then opened it. But nothing came out.

Patrick gave a faint smile. 'You're doing it again. Staying silent when I need to know what you're thinking. I never thought I'd have to say this to you, but could you please start talking?'

'Patrick...' Words failed her and he sighed.

'That night in Chicago was incredible. I couldn't stop thinking about it. I couldn't stop thinking about *you*. I even contemplated getting in touch with you but I had no idea what I'd say. I'd decided that it wasn't fair to drag the children to the States, and I couldn't ask you to come here. And when I opened my door on Christmas Eve and you were standing there...'

'You thought I was pregnant,' Hayley whispered. 'And you were shocked.'

'Yes,' he said honestly. 'I'd made that mistake before and I wasn't going to make it again. But then I got to know you.'

'It's only been a couple of weeks—'

'Yes. And those weeks have been incredible. You transformed our lives with your sunny personality, your goodness and your non-stop chatter. You made us happy. And I thought you were happy, too.'

Her eyes stinging, Hayley smiled. 'I was happy. Very happy.'

'Then why are you leaving?'

'Because I'm pregnant and that changes everything.'

'I asked you to marry me because I love you. *Not* because you're having my baby. And I'm asking you again now, for the same reason.' His hands shifted from her arms to her face and he gazed down at her. 'I love you. I want to be with you. Will you marry me?'

'Say yes, love,' Jack yelled from the taxi, and Hayley gave a gasp of horror and buried her face in Patrick's coat.

'He can hear us?'

'Every word,' Patrick said calmly, 'and I really couldn't care less. It's your answer I want, not his.'

'Patrick—'

'Answer me one question.' He lifted her chin with his fingers and for once his voice wasn't completely steady. 'Do you love me?'

She gazed into his blue eyes, suddenly shy. 'Yes, of course I do. You know that.'

'How much?'

'As much as it's possible to love someone. I'm crazy about you. Do you really have to ask? I gave up everything to come here, Patrick. I gave up my job, my flat—I made a complete fool of myself over you. I followed my dream.'

With a groan he lowered his head to hers, his kiss unusually tender. 'Now answer me another question.' He murmured the words against her mouth, his eyes holding hers. 'Do you love my children?'

'I *adore* your children!'

'Then what's the problem?'

Distracted by the kiss, it took Hayley a moment to answer. 'Pregnancy isn't a good reason to get married.'

'We've just established that I proposed *before* I knew you were pregnant.'

Unable to argue with that, she pulled away slightly. 'It isn't just you, Patrick,' she confessed softly. 'It's me, too. I mean, I was brought up in a stepfamily and frankly it was *awful*. Dysfunctional just doesn't begin to describe it. All right, we love each other—but that might not be enough! It isn't just about us, is it? It's about Alfie and Posy and how they might feel about the baby. What if they resent it?'

'We won't resent it!' Alfie was standing in the doorway, shivering in his dressing gown, Posy in his arms. 'We can't wait for you to marry Daddy and give us a baby brother or sister, can we, Pose? Well, Posy doesn't really know, of course, because she's still little and only interested in her blanket, but also because she hasn't had a sister yet, and I have. It's great.' He frowned. 'Well, maybe not the nappy part, that's pretty gross actually, but the rest of it is cool.'

Hayley gave a cry of concern. 'How long have you been standing there? Alfie, you must be *freezing.*'

'We've been here long enough to hear everything. We're a family, Hayley. Team Buchannan. You should join our team.' Alfie shifted Posy awkwardly. 'Dad is a pretty good catch. All the women around here want him.'

Hayley bit back a laugh. 'You've only known me for a couple of weeks. Why would you want me to be on your team?'

'Well, there's the obvious stuff of course—you can cook well, and you're great at clearing up after us. And then there's the fact that two of the kittens are yours so if you stay we get to keep all four, which would be cool. But the real reason is because we love you and we know you love Dad.' Alfie hitched Posy up in his arms. 'I heard you say you love him. Mum never said that. Not once. I heard her say loads of stuff to Dad, but she never said *I love you.* You *do* love Dad, I can tell. And he loves you. And so do we. And do you mind if I go in now, because Posy weighs a ton? It must be all the turkey she's eaten.' Staggering slightly, he backed into the house, leaving Hayley with tears pouring down her cheeks.

'I can't believe he just said all that.' She was humbled by the children's warmth and acceptance.

'Do you really think our family isn't going to work?' Laughing, Patrick took her hand and slid the ring back onto her finger. 'We're not going to let you say no, Hayley. We want you on Team Buchannan. Say yes. Come on—of all the words I've heard you say, that's the one I want to hear.'

Hayley looked around her. She looked at the beautiful barn, the mountains and the snow-covered trees. And then she looked at the man standing in front of her—*the man she loved*.

'You do realise that Alfie is right—if you marry me you'll end up keeping all four kittens,' she said, and her voice wobbled. 'He gave them to me as a present and I won't be parted from them.'

Patrick rolled his eyes, but he was smiling. 'I think I can probably cope.'

'You're sure you don't want more time to think about it?'

'I'm sure. I love you, Hayley, that isn't going to change.'

'In that case, yes,' she said in a choked voice. 'Yes, of course. I'll marry you. Oh, Patrick...' She flung her arms round his neck and Jack beeped the horn madly and cheered.

'Good job I don't have any neighbours,' Patrick drawled, his mouth against hers as he kissed her again. 'Given that he knows such a lot about your underwear, I think perhaps we'd better invite Jack to the wedding. What do you think?'

'I think I love you, Patrick Buchannan,' Hayley said huskily. 'I think I love you with all my heart.'

★ ★ ★ ★ ★

ReaderService.com

Manage your account online!

- Review your order history
- Manage your payments
- Update your address

*We've designed
the Harlequin® Reader Service
website just for you.*

Enjoy all the features!

- Reader excerpts from any series
- Respond to mailings and
  special monthly offers
- Discover new series available to you
- Browse the Bonus Bucks catalogue
- Share your feedback

Visit us at:
ReaderService.com